Two to Tango

Also by Nuala Woulfe

Chasing Rainbows

Two to Tango

Nuala Woulfe

POOLBEG

Published 2010
by Poolbeg Press Ltd.
123 Grange Hill, Baldoyle,
Dublin 13, Ireland
Email: poolbeg@poolbeg.com

© Nuala Woulfe

The moral right of the author has been asserted.

Copyright for typesetting, layout, design
© Poolbeg Press Ltd.

A catalogue record for this book is available from the British Library.

ISBN 978-1-84223-434-1

Typeset by Patricia Hope in Sabon 11/14.5

Printed by
CPI Cox & Wyman, UK

www.poolbeg.com

Note on the Author

Nuala Woulfe lives in Tipperary with her husband and three children. In her early days she worked as a reporter, before going back to college in her mid-twenties to do an Arts degree full time. Like Julie Walters in *Educating Rita*, she had no idea what she was going to do once she had this degree and just had a vague idea that she might become some kind of "ologist". Having worked in research for a while, she relocated to the mid-west about ten years ago and in between having children started to write books. Her debut novel *Chasing Rainbows* was published by Poolbeg in 2009.

Acknowledgements

First of all, a very special thanks to all the rugby girls, from all walks of life, of all shapes, sizes, ages and abilities, who answered my uneducated questions about rucks and scrums and everything else to do with the game. I was really taken by your sense of camaraderie and fun. Thank you for your time and for letting me watch your practices and games. Thanks to my "beauty source" for telling me how salons and spas might be run and thanks to the Arklow girls for telling me about the existence of pink fake eyelashes – it made the Sexy Lingerie scene, further into the book!

To Gaye in Poolbeg, everyone says you're just fab and the thing is you really are and so funny too! Thanks, Paula, for telling me you thought *Two to Tango* had a lot of originality – your endorsement meant a lot and thanks for giving me a cover which I think really reflects the mood of the book. Heartfelt thanks to all the Tipperary girls (most of whom are not from Tipperary) for keeping me sane on a weekly basis. I'll never forget the Bellydance workshop. What a great Saturday morning!

Thanks to everyone who helped out, either with research and encouragement for *Two to Tango* or in helping to get *Chasing Rainbows*, my first book, off the ground. Thanks to my family for your part in the PR effort of *Chasing Rainbows* and just for putting the word out there for me. I really appreciate your never-ending support and love.

For women everywhere, dream, dare, do
and
if you have it in you – dance.

One

Through the kitchen window Jennifer O'Malley spotted her husband Dan pottering around the greenhouse, moving pots and cleaning the winter mould from the glass with a cloth and spray, in oversized washing-up gloves. Out of badness the thirty-something mother-of-three dialled Dan's mobile and watched as he fumbled about in his pockets for his phone. He was still a handsome man, she thought, as she waited for him to answer – lithe, sallow-skinned and blond with just a touch of daddy-grey about the temples.

"What are you wearing?" she asked, trying to sound sexy but aware that her voice mostly sounded hoarse and just a little bit desperate.

"Jennifer? That you? What do you mean what am I wearing?" his Newfoundland-Canadian accent, which had a strangely Irish twang about it, broke through on the phone.

"Right now – what are you wearing?"

"A fleece – it's chilly in the greenhouse, even though it's warmer inside than out," he said, completely unaware that his wife's dark eyes were studying his every movement as she wound a wayward strand of dirty-blonde hair round her index finger.

"What else?"

"I don't know – dirty socks? Where are you?"

God, this was useless. Dan didn't even have the brainpower to ask her what *she* might be wearing – not that she had anything sexy to boast about these days – not in big sizes. Perhaps it was no harm; slinky drawers might give out the message that she was frisky, which she was in a surprisingly uncomfortable sort of way. Running a spare hand down her flabby mammy bits, which she'd liberally sprayed with perfume (the only thing sexy she currently had to cover her pelt), Jennifer knew what she needed right now was earth-shattering excitement. Right now at this very moment on a January morning she wanted something momentous to happen, like a Hollywood movie star bursting through the door pursued by fast cars and helicopters, telling her that in the interests of national security he needed to have sex with her now – on the couch – with all her clothes on and with helicopter searchlights pinpointing her every move and relaying images back to live satellite TV in the interests of – well, in the interests of national security.

Feeling all hot and bothered, Jennifer's eyes glanced back through the double doors at her couch, wondering would it be up to any kind of national-security action. Chance would be a fine thing. Then her roaming eyes returned to base, alighting on the remote control which was just about to be stuffed into her eight-month-old son's mouth.

2

"Forget it, forget I even asked!" she sighed as she hung up, pulled her baby son onto her knees to breastfeed, switched on some international TV and tuned in to France's loveliest weatherman, the soft-spoken, dimple-cheeked golden-haired weather babe du jour, Pierre Dubois. She listened raptly as Pierre in his native French tongued a few weathery terms which might one day come in useful at her daughter's experimental French-speaking primary school, started by Irish parents of Norman descent. Straight after the weather Sophie Lloyd, the nation's glossy-haired culinary wonder came on, and was just sticking one buffed shiny finger into a chocolate pudding, licking it and having a pretend culinary orgasm for the camera when Dan appeared and hovered nervously beside the double doors near the TV.

"Everything okay?" he asked slowly, peeling off a dirty man-sized washing-up glove just as the brunette chef let forth another strangled *miaow* of fake pleasure.

"The baby's not bawling – what more could a mother ask for?" she answered briskly, not allowing her eyes to wander from the screen.

"Sure you're okay?" he tried again very tentatively.

"I'm *fine*," she snapped as she fisted a cushion into an acceptable shape before slipping it behind her back.

"Is it because I'm going away and leaving you with the kids for two nights?" he asked, not willing to give up his investigative line of questioning just yet.

"It's not your fault, I understand work is work, your computer company owns your ass, what can you do, right?" came her sardonic response.

"Jeeze, you know I hate Intech's team-building days away – I'd gnaw my own arm off if I thought I could get out of this buddy-building nonsense," he insisted as he deliberately moved a fraction in front of the TV, directly into her line of vision.

"You want to be in Galway for lunch, right? You'd better go," she said frostily. Then full of guilt she forced herself to smile until it seemed her face might crack.

God, she was such a bitch these days. A long time ago she used to be the kind of girl who'd blow kisses at herself when she passed mirrors, who'd wiggle her hips and shake her boobs just for fun, but that was such a long time ago it might as well have been a completely different person. In fact, now that she thought about it, it *was* a completely different person, somebody young, somebody fun and somebody most definitely free.

When Jennifer O'Malley was angry, she baked, which was somewhat surprising because the results were never pleasing and only led to further irritation. It was madness, she knew, but as Abby was home from playschool today (she was on probation on account of her need to taste her fellow students with her teeth) and with time on her hands before collecting Emma from 'big school' the baking urge had come upon her and she'd decided to hit the flour – hard. Today her nerve wasn't up to the dreaded scones, but she felt she had been close to success with the muffins the last time she'd tried.

So, she and Abby mixed all the ingredients together, slopped them into paper cases, then placed their gooey achievements on trays in the oven and hoped for the best.

"Mammy, this is fun," her angelic-looking three-year-old lisped.

"Isn't it just?" Jennifer laughed as she kissed the child on her soft white blonde hair. "You just stay here a moment and watch our lovely buns while I check on Adam in the bedroom." Jennifer left the kitchen to check that her son, who'd fallen asleep in his car seat, was still breathing. It was while tenderly stroking her sleeping baby's flushed cheek that that she heard the crash and a shrill-pitched scream that turned her into an Olympic athlete in three seconds flat. Oh hell, what had the little minx done now?

Back in the kitchen Jennifer's eyes swooped on the scene and her brain proceeded to check all the relevant boxes. Hysterically screaming child – check, blood flowing from the head – check, child in need of medical attention – further investigation needed. Zooming in on the hot spot, Jennifer took Abby's head in her hands and surveyed the damage. Shit, up close there was a half-inch slash on the child's forehead near the hairline and Jennifer knew that only stitches would solve this problem.

"Were you climbing again?" she half-scolded, half-consoled.

A little sniffle and Abby pointed at the mixing bowl that Jennifer had pushed out of the way – she'd been climbing the kitchen counter to find and lick the bowl.

As she tried to calm her hysterical tot, Jennifer fired two emergency bananas, a half-packet of biscuits, several cartons of juice, soothers, baby toys and her purse into her mammy bag-sack, placed the baby in the hall in his car seat with a blanket over him to guard against the January cold, and lastly switched off the cooker knowing that the action would cause her muffins to collapse from promising mounds into a sorry soggy mess.

Reversing her car at lunatic speed out the driveway of her small three-bed bungalow and watching her middle child in the mirror with blood trickling down her face, Jennifer rang her friend Helen and prayed she'd not be working one of her mornings at the local butcher's.

"Helen, you around? We're on our way to Bannestown Hospital . . . Abby, wouldn't you know . . . cut to the head . . . it's just with Dan away I wondered could you collect Emma from school . . . are you sure? Thanks, you're a star."

Bursting through the hospital doors Jennifer's eyes scoured A&E and her breathing improved just a bit. Thank heavens – the place wasn't totally jammers, with a bit of luck they should be seen within the hour.

Helen was outside talking to Emma when Jennifer finally pulled into the sweeping driveway of her friend's enormous terracotta-painted farmhouse bungalow.

"Acting the monkey again, was she? What was it the last time?"

"Raisins up the nose," Jennifer sighed, rolling her eyes in exasperation.

"Sweet Jesus – there's no end to that one's imagination!" joked the captain of the parish rugby team, a woman with rosy cheeks, playful eyes, a swinging raven plait down her back and a fit, toned body that was always chasing action. "So, where's the stitches?" Helen stuck her nose in the car and surveyed the three-year-old's skull.

"There's none – they glued the cut – no old-fashioned stitches necessary," Jennifer answered, feeling relief that the slit looked much less intimidating now it had been cleaned and sealed.

"Glue . . . seriously? Well, fancy that," Helen smiled as she smoothed Abby's hair back from her forehead.

"Thanks again, Helen, for taking Emma," Jennifer said with genuine gratitude.

"Oh for God's sake, will you say no more! She wasn't an ounce of trouble." Helen smiled at a blushing Emma.

Of course Emma was no trouble, Jennifer thought, not her five-going-on-fifty Emma who was always adept at seeing what needed to be done and just doing it, her blonde Emma who never complained, her Emma who was always smiling – either that or biting her nails.

"You'll come in and have a cup of tea so?" Helen coaxed as her scruffy black-and-white cat moulded itself into her shins and mewed plaintively, demanding attention.

"Believe me, I'd love to, but if it's not too ignorant I think it would be better if I just hit the road, get them fed, do the laundry . . . clean the kitchen . . . ha, ha, ha, no, maybe cleaning the kitchen is just *too* optimistic!"

"Tough call looking after kids when Dan is away travelling," Helen sympathised.

"He's not travelling this time . . . well, I suppose he sort of is but it's nowhere foreign, just Galway at a team-building love-in – basically the company try and get people who normally can't stand each other to 'bond' and all the employees do their best not to reveal any secrets. I can't see Dan enjoying it much – so I suppose it's rough on him too."

"You reckon? You're such an understanding wife, I bet it's a blast," Helen teased, then cursed the cat for making a good attempt at tripping her up from under her feet.

Cross at being shooed, the cat jumped on the bonnet and Helen ignored him as she opened the door for Emma and helped her get into her car seat. Then her quick eyes fell on the latest *Slinky Bunnies – Sex Toys and Lingerie Special* magazine – and she began to chuckle. She scooped it up, eagerly released it from its cellophane prison and began to thumb through its saucy pages.

"Good Jesus, all these frisky young ones in sexed-up gear with not a patch of cellulite in sight! Your pal Sandra still in the *Slinky Bunnies* knicker-and-bra game then?"

"Yep – business is booming – she says sex is a cheap night in and never goes out of fashion," Jennifer quipped as she pulled Abby's awkward safety belt super-tight. It was a frustrating car seat, probably designed by a twenty-something male engineer who'd rather be concepting high-powered sexy cars instead of boring kiddie equipment.

"Well, now I've got a glimpse of all this young smooth flesh I'd better check into the beautician's myself."

"Why, what are you getting done – a facelift?" Jennifer teased.

"Ha bloody ha. No, a Brazilian actually – wasn't I in the scrum only last week when I was locked in and couldn't move and a team-mate grabbed a hold of my . . ." Helen's voice dropped to a whisper, "hair . . . and I'm not talking the plait on my head, Jenny!" Helen gestured at her crotch.

"That's gross, Helen, *please* don't tell me any more!" Jennifer pantomimed a scandalised face.

"Well, gross or not, as captain I can't leave anything to chance this year – we've a tough season ahead and if we play well Bannestown might even move up a division!" said Helen with feeling as she threw the catalogue in the boot, gave the car a friendly smack, shooed the cat from the bonnet and waved goodbye from the steps of her house with the number of her local beautician's pounding in her brain.

Jennifer drove off, realising that something about the raunchy catalogue really bothered her as she'd deliberately avoided opening it and seeing the bunch of skinny young harlots parading around in their sexy drawers. Of course *Slinky Bunnies* did plus-size lingerie too, as well as comfy pyjamas, but no one with a big arse or flabby thighs actually posed in the magazine – that would have been far too depressing.

Driving home, with the stereo turned up high, Jennifer tuned into some powerful hits from the eighties and nineties, songs that lit her up from the inside. Despite Adam's bawling and the girls' bickering, it reminded her of a time when she was full of energy with a sassy demeanour and a trail of tongue-tied guys collapsing around her feet. *That* girl didn't own a single pair of cuddly pyjamas. *That* girl only wore G-strings, if she wore anything at all. *That* girl could have posed for *Slinky Bunnies* herself with or without knickers and bra, she thought, as she pulled into her driveway and took a very deep breath.

Lunch was served late, laundry washed, ironing tackled, fights broken up, an Arctic Dinner of frozen fish and chips which Sophie Lloyd would never approve of served up, and close to nine Jennifer got them all to bed.

Dimming the lights to low she placed a slim white candle on the table, poured a glass of red wine into a long-stemmed crystal glass and knocked it back in one go. Then selecting a CD from her collection, she allowed a loud and silly belly-dancing track to fill the room with exotic sounds until her body began to sway in time with the beat.

As the music swelled a mood of seduction washed over her and in a moment of hip-hitching excitement she did a little dance of the seven veils with her multi-coloured winter scarf, a beautiful mesh of soft brightly coloured felts interlaced with delicate gold thread, and laughed as she practised a seductive look with her caramel-fudge eyes, then blew a flirtatious kiss to the mirror on the wall. Drunk with anticipation and with the first glass of wine already making her head spin, Jennifer padded past the kitchen into the utility room beyond and unloaded fifteen giant bars of chocolate from her store cupboard, then spread them on the floor of her living room like a shiny new pack of playing cards.

Huge, playful giggles reminiscent of childhood built up inside her as she slid her fingers along the luxuriant paper and brought the bars to her nose one by one to smell the traces of seduction within. Each bar she handled carefully, studying the ingredients – dark, milk, white or plain, filled with fondant or raisin, biscuits or nuts. Finally, her hands settled on one bar and she spliced open its shiny covering with her nail and snapped off a huge chunk of milk chocolate with hidden fondant inside. The chocolate broke in a jagged triangle and her tongue marvelled at the initial sharpness and then the velvety texture of melted sweetness. With artificially controlled calmness, Jennifer opened two more bars, getting down on her hands and knees to smell each one, bringing each up to her nose and inhaling deeply until her brain caught the scent and registered crazed and sudden interest. Organic chocolate, fair-trade chocolate, exotic chocolate; this should have been a pleasure shared, but then again needs must.

A soft and seductive belly-dance track played on the stereo and Jennifer swirled as she munched, swirled as she sipped her wine. How daft, how ridiculous – but what did it matter? The chocolate orgy, now wildly out of control, felt good. In less than half an hour she broke chunk after chunk off each of the bars until at a conservative estimate she'd inhaled, licked and swallowed three or four giant bars in all, washed down with more wine. Hers was an experiment in gluttony but strangely she didn't feel guilt, all she felt was joy. It was like being little again, like overindulging at Christmas or Easter, when eating nothing but chocolate was the right of every small child with a full set of milk teeth and no knowledge of disapproving dentists.

As she pranced behind her scarf, the candlelight glinted off the glass on the table; then mid-tummy-jostle she sauntered to the answering machine and found several unheard messages vying for attention.

"Baby, it's me, Dan . . . Jeeze, I'm such an ass. No wonder you were so quiet . . . well, I'll make it up to you, I promise. Where are you?" The message beeped into nothing.

"Jennifer, it's Dan . . . sorry, couldn't ring for ages – it's like being a Navy Seal here – they've got us drilling

every moment. We're being corralled into another meeting now. Why aren't you answering your texts?" Message two faded with the first.

"Hi again, look, what I meant to say is I'm sorry and Happy Anniversary and I love you, honey. Maybe if you get a chance you'll call me back?"

As the greetings died, Jennifer mused just a little. As husbands went, Dan was a good guy, a steady guy, but she knew that she wouldn't be ringing him back – not tonight.

"Happy Anniversary, Jenny," she whispered as she blew out the melted candle, corked the wine and trudged off to her king-size bed to an acrobatic baby who had long since forsaken the cot as his natural birthright.

Taking off all her clothes, Jennifer lay down beside her baby son who was curled up peacefully beside the wall, but her own body refused to rest. Her sinews, her muscles, her very skin were charged as she remembered her wedding night seven years ago, when she was dressed in expensive white underwear from silken toe to satin lace-trimmed bra, but tonight she'd nothing of satin or lace that fitted or flattered her figure, but that was all right because there was no man to please, there was only herself.

All night, while her husband was away Jennifer was like a taut elastic band as chocolate, wine and intense primitive desire played havoc with her brain. In her fantasises she was the most beautiful woman on the planet and the sexiest guys on the planet were driven wild by her presence.

"You're *so* gorgeous, *so* funny, *so* hot," hard-bodied Hollywood Lotharios would whisper in her ear as she'd sip exotic cocktails with harlot names and flirt outrageously from under expertly glued eyelashes.

"Could you hang on a sec, Elvis? I have Paul Newman waiting for me in the other room!" she said to herself in a suppressed giggle. Hell, it was her fantasy and who said the bloke still had to have his vital signs intact? Part of her worried that the only sane part of her left was descending into insanity, part of her didn't care for any such diagnosis, because until dawn broke Jennifer O'Malley was lifted out of the monotony of her world and transported back to her past to watch that fabulously sexy girl who blew kisses at mirrors and wore G-strings every day – that is, if she wore anything at all!

Two

"I'm not paying for this substandard work! Look at my bloody tan – it's as patchy as a hooker's CV!" Mrs Elvery was screaming, all trace of pseudo-poshness out the window as she threw a hissy fit in Carrigmore's County Hotel salon like a child demanding sweets at the supermarket checkout.

Hearing one of the salon's best fee-paying clients having a meltdown, beautiful Rebecca Gleeson massaged the top of her pretty nose with her own perfectly manicured fingers and sighed deeply.

It had been a wicked day on reception at the ridiculously named Tranquillity where Rebecca worked part-time. Groaning and looking through a mesh of fingers and her own groomed and gorgeous long red hair, Rebecca saw Dympna, the mousey-haired timid beautician, standing in front of her, her face crumpled in fear, her brain disengaged, tears threatening.

"What'll I do? She's going mental in there and there's

nothing even wrong with her bloody tan," the young, just-out-of-college Dympna asked in a panic.

Rebecca rolled her chocolate-brown eyes and gnawed her lip in frustration. She'd seen it all a hundred times before – middle-aged wrinkly with an expanding waistline going to a 'do' ends up in a depression when she realises she no longer shares even a passing resemblance to a Hollywood B or C-lister, fake tan or no fake tan.

"Well, obviously we can't bloody charge her the full whack now – she knows everyone on the rubber-chicken social circuit. Tell the mean old cow we won't charge her a penny since she's such a *valued* customer and throw in a few vouchers to get shot of her."

A calmed-down Dympna disappeared back into the cubicle where the wails eventually subsided with the news of some nice little freebies.

"What's up with Elvers?" Keelin, Tranquillity's veteran beautician, asked as she waddled on tacky white high-heels towards Rebecca's desk.

"Nothing, it's all been sorted," Rebecca said shortly and Keelin's body language immediately went huffy. Not that Rebecca cared – she didn't like Keelin, finding her far too nosey for her own good.

"I never let the old bat throw a wobbly when she's with me, but that Dympna's not a cool head under pressure – she finds it too hard to concentrate," Keelin said meanly, deliberately ignoring Rebecca's aloofness.

"Yeah? Well, speaking of heads, what the hell possessed you to try and wax the hair off that biker's head today? We'll be lucky he doesn't sue us, with all the blood that oozed out of his scalp," Rebecca hissed.

"As it happens," Keelin defended herself, her massive

mammaries puffed out in defiance, her big hips and rear end wiggling for a fight, "his girlfriend told him hair grows back much slower if you wax and, since he believes no hair is far more aerodynamic for the bike and he's fed up shaving, he thought he'd give waxing a go. Don't worry, he won't be suing – he knows himself what he was asking was a bit revolutionary for this place."

"All I'm saying is if we're not careful this whole place could go down the tubes fast – all it needs is a few dissatisfied customers – word travels fast around a small provincial town. Did you know the hairdressers in here had to discreetly chuck out a young one who turned up today for a cut and blow-dry – she had nits!"

"Well, we can't be as picky as *you* would like us to be with the clients, Rebecca. There's no royalty around here. In the sticks, cash is king, and the last time I checked you didn't own the bloody salon!" Keelin tried and failed to toss her dirty blonde locks sulkily, an impossible task since they were held rigid with industrial-strength hairspray.

Idiots, I'm surrounded by country-bumpkin idiots, Rebecca thought as she faked a sympathetic goodbye for Lady Muck Elvery (a simple task as Rebecca had faked a million smiles in her pre-marriage air stewardess days), shut up the salon, grabbed her handbag and stormed out the door.

"Hello, baby, have you missed me?" she greeted her two-seater soft-topped roadster as she opened the door, eased her tall, svelte figure onto electrically heated leather seats and turned the key, allowing her beautiful high-powered motor to roar then purr.

Fifteen minutes later Rebecca stopped outside her newly built stone mansion and waited for the enormous electric gates to open. Once inside the imposing front door of her home, she threw her keys on the hall table and hit the messages on her machine. *'Out tonight – don't wait up,'* her husband's voice growled. Passing by the familiar silver-framed photo of her wedding, she glared at her husband's image before bounding up the stairs and leaving a trail of practical well-cut work clothes from landing to bedroom.

Having showered and dried, a naked Rebecca fumbled for the hidden catch behind the lingerie drawer in her walk-in wardrobe and, not for the first time, was glad that Mark had let her oversee the building of her personal wardrobe. The false door might not have been the most unusual job that the carpenter had ever done but Rebecca had tipped him well anyhow to guarantee his secrecy. At the time she wasn't quite sure why she wanted a secret compartment or what exactly she'd put in it – all she knew was that every woman should have a private place for private things and marriage didn't mean revealing everything about yourself to that 'till death do us part' other person.

Eagerly Rebecca sought out her most valued possessions: skyscraper, thigh-high black-leather boots. Zipping up her sexy footwear, Rebecca tossed her beautiful hair – a mesh of hot red gold, powdered cinnamon and clear blonde honey – then admired her reflection in the mirror. Gorgeous, you're bloody gorgeous, she told herself, running her long fingers over the curves of her hips, smooth and perfect except for some raised silver speckles on one outer flank and her special lucky silver scar in the shape of a leaf near the top of her pubic bone.

Admiring her lightly tanned skin in the mirror, the results of a recent sun holiday, Rebecca's dark eyes were pensive as she considered her chosen underwear – a black satin thong with pink and red jewels along the edges and a diamante under-wired bra – proof that Rebecca Gleeson was a thirty-year-old beauty who underneath it all was literally always ready for adventure.

Throwing a black satin gown over her shoulders, she clopped down the stairs and into her gleaming white Italian-marble kitchen which had every kind of oversized expensive appliance – appliances which Rebecca never used, bar the microwave.

Reaching for her flashy corkscrew, Rebecca eyed up a bottle of red wine and poured a half-glass, took a day-old carton of home-made soup from the fridge, bought from the local posh deli, and stuck it in the microwave to heat, careful not to bang her French-polished talons against any of the equipment, then piled a plate high with salad from the plastic bag in the fridge and topped that with a rolled slice of ham. Hungrily munching three types of lettuce, Rebecca was walking back to the hall to fetch a miniscule bar of organic chocolate from her bag to have as dessert with the wine, when her mobile rang.

"Hi, Rebecca, it's Lou, really sorry but I was wondering if we could switch tennis to Tuesday?"

"No way – we always play Monday!" Rebecca snapped disbelievingly.

"Sorry – I've got an appointment and it slipped my mind to tell you," Lou trilled, ignoring the irritation in her friend's voice.

"Well, we mightn't get Tuesday at such short notice,"

Rebecca sighed, making sure her disapproval was obvious as frost down the line.

"Like I said, I'm very sorry," Lou asserted confidently.

"Oh well, if you can't you can't . . . look, if there's nothing else I'd better head. I'm a bit achy from being on my feet all day and I've just run a nice bath," she lied.

"Be sure to add in a few oils to help you relax . . . I must do an Indian Head Massage on you too sometime – it's great for all those niggly end-of-week aches and pains!" Lou gushed and they said their goodbyes.

Rebecca rolled her eyes. Lou was an aromatherapy masseur who worked part-time for the salon and she was always adding to her repertoire, Indian Head being the latest in her bag of tricks. Rebecca knew what would really help in her relaxation right now: right now she'd like to punch a hole in a great big wall, kick open a door FBI-style or maybe just walk all over her husband with her scary big boots then karate-chop his head clean off his shoulders for added fun.

"Out tonight – don't wait up" . . . she replayed the message in her head and felt the muscles in her shoulders tense, her jaw tighten.

Back in the kitchen she topped her glass to the brim, smeared some goat's cheese on a cracker and tried to remember the last time she was out with her husband Mark, eight years her senior, on a Friday night, but for the life of her she couldn't remember.

Plonking herself on her precious white-leather sofa, her boots stretched out on the coffee table in front of her, Rebecca turned on the TV and flicked through the usual rubbish – depressing soaps that she knew the girls in work would be discussing on Monday – but there was also an interesting documentary on ancient Egypt and then she came across her favourite car-makeover show and was hooked. Rebecca loved cars, always had, anything fast and zippy with a beautiful interior and a nice range of gizmos, and she wasn't a snob about makes or years either – Hyundai, Mercedes, Porsche, BMW, Audi TT or Saab convertible – so many makes and models, so little time, and that's before she even factored in all the American or Italian lovelies. Every year she thought about going to some big international car show. What she wouldn't give for a sexy Lamborghini! God, what would they make of that in this boring little backwater where she lived? Yes, Rebecca Gleeson salivated over cars with shiny new alloys like some women covet the latest pair of shiny new designer shoes.

With intense pleasure she watched the car makeover until it was over, then her bored eyes strayed from the screen and swept over her perfect home where every idea for every cushion, every drape and every tile had been her own. The antique blackened iron stove, which nestled into the Mexican-style fireplace, had been sourced over the internet, the wooden boards and slate floors through salvage companies. It had been a real trial but Rebecca had toured the length and breadth of the country to have unique features – hand-painted tiles on the virgin kitchen walls, hand-made stained glass to her own design over the doorway – everything exotic, everything unusual, everything perfect, everything a conversation starter and ultimately everything completely and deeply unsatisfying.

Distracted by her interior-design memories and simmering with unexplained discontent, Rebecca made the mistake of answering the telephone when it rang and the line instantly went to ice as the two connecting life-forms recognised each other, then willingly allowed their distaste to permeate their conversation in subtly obvious ways.

"Oh, Rebecca – hi, it's Dee. Sorry to bother you – it's just Mark isn't answering his mobile."

"He's out – Kenny's, I think, told me not to wait up," Rebecca said quickly, eager to get her mother-in-law off the line.

"Well, I was just ringing to invite you two to dinner on Sunday – a bit of a last-minute event. Can you believe it? Roy and I are married thirty-nine years!"

Rebecca rolled her eyes, locked her lower jaw into a grimace and impaled the phone in her head, finding some strange comfort in the pressure and pain.

"All the gang will be there," Dee rambled.

So that would be Linda (younger version of her mother – reinforced steel from the ends of her finely coiffed hair to the tips of her fuck-off pointy toes), Linda's twin Tom (pain-in-the-ass, lockjaw, boring country solicitor) and Elaine (bloated form of her sister complete with matching metal hair and pointy toes shoved onto swollen feet).

"And *all* the kids, of course . . ." Dee emphasised, knowing that despite years of marriage Rebecca still wasn't any trouble in that department.

"How *lovely!*" Rebecca enthused with as much forced sweetness as she could muster.

"Yes, it'll be great to have all my grandchildren around me – it makes me feel so – I don't know, fulfilled, I suppose. So we'll see you both there?"

"Well, sure, I'll pass on the message to Himself," Rebecca said in a forced up-beat manner, feeling her jaw almost lock with the super-sweet tension as she focussed on the spindly heels of her boots with their wonderfully pointy toes, so good for kicking ass, whether it be mother-in-laws or husbands.

"Well, dear, I can't see how my firstborn can refuse."

No, Rebecca couldn't see how he could either – which was a pity because she just despised Mark's mind-numbingly boring, social-climbing, dull-as-ditchwater family.

Irritated that her precious weekend time would be eroded now by Dee's party plans, Rebecca said a brisk goodbye and hung up. Then she broke her own rule about goat's cheese crackers and had two more in succession complete with even more wine and then two full-fat digestive biscuits as well as a mini chocolate bar – and her body, used to simple-carbohydrate deprivation, was almost giddy from the morsels of sugar she was throwing at her blood stream.

Bored now by TV, Rebecca angrily climbed the stairs to her sumptuous bedroom, her disinterested eyes sweeping over the floor-length green-silk drapes, her six-foot-wide four-poster bed and her trendy wicker-basket seat swinging from the ceiling.

Feeling powerful but furious, she unbelted her silky robe, letting it fall to the floor in one movement, then headed for her walk-in wardrobe once more. Hauling off her boots she crouched down like a cat and pushed the catch behind her underwear drawer to reveal the secret compartment for the second time. It contained all manner of exotic things, such as wigs and DVD's but this time what she wanted was some black nipple-tassels, red-satin hot pants, a killer pair of open-toed purple suede heels and her shiny silver dance-pole that she easily assembled and which was suctioned in place between ceiling and floor. Fixing her gaze on her CD collection, Rebecca debated what angry young female artistes should accompany her in tonight's dancing: Pink, The Pussycat Dolls, Beyoncé, Blondie or Madonna? All of them were worthy kick-ass women whom she'd worked out to in the past, but tonight the choice wasn't at all hard as she sank her toes into her purple weapons of choice. Not a woman after all. Purple shoes – Purple artist – Prince – tonight nobody else would do.

There's so much you don't know about me, Mark Gleeson, Rebecca thought as she grabbed the pole with her strong arms and did a few swift twirls just inches off the floor. There's so much you don't know about my likes and dislikes, she ranted silently, as she tensed her abdominal muscles and effortlessly gripped the sexy metal spire with her long toned legs, easing out all the tensions of the day.

Her flame hair tumbled upside down as she gripped the metal with the strength of a python and cursed her husband under her breath. Mark Gleeson, if you could see me now I wouldn't let so much as a finger of yours touch me, she fumed as she writhed to the sounds of the diminutive pop star preaching that she should act her age not her shoe size. Fire coursed through Rebecca's veins but glass froze her heart as she writhed.

Men would pay big bucks to see her do this erotic display of power and strength, she knew they would. "Come on, Rebecca, take the tassels off, just the one – throw us just the one, love!" they'd chant, desperate to see a bit more of her beautiful, supple flesh, but her cold inner bitch would ignore their pleas. Carried away by the imaginary image of control over all mankind, Rebecca pushed her body into a basic kick-up invert, crossing her feet together, letting her abdominals do all the work then letting her thighs straighten up – stretching out while fully inverted and sliding down the pole slowly and skilfully.

Charged up now she repeated the whole exercise, sashaying and prancing around the shiny silver love-magnet that took all her frustrations away but then something went wrong – there was a dull thud as Rebecca Gleeson – shoe-size six – collapsed on the floor bum first with a shriek of pain.

Standing up and rubbing her sore spots, Rebecca smiled to herself, then laughed out loud. Well, it had been only a few months since she'd started the old pole-cavorting, learning every move off the internet and from her specialist DVD and naturally she still made the occasional mistake. Maybe men wouldn't be chanting too hard for her yet, she mused as she yanked up her hot pants, rubbed her lower back and buttock-cheeks and resumed her secret dance passion to the wails of the Purple One.

Three

"Hello!"

"Daddy, Daddy!" two little girls jumped on Dan affectionately and began to babble excitedly the minute their father appeared at the door.

"Daddy, Daddy, the doctor stuck my head back, see!" Abby showed off her war wounds, then screamed, "What you buy us, what you buy us – we want pressies!"

"Girls, girls, your dad didn't even go on a plane," Jennifer admonished them.

"It's okay – I stopped off and got presents anyway," Dan said as he dropped his bags on the couch, dished out some dollies that looked like prostitutes and watched his daughters scarper for their bedrooms. "So how's my best girl holding up?" He stood before her sheepishly, not sure whether to go in for a bear hug, apologise again or wait for a scorned-wife tirade. Despite the fact that Jen had already sent him a 'don't worry about it' text, deep down in his primitive man-brain Dan thought this might be one of those female phrases to fear, along with 'fine', 'go ahead' or nothing followed by a disbelieving arch of an eyebrow.

"Put it this way, I've survived without your presence yet again," Jennifer smiled sardonically, "but then again I'm a veteran at surviving without sleep, barely eating, basic washing . . ."

Sniffing under her arms, Dan laughed. "At least you don't smell too bad but the day the Special Forces Marines come to give you your secret mission, I'd say you'd be more than ready, like that actress in the film with Arnie – you know, *True Lies*?"

"Jamie Lee Curtis – wish I had her body – I might have too if I managed to stay awake long enough to care about going to the gym." She smiled politely as she plonked herself down on the couch with Adam.

"Jeeze, didn't he sleep at all?" Dan asked, gazing at the eight-month-old troublemaker in his wife's arms.

"Not much, you know what he's like – oh wait, except the night of our anniversary when he slept like a log but I'd eaten just a little bit of choc and couldn't switch my mind off –"

"About our wedding anniversary – I really am sorry and I know you must have been pissed not getting a break from all the cooking and cleaning –"

"Or doing the school run – how am I ever going to sign up for French lessons at Emma's primary school when you're never around to baby-sit?"

"You're the one who wanted to send her to that start-up French-speaking school," he said as he shifted his bags to the floor and flopped onto the couch beside her.

"You shouldn't have bothered if it's getting you stressed."

"But it's *so* cutting edge," she gushed, "and I'm in the bad books for never getting involved and you are disadvantaging Emma by refusing to speak the French you have, that is when you're here!"

Dan gave her a strange look, shook his head slowly and laughed.

"Stop laughing, Dan! You know I can't speak French. And you know the kids in there in their early years are meant to only have access to natural, wooden toys and they're going to start hassling me soon especially since you told them you'd help out with making a few wooden playthings –"

"No, honey, *you* told them that at the interview, thinking it would help get Emma in, remember, along with the big stinking lie that my long-dead grandmother was French Canadian? I don't feel at all obligated by any of your little fibs. You know how I feel – Emma will learn French if she ever needs it for real. That school was never my idea."

"Easy for you to be so flippant about our children's education," she sniped. "You leave it all to me and I can't be doing everything, not while I'm still breastfeeding Adam and getting no sleep –"

"Ever, yeah, I know," Dan sighed.

He didn't know actually, she thought. Dan wouldn't recognise a vacuum cleaner if it stabbed him and he was often away so much travelling that it was just faster if she did everything domestic. Besides, with only one income in the house, Dan couldn't show up bleary-eyed to meetings. His career was really 'their' career; they'd decided that after Abby was born when Jennifer chucked in the most boring job in the world working in a lab, the great big payoff for her hard-earned science degree.

"Okay, so tell us about the interrogation methods Intech used and who cracked," she sighed wearily as, realising once again that he would never be any use on the school front, she gave up the argument.

"Oh Christ, you don't want to know! One of the girls broke down in tears and told us her mother has breast cancer and all the pressure is on her because she's an only child, and one of the marketing guys broke down and told us his marriage is on the rocks, that his wife has run off with a lesbian and he doesn't know what to do. Awful, awful stuff and then after all the waterworks there were happy smiles and claps on the back all round and 'we're here for you, buddy' promises. Such a load of schmaltzy crap you wouldn't believe." Dan visibly cringed as he remembered.

"So what about you, tough guy, did you crack?" Jennifer teased as she jostled Adam in her arms.

"Me? I told them straight up they hired me for my logical brain and people with logical brains don't do tears. Fuck, what was wrong with the good old days when work was work and home was home? What's wrong with men *not* wanting to have a nervous breakdown in front of their colleagues? This wanting to know everything about the guy next to you, who frankly you'd never have a beer with under *any* circumstances – it's just plain fucking creepy if you ask me."

"So you didn't crack then – bet that means you got something nice, bright and a just a little bit tacky to put on our mantelpiece to join all the other employee stuff you've won over the years. Come on, show us this year's trophy for being Intech's Mr Amazing." Jennifer shot her husband a coy smile and, with Adam gripping her side like a baby gorilla, she made a show of bending over and rooting for tacky treasure through Dan's bags on the floor.

"Stop, will you?" he snapped as he slapped her hands away from her jokey rummaging.

"I'm only having a laugh," she said. "What's wrong with you?"

"Nothing. I just want to forget all about this weekend – hand the kid over, will you?" Dan stretched out his arms and took Adam, then seeing Jennifer's eyes registering hurt and puzzlement and knowing she wouldn't let go till she was satisfied, he sighed. "Let's just say, this year – well, the focus wasn't on awards this year."

"Never mind, sure we're running out of space for your awards anyway." Jennifer spoke lightly but underneath she felt anxious.

Dan was the rising star at Intech Computer Systems; he was a company man, was fun and uncomplicated in a North American way. Whenever she got to a company dinner, everyone from the girls on reception to his bosses raved about his fab brain and nice-guy attitude. Surely nothing had changed?

Seeing the tension on her face Dan offered an explanation for his lack of company rewards.

"I'm not the new kid on the block any more, Jen. I'm nearly thirty-seven and whatever way you cut it, I just don't have the enthusiasm any more that I did in my twenties. It's young guys these places want, guys who have no family, no ties, who are hungry, eager to shine, the way

I used to be . . . and to think we were meant to be team-building . . . what a laugh that turned out to be!"

"Well, what about your chances of promotion – was there any talk of that, maybe at dinner?" Jennifer said briskly, only interested in the future. It was 'their' job after all.

Wearily, Dan shrugged his shoulders. He handed a grizzling Adam back to her, hauled off his expensive casual work-shoes and with a half-smile and some ill-concealed impatience began to surf with the remote control, before deciding on another course of action.

"Honey, do you mind if I get changed and go outside and finish organising the greenhouse? Being out there helps me unwind and there's a lot to get ready for spring. When I was away I thought maybe we should get a polytunnel too, grow some lettuce, some herbs maybe. We've got so much land around the bungalow going to waste."

"Yeah, sure, you go ahead. I'll make you a cup of tea to drink out there."

With the baby perched on one hip, Jennifer made the tea while her husband changed into some grubby gardening clothes in the utility room. Adrenaline pumped through her veins as she worried about the possibilities of Dan's promotion and the reward for years of being a good wife – her big posh house in the future. Jennifer even knew which four-bed detached beauty she wanted – she passed it every day on the school run – a modern beauty of cut stone, walled gardens and huge bay windows. Every time one of these lovelies came on the market Jennifer would press her nose up against the windows of the local estate agent's and dream. "Oh, by the way, there's a present for you in my travel bag – something pretty to cheer you up, seeing as I missed our anniversary," Dan said as he took the tea and planted a kiss on her cheek.

Her curiosity piqued, Jennifer walked back into the living room and found herself getting quite excited. Maybe he'd bought her jewellery, something modern and expensive, something sophisticated, trendy and extravagant all in one go, or maybe some gorgeous perfume or even a huge box of handmade chocolates – legitimate hardcore drugs which might keep her awake long enough to unload the dishwasher. No, it couldn't be chocs – chocs were never pretty and he had said it was pretty.

When Jennifer's eager hands felt the parcel, her heart sank. It was soft and squishy and she knew what it was in an instant.

Dan had followed her into the room to enjoy her reaction.

"Thanks," she smiled weakly as she surveyed the expensive red lacy knickers and bra inside that would hardly fit an adolescent. Why did her husband and Sandra in Dublin think sexy knickers were the solution to all her life problems?

"You're welcome, honey." Dan kissed her on the nose and went outside in his scruffy jeans and his gardening fleece to do something worthwhile with his hands.

Watching him through the kitchen window as she lapped up a hot chocolate and munched on a crumbly HobNob, Jennifer thought that this greenhouse really was like his barren womb. Every year for the last two years he promised himself he'd tend and plant and nurture living things and last year he'd even got round to starting some seedlings but work and tiredness got the better of him in the end and nothing had been fruitful. But it was a yearning in him, this wanting to literally see the fruits of his own labour, to hold something he had nurtured in his own hands. Gardening was for him his baby yet to be.

Feeling uncomfortable, Jennifer moved away from the window. There was something overly needy in this gardening business, something desperately primitive, and she was thankful when the phone rang to distract her from her worries.

"Ach, Aunt Birdie, when you coming to see us?" Jen had virtually lost all trace of her Northern Ireland accent over the years, but somehow it was still rooted deep in her brain.

"Ach, don't 'Aunt Birdie' me! When am *I* coming down to see you? Don't you know *I'm* the pensioner, alone up in Belfast without any children of my own for comfort," Birdie said good-naturedly. "How are the wee pets anyway? Is that poor child Emma still learning French in that daft school? Seems pointless when the 21st century belongs to the Chinese, that's what a documentary I was watching was saying only last week . . . "

Jennifer bristled; she really wasn't in form for her sixty-year-old aunt's life criticisms.

"Abby's fine, Emma's fine and she just *loves* school," she lied through her teeth.

"Do you know, I haven't heard from your brother Lee in America in months. Is he still working in the rodeo business over there? Not that I know where he ever learnt to ride a horse."

"*Roadie*, Aunt Birdie – he's a roadie with a rock band – there's no horses involved."

"Still, I worry about him and the life he must be leading," Birdie fretted.

Jennifer could just imagine the kind of lifestyle he was living, lucky single bastard.

"And he sent a postcard from Mexico only two weeks ago. Don't you think that's a bit suspicious? What if he's not a rodeo at all but is in prison, Jennifer?"

"Aunt Birdie, if my layabout brother was in prison he'd hardly be able to send a postcard, now would he?"

"Yes, but maybe he got someone on parole to post it for him!"

Jennifer rolled her eyes; her brother was thirty-two and should be able to buffer himself against the world by now. Really, her aunt watched far too many North American crime dramas.

"Ah, Birdie, you always worried about us all far too much."

"Ach, it's only because I never had any wee wains of my own."

"Mammy, come quick! Abby's made a real big mess!" Emma cried as she burst through the doors.

"Birdie, gotta go. I don't know why you keep ringing me on my mobile anyway."

"Well, that's because –" There was an enormous crash and Jennifer cut her aunt off mid-stream and bolted out the door.

In the kitchen Abby's bare feet were surrounded by a puddle of apple juice and the bread bin and in her little hands she held an empty litre carton of juice and a box of Krispies.

"I'm hungry," whined the little scavenger.

"You're always hungry," Jennifer snapped as she cleared up the destruction.

Ridiculous knickers had been bought, so when the kids were finally put to bed, sex was a given, at least in Dan's mind as he began stroking Jennifer's arm and kissing the back of her neck as they sat on the couch together watching TV.

"Fancy an early night?" Dan whispered in her ear as he nuzzled in close.

"I'm so tired, Dan – with you away there never was a minute," Jennifer said, faking a yawn, hoping it was the only thing she might have to fake that night.

"But if we don't make the time for sex, honey, we'll never have any . . . when did we do it last?"

Jen did a mental calculation: it was about three weeks ago just before Christmas in the sitting room with the lights switched off and the Christmas lights doing a manic dance, illuminating the tinsel and throwing up spidery shadows on the ceiling. Still, she hated these 'making time for sex' requests – it was like bringing business to the bedroom, being asked, 'Do you have a window available sometime this week between ten and ten fifteen?'

"And I don't want to seem ungrateful but I don't think your new underwear will fit," Jennifer said, still trying to side-step Dan's sexual intentions.

"That's okay – it only has to be on long enough for me to rip it off," he joked, making her feel panicky.

Tonight was a night when he didn't seem to want to back down but her unpredictable libido had scarpered and besides she didn't want to wear his present of pants and bra – they would cut into her bum and ribcage and emphasise her soft body, still two stone overweight since the birth of her babies.

"So do you want me to move Adam in with the girls?" Dan continued as he nibbled the inside of her elbow, slowly, delicately, in a way that made her want to scream not from pleasure but from irritation because she knew he thought her inner elbow was some kind of magic sexy button that once used would always work.

"Ehm . . ."

No, tonight was not a night that Dan O'Malley was likely to back down.

Their marital room was full of baby junk and piles of family laundry heaped on the dresser. Dan threw himself into the bed, now minus the baby, and patted the mattress for her to join him on the lonely sheets. Feeling every inch the shy but frumpy virgin, Jennifer stripped naked, hid her flesh underneath an oversized baggy T-shirt and never even looked once in the direction of the new lingerie, a fact which disappointed Dan though he tried hard to hide the fact.

"Why the glum face?" he asked, seeing that she wasn't exactly burning with anticipation.

"Let's just say I've had a real bad-hair kind of few days since you've been away."

"Kinda like the bad-hair day Helena Bonham Carter had in *Frankenstein,* where she ran around screaming with her hair on fire?" Dan teased.

"*Frankenstein?*" Jennifer glared. "I know my hair's a state but it's not *that* bad. *Frankenstein*, Jesus, you'd want to start being nice to me or I'm putting my clothes back on!"

"Okay, okay, I can do nice," he promised as his hands swept the sheets salaciously in long, suggestive movements.

"And lights off, okay?" she told him, annoyed by the leer on his face

"For fuck's sake, Jen, I'm fed up telling you you're still hot!"

"Lights off, or deal off!" she snapped at him definitively.

"Any way you want," he sighed, throwing his hands up in the air like an Italian gangster trying to placate all sides, trying to get the big deal to go down without bloodshed.

Still, every bit of her wanted to scream as he touched her, because he knew her so well, because it was the same-old same-old sex that would end in a big crescendo of enjoyment for him as he died and went to heaven, leaving her feeling alone and inexplicably sad.

"Jen?"

Her body was rigid, frozen from her cold thoughts. Maybe she, who used to have the wildest sex of her life with Dan, all-night hormone-fuelled sessions, was actually turning frigid as she entered old age. Maybe she should investigate convents now for when the menopause reared its head and the children were grown and she would be free to shut herself up in a nunnery away from the attentions of all men.

"Jen, do you think you could try and get in the mood?"

His erection was throbbing and she knew he wanted to bury himself in her flesh.

"No!" she snapped at him as he grabbed her round the waist and went to take her from behind. "I want to be on top, okay!"

"Okay, anything you want, babe," he said soothingly, making her feel guilty.

She knew she was being unfair. If he tried any familiar techniques these days it irritated her – if he tried anything new she despised his creativity.

On top of him, moving slowly and rhythmically, she felt herself relaxing, felt his hands reaching up tentatively and massaging her breasts and stroking her buttocks. He barely moved; she knew he was almost afraid to in case he upset her, upset the mood which was charged not with sexual tension, but with something else, something more dangerous.

Gradually she felt the tension leave her shoulders and she arched her head back and let her hair tickle the back of her neck and then she leaned forward and ran her fingers through his hair. It was the softest hair, sleek like a newly bought cuddly toy. In the darkness she could feel him breathing hesitantly. Orgasm was only seconds away, she could feel it building, an energy starting low and rising to her chest, oh God, let it not elude me, she begged, it was like chasing shadows, shadows that she needed, that she surely deserved.

Her hips ground into him and she didn't care for his pleasure at all as she came and afterwards he touched her arm and rubbed it gently as she threw herself off him and collapsed onto the pillow, gasping for breath, feeling the warmth of orgasm rushing upwards. When she began to breathe more steadily he went in search of his own pleasure and came quickly, lying back on the pillows with one arm over his face and underneath that arm she knew the corners of his lips would be curled in pleasure. Then she had a malicious thought – maybe Dan had only suggested sex because it always gave him a sound night's sleep when something was on his mind.

Almost as if he could see the scowl on her face, Dan reached out in his sleepiness and squeezed her hand firmly and she understood the gesture in an instant: it was their code without words and meant many things. It meant, 'I'm your friend, things will be all right, the labour pains will be over soon, don't be too hard on yourself' and lots of other small, private things but more than anything else it meant, 'I love you'. Automatically Jennifer squeezed his hand back, confirming the connection between them, and anyway it was true, she did love him – most of the time anyway. With a somewhat comforting silence blanketing them both into sleep, Dan's next mumbled words didn't make any sense when they seeped into her sleepy brain and demanded recognition.

"Jen, I've been made redundant – don't worry – everything will work out fine."

Her eyes snapped open for a moment. Then he squeezed her hand again, the gesture that had always been really for her, to reassure her, to comfort her in times of trouble. Dan began to snore as he instantly fell asleep and despite her mind's protest Jennifer's weary body slipped into sleep too, a sleep which was littered with dreams about having holes in her shoes and not having enough money for milk.

Four

On Sunday afternoon Mark dragged Rebecca out the door like a child heading for the dentist. Before he left the hallway he grabbed her firmly by the shoulders, gave her a squeeze and said "You can do this!" with a wry smile on his face and more than a hint of badness in his piercing blue-grey eyes.

He was such a maddeningly handsome man. Tall and well-built with thick dark-brown wavy hair and a sallow complexion, Rebecca loved the way he carried himself. He had the stance of a fighter, big but fast on his feet if need be – agility and power all in one raw, sexy male package.

"So what do you think? Do you think you can survive us Gleesons for an afternoon?" he teased, pushing a lock of Rebecca's lovely hair behind her ear.

Rebecca shrugged off his paws and glared at him dangerously. In-laws – an awful bloody invention that pushed the word *tolerance* to the limit. And nieces and nephews through marriage – annoying sticky little things that flew around like demented wasps and got between your legs and tried to trip you up. The thought of the hours ahead with the Gleesons hit Rebecca hard in the gut.

"Look, it's Dee and Roy's anniversary – we have to go – but I'll even drive so you can lose yourself in a haze of alcohol," he placated her.

"Thanks! I know you're only offering because you're bollixed from the weekend and can't risk another drop in case you die of alcohol poisoning!" Rebecca scratched him with her words but tension was carved between her brows and something in her manner made Mark feel unexpectedly sorry for her as he planted a little kiss on her forehead.

"Relax, they're not monsters– they're just *people*," he tried to cajole her.

"They're *your* people," she lashed back at him as if he came from some weird alien stock that ate outsiders like her for breakfast.

"Oh for God's sake, you're such a bloody drama queen sometimes!"

"Well, if I don't inflict my family on you, I don't see why I have to suffer yours even for an afternoon," she blazed.

"Yes, you and your family – we all know why we don't have to suffer *your* blood relations, darling!" He gestured towards the door, suddenly impatient. "Shall we?"

Outside large drops of rain were jumping in puddles, causing big sprays of dirty water to splash up from the gravel. The day had a suffocating warmth about it, that made Rebecca's breathing feel laboured and she felt that at any moment she might even throw up as the car pulled away and they headed for his mother's country mansion.

Fifteen minutes later Rebecca was looking up at the big black wrought-iron gates of her mother-in-law's palatial home. The driveway was long and winding with miniature hedges either side but soon Rebecca was looking up at the big grey palace of stone with its amazingly vulgar fairytale turrets, latticed windows and pretension at every architectural turn. Dee's home was legendary in the locality with most of the gossip centring on the fact that Gleeson Manor was fitted out with no less than eight themed bathrooms or en-suites – each one more outrageous than the next. Rebecca's own favourite was the downstairs Taj Mahal although the upstairs Moroccan harem loo, Dee's own personal favourite, came a close second in the vulgar stakes. It was a standard joke in Carrigmore town that Dee had more thrones than the queen on which to plant her trumped-up regal rear end.

Opening the majestic door with his family key, Mark walked into the enormous hallway and tiptoed round the large Persian rug – a family heirloom brought home from Saudi by a maverick uncle twenty-five years ago. Taking Rebecca by the hand, he headed for Dee's enormous, interior-designed kitchen where the designer's brief had been to inject warmth into the living space – ironic since Dee herself was so cold she could immobilise her victims within the time it took to open her lips and breathe out a brittle greeting.

"Mark, darling, how are you?" The brightness of Dee's cosmetically whitened teeth was blinding as her lips parted in a smile for her first-born. "And Rebecca . . . you're keeping well, I hope?" The chill of Dee's words cut Rebecca's cheekbones as the glamorous mother-in-law dealt out a perfunctory peck and brazenly checked Rebecca's abdomen for the slightest chance of swelling. "Get yourselves a glass of wine. I'm cooking a lamb roast so I'm keeping myself busy!" Dee stomped around the kitchen island, looking for her oven gloves – she hadn't a clue where they were since in real life Mrs Deirdre Gleeson was more a hardnosed auctioneer and small town developer than a domestic goddess and a doting sixty-something granny.

Although nowadays Mark was managing the business almost completely and Dee was back managing the family pub. Watching Dee walk away Rebecca was struck by the senior citizen's fabulous figure. Dee had never watched what she ate or needed to exercise to keep in shape; being focussed on business from the moment she woke up for the last forty years was all she needed to burn truckloads of calories every day.

"The pub business must be slow if she has time to do her own cooking now," Rebecca whispered snidely to Mark over her glass of wine.

Still, the Gleeson collective family wealth stayed constant thanks to their investment shrewdness. Mark's extended family had their money diversified in property, petrol stations and even start-up knowledge-based companies amongst other things.

Feeling trapped already, Rebecca looked towards the back of the kitchen, where the entire corner was wall-to-wall glass where two massive sliding patio doors met. Through the glass she could see Dee's 'JCB Art

Installation Project' – a muck mound, seeded with grass, which was meant to represent Dee's naked body profile – and Rebecca felt the corner of her mouth twitch in laughter as once more she took in her mother-in-law's latest ego trip. The Big Momma had seen a gardening programme where Jerry Hall had posed as a model for hills in a giant back garden and decided that she too would immortalise her own figure in earth and grass – but on the cheap.

"It's just fabulous, isn't it?" Dee insisted as she hemmed Rebecca in like a wayward sheep with a platter of cheese and crackers.

"And so *you* too," was the best Rebecca could mutter, knowing well that Dee loved nothing better than eliciting compliments for her muck-and-grass sculpture and was oblivious to all her grassy flaws – one earthy boob was unbalanced and the curve of her hip down to her backside had become lop-sided from a mini-landslide due to an unexpected deluge of summer rain.

As predicted, the sticky-fingered little nephews and nieces, whom nobody seemed interested in controlling, reigned supreme – shattering Rebecca's ears with wails and tantrums, doing cartwheels in the most inappropriate of places, fighting, pulling hair and dribbling goo and snot non-stop. It had been hard picking the right outfit to withstand the ravages of the young Gleeson brats, and no matter what Rebecca wore, she knew it would be torn to shreds (metaphorically speaking) by Mark's two bitchy sisters the moment they got her alone.

"Rebecca! Lovely top – designer, is it? Some obscure name we've never heard of, I bet – purple's a bit intense though, isn't it, for someone with your colouring?" Big

Shark Sister Linda took the first bite, displaying an eclipse of white dagger teeth, similar to her mother's, in the process.

"It's a one-off piece from an up-and-coming Irish designer and the colour is *mulberry*, Linda – mulberry silk – and actually I think it really brings out the colour of my eyes," Rebecca smirked back.

"Ah sure, you're too posh for us, Rebecca – you're still a city girl through and through. We'd call that *purple* down here in the sticks." Elaine, sensing the blood of her sister's attack, was getting whipped up now in her own frenzy. Yes, the Shark Sisters were circling and Mark had already scarpered for calmer waters.

"I'd say you'd have to work a fair few days at Tranquillity to pay for the likes of that," Elaine swiped again and the tone was half-jokey, half-loaded-with-venom.

"Well, Mark doesn't like me working *too* hard. He says women who spend all their time working end up with *awful* crow's feet and flabby backsides." Rebecca smiled as Elaine tried to stand up tall, suck in her belly and appear two stone slimmer while Linda nearly burst a blood vessel trying to loosen the permanent groove between her brows.

Both sisters grimaced through their too-white teeth and tried to stop themselves turning their own exclusive shade of mulberry from rage. Mercifully both of them were distracted by their collective brood who were murdering each other on Dee's 'look-no-touch' Persian carpet in the hall.

Rebecca's relief was short-lived however as boring brother Tom moved in to fill the vacuum – malt whiskey in hand and tales of woe from the courtroom.

"Rebecca, well, well, a long time since we've seen you," he said in a practised theatrical voice as he put his hand on her forearm and gripped it tightly in mock affection.

A little squeeze more and she'd sue him for assault or, at the very least, for harassment.

"So how are things with you at the salon?" he cross-examined.

"Nobody suing this week, Tom, but you can be sure if they do I'll pass the case on to my *favourite* brother-in-law at law!"

He threw his head back and roared with far-too-loud laughter at her little joke. "Oh do, do – business is devilish slow – there's not enough criminals down the country to keep a poor country solicitor like myself in decent sports jackets!" Laughing raucously at his own joke, he tidied the sleeves of one of his boring tweed constructions with his fidgety little fingers, gave her a peering look over his half-moon glasses and pushed his long black greasy locks behind his ears. Tom was only thirty-six but was one of those individuals who is born old, delights in it in fact. Rapidly approaching thirty-seven, he moaned about not having a woman in his life, which was no surprise, considering his appearance, his sacrifice to his profession and his dedication to mind-numbing solitary activities such as fishing and clay-pigeon shooting.

Rebecca shot Mark a 'get this idiot off me now' look but her good-looking husband was sitting casually on Dee's Italian burgundy leather couch, one hand leaning on the armrest, cradling a glass of wine, and on his knee and filling the other arm completely were two of his nieces who were looking up adoringly as their fun-loving uncle chatted to their equally fun-loving Granddad Roy. There was no escape from Tom's boring prattle until Dee's booming voice announced dinner was ready and everyone was seated at her grandiose mahogany dining table. Rebecca hated the way the snotty-nosed dribbling children weren't shipped off to a table by themselves but were interspersed between the adults and mollycoddled at every opportunity, except for Linda's eldest boy, the un-cuddly Peter, who at twelve was stockily built and was entering sulky-teenage territory.

"What's that you've got there?" Mark asked as Linda's eldest daughter Mia played with something in the palm of her hand.

"A DS, Uncle Mark – I like it because you can play this fashion-designer game on it and that's what I want to be when I'm grown up – a fashion designer!"

"Well, isn't that brilliant, although I think you should maybe put it away now that we're eating or your mum might get cross," Mark said gently.

Mia blushed from her favourite uncle's attention and, clicking her game shut, flicked her hair and looked at Mark through her eyelashes as she told him that she might also want to be a ballerina when she grew up, she hadn't quite decided.

As Mark patted the little girl's hand with affection and smiled, Rebecca experienced a stab of jealousy, which unnerved her so much it diverted her from Dee's shrivelled-up roast and squished vegetables.

For the next few hours, Rebecca soldiered through the bland food and bland conversation and watched as the clock over the solid wood fireplace pushed forwards at a snail's pace – every half-hour gone by was like a minor victory, and every half-hour was exhausting as Rebecca feigned interest in the banalities of Gleeson life. Somehow it got to seven o'clock and Mark's people were slowly moving towards the hall, packing off children into car seats.

Then Elaine, in the midst of a mini child emergency with her toddler, shoved her five-month-old baby girl into Rebecca's arms.

Rebecca watched the small human life-form in her care with suspicious eyes but when she saw the little body spasm she somehow knew the baby-milk volcano was about to explode and feared for her Mulberry silk blouse. Quick as a soccer player, she held the little thing at arm's length until the child posited up some milk and then made strange gurgling noises in the back of her throat. In an instant all the Gleeson eyes were turned on Rebecca in appalled shock before a screaming Linda rescued the gasping child from Rebecca's overstretched and stiffened arms.

"What's the big deal?" Rebecca asked as Mark drove her home, his face set in stone. "Okay, I know the baby puked a little on the famous rug but I thought the baby wipes got everything off."

Mark was like ice, too furious to respond to her questions for what seemed like ages.

"It's not the fucking rug, you stupid woman! It's that you would be willing to let a child nearly choke on its own vomit than risk it puking on your stupid blouse!"

For a split second he took his eyes off the road and shook his head as if he wondered about her exact biological make-up.

Rebecca always said her father was "a cold fish" although Mark didn't actually know – he'd never met the man in the flesh and had no real urge to either.

"What the hell is wrong with you, Rebecca, that you'd feel so little for a tiny human being?" he shouted at the road ahead. "I don't know, sometimes I wonder if you're made right – sometimes I wonder if you're natural at all!"

Rebecca pretended not to hear him as she checked her flawless make-up in the passenger mirror, still unsure what exactly was upsetting her husband so deeply. So she didn't like babies and she didn't like his family. What the hell was wrong with that? Didn't thousands of other women feel the same about their in-laws? She fumed as she snapped the flap of the mirror shut and stared at the wipers which were brushing back the evening rain.

"I'm turning in for an early night," Rebecca announced coldly as Mark went to make himself a sandwich in the kitchen.

Hearing the blare of the downstairs TV, a seething Rebecca began her intensive night-time routine as if her sanity depended on every detail being carried out exactly. Then she took a shower and enjoyed the smells of aromatherapy oils and delicious creams rubbed into her body and hands. For more than an hour she read a book and when she plumped the pillows and turned off the lights she couldn't sleep. The scene of Mia and Mark kept coming into her head and Rebecca didn't like to admit that the emotion she felt towards her niece was jealousy mixed with anger, feelings which confused her somewhat.

Some time later Mark came into the bedroom and padded about quietly in the dark as he undressed. In the bed, pretending to be asleep, she could hear his uncertain breathing as he stroked her arm and thigh underneath her satin negligée.

"Rebecca?" he whispered hopefully as he snuggled up close.

Resolutely she refused to answer. She suspected Mark knew she was faking tiredness but she didn't care as she rolled over, elbowed him deliberately in the ribs, stole the duvet and hugged the edge of the mattress like it was all that was keeping her from falling off the edge of marital life.

Five

At ten o'clock a 'sick' Dan was lying prostrate on the couch in the living room, wearing just his faded boxers and a black fleecy dressing gown, fuzzy golden chest-hair bursting out from the soft lapels. He was drinking his second cup of real coffee (made for him by Jen), munching on pancakes and maple syrup, and from time to time moaning – loudly.

"I feel really crap – maybe I should throw some more Paracetamol and vitamin C at the bastard bugs – bloody employees sobbing and snotting all over the place – it's no wonder I picked up the flu at that team-building fiasco. God, it even hurts to talk."

Jen almost smiled. He was worse than Emma angling for a day off school, but then she remembered he'd been made redundant and she injected a sharpness into her voice. It wouldn't do to show him any softness, he needed to be strong, he needed to find his backbone, he needed to find another bloody job for heaven's sake and soon.

"Grow up, would you, Dan? Your nose isn't even red," she snapped. Someone had to raise Dan from the dead where he'd watched nothing but moon-landing documentaries the last 24 hours.

Displeased with her unsympathetic response, Dan rubbed his hand over his stubble, moaned a bit more, then began to root around on the shelf for his DVD special on Antarctic exploration. It was clear he was planning to settle down for a long, comfortable expedition on the couch.

"Dan, the girls are coming round for the mother and toddler meeting? I mentioned it last night and again this morning – remember?" Jennifer sighed as he looked confused. "Your trousers, do you think you could make yourself decent or maybe you could even disappear to that place beloved by all bearded grunting Neanderthals?"

His brain appeared to have stalled so she had to spell it out.

"Your cave – otherwise called bed – will you shuffle off and die in it at the very least?"

Silently he turned off the TV and dragged himself along the corridor.

Flying around like an over-excited puppy, Jen gave the kitchen work-surfaces a quick clean and from time to time she opened the utility door and fired in anything that she found particularly difficult to tidy away, like Abby's scooter, a space hopper and the local phone directory.

Jen had been dreading this committee meeting of the mother and toddler group because the tidy-up had to start the night before and took hours, but it was her time to host the mammy-baby love-in, complete with biscuits, tea and non-tooth-rotting kiddie juice. Despite the manic tidying she was looking forward to seeing the girls – it would be a break from having to think about scary real-life stuff and scary real-life consequences.

Dark-haired, red-highlighted Sexy Sadie the Scottish lass with the big throaty laugh was first through the door with her six-month-old baby girl Lisa in a rock-a-tot and big brother Mikey hanging out of her trouser legs with every step. Sadie had a bit of an arse, a slight pot-belly, huge boobs, a nipped-in waist and dark eyes that ten years ago were adept at wooing men into bed – and they'd still succeed, given half the chance.

"I hate this limpet-leg stage they go through – it's like having a rabid dog stuck to you that you can't shake off," Sadie moaned as she grabbed a biscuit and fed it to Mikey under the table.

Helen stormed through the door next, childless, with two home-made apple tarts.

"I can't believe I'm still secretary on this fecking committee when my own are all in school. I swear I really, really will move on one day and give my all to the rugby."

"Ah Helen, if you do who'll make the tea for all the mums who come to the group and suss out any rugby potential?" laughed red-blonde curly-haired, tall and willowy Yummy Mummy Vicki who had given birth three weeks ago to her second and had no tummy at all to show for it.

It was disgusting how she fitted into her pre-pregnancy jeans as soon as she left the hospital, thought Jen. Still, her back had been in bits before and after the birth and she was still hobbling around on one crutch.

Helen, full of concern, helped the walking wounded to a chair. "Weren't you brilliant to have a natural birth all the same and you on crutches in the delivery room with the bad back?"

"It's not like I was making a deliberate stand, Helen – it's just my babies come so fast there's very little anyone can do," Vicki laughed. "My poor husband was the one in need of medical attention after we got the police escort all the way in!"

"Still, it's girls like you we need on the team – warrior women!" Helen punched her fist in the air passionately before she switched on the kettle and started to hack up a pie.

"Helen, do you ever stop yakking about rugby?" Vicki laughed as Helen pushed the first piece of homemade pie and fresh cream her way.

"It's just we're badly stuck this season – on a skeleton team, we are. One of our best is lost to us – playing rugby for university now instead of coming home weekends. And Jackie Lynch, all five foot three of her, is up the duff again – if I ever meet her husband I'll tie a knot in his boy bits, I swear – one of our best players she was, just like Sadie could have been if she'd stayed the course!"

"Ach, don't tell me you're still sore because you lost me on my first game out when I found out I was three months pregnant?" laughed Sadie. "I'm in my mid-thirties, Helen – I'm too old for it all now anyway!"

"Mid-thirties old? Speak for yourself! One training season – I can't believe that's all I got out of you, Sadie, and you had a real thirst for the game too – don't tell me any different!"

A knock on the door and eco-warrior mum Laura arrived, followed by 'I'm knackered I've had four of them just look at my grey hair' Betty and several more interchangeable chubby tots who invaded Jennifer's house and managed to take it apart in minutes.

"Right, what's on the agenda?" asked Laura, smoothing her brown pixie-girl hair with her long fingers.

"Jesus, I've just had the strangest urge come over me," Vicki said, her face almost trance-like as Jennifer handed her a milky cuppa.

"People, can we not get distracted, please?" Laura asked, checking her watch.

"What is it, what kind of urge?" Jennifer queried, eager to fulfil her hostess duties. "Is it chocolate? Do you want chocolate? I have chocolate – just give me a minute to sniff it out."

"No, not chocolate. I've just had the strongest urge to fire a gun, isn't that funny? I haven't fired a gun for years but I swear right now my fingers are just itching to pull a trigger." Vicki squeezed the handle of her cup slowly with her finger.

"Jesus, you can't make a statement like that and not explain yourself," Laura said, all agog.

"Yeah, Rambo, what's the story with the guns?" Sadie asked, her dark eyes puzzled.

"Guns? Oh, I used to be in the FCA when I was a teenager – that's the Territorial Army to you, Sadie. For two years I was Private McCarthy, I used to sleep with my gun and all when we were on manoeuvres. God, I loved my gun!" Vicki sighed nostalgically.

"You, you had a gun?" Betty laughed and laughed till tears fell down her face.

"Yeah, what's strange about that?" Vicki asked as she ran a manicured baubled hand through her curls and glared menacingly, her finger still on the trigger of her cup.

"You're just so girlie-girlie *and* you're doing an aromatherapy massage course," Laura gasped. "I never would have taken *you* for a soldier girl – you're just, well, frankly you're not the type!"

"See, this is what I'm talking about! Women who have stamina, women who have grit, can still be girlie-girlie women who wear make-up *and* play rugby," Helen gushed.

"*Helen!*" everyone shouted together. "Would you ever shut up about the rugby!"

"Right, girls, this agenda – will we just wing it?" asked Sadie the Chair, as she plugged her babe with a soother and began changing the nappy of her two-and-a-half-year-old underneath the kitchen table. "Okay, there's the grant application – Laura's agreed to sort it – thanks, Laura. And someone needs to renew the insurance?"

"I'll do that," said Betty with a nod of her head.

"Great . . . so now the boring stuff's out of the way, let's get down to the real business," said Sadie. "Where are we going for our night away?"

"*Galway!*" screamed Vicki and Laura in unison.

"For feck's sake, girls," chided Sadie. "Just because Galway is on the edge of the Atlantic, don't lose the run of yourselves and think you're actually going somewhere flash!"

"Like Biarritz," Vicki cooed dreamily.

"Can we just say somewhere central in *Ireland* and can we please go soon? I have a full-time job to go back to, ladies – maternity leave doesn't last forever, you know." Sadie sighed dramatically, her massive boobs heaving with the slight exertion.

"Okay, if there are no *serious* suggestions, I'll look into Kilkenny for Miss 'Time is Money High-flying Bigshot' here and Betty can check out Galway," said Helen, determined to get something sorted.

Laura had begun to look through Jennifer's magazines which were in a pile ready for recycling when she came across the *Slinky Bunny* catalogue.

"Oh now, *this* is a bit more like it for entertainment! Where did you get *this*, Jenny?"

"Have you still got that filthy catalogue – what did you order in the end?" Helen quizzed.

Jennifer blushed with embarrassment as Helen flicked through the sexy knickers and bras and took in the fancy-gadgets section with a low whistle.

"Does your man on page twenty come with the Tarzan briefs included or would that cost extra?" laughed Sadie as she squeezed in beside Laura for a nose.

"The pair of you are sex-obsessed," Helen scolded in mock horror.

"Damn right we are – we're in our mid-thirties now and that's when all the magazines say women reach their sexual peak," Sadie said, running her tongue along her teeth.

"That's true – don't they say women in their mid-thirties are actually ideally paired with seventeen-year-olds? Imagine all that toned, willing, perfectly legal young male flesh!" Laura placed her finger in her mouth and licked it slowly for show.

"For God's sake – if more of you would just commit

to the rugby I'd run the lust out of you in a training session, I would!" Helen said, rolling her eyes.

"Is it just me," moaned Betty, "or are we all a bit sex-obsessed these days?"

"Never mind sex – do you remember romance, girls?" sighed Laura, who currently had custody of the sex catalogue and whose saucer eyes were glued to the bondage section.

"Bloody babies suck the life out of more than just your tits," moaned Jennifer.

They all knew what she meant – even the bottle-feeding mammies. For a minute Jennifer thought her friends might fill up with tears if it wasn't for the pragmatism of Helen, who suggested another round of tea as distraction from daft feminine emotions.

"So tell us, Jenny, how is the Man Cold progressing with Dan?" asked Helen jocularly.

"Things are *very* bad there. I might have to ring the emergency services – get him carted away in an ambulance." Jennifer rolled her eyes to heaven and everyone sniggered.

Down the corridor the floorboards creaked and Jennifer could hear the sound of footsteps outside the kitchen door before Dan waltzed barefoot into the kitchen, thankfully in a pair of jeans and a white cotton shirt, although the stubble was still intact, giving his jaw a surprisingly sexy definition that demanded instant female attention.

"Ladies!" Dan nodded as he practically sashayed towards the dishwasher to get a cup and stuck the kettle on to boil again. Talk about rising from the dead, thought Jennifer in amazement. At the mere hint of raging female hormones in his kitchen?

Vicki bounced her curls and Sadie wiggled in her chair a bit and stuck her boobs out. It was funny, thought Jennifer, the effect a man, any man had on a bunch of women. It must be a primitive thing really, this need they all had to be noticed. Expertly Sadie crossed her long, sexy, curvy legs, showing off a flash of patterned tights and emphasising her knee-high black-leather boots with buckles at the ankle – those boots were dangerous, Jennifer thought, Jennifer knew all about men and boots (theoretically speaking).

"Good to see you up and about, Dan – heard you were at death's door," flirted Sadie.

Jennifer noticed her friend's top was far too tight for decency really. Those little buttons on the front were undone almost to the point of being an arrestable offence.

"Rumours about my demise, as they say, have been greatly exaggerated," Dan flirted.

Yes, definitely flirted back, and Jennifer frowned again. Sadie was getting dangerously close to being struck off the Christmas-card list.

"Making your own tea . . . despite your *terrible* affliction?" Vicki took up the teasing.

"Yes . . . well, us guys, you know, we struggle on," Dan assisted in his own dissection.

"So brave, wouldn't you say?" added Laura for effect.

Dan leaned against the cupboard doors, his hands pressed against the counter top, his tanned forearms peeking out from underneath his cuffs. He was born tanned; it was part of being Canadian. A little bit of fair curl peeked out from the top of his shirt – the curl was sprung tight and glistening the way Jennifer remembered his chest hair always was after a shower, when she'd always wanted to put her arms around him and pull him towards her tightly.

As they teased Dan mercilessly he began to smile, his lips curling slightly at first and then his mouth breaking into a broad grin. Most men would have run by now but not Dan, he was wonderfully open around women – always had been in fact.

"It must be *very* pressurised being such a high-flying executive like yourself, Dan – I'm sure catching a Man Cold must be an occupational hazard," Sadie baited playfully. "You know, I'm going back into the workforce myself soon . . . but things change so fast I don't know if I'd be able for all these new strategies that top people like yourself get involved in."

"Oh, like when we all get into the Jacuzzi butt naked and bond? That kind of thing?"

"Jesus, I'm going back to work tomorrow!" Vicki whispered under her breath to Helen. "Don't worry, Sadie," said Dan. "When you finally get back to work after your maternity leave I'm sure you'll cope with any touchy-feely crap your workplace has dreamt up for you in your absence. For example, at our recent employee-bonding session, this is what we all had to do for our team-building . . . Come on, ladies, everyone in a circle! Try to pretend you all like each other!"

Jennifer was about to bolt for the utility room to complete any kind of 'urgent job' to avoid being snared into Dan's mind games.

"You too, Jen!" Dan insisted, stalling her. "Laugher Yoga, ladies – ever tried it? Right now, let's open up the breathing – everyone say '*ho ho ho, ha ha ha*'."

Ten seconds later Jennifer's home was full of prospective Santa Clauses.

"Now, people, we're going to progress to some clapping and some chanting of 'very good, very good, yeah!' and on the 'yeah' give the thumbs-up sign and smile till it hurts. So, let's get moving! It's time to reach down, pull the imaginary cord on your imaginary petrol lawnmower, make the farty start-up noise and run around in circles."

Off they went: six crazy women, four mobile tots, several babes in arms and one member of the male species on a mad dash around Jen's house, through the double doors of the sitting/dining room and back to the kitchen until they were all rocking with laughter.

"A gas man, a truly gas man," said Helen as she left Jen's home ten minutes later with glowing cheeks. "Do you think he'd be interested in taking up the rugby himself? Sure it can't be much different from American football – and sure they play rugby in Canada as well?"

"How about we scrap the committee meetings altogether and just do this lark from now on," laughed Betty, air-kissing Jennifer goodbye.

All of a sudden, the front door became a bottleneck of mums, tots and buggies as the giggling guests tried to beat it out the door in time for feedings, naps and pick-ups from playschools. Outside, with Adam stuck to her hip, Jennifer caught sight of a woman kitted out in trainers and a funky tracksuit bouncing down the road toward the house with a baby buggy.

"Who's that, Jenny – a neighbour?" Helen asked, spotting obvious rugby potential.

"Oh, that's Fiona, came last week to the group for the first time with her six-month-old, ran all the way. That's a special jogging buggy she has there – we've already christened her Fiona the Pram. Mad to come to a committee meeting, wants us to do more hardcore activities like going to indoor playgrounds with the kids, maybe buying a small trampoline, anything with a bit of jumping in it in fact."

"Wouldn't her baby be a bit young for that high-activity stuff yet?" Sadie queried.

"Oh, eager is this Fiona one! She's even suggested we meet at the local playground once a week and do a workout with the equipment – press-ups, leg-curls, star-jumps – while the kids are running about." Sadie nudged Helen in the ribs. "Wait'll you meet her!"

"Oh, don't say I've missed it!" Fiona was very distressed to see the gang of women at the front door, obviously on the move en masse like a herd of gazelles.

"I thought you said eleven and it took me longer to jog here than I thought," Fiona panted.

"Sorry – it was ten – we're packing up now, I'm afraid," Jennifer smiled sympathetically.

Fiona's brow was glowing, her blue eyes bright from exercise, and obvious disappointment showed on her heart-shaped face. Distractedly she placed her hand upwards to re-adjust her red bandana which was keeping a horde of fat black puppy-tail curls away from her flushed cheeks and forehead.

Having assessed the situation, she didn't waste a minute now that her chance at influencing a committee meeting was temporarily scuppered. "Okay, well, I'll catch you all at group tomorrow. Just to let you know I've made inquires over the phone about doing baby gymnastics for mums and tots if you're interested."

"Great stuff, sure we'll see you then and talk about it further," Laura said, smiling stiffly.

"See what I mean – eager," said Sadie as they watched Fiona bounce out of view.

"Eager's what I want. I'd say she's no more than late twenties as well – she'd make a great little winger," Helen mused.

"Oh for God's sake, Helen, would you ever shut up about the rugby!" everyone roared together as they headed for their cars and on to the obligatory crèches, super-markets and playschools.

Shutting the door after them, Jennifer could nearly feel the stillness settle on her home like dust descending from the ceiling and her sharpened senses knew Dan was nearby. Turning around she saw him right there.

"They've all gone? Hope I didn't freak them out too much with all that team-building stuff," he apologised.

"No, I think they actually enjoyed it," she said, smiling till her cheeks ached and wondering why she felt so awkward around someone who had known her for so long.

He shrugged his shoulders, then winced as he rubbed his temples with his thumbs.

"Feeling really crap after all that madness – would you bring me an OJ?" He didn't even look at her as he shuffled off to the higgledy-piggledy spare bedroom-cum-office-cum-computer/store/junk-room to expire gently on the futon and nurse his germs in private.

Behind his closed door she heard him cough and put on some mindless midday radio. As she went to pour a glass of orange juice, she heard the post snap onto her parquet wooden floor – a belated Happy Anniversary card from the lovely Aunt Birdie and another blue-skied postcard from the despicable Jimmy. Jennifer didn't even read it, just noted the inscription scrawled across the front and the Spanish postmark. Angrily she ripped the unwanted card apart and tossed the little pieces into her kitchen bin. All men were heartbreakers, all men were selfish, clueless and frustrating but then again who said she had to give them all an easy ride?

Walking into Dan's room she handed him his orange juice and felt half-angry, half-fearful. She wanted to talk, needed to talk about them, about their future but the words just wouldn't make the journey from her brain to her throat.

"Think I'll lie down for a while, take it easy, get some sleep," Dan said after the first sip of juice.

"When do you want me to wake you?" she asked briskly as she took back the empty glass.

"Don't know – guess I'll rest as long as I need," he said flatly as he rolled over on his stomach and hid his face completely underneath the duvet, burying in tight, like a man trying to burrow to the very centre of the universe to find some safety and solace.

Six

For a while it seemed as if the rain would scupper the morning tennis session but the showers were fleeting and the winter sun won out in the end. Driving down the main street of Carrigmore, Rebecca shivered and turned the heating up a fraction. The black mountains, which hemmed in the town's inhabitants in a claustrophobic way, looked even more menacing than usual – their moody presence always gave Rebecca the chills.

As she waited in traffic Rebecca diverted her eyes to the dramatic castle high up on the big, black rock – the landmark which gave Carrigmore its name. Tapping the pads of her fingers on the steering wheel, she took in the period houses, massive grey structures set back from the road with chunky steps and grandiose railings leading up to impressive front doors. The buildings were a reminder of something irritating but something that escaped her memory for now as she waited for the line of cars at the traffic lights to clear.

At the end of the terrace was a house where the paint was peeling from the railings, where ivy overran the pillars and walls. The front door was bubbled from rain damage and great clumps of moss took up proud residence on the roof and windowsills. This was a house where the occupants were so self-assured of their position that they didn't need to impress like the nouveau-riche bankers, solicitors and traders; indeed this was a house where the need to impress with freshly painted house exteriors would be judged to be a vulgarity.

As she stared, the fossilised exterior finally jogged her memory and she groaned as she remembered it was Audrey Russell's defiantly grubby property (shared with her pompous bachelor brother Herbert). Shrill-voiced Audrey of sensible shoes and ugly cardigans, who wore her mother's ancient pearls to every stuffy little do around town, was the Chair of the local tennis club and the irritating thorn in Rebecca's side.

Pulling her car into the driveway of the tennis court, and parking in a discreet corner, Rebecca prayed she wouldn't bump into the club's Sergeant Major who would, as always, be looking for an up-to-date progress report on all matters outstanding from Rebecca, the club secretary. But, hopeful of sprinting to the locker rooms unmolested, she knew detection was a certainty when she was overtaken by Wellington, then Nelson, Audrey's hyperactive red setters and then heard a booming voice from behind call both her and the beasts to attention.

"Ah, Rachel – a word," barked Audrey, a tall, sinewy spinster with a neat grey bob who always dressed for the country in laced, low-heeled, ugly shoes, tights like liquid mud and tartan skirts which were generally brushed with dog hair. Today she completed her look with a vile brown woollen jumper with patched elbows, a green padded gilet and a mauve silk scarf at her throat which clashed wildly with her entire ensemble. "I am putting the final touches to the vintage opera night and was wondering how the fundraising was shaping up your end – that salon of yours, have you secured any funding yet?"

Rebecca had opened her mouth to respond when Audrey barked again.

"The salon, Rachel, have you heard?"

Rebecca bristled from the incorrect address, though she had long since given up trying to get Audrey to remember that her name was actually Rebecca. 'That's because the old bitch doesn't *want* to remember your name because she doesn't *want* you to ever think you're important to her,' Mark had laughed when Rebecca told him of her stinging encounters.

"Oh Audrey, hello, yes, the salon has promised involvement this year again." There was strength in Rebecca's voice although underneath she was shaking – Audrey always made her feel inferior somehow.

"So will that Tranquil place give cash or are they insisting on vouchers again?" Audrey continued in her emotionally unaware, military-style rant. "The cash is far better as far as I'm concerned."

"I'm still finalising the details." Rebecca was smiling so much her jaw ached. Up close, she could see how beauty vouchers would be lost on Audrey and her band of equally leather-faced tartan-wearing friends – a dying breed in the club but a forceful breed yet. Audrey's crowd didn't really go in for a lot of facial maintenance, especially after the age of thirty when they'd been securely married, had belted out a few brats and could concentrate on more interesting pursuits like dogs, point-to-points and foxhound racing.

"Well, tell them in *there* that we're not interested in vouchers – like I said, cash is what we want," Audrey thundered.

Momentarily the old crone was distracted by her younger brother, Herbert, dickied up in a bow tie and waistcoat and green farmer's wellies, rounding the corner with a beautiful red-wheaten Rhodesian Ridgeback at his heels. The two siblings merged silently, an air of superiority surrounding them like a kind of impenetrable radar and the dogs bounded off in the direction of the clubhouse, knowing as well as their masters that a quick game of cards was routine before elevenses.

"I'll see what I can do," Rebecca yelled after Audrey but her nasty brown tights and tartan skirt strode around the corner without any acknowledgement.

As Audrey disappeared from view Rebecca felt she could breathe again – at least until the old biddy got back on her case – probably by tomorrow at the latest.

Lou was already waiting in the locker rooms, tying back her long flaxen hair with a soft pink fluffy band. Rebecca flashed her companion a quick smile and Lou looked up briefly, then tapped her racquet in pretend competitiveness.

"All set? Bet I take you today," she joked.

"Doubt it," boasted Rebecca playfully as she tightened a loose shoelace on her tennis shoe.

When it came to tennis, as in all things about their relationship, Lou was firmly stuck in second-best position. Rebecca had the edge on fitness and tactics just as Rebecca had the edge on hair, legs and bum.

"Come on, Louise, let's get out and about before the rain spoils our fun," Rebecca urged as she jumped up and down on the spot for a few moments, warming up her legs in anticipation.

"In a minute – have you heard the scandal from the weekend?" Lou asked with a smirk.

"Not the teenage disco again?" Rebecca groaned.

"Apparently this time there was mayhem. Three young fellas in tinsel wigs from the town streaked round the clubhouse just as the kids were leaving. Audrey, who was upstairs with Bert, saw it all from the bar."

"Always surprises me why he's around for the discos," Rebecca sniped. "I think he just likes to lech at the young things in their too-short skirts."

"Yeah, I know what you mean – he's definitely a leg-man – doesn't even bother hiding it, the pervert. Remember those fab green heels you wore to the cocktail party last summer? He couldn't stop staring at your legs all night!"

"*Please*, don't remind me."

"Anyhow Nancy Drew and her pervy bruv called the cops and Audrey set the dogs on the young guys with a roar for the mutts to take 'a big bite out of their hairy behinds'."

"What? Sure those dogs would only lick you to death, especially the bloody Ridgeback!" Rebecca laughed.

"And apparently Audrey is threatening to call one of those emergency or extraordinary meetings, to finally blow the teenage disco back to the Ice Age."

Rebecca bit her lip. The once-a-month teenage disco had been a source of contention ever since the exclusive tennis club opened its doors to the country's new and vulgar money and their brat teens in exchange for a totally refurbished clubhouse complete with ultra-modern showers and a members' bar.

Being new money herself, Rebecca understood the attraction of the tennis club for the local social-climbers but despite several years of being on the committee, the old guard who still held the real power never really let her join their ranks. In the summer when Audrey and her cronies would be busy saving pence by trading home-grown fruit and veg, Rebecca was never included in the prize booty swap and she'd bristle when Mark would ask her summer after summer, "Any home-grown veg for my dinner yet? Thought not!"

But Rebecca refused to be disheartened. She was addicted to the place and it started the minute her car swept up the gravel path to the tasteful stone, glass and steel building which cleverly incorporated part of the old clubhouse into the design. Although sometimes Rebecca's pleasure was dulled when she thought of how Mark had lost out in the refurbishment of the buildings. Lou's husband Oliver, an architect and friend of Mark's, had designed the structure but Mark had stubbornly refused to have anything to do with the project. "Wouldn't bother my arse – that crowd are nothing but trouble – they'd argue with you over the final build right down to the last fifty cents – bet you any money Ollie will regret getting involved," he had told an irritated Rebecca who wanted the kudos of having her name attached to a project which was a showcase for the region. Her husband really could be an awful stubborn oaf, she thought as she remembered.

"Hey, you're daydreaming," Lou teased.

"Am I? Sorry."

"So how is Audrey's vintage-ball fundraiser working out?" Lou asked as she pulled on her tracksuit bottoms over her perfectly spray-painted legs.

"Oh, don't get me started. They think dressing up in granny clothes with long pearls and feathers in their hair is the height of excitement. I've *finally* got them to agree to the mini fashion show as well but they virtually squirm every time I mention the word *fashion* as if showing an interest in the contemporary clothes scene is somehow vulgar and despicable."

"That's because most of Aud's crowd look like they've been dug up. We all have to move with the times and if the younger crowd want fashion than Audrey and her *Addams Family* friends will just have to accept it. Of course I'm sure you'll be fab as compère on the night."

"To tell you the truth," said Rebecca, "I'd prefer to be sitting down getting discreetly locked on wine and champagne."

"Ah yes, but you enjoy the razzmatazz too, don't you? It's your kind of thing – dressing up, annoying the old biddies who are all worked up with longing and envy wondering about your rocks."

"Most of them are man-made industrial diamonds anyway," Rebecca laughed.

"Ah yes, but they don't know that, darling! New money drives them insane with jealousy and I really do think it's great *you're* compère too. If it were me I would be tripping over myself with nerves." Lou bent down and quickly laced up one shoe.

"Oh, you know what they say, fake it until you believe it yourself," Rebecca quipped.

"Or fake it till you make it," Lou bounced back.

Or fake it until it hurts. Rebecca had been doing that all her adult life.

"So how are things with Mark? You seemed a bit tense the other night when I rang?"

"Did I?"

"A bit . . . ah, sure, don't worry – I'll go easy on you since you're probably wrecked from cleaning that big house yourself now that your cleaner has left," Lou said, smiling cheekily.

What the hell was she talking about? True, their Polish cleaner Mariola hadn't been at the house since the Christmas party and then she had taken off for a quick trip home, but she hadn't left, had she? Christ, she hoped not – the replacement Mariola had sorted for them in her absence had turned out to be a real slacker and Rebecca hated a dirty house but was loath to lift a finger herself even to keep the place from falling down.

"You must be mixed up, Lou – Mariola's not going anywhere."

"Are you sure? Mark told Ollie last week she was looking for cleaning work and that she'd prefer business to domestic. He said he'd put the word out. Hey, sorry, like you said I must be mixed up – either that or I'm losing my mind."

Throwing her gear bag in the locker Rebecca tried to seem indifferent; it wouldn't be appropriate if she seemed irked about the working habits of a cleaner and she never liked people to think that she and Mark were anything other than a united front.

What the hell was he playing at though? Things hadn't been great with property the last while – the days of selling one big house without effort and living off the earnings were gone. It was all about turnover now, the need to sell the little grubby semi-d's fast, the reliance on a measly percentage from the rental market – the scraps of the trade only a few years back but the stuff of survival now. True the Gleesons were savvy and had their fingers in a lot of pies when it came to business but maybe Mark was cutting back on their own expenses and the cleaner was the first luxury to go? Well, he could bloody well reinstate her – immediately. If money was a problem she'd be willing to work more hours at the spa – better that than donning a pair of rubber gloves and lugging a mop around the house herself. No, she'd be putting her foot down – you had to with Mark. If he for one moment thought she was a pushover, God knows what other changes he might implement – he might sell the house from under her and downgrade her to a caravan if he thought he could get away with it.

"Right, can we stop talking and finally hit the court, Lou?"

Fuming but hiding her anger under a smile, Rebecca open the wired gates to the omni-surface artificial grass court and pounded the ball off the ground. With her first serve Rebecca produced a smashing ace that nearly cut the legs off her surprised opponent. Good, she thought – thundering aces meant she was angry and if she was angry, as with everything else in Rebecca Gleeson's life, that meant she'd win.

It was nearly eight when Rebecca heard the key turn in the door but she was waiting for him, ready to pounce.

"Well, what's this I hear about you giving our cleaner

the sack, Mark?" she assailed him, knowing full well she was acting on instinct and not on fact, but then again he never gave her the full facts when it came to business and she reckoned provoking him might shake him into the truth.

"For fuck's sake, I'm only in the door from showing a house," Mark defended himself as he threw his coat on a kitchen chair and poured himself a beer from the fridge.

"So? Is it true?"

"Is what true?"

"That we no longer have a cleaner?"

"Oh that . . . what do you care . . . she was just a pair of extra hands around the place." Mark was watching the head of his light ale settle and pursing his lips for the first taste.

"Well, firstly, I don't like to hear my own business coming from Lou – it makes me look an idiot – and, secondly, it was *my* house she was cleaning – if she had a problem or was leaving she should have told me, *not* you, before she disappeared on her holiday. So I wonder did she really quit or did you have a word with her and ask her to leave. I know your style. What are you up to, Mark?"

"What? Are you worried that I'll have you waxing your own legs soon? Don't worry, sweetheart. We're not on the scrapheap yet. As I said, she was just an extra pair of hands – easily replaced."

"But why replace her in the first place when she did such a good job?"

"I didn't. Her choice – she wanted to move into business – more hours," he shrugged. "We'll get another cleaner. You can look for one yourself tomorrow."

Rebecca bit her lip and crossed her arms, not satisfied with his explanation and not sure if there was a bit more fighting to do. He was irritating her to hell these days . . . up to something in business, winding down other concerns and telling her nothing as usual.

"Still, you should have told me first about her leaving as soon as you knew," she lashed out at him. "I don't like secrets, especially ones that my friends seem to be in on before me!"

"Yeah, right . . . no secrets," agreed Mark mantra-like, not at all moved by his wife's whingeing but too tired to let her mini-tantrum escalate into a heated fight.

"So – have you eaten?" Rebecca added somewhat sulkily after a minute's awkward silence, not sure what to do with the adrenaline that was bursting through her veins demanding an immediate outlet.

"Grabbed a bite in the pub earlier on."

Rebecca shrugged and left the room.

Mark busied himself buttering a few slices of bread, rolling them around a few slices of packaged ham that he retrieved from the fridge. When it came to culinary pleasures there was never much point in bothering his pretty wife. Before the bespoke solid oak, marble-topped kitchen and the top-of-the-range appliances were even installed he knew they'd be purely for show – nothing more.

As he ate his sandwich Mark noticed that a bunch of bananas lying at the corner of the kitchen counter were beginning to over-ripen. In a day or two they'd be thrown into the bin – yes, that was his Rebecca, his Rebecca who loved the idea of an overflowing fruit-bowl in her designer kitchen, but who only ever ate expensive pre-packaged fruit salad from the chill section of the local supermarket, that is if she ate at all.

Rebecca reappeared at the door. "Are you staying home tonight? We could watch a movie," she asked huffily.

"I'm off to play poker."

"On a work night?" Rebecca snapped, feeling angry all over again.

Mark threw her a knife-edge look and she clenched and unclenched her fists, digging her manicured nails into the palms of her hands so it hurt.

"Coming home, reeking of booze and stinking up my house with the smell of stale fags!" she ranted, unable to contain herself.

"Jesus, sometimes you're such a bitch, such a nag, but then you're such a cold fish at the best of times that your bad humours don't really surprise me any more!" Mark abandoned his sandwich and made for the door.

"I'm *not* a nag," said Jen, following him. "I just think you might spend some time home with your wife now and again. It's such a big house to rattle about in on my own."

"Well, if you had more *real* friends you could be throwing parties every night of the week!" Mark grabbed his coat and car keys. "Then again, we could always fill the place with children if it's company you're after!" He went out, banging the front door shut, causing her beautiful hand-painted glass to shudder dangerously.

Moments later she heard him start up his Merc, the wheels crunching on gravel as he disappeared into the night.

Chewing her lip in anger, part of her hoped he'd have enough Dutch courage to drive the car home after his session of booze and cards. Part of her even hoped he would end up in a ditch somewhere dead by morning. How wonderful to be a free woman wallowing in so much life insurance that her grief would surely be short-lived? Not that any of this would happen. Mark would stay over and make his own way to work: she wouldn't see him till tomorrow evening. Biting her knuckle, she wondered if she had a few sociopathic genes in her make-up that allowed her think such dark thoughts about her husband – if she had it would definitely be from her father. Selfishness was at the core of who he was, just as it was at the core of her being too, she supposed.

Seven

Jennifer came home from the supermarket and the school run one afternoon to find her husband risen from his bed, where he'd lain for a week. Now in miraculous good health he was out in the back garden in worn clothes and wellies, digging a bloody big hole on the lawn, up to his knees in muck with no sign of stopping. Smiling broadly, he waved and cautiously she waved right back.

What the hell was her unpredictable obviously-on-the-edge husband up to now?

"Fancy a cup of tea, Dan?" she yelled as she opened the kitchen window and tried to play casual.

"No, got a hole to dig," he shouted back.

Right, this was bloody serious so. Fearful, Jennifer knew she needed to talk to the one person whose advice she really needed; unfortunately it was also the one person whom she often couldn't stand. Sticking on a DVD for the girls, Jennifer went to move her sleeping son from his car seat and into his cot with the fiddly catch (undoubtedly designed by a twenty-something childless male engineer) and dialled the number of the long-time cow of a friend she'd repeatedly sworn to cross off her Christmas-card list every year.

"Hello – Sandra from *Slinky Bunnies* here," the cow answered breezily.

"Sandra, it's me, Jen."

"Oh hello, you! Hubby back from his Gestapo interrogation session in the West then?"

"What? Oh yeah, Dan did his team-bonding session thingy . . . it was kind of . . . eventful."

Jennifer could hear her friend tapping away on a keyboard and was irritated at the sound of every little click. For God's sake, didn't she deserve Sandra's full attention from time to time? With Sandra time was always money and Sandra was always consumed with money-making ploys, and had tried it all, especially anything home-based or flexible to fit in with the rearing of her three demon boys.

First there was the mobile nail clinic where she organised 'nail parties' and did 'discount' nails for weddings and hens – not that the whole operation ever cost much as Sandra bought the stick-on nails in bulk from eBay and she never bothered with any kind of legitimate 'nail course'. "Nails – how feckin' difficult could they be?" Sandra reasoned and, in fairness to her, she was probably right.

Then, when her own kids grew up a bit, Sandra reckoned other stressed-out parents would pay any amount to escape from their little rug-rats, especially for birthday parties, so she bought a tinsel wig and some face-paints (courtesy of the cheapo pound shop) and went into business doing party games for ridiculous amounts of money. These days, however, Sandra was in the knicker business and it was a perfect career choice as Sandra was the randiest person Jennifer had ever known and knickers brought in lots of lovely money now that the Irish had finally lost their Catholic guilt and had become wildly experimental between the sheets and everywhere else.

"So, did you get a chance to look at that catalogue I sent you?" asked Sandra, still only giving Jennifer half her attention as she tapped furiously on her keyboard.

"Ehm – lost it actually," Jennifer lied. In fact, after the girls had thumbed it to death at the committee meeting, she'd slipped it into the recycling and had consoled her less than svelte figure with a few chockie bickies and an instant packet latte.

"No matter, I'll post you another – I hope you're not in those nursing bras 24/7?" The tone of disapproval was unmistakable.

"No, of course I'm not in nursing bras . . . well . . . not all of the time anyway." Jennifer peered down her shapeless, faded T-shirt at her once white and now grey-blue underwear which had been holding her bits together since giving birth. Now that she thought about it, this wasn't even a new bra – it must have been from Abby's or even Emma's nursing days. On close inspection she saw a few dried crumbs, probably breakfast toast, lodged in the valley between her heavy bosoms.

"You know, Jen, if you don't get out of that shabby underwear and into something a bit racier Dan will lose interest in you completely," Sandra warned.

Jennifer bit her lip. No sex mightn't be a bad thing . . . sex was for people who were at peace with life and had no worries, not for stressed-out wives with redundant husbands.

"It's just that I'm waiting for my body to get back into shape first, you know, before I splash out on new underwear," she rationalised as she picked out a scratchy crumb which was stabbing her left boob.

"Oh, are you going back to the gym and working out then? Some of the gyms here in the city offer great programmes to help mums lose the flab. Sure how old is Adam now anyway?"

"Eight months."

Eight months and she hadn't lost a pound of her pregnancy weight and the breastfeeding that most mums swore by for melting the fat had had no effect on her. Besides, she couldn't stop eating and unfortunately when she ran out of the good stuff she naturally gravitated towards the kids' Milky Bars and Smarties and sometimes, most shamefully of all, even the baking chocolate for the Rice Krispie buns, and now that Dan had been made redundant, she was eating all the time from nerves and part of her thought she might as well keep on eating while she could afford to have a serious chocolate habit.

"Yeah – see, the thing is," she went on, "there's no point in buying anything nice when I'll *definitely* be finished breastfeeding soon and my boobs will be deflating."

"Well, you could go for something adjustable – you know, something that would do you now and later on . . . a nice little corset or basque would suck all your bits in *and* allow you to be a *real* Mammy Von Tease in the bedroom," Sandra suggested smuttily.

"Oh . . . do you think? I just don't know," Jennifer fretted as she squeezed her tummy.

"Or then again you could go for something more roomy while you're waiting to lose the pounds . . . a nice floaty cammy, a baby-doll nightie, some crotchless all-in-ones –"

"Sandra!"

Jennifer heard her friend cackling down the phone and she couldn't resist laughing too. For a moment the *click-click* on computer keys stopped completely as Sandra enjoyed a good old bellyache and for that moment it seemed as if the ice was broken and they were back to the old days, when they were both in their early twenties and off on some adventure. Great times – when the two of them pretended they were nymphomaniac twins to get the guys all wound up (they did have matching blonde bobs at the time). These days their relationship seemed so stilted, defined by the obligatory Christmas and birthday card, the check-up phone call once a month and the boredom and monotony of what was once an electric, spontaneous friendship.

Abruptly the magic laughter ceased and Jennifer could hear Sandra revert to her tapping, getting the accounts together for the end of the week no doubt, sending emails to her *Slinky Bunnies*, telling them to get their figures in, planning parties for the next few months, being productive, being busy.

"Did I tell you I've just come back from Belfast from our Spa Weekend Special awarded to the *Slinky Bunny* unit with the best sales?"

"Seriously? Wow, that must have been great for winding down and relaxing!"

"Suppose . . . we mostly just got our nails painted. No point in wasting too much drinking time. We've another weekend away to go on soon, just the top managers this time. We have to vote Copenhagen, Barcelona or Prague – what do you think?"

"God, I wouldn't know. It all sounds so exciting."

"Trouble is, I've been to all of them before. Hate going back anywhere twice," sighed Sandra wearily with the boredom of the seasoned traveller.

"You know, I realise you're always up to your eyes but I was thinking we really must meet up soon, Sandra. You haven't seen Adam since the christening . . . so maybe when you come back from Prague or wherever else you'll be heading . . ."

There were a few non-committal mutterings down the phone and an awkward silence froze the line.

"So, nothing else exciting then?" Jennifer could hear her friend inhaling deeply on a cigarette now. She could nearly feel her friend's boredom ooze down the line.

"Well, you know me – I'm not exactly being chased by the paparazzi!"

"Right, you won't mind if I head then? I've got a parent-teacher meeting this evening and I'm in a bit of a rush."

It wasn't a request really. That was it – she was definitely crossing that bitch off the Christmas-card list forever. For a moment she thought back to the days when she and Sandra were on their first great adventure, working in Chicago on a J1 Visa, rollerblading down Navy Pier on the shores of the great Lake Michigan, partying on the dodgy side of the Windy City to the horror of the American girls who warned that America was awash with serial killers. Back in those days Jennifer and Sandra had roared with laughter at their concern. They were two mad cows who had met when they both enrolled for university: Jennifer semi-serious about her studies since she was the first of her family to hit third level; Sandra neither knowing nor caring where she was heading in life so long as she was having fun and had a bit of cash at the ready. The mad girl-power days just before Jennifer fell for a Canadian busboy in the Chicago restaurant where she waitressed, a boy with a huge smile and laid-back attitude, a computer student who liked to laugh a lot.

"Dan's been made redundant," Jennifer suddenly rattled out for dramatic effect and for a moment she thought Sandra had crashed off her chair and taken the laptop down with her. Something definitely fell and she distinctly heard Sandra gasp.

"He's been let go?" The clicking of nails on the computer keyboard was killed as was the posh phone voice as Sandra's vowels flattened out with the excitement.

"The whole company is restructuring – they're relocating to Eastern Europe. In fairness, they've been building the bloody plant for the last three years so it's hardly a shock they want to now put people in it . . . except it was a shock when the news actually came."

"But surely the plan was always to keep a core operation here?" Sandra asked excitedly.

"Plans change, Dan says that's the way business is these days – the whole world is changing. It's not even about making money any more – it's about making *more* money," Jennifer sighed.

"Cash is King all right – it's the reason I never

finished my degree – my love of filthy lucre. So how's he holding up since he got the news?"

"Yeah, well, that's the other thing. I'm worried he could be depressed because he's kind of suffering from some sort of totally inappropriate insane happiness – I can see him from the window this very minute, hear him too – and I think, yes, he is, he's definitely whistling."

"You know, I heard of something like this on the radio last week. Men are going through their mid-life crises much earlier, having heart attacks earlier too – and being redundant and maybe even being depressed, sure that would only make it ten times worse."

"Yeah, well, like I said, he's taken to the bed . . . well, he had taken to the bed . . . I've been out all morning and just got home and now he's started to dig a bloody big hole in the garden."

A deep breath told Jennifer that Sandra was lighting up another fag to match the best drug of all – excitement.

"How big exactly, this hole?"

"It's past his knees now."

"Jesus, you're not saying, you don't think . . ."

"I don't know what to think, that's the problem, he's barely said a word to me about the whole thing –"

"What are you doing next week?" Sandra interrupted, her mind razor sharp.

"Couldn't tell you, sure you know me, always being chased by the paparazzi!" Jennifer barked out a laugh that sounded quite scary.

"Next week so, I'll come visit you. Sit tight and in the meantime do whatever you do to relieve stress," Sandra warned before she hung up.

Stress relief? Right, it was time to bake buns again so. Time to pretend that everything was all right in the world, time to have a go at being the perfect mother and hope that the world would stay still and perfect too. Besides, Emma's school was having a bake sale and home-made and organic were absolute requirements for ambitious middle-class parents and, while Jen might be deficient in lots of respects, when it came to Emma's school surely she would eventually crack the baking of buns?

"Abby, Emma, Mammy is making buns – do you want to come help?"

The two children looked at each other – it was a look between fear and excitement.

"Come on, it's a good time just before dinner and thankfully Adam is asleep."

"What we making, Mammy?" Emma asked excitedly.

"We'll have another go at some muffins, will we? I still have most of the stuff from the last time," Jennifer told her offspring calmly and assertively.

A quick visual check round the kitchen told her she was indeed well up on eggs, milk, flour, apples and muffin-cases. Muffins – what was there to do, only mix flour, peel and stew apples and add in some milk with ground cinnamon? It was then that Jennifer realised she had no ground cinnamon. Never mind, she would improvise. She would problem-solve just like in the world of work, her pre-mammy problem-solving brain fired up – but definitely not on all cylinders. There were cinnamon sticks left over from Christmas from her mulled-wine experiment, she remembered. Right, she would grind the papery sticks down with her under-used mortar and pestle until she got the required two teaspoons of powder. It was a sound plan – Jen felt quite proud of her just-about-still-intact problem-solving ability.

Fifteen minutes later she was still grinding away, her neck hurting from being bent over the bowl in concentration, her hair falling over her eyes as the sweat beaded on her brow, and then panic began to build as the hand of the clock leapfrogged towards feeding time at the zoo and the kids became antsy for real hunger-blocking food.

"Mammy, my tummy hurts, I think it's hungry," Abby, the fly-weight human eating-machine, whinged.

"Okay, pet, nearly there . . . look, Mammy has a teaspoon of spice now, isn't this fun?" Jennifer tried to console her in a hyper-upbeat voice. As she nearly ground her knuckles into the mortar bowl she was disheartened to see that she was still well behind on the second teaspoon.

Suddenly, Adam roared into life and a flustered Jen dashed down the corridor and rescued him before he sprang from his cot – again. Back in the kitchen, the jiggling red-faced baby on her hip kept trying to snatch at her mixing bowl and lick raw egg off the eggshells. Frustrated, Jennifer dumped her son on the floor and his sharp little fingernails dug into her legs in revenge as she worked the mortar and pestle furiously until she finally got her required two teaspoons of spice. Muffin goo was then lashed into the paper muffin-cases and the whole lot thrown into the hot oven and Jennifer watched in fascination as the mixture began to rise and rise and rise and taunt her with possible perfection. Fifteen minutes later the muffins had morphed into enormous misshapen domes but when she checked she found they were still soggy in the middle. Ten more minutes and they were just the same: soft, soggy, ginormous and defiant.

Another ten minutes passed, panic building and the children's noses pressed against the heatproof oven window. Then Jennifer checked again and the muffins were still a mass of goo in the middle while beginning to burn on top. Heart aching, and totally mystified, Jennifer hauled the twisted bodies out and let them expire on the wire cooling-rack before they left for their final resting place – the bin.

"Oh, Mammy, some bun bits – can we lick some, please?" Abby begged.

A frazzled Jen broke off any edible crumbs from the sides and fed them to her children like they were starving baby birds.

"Dinner's going to be a bit late, kids – how about fish-fingers, beans and chips?"

Emma shot her a 'for God's sake what kind of mother are you?' look, then went into the sitting room to watch telly, reappearing to drag her mother in there in front of the TV screen.

"Look, Mammy, Sophie's making muffins tonight – *her* muffins look *real* nice," she announced excitedly.

Evil, evil woman, your muffins do look bloody perfect! Jennifer tried to communicate her hatred through the TV so she could inflict some mortal damage on Sophie Lloyd's muffins. Sophie was now icing the blasted things, her perfectly made-up pretty face going into spasms of *ooh* and *aahh* as she shook her dark, glossy mane seductively, placed a dab of white, runny sugar on her finger and licked it in slow motion for the camera.

A little hand reached up and gently patted Jen's

stomach as she stared at the TV speechless with envy, hatred and desire. Looking down she saw Abby's angelic face turned up towards her, her eyes all mournful pity and unbelievable understanding.

"Poor, poor Mammy, you're sad because you're not pretty like Sophie and you have a big tummy. Sophie has no tummy, 'cos she has no children – we made your big fat tummy, didn't we, Mammy?"

Jennifer was fit to explode. It was well known that culinary wonder, Sophie Lloyd, had *five* children under the age of eight and got better-looking with every little bundle that came home from the hospital and appeared on the front of all the Irish glossies. What the hell was she, a mother of just three, doing wrong?

"Don't worry, Mammy," Abby beamed, "you make fish and chips and I'll help Daddy dig his hole – he'll have lots of fun stones and worms – I love worms!"

From the kitchen window, with yet another non-nutritious dinner blasting away in the oven, her hands gripping a hot cup of tea, and a freed Adam gnawing at her shins, Jennifer watched father and daughter digging, one with a heavy-duty spade the other with a cracked red plastic shovel. Every now and then Abby would find a worm and hold it up for her daddy to inspect. Dan would look at the beast carefully, then much to Abby's delight bring the creature to his mouth and pretend to eat it. Then both of them would throw their heads back and laugh and laugh and laugh.

Jen went back to switch off the TV.

"Next week we'll be doing some quick and easy recipes for all the family for when you are out and about spring-picnicking!" droned Sophie.

Picnics! What planet did this woman live on? Jennifer switched off the TV with a snort.

Back in the kitchen, with her children waiting to be fed some dinner, Jennifer wondered when exactly her flat-as-a-board stomach had gone saggy and how long it would take for it ever to go back firm and would the Jen of the future ever be remotely like the Jen of the past with a need for a sexy bit of anything out of Sandra's saucy-knickers catalogue?

Eight

Brooding on her lastest major row with Mark, Rebecca padded to the snug off the kitchen. His words had stung and, as the days passed, she found her mind constantly returning to them. How dare he imply that she had no friends, she thought as she flicked on the downstairs computer. Besides, friends were easily acquired. Lou had been more than willing to fawn on her when she first arrived in the provinces.

"It must have been *so* exciting being an air stewardess!" Lou had gushed within minutes of meeting Rebecca in the County Arms Hotel six years ago.

It wasn't, actually. Being an air stewardess was often unbelievably boring: doing that daft exit routine for passengers who couldn't give a toss if the plane went down so long as they were well sauced, reassuring mothers with screaming babies that their children's ears wouldn't explode on take-off and settling disputes with infantile passengers over ownership of arm-rests. Then there was also the loneliness of sterile hotel rooms.

No, Mark turned up at just the right time – just as passengers were getting more stroppy and more lower-class by the day. She remembered that first trip to London, when he was over checking on his UK rental properties. She'd caught his eye when she smiled wryly at his saucy little comments and double entendres while staying completely cool and professional. He was a naturally funny guy, had unmistakable presence, a sexiness that he was very aware of, so naturally he didn't think twice before slipping her his business card . . . which she promptly dumped in the bin.

Driven demented by her coolness, and occasional warmth, Mark asked her out to lunch the next time he saw her, an invitation she'd declined. Then he upped the stakes to dinner in an over-priced Dublin hotel, which she also refused – she didn't want him to think she was overly impressed by money. Until one day she bought him a cup of coffee at the airport and afterwards she made him work for every morsel of her time and attention.

Within months they were engaged, and in just over a year they were married and then, most blissfully of all, Rebecca was able to give up the air stewardess game to become the cosseted young wife of a big name down the country with something of a glamorous 'hobby' job. A year of beauty school had been all it took to put that plan into action.

Sighing, Rebecca forced herself to forget the promises of the past and begin the tedious task of uploading her Christmas photos from the digital camera to the computer screen. There were a few shots of Lou looking a little bit tired and emotional and far too many of Mark's dodgy town acquaintances. The party had been a real late night and it had been a good idea to have their cleaner Mariola over to tidy the kitchen and to ensure there was a ready supply of sparkling glasses and cutlery available to their guests.

Rebecca stared at the familiar pretty face of the twenty-something blonde who'd come to clean her house once a week for the last two years. She'd been a great worker, Mariola, dependable but thankfully quiet. Then as Rebecca flicked through the remaining photos her heart froze. It wasn't anything in particular, not a kiss or a touch but just a small look of familiarity as Mark turned his head towards their employee. In his eyes was a warmth that Rebecca hadn't seen come her way in a long time, an affection frozen in pixels, as he placed one protective arm around Mariola's shoulders.

Shyly the Slavic beauty gazed up at Mark through long blackened lashes like a Polish Princess Diana who knows when a man has been entranced and the computer whirred as Rebecca stiffened in her seat with fear, hurt and jealousy. No, experience had taught her that contrary to Mark's advice it was better not to need companionship. People were obligations, people always let you down and men-people were worst of all.

Determinedly Rebecca got up from her seat, walked up the stairs as if weighed down by lead, peeled off all her clothes and slipped into some Egyptian-cotton pyjamas before escaping into bed. If Mark was having an affair, she'd pick up her life and move on, she'd find another man to woo and this time she'd stay on the pedestal. Experience showed that the only way to keep a man interested was to stay aloof, to always be somewhat unattainable. Rebecca was a smart girl – how had she forgotten the golden rules of treating them mean to keep them keen, and when exactly had Mark stopped looking at her like she was precious and started looking at other women as if they were something more?

If she'd been any other kind of girl, this would have been the moment for some kind of romantic movie, a big box of hankies and a fishbowl of wine but Rebecca didn't want to feel vulnerable – she wanted to feel strong. Kick-ass car movies always made her feel that way. Which one would she select, which persona would she adopt? Car thief Angelina Jolie in *Gone in Sixty Seconds*? As she looked through her personal DVD collection the phone rang and she let it ring without answering.

"Hi, Rebecca – just wanted to say I know you thought I was being a bit coy about changing our tennis day last week . . . it's just, well . . . oh, I'm so excited just even thinking about it . . . I had a doctor's appointment because, well, I'm pregnant! I can't believe it myself to tell you the truth – I don't even feel sick! Anyhow, all's well with me and the baby, and Ollie and I are so, so excited . . . call me! Byeee!"

Cars were stuck in Rebecca's head as her brain filtered Lou's news; Lou'd be straight into mundane mammy-cars now as quick as she could – jeeps, MPVs, horrible, sensible fuel-efficient mammy-wagons – those awful big, ugly, sexless metal bricks on wheels.

The thought of Lou's upcoming domestic bliss gave Rebecca the chills as her hand fell on her *Pretty Woman* DVD; she'd always been a bit partial to that scene where Julia Roberts hops into Richard Gere's Lotus and shows him how it corners like it's on rails but she dithered over the choice. Unconsciously her hand fell on the movie she wanted, super-ass-kicking Uma Thurman in *Kill Bill* – there was nothing like watching sword-legend Uma slashing through men with Japanese steel to make a woman feel invincible and if she couldn't sleep she could always watch *Kill Bill 2* and plan strategies for killing her husband with maximum pain. Sticking the DVD into her recorder, Rebecca snuggled under the duvet and wondered if her husband, he of the roving eye, had already heard the 'baby news' from his buddy Ollie and, considering his quiet anger these days, maybe he had.

Nine

"Now I know you're probably a bit worried about me but there's really no need – I have *everything* worked out," Dan told Jennifer over breakfast as he sat around in his boxer shorts drinking his second industrial-strength cup of coffee and munching jam and toast.

"Oh? That's good to know," Jennifer answered in a forced singalong voice as she looked out the back window of her kitchen. At least the matter of the large hole in the garden had been solved: Dan was building a super-duper sandpit for the kids; he'd be laying the concrete blocks soon and Sandra's interest in visiting had lapsed once again now the O'Malley digging mystery had been solved.

"So I've decided to just take it easy for a while and see if I can figure out what it is I want to do with my life . . . go for walks . . . have fun . . . did you know that work is meant to be *fun*, Jenny?"

"Is it? And what *exactly* are we meant to live on

while you find yourself and have fun?" Jennifer asked, just about keeping her hysteria under wraps.

"Well, I've calculated that with the redundancy and our savings we'll have enough cash to live for six months – maybe seven – to pay all the bills including the mortgage – thankfully we've got a good one and at least we had the sense to buy our own place years ago –"

"Six months, did you say six months?" Jennifer gasped.

"Lucky, aren't we? Some people have no savings at all!"

"Dan, have you completely lost it? We can't postpone life for six months – you've got to apply for jobs today, ring recruitment agencies today! Our savings are not for having fun with! Our savings are meant to be for a rainy day!"

"Haven't you noticed it's been a rainy day in my life for years, Jen? Besides, I can't just become a nameless suit in another company overnight – I don't know if I can do that *ever* again. You give some place the best years of your life and what happens? They take your job from you like that!" He snapped his fingers angrily for effect. "We're out of bread by the way. Could you go to the shops and stock up? I want to search the Net . . . I'm all fired up about flexible employment and having fun for a change . . . maybe even doing a diving course . . . doing something different, doing something definitely not me because I don't think I like the Old Dan any more . . . he's *no* fun!"

Afraid of the faraway look in his eyes and his fast-paced excitable rantings, Jennifer decided not to push her financial interrogation. This lunatic version of her husband was talking so joyously that he had to be stressed and she didn't want to push him so far that he started to camp in the garden and stalk neighbourhood cats thinking they were big game. What in God's name was going through Dan's mind though? Wasn't he a bit young yet for a mini-meltdown? Why did men think they were the only ones allowed to have mid-life crises anyway? Damn it, her husband was being an unreasonable child and she would tell him as much when she was certain that he wasn't actually mentally unstable. And Intech might still ring and ask him back, telling him it was all a big misunderstanding and that something good would be coming his way soon.

"I'm buying a Ferrari!" Dan shouted excitedly as she came through the front door, her arms nearly dislocated from the weight of both Adam and the shopping bags.

"What?" she asked, certain she must have misheard.

"An old one obviously – you can buy them for *nothing* these days – of course the best selection is in the UK. I can even get classic insurance so driving it won't cost a fortune!"

The insanity was more than she could bear. Jennifer exploded.

"But you don't even *like* cars! Anytime I ever heard you talk about cars it was about their safety, their reliability – snow-chains on the wheels of heavy-duty cars for Canadian winters, functional cars plugged into the garage overnight so the petrol didn't freeze by morning. You don't like penis-substitute cars, Dan – you never did, remember?"

He looked at her as if she'd lost her head. "Jenny, *all* men like penis-substitute cars, it's just some of us are in denial for longer," he said in his Wise Old Wizard voice that was seriously beginning to get on her already fraught nerves. "Now I've just got to figure out which one I need to buy to feel happy."

The new 'exciting' Dan was going away for the night to have a drink with an old work pal (also a thirty-something stressed-out executive type, currently in employment) whose no-nonsense wife had agreed to let him off the leash for one night. Naturally the new flash-cash Dan was spending a night in a posh hotel, rather than roughing it on his friend's couch being driven demented by somebody else's brood.

"I need a break from kids' wailing if I'm ever to think about my future," Dan breezed as he kissed a peeved Jen on the cheek and ran out the door with an armful of sports-car printouts under his arm.

"Well, good luck so," Jennifer said sulkily, not that the escaping Dan noticed. "Flash cars!" she cursed – what an insane indulgence! Picking up a printout of one of Dan's desired boy-toys and pushing the paper close to her nose she felt blinding anger . . . and then she was overcome with something worse – panic, big, black, all-consuming, all-over-choking panic.

Fretting, she checked the on-line bank account and her inner wimp had a seizure when she saw for herself the holes that were being made in their finances from both necessities and fun purchases.

Shopping. The supermarkets were still open and some cheap shopping would distract her fevered brain from impending financial disaster and a husband on the edge.

"What are we here for, Mammy? What's for dinner?" Emma asked suspiciously as Jennifer slipped two enormous organic fair-trade bars of chocolate into the shopping bag hanging from the back of Adam's pram.

Guiltily, Jennifer slipped one of the bars out again and put it back on the shelf.

"That's grown-up chocolate, Mammy – are we having a party?" Abby probed as the chosen bar was concealed under cans of beans and jars of stir-in sauces.

"A party – no, honey, although we can have a bickie after dinner if you want," Jennifer replied breezily, trying to distract her children from their policewoman questions.

Passing by the Tex-Mex section Jennifer caught sight of some fiery chilli beef-enhancing products and was instantly smitten. Exotic food, kiddie-unfriendly food, her mouth began to water – it had been so long since she had eaten anything more interesting than Shepherd's Pie or plain old fried chicken. Tex-Mex chilli beef, melted cheese, tacos and chilli beans; the ethnic culinary notion had been tried out in her brain and accepted as a sexy dinner option for one. In seconds the hot stuff was in the shopping bag along with the chocolate. Chilli and chocolate, a perfect combination – weren't they both from South America? South America, that unanswered question, worried her mind even now as she negotiated the checkout and ignored the smug smirks of the cashier who noticed the bar of gourmet grown-up chocolate was already defiled.

Later that night, when the kids were all asleep by ten, good going in the O'Malley household, Jennifer fired the chilli-powder mix into the pan with some minced beef, and boiled some express rice. While her exotic dinner simmered, she grated cheese and prepared salad. For some reason she rejected all notions of wine and went searching for Dan's beer instead and wondered when had it become *Dan's* beer. When had she gone all boring and respectable, drinking nothing but girlie wine?

Lighting a chunky half-melted candle, Jennifer guzzled the beer by the neck and remembered the first time she'd tried Mexican food, eating with the Mexican chefs in America at one of their after-work car-park parties, serving up beans, burritos, tacos and the extra-hot chilli soup they made especially for the *gringos* – a culinary inferno which only beer could extinguish. As the beer bubbles burst on her tongue, Jennifer suddenly itched to put on Johnny Cash, the Man in Black who'd been their constant companion when she and Dan took a road trip to Kentucky. Closing her eyes she listened as Johnny belted out the blues and remembered the days of sunshine, riding horses American style by the lazy Green River, snoozing outside Mammoth Cave in sparkling sunlight while Dan tickled her flat brown belly with long-stemmed daisies, eating refried beans and Kentucky Fried Chicken under a bejewelled black-satin Kentucky sky just for kicks, being just a little wild, just a little young, drinking nothing but beer or whiskey, neat or on the rocks . . .

Ten

The universe demanded that some kind of action be taken, a plate smashed against a wall, something broken with force and determination – the very air was heavy with tension when Rebecca finally let loose on first sighting her husband and screamed that he was the biggest bastard in the whole world.

"Jesus, what's your problem, PMT?" he said, genuinely startled as his wife returned home and interrupted his evening TV and steak-eating experience.

"*This, this* is my problem," Rebecca fumed as she shoved a picture of himself and their former cleaner under his nose. "How long have you been getting down and dirty with the Polish cleaner, Mark? No wonder you fired her. I just knew you really fired her or came to some agreement for her to leave before I found out. Did you think you could keep everything in this picture a big secret forever?"

Mark whipped the piece of paper from her shaking hand, stuck it under his nose for inspection, thrust it back at her and laughed.

"What in God's name are you talking about? It was Christmas! I wished her well and told her what a good job she did around the place – nothing more."

"Yeah, right. You certainly had a good enough grip of her in this shot. How could you, Mark – she must only be twenty-three, twenty-four?"

"Same age as you were when I met you, more or less – you were nice then, sweet even – the years weren't long making you bitter, were they, Rebecca?"

His words were like lemon to an open cut but she hid her discomfort well.

"So you deny that there is anything between you then! How convenient for you that the night she came to clean also happened to be the night I usually worked late in the salon!"

"Would you ever relax and book yourself into the spa for the morning or take yourself off shopping and buy some new shoes," Mark answered, exasperated by her tenaciousness. "You're talking more crap than usual, Rebecca, and I'm not in form for your jealous antics."

"My *antics* – this is our marriage here, Mark, our *marriage* and all you can say is *I'm* talking crap? Look at this photo. Go on, look at it! What you want is written all over your face, what I want to know is did you get it, because if you did I swear I'll –"

"You'll what? You'll leave? And where will you go, which 'friend' will you even call to bitch about me to?" he said savagely. "Let's face it, Rebecca, your lack of friends even influences your choice of car. You drive a two-seater because you don't have enough friends to fill a proper car, do you, sweetheart?"

Without glancing at her, he poured himself a beer

from its can and focused on the sports channel. Stiffening in his seat and not even noticing a small spill of beer dribbling onto his shirt, he watched a player race down the pitch and make a fabulous pass to the celebrity striker who scored a goal in seconds, then punched the air with his fist.

Incensed, Rebecca left the room and thumped upstairs, not sure exactly what she was angry about – after all he'd denied everything – but still she felt raw, angry and insecure. Gently she removed every trace of her perfectly made-up face and, gazing at her reflection in the mirror, she fretted terribly. Where would she go if Mark was playing away from home? Who were the friends who might support her? The beautician who did her nails, the hairdresser who washed and blow-dried her hair twice a week, the local old crones whom she lunched with, discussing ideas for fundraising events? No, she was quite sure that if she screamed hysterically to any one of these women, 'I think my husband is having an affair!', she would redden to her ears, make her excuses and run.

The only possible contender for the Best Friend position was Lou and Lou wouldn't want to hear any news that rocked the status quo especially if it started any tension between Mark and Ollie – who'd been school friends and occasional partners in life since they both took on the revamping and redeveloping of property in Ireland and the UK during the summers with a bit of start-up cash from their dads, while still only in their early twenties.

Feeling shaky, Rebecca picked up the handset of her phone and traced her fingers over the number of the woman who lived only forty miles down the road, but there was such emotional distance between them they might as well have lived on different planets. Unsure, Rebecca held the phone to her ear until the dial buzz became an urgent beep and, as the fear rose in her belly, she returned the handset to its cradle. Another time – when she felt braver – she'd make the call to her sister Jennifer, another time when she felt more desperate and more in need of sisterly care and protection. Hell, it had been so long now, another year would hardly make any difference.

Downstairs she could hear the roar of the television as her husband watched TV. In front of her full-length mirror in her bedroom, she unbuttoned her pink satin work-blouse and slid her hands to her hips, pausing at her waist long enough to release her skirt button and unzip the skirt, slowly, enjoying the glimpse of toned leg from underneath the slash of fabric. Noiselessly, the skirt fell to the floor and Rebecca took pleasure in the spectacle of herself wearing a beautiful lace and satin twin-set in sensual dusky pink.

Would she dare dance with Mark nearby? It took only minutes to assemble and disassemble that gorgeous pole. Spurred on by the risk of discovery she thought about dancing noiselessly in her underwear, springing off her toes, using the metal as her friend and her enemy, feeling the delicious tension in her arms and legs as she'd hold a position for a few seconds, testing her suppleness, strength and growing skill. If Mark discovered her writhing around the pole, she'd take pleasure in driving him insane with desire; with every calculated move she'd let him watch, but definitely absolutely definitely, not touch.

Sighing, Rebecca settled instead on the extremely boring, but highly effective body-strengthening Pilates.

Rolling out her rubber exercise mat, she closed her eyes and attempted the art of pulling her stomach muscles through her rear end while trying not to pass out from lack of oxygen.

Forty minutes later Mark showed up at the door ready for bed and cursed as he almost fell over her en route to the en-suite bathroom. Re-emerging five minutes later in cotton boxer shorts and a white cotton bathrobe, he plonked himself on the bed to read a travel supplement from the paper, obviously seething.

Verbal communication was zero, but as Rebecca held her body taut, letting her knees fall slowly to the side and rocking them back to her centre, she read her husband's body language and knew he was hopelessly turned on despite pretending to be engrossed in his reading. From time to time she caught him looking at her but pretended not to notice, and when she moved on to yoga and was arched into the cat position she knew Mark was tense with anticipation, and that knowledge made her feel powerful and more than a little cruel.

"Come to bed, will you, I'm away early tomorrow," he growled, pulling off his bathrobe and throwing it roughly on the floor.

She ignored him.

"Rebecca, come to bed for fuck's sake!" he snapped.

Like a snake Rebecca slithered off her mat and deliberately spent ages in the bathroom, keeping him wondering whether he would be in line for any of the sexy stuff tonight. Brushing her long red hair she took one last look at her toned body in the mirror, then switching off the light sauntered out in Egyptian cotton pyjamas. As she walked towards the bed she could see the disappointment in his face; he knew her attire meant all bets were off for a night of passion.

"I can't believe you're still lying there brazen. If you had any decency you'd know to feck off to another room," she said, throwing a spare pillow directly at his head.

"Why, because you've got a vivid imagination, about me having the 'hots' for another woman? Besides, I built this house, some of it with my own hands and I'll be damned if I'll go elsewhere just because you want it that way!"

"You're such a shit, do you know that?" she hissed at him but she decided she wasn't giving up her beautiful super-king-size bed with its outrageously expensive memory-foam mattress either so, jumping in and banging the pillows, she glared at him ferociously. "Keep on your own side of the bed, don't even *touch* off me! I don't even want to feel your breath on the back of my neck, do you hear, Mark Gleeson!"

"Jesus, to think it has all come to this! I suppose there's not a chance now of your wearing that air stewardess uniform you keep hanging in the wardrobe?" Mark retaliated wickedly before groaning as she elbowed him mercilessly in the ribs.

Somewhere in the early morning with dawn breaking through a chink in the curtains her body betrayed her and she found she'd abandoned her extremist 'outraged wife' position for the middle of the bed and Mark had happily followed. His arm was like a dead weight around her and his leg was wrapped possessively around her outer thigh. They were both half asleep but, aroused by his scent, she wiggled in animal comfort and instantly he awoke, like a man who had just had a sudden shot of adrenaline. Rebecca was still dozing in the half darkness when he slipped off her pyjama bottoms, kissed her flat stomach and began to move downwards with his warm lips and mischievous tongue.

"You're so fucking tense!" he whispered.

He knew she didn't like this; that not tasting her was their unwritten rule, because it was too intense, made her feel vulnerable, but she was surfing the waves of pleasure before she was really conscious of what he was doing. Sleepily, she tried to turn on her tummy but he held her wrists gently and resumed his torturous kisses below her waistline until the tension inside her finally snapped and she swore she left her body and floated towards the ceiling.

"You tricked me into that little game," she half-scolded as she switched on the bedside lamp, arched an eyebrow and glanced at the alarm.

"Baby, I'm just giving you what you crave but won't own up to – best breakfast in bed I've had in a long time," Mark laughed as he fell back on the pillows and smirked.

For a moment she laughed with him and then she pounded his head mercilessly with a pillow and they tumbled around the mattress until he was on top of her, looking at her with a tenderness that she had rarely seen in recent months and it satisfied an intense longing, a craving deep inside.

Clearing his throat, Mark began to deliver a hasty speech and for once she really wanted to listen.

"Rebecca, last night . . . saying that thing about having no friends," he began. "I was angry and I knew it would hurt you – I was out of order and I'm sorry."

Pushing him away, Rebecca sat up and hugged her knees, then shrugged her shoulders indifferently. "It's not the first time you've said it – besides, it's the truth. I am a bit of a loner," she answered quietly.

For a second there was an uncomfortable silence that Mark knew he would have to be the first to break and, putting his arm around her cautiously then protectively, he felt her upper body gradually lean into his chest.

"Rebecca . . . you didn't really think that there was anything between me and the cleaner, did you?" he asked as he rubbed her arm gently.

Sighing softly, Rebecca met his gaze. "No . . . I don't know . . . it's just . . . something about the way you looked at her made me really angry."

"Ah . . . the green-eyed monster. It's nice to think you still like me enough that you don't want another woman to get her claws into me," he teased.

"Don't get a big head about it, Mark Gleeson, it's only because you're mine – let the cleaner feck off and get her own man. I've spent years trying to put manners on you and even then I'd say I've only had limited bloody success!"

"Oh for God's sake, woman, will you stop looking for a fight? You ever notice, Rebecca, that when we fight our bodies end up together in the morning?"

"I wouldn't read too much into it if I were you, Mark. I think your big ass is wearing a hole in the middle of the bed and that's the only reason we're sliding together," Rebecca sniped playfully as she rolled contentedly on her super-expensive mattress.

"Stay," he commanded suddenly, aroused by her spontaneous playfulness.

"Feck off – I'll be late for the salon!"

"Stay, let them fire you, you don't need their job anyway," he wheedled.

"Mark!"

"Sorry, I've decided, you're not going anywhere until I fuck you properly," he announced as he pulled her top over her head and chased her round the bed, grabbing her from behind and playfully biting her ankles and shins while growling like a guard dog.

Exhausted and laughing, she collapsed on her stomach and let him press her arms above her head so he could kiss and feel her from her wrists to the curve of her elbows, nuzzle her neck and bury his head in her beautiful red hair.

"Rebecca – my Rebecca, my little wild cat!" His eager hands explored her like she was some sort of exotic being, squeezing her breasts then buttocks together from behind, holding the small of her back while she arched in pleasure at his kisses.

Releasing her, their eyes met. Then sitting up and locking her legs around him, Rebecca kissed him hard on the mouth, then fell backwards onto the pillows, pulling him with her, laughing as he kissed her throat and shoulders and began to slyly work his hand between her legs.

His touch was electric and she hadn't felt so turned on in such a long time. Weeks, maybe months had passed since she had wanted him so badly, had appreciated him so much, she thought as patterns of morning light danced in front of her half-closed lids . . .

But abruptly she sensed a difference in his lovemaking, felt him kiss and rub her stomach several times, slowly, gently, and somehow it just felt very wrong. Opening her eyes Rebecca saw Mark hovering over her stomach and, overcome with rage, she kicked at him hard – hoping only to knock him off the bed, but instead she kicked him right between the legs and in shock he fell over the side and whimpered in pain and disbelief on the carpet.

"What the fuck was that for?" he panted when he had recovered enough to speak.

"For *looking* at me," she snapped as she watched him still writhing in agony on the floor.

"For fuck's sake, can't a man look at his wife without getting murdered?"

"Not just for looking at me but for looking at me like – like I'm some kind of brood mare for you to inseminate!"

"Well, what's wrong with that? You've had the fun of your twenties and you've been off the pill six months –"

"And it can take at least twelve to get pregnant – I've looked it up!"

"And I'm sure everything is fine . . . but you know Lou and Ollie are expecting and I just thought maybe you . . . I mean maybe we both should get checked out just in case –"

"No, I'm not listening to a word you're saying and I don't care who else on the planet is pregnant – there's nothing I have that needs checking out," she said stiffly. "Now, if you don't mind I'm having a shower and by the way there's only enough milk in the house for tea so don't take it all in your cornflakes or your life won't be worth living!"

"Rebecca!"

Fuming, she stormed into the bathroom and once inside

leaned against the door. Outside he was still calling her name and cursing loudly. Babies, babies, babies – he wanted one so badly – would she ever be able to satisfy his raw paternal need?

Eleven

Jennifer's head felt like it was full of rocks when she awoke the next morning after her Mexican night. Sleep deprived and feeling shaky, she knew she was not with it enough to drive a car so she decided to blow the cobwebs out of her brain by dragging the family on a bracing walk all the way to Emma's school. It was a good decision, she reasoned, as she hid the giant chocolate wrapper from the previous night in the bin and covered it with kitchen roll.

Puffing and blowing to make school on time, Jennifer saw Emma to the school gate where her first-born was snatched up by her eager teacher and led into her forlorn and weather-beaten prefab. As Emma disappeared, Jennifer watched the mums in their big four-wheel drives, with year-round sunglasses, battle for a last-minute parking spot. With a struggling Abby in tow – she was still on probation from playschool – Jennifer caught sight of Fiona the Pram, now a regular at the mums and tots, and was forced to stop and exchange a few civil words.

"Do you really think he likes all the jiggling around in that thing? If he was mine I'd be worried that he'd throw up," she asked as she took in Fiona's stunned-looking toddler.

"Dara – no, he *loves* it – he always laughs when I jog. You just caught him at a bad moment." Fiona pressed a non-tooth-rotting organic rusk into a fat little fist, then ran her other hand over a yellow bandana, today's little hip-mummy fashion statement. Despite his rusk, the "always laughing" kid still looked very grumpy and started to hiccup.

"So what has you up and about so early, Fiona? You don't have any kids in the school that I don't know about, do you?" Jennifer forced herself to be cheery when in fact she was acutely aware that her trousers were too long and fraying at the ends, her cotton top had shrunk in the wash and was riding up her fat belly and her hair looked like it had recently survived an Australian bush fire.

"No, no, Dara's the first – just putting his name down for Junior Infants in four years' time. I met Madeline at intensive aerobics last week and was a bit worried when she said I really should have had his name down from birth. Isn't that right, Madeline?"

Jennifer hadn't noticed she was in the presence of Perfect Mum with the perfect Norman-French name, Madeline De Burca, but one look at the no-nonsense, clean-cut, manicured, surgically-implanted-sunglasses-on-the-head mother, told the world that this mum was likely to know all about school procedures and important parent strategies, especially as she was on the school board. A groomed Madeline cast her eye over Abby, who at that moment was trying to contort herself into an octopus while balancing against the pram, and Jennifer knew what the other mum was thinking: problem child, lack of discipline, wouldn't happen if she was mine. Madeline's children were model children – Jennifer had seen them all line up regimentally in front of the four-wheel drive before being rushed off to numerous brain and body-strengthening after-school activities.

"So, little girl, are you not going to playschool?" Madeline asked the champion on-off playschool-biter directly.

"Not every day . . . I'm on pro . . . pro . . . what's the word again, Mammy?"

"Pro-biotic yogurts, really good for the immune system, she needs a bit of building up before we send her off every day," Jennifer swiftly supplied. "Playschool, where would we be without it – it's great to get them out of the house, isn't it, just for the sanity?"

"Is she going to the bilingual French-speaking playschool? It helps in the transition to the big school when she's four or five," Madeline said, giving Jennifer a knowing wink-wink-don't-you-know-I'm-on-the-board smile.

"Eh, no . . . but she has a sibling in the school already, so I'm not that worried." Jennifer shuffled around on her feet trying to hide her scuffed mules and frayed hems from Madeline's beady eyes.

"Yes, but you can never tell what judging criteria will be used in the future. There's talk of giving extra points if parents do the entrance interview in French and extra points being awarded for every French-speaking country the child has visited pre Junior Infants. Did you know that from next month the new crèche near the church is hiring two Gallic-speaking carers who will be talking in their native tongue from the moment you drop your baby in, and during the day the crèche will be playing Chopin as well as Baby Mozart. Just think how fantastic that will be for pre-speech comprehension and musical ability! You should really think of booking your little boy in there for a few hours a week just to get him going." During this speech Madeline seemed to be taking in for the first time how ordinary Jen's pram was, judging from the way she was staring at it and wrinkling her nose. Jennifer remembered Madeline's last baby pram, from the few times she'd seen her walk to the school gates; it was like a mini-space-pod, had undoubtedly cost the price of a small car and was probably designed by NASA.

Conspiratorially Madeline dropped her voice to a whisper and, checking that she wasn't being overheard, added that the town's latest crèche was apparently instructing staff in baby sign language.

"Imagine, they'll be able to talk to pre-verbal children with their hands and once a month they're going to allow parents to come in and practise baby massage on the premises with that Baby Mozart brain-music or possibly Beethoven going on in the background."

"Oh God, I'm going to book Dara in today!" Fiona said with a squeal of anticipation.

"It might be no harm, *especially* since you didn't get him down for the big school from birth and since he doesn't have a French name." Madeline gave the knowing little wink-wink smile again and Fiona said a hasty goodbye and jogged off to the super new crèche as fast as her bouncy buggy would allow while Madeline slunk her designer-track-suited ass into her tank of a car and drove off in style, sunglasses firmly perched on her disapproving button nose. Jennifer looked at her own two youngest children and worried – worried that she was out of the loop, not knowledgeable about the 'in' things and that she was already ruining her kids' lives through neglect, neglect, neglect!

Resolved to conquer her maternal flaws straight away, she decided to walk to the town library and read Abby a nice story about a duck or a tractor. Unfortunately she had only taken a few strides when her stomach began to cramp – badly. Maybe chilli, chocolate and early-morning exercise wasn't such a good combination after all, she thought, as she felt her guts gurgling. Thankfully, the library with its pristine toilets wasn't far away – she could see the pretty redbrick building from the school. Sweat breaking out on her forehead, she walked like a duck with appendicitis and shuffled through the library door, heading straight past the eye-catching kiddie section for the sanctuary of the loos.

"But, Mammy, I don't *need* to go," Abby cried as Jennifer dragged her into the toilet, bolted the door and swore from now on she'd live on nothing but rice and potatoes.

God, if this was what colonic irrigation was like they could keep it, Jennifer thought afterwards as she nearly collapsed into the sink and splashed some water on her face. Feeling as weak as if she'd just given birth, Jennifer beat a track past the kiddie-book section, killing Abby's pleas for duck-and-tractor reading, and tried to shuffle home as fast as possible. Wrestling with a screaming

Abby was enough to set her insides off again and with some fear she headed for the supermarket for immediate and discreet relief.

"Mammy, I don't need to go – I haven't weed in my pants!" Abby repeatedly protested right up to the point where her mother was again splashing water on her cheeks and taking deep breaths.

"So what are we buying?" the tot asked innocently as they both exited the toilets.

"What?"

"This is *Tesco*, Mammy, what are we buying?"

This was indeed Tesco and the child was correct: when in Tesco the buying of something seemed entirely appropriate, especially as they were passing the frozen-food aisle anyway and chips were always in short supply in the O'Malley household.

"Fancy a pizza tonight, Abby, maybe with some of your favourite chips?"

"Don't care. Hurry up, Mammy! Why are you spending so long looking at chips?"

"Don't rush me, Abby, I'm trying to find the right ones," Jennifer answered in pleasurable relief. The coldness of the chill-section fridges was like a compress on her nether regions, and when no one was looking she pushed her butt cheeks out a bit so she could feel the caress of the cold air where it was most needed. You are a lunatic woman who should not be in charge of children – especially little ones, her nagging inner voice protested.

"How about Hawaiian, Abby? Yes, let's have Hawaiian," she said as she opened the chill-cabinet door and took out a cardboard box of dough and cheese and a zillion little chemicals in the plastic ham. Not like the freshly baked pizza of her US days. Funny, every time she saw Hawaiian pizza it reminded her of the first time she had met Dan . . .

"Circle, okay, see circle . . . " Jennifer drew an imaginary circle for Javier the Mexican chef, then sawed it down the middle with her finger, "this bit Hawaiian, this bit cheese, understand?"

"He doesn't speak English," an annoying blond busboy with annoyingly white teeth, who she had never seen before, butted in happily.

"I bloody well know that," Jennifer snapped, feeling stressed.

"Hey, you're Irish!"

Irritation built up in Jennifer. She had three other tables to wait and two checks to drop and this guy wanted to annoy her by making stupid Paddy-Irish observations.

"Yeah, I'm Irish, you're American – big deal."

"Hey – nice to meet you too! My name's Dan – I'm Canadian, from Newfoundland actually, the most Irish place in the world after Ireland, and if you don't want my help that's fine by me."

"Okay, Mr Almost Irish, so how exactly *can* you help me?" Jennifer asked brusquely.

"I speak a little Spanish."

"Oh, okay, I guess that would help all right," she acknowledged with a grin that broke the ice.

"Crazy Americans," Javier spat out a rare English phrase as he understood the problem for the first time and began to get busy with the bizarre pizza request.

One summer long ago, passion bubbled in an

American kitchen and all because of Hawaiian pizza. Hawaiian pizza – an excellent choice, vaguely exotic, but safe – just like Dan.

At home there was a ridiculous message from Dan saying that he was getting the ferry to the UK to look at a sexy car that was going cheap but she hardly heard. Her food splurge from the night before had left her with a thumping headache as well as dodgy bowels and Adam was definitely fussing at her breast where her nipples were strangely hot and itchy. At dinnertime Adam was cross and wouldn't feed at all and, sticking a finger between his soft baby lips, Jennifer realised the inside of his mouth was covered in hard, white patches. Thrush – no wonder her nipples were on fire, along with her digestive system.

"Oh, the live yogurt is very good for that if you can't get to the doctor what with Dan being away," Helen said knowledgeably over the phone when she heard Jennifer's predicament. Being a country girl Helen was well up on everything beneficial that came out of a cow. And so, nipples smeared in cold cow goo, Jennifer went to bed. In her fractured dreams she was a Page 3 model of perfect form and face, teasing the tabloid readers with dabs of whipped cream strategically placed on her famous football-proportioned knockers. For some reason the tabloid was running a nationwide competition and the lucky winner would get to lick the cream off her boobs on live TV with all the proceeds going to charity. Naturally her head liked the sound of that – the charity bit of course.

Dan was in the driveway walking round and round his new toy as if he were a big cat bringing home the kill when, two days after thrush reared its ugly, itchy head, Jennifer got home with her pharmaceutically approved nipple-cooling creams from the doctor.

"Well, what do you think – a beauty, isn't it?" he asked, encouraging her approval, but with itchy boobs Jennifer wasn't much in the mood to be gracious.

"Wow, Dan, as a husband this time you've *really* gone and surpassed yourself," she said sarcastically as Adam tried to paw at the contraption from the comfort of her hip. "I only hope you got a discount since your new flash car seems to be missing *all* of its wheels!"

"Ah yes, I thought you might notice its unusual appearance," he grinned sheepishly.

"Oh believe me, I noticed, because while I admit I'm a bit of a girl when it comes to these things, even I can clearly see that your flash car seems to have morphed into a boat – and a pretty crappy boat at that!"

"Hey, it's not that bad. The shell is actually in good condition . . . needs a bit of cosmetic work of course but I'm *really* excited about just pulling bits off this baby, rebuilding her, just getting down to it with some elbow grease!"

Affectionately, he rubbed his hand down the belly of the craft and Jennifer couldn't help but notice several big holes in its structure. An idiot could tell this contraption with big black lesions on its flaking blue skin needed much more than a bit of cosmetic reworking.

"And the *best* thing is – I got it for a great price too," he added happily.

"Naturally you've seen the gigantic holes in this tub of yours," said Jennifer, putting her hand up to inspect one hole before it crumbled to the touch.

"Oh these ones, they're not as bad as they seem." Dan deliberately put his fist through one hole and watched it implode in a heap of dust. "The big one now, that'll be a fairly sizeable repair, but until I cut the rotten bits away I won't know how bad it is exactly." Casually, he fingered the ragged black edges and plucked away its softened tissue until the wood cracked like a rotten egg.

At this rate the whole craft would end up being more hole than boat, Jennifer thought as she watched the faraway look take him over.

"Of course until I sand her down there's no way of knowing just how much is rotten – it might be much worse than I thought," Dan mused happily.

"And would you mind telling me how you actually came to be in possession of this – this *boat* when I thought you had your heart set on a flash motor?"

"Love."

"What?"

"Spellbinding, all-consuming love at first sight . . . I was about to board the ferry when I saw her and I realised what you said was true. I don't need a flash penis-substitute car, I just need something to feel passionate about . . . and all the memories of growing up in Newfoundland came flooding back, the smell of the sea, lobster pots, fishing boats . . . my grandfather taking out tourists whale-watching or upholstering some bit or other of a boat . . . it all came back to me when I saw her for sale in Mrs McAllister's front garden – her husband died last year, it was his boat. Mrs McAllister wanted rid of it – found looking at it every day too upsetting."

"I can see why. Dan, bloody hell, you don't know the first thing about boats!"

"Course I do – didn't I just tell you it's in the blood? I'm going to rip this baby to bits and bring her back to her former glory – wait and see. One day, my son, all this will be yours!" he said grandly as he grabbed Adam from Jen's arms and kissed him tenderly.

Adam dutifully smiled a gummy smile and Jennifer rolled her eyes in irritation.

"As if any son of mine would ever want anything so archaic," she said acidly, swanning off, leaving the love-struck boatman outside with his glorified piece of firewood.

Seeing Dan blowing money enraged her so much that she immediately resolved to spend some on herself, before they were totally broke and Dan was having a relaxing holiday in the mental hospital. All fired up, she punched in the code for the Leinster Headquarters of Slinky Bunnies, otherwise known as Sandra's kitchen.

"Sandra, I've decided to leave my husband and you're going to help me do it!"

Jennifer knew her city-slicker friend wasn't expecting that.

"What, are you looking for a safe house or something? He hasn't gone dangerous, has he?"

"Well, if you'd bothered your arse coming down to see me you'd have been able to judge yourself. Relax – I'm only talking a few days. We're going to New York, as soon as possible, and since I'd get a rubbish deal you're going to book it all on the Internet."

"New York! Do you know how many times I've been to New York?" Sandra said indignantly. "Now Buenos Aires, that's the place to go – one of the girls told me a while back how they danced the tango on Florida Street and had a gas time going to a restaurant which turned out to be a strip club and were served dinner by a woman in the nip – "

"Sandra, listen up. It's New York!"

"Well, excuse me, I haven't said anything about going yet," Sandra said snottily.

"It's New York or nowhere," said Jennifer, feeling strangely powerful. To hell with fitting in with other people's plans! From now on she was setting the agenda. Down the phone she could feel the tension building – could nearly hear Sandra's heart beating, her quick brain thinking. After all, they both knew this was more than just a conversation – this was about the state of their friendship. That is, if they really had a friendship worth valuing any more.

"Well, would I be going with the present day Jenny or the old fun Jenny?" Sandra asked, her question a cocktail of coquettish playfulness laced with venom.

"I don't know. All I know is this Jenny at the end of the phone is in a mad rush to take a big chunk out of the Big Apple and would leave tonight if she could."

"New York – why New York? Boston, Santa Monica – I haven't been to them yet."

"It's New York! Look, on account of the short notice I'll sweeten the deal. You book it and I'll pay for the hotel, I'll pay for the flights too if they're crippling." What the hell, she might as well blow the family finances completely before her husband bought a helicopter and parked it on the front lawn.

The phone line was eerily quiet but Jennifer waited calmly, confident that Sandra couldn't resist her fabulously generous offer.

"Oh feck it – when are we going then?" Sandra gasped.

Dan's reaction was disappointing – infuriating even.

"Sure I can cope, especially since Adam finally weaned himself completely after you got thrush. Baby-sitting three kids, just how hard can it be?"

Jennifer was hoping he'd find out.

The art of forgetting she was a mother began as soon as Jennifer pushed her way through the airport doors in Dublin but fear set in as soon as she saw the Departures crush.

"What's customs like for the States? Do they still clear you at Shannon, Sandra?" she fussed.

Sandra rolled her eyes in amazement. "How long has it been exactly since you were on a plane, Jennifer?"

"My honeymoon."

"Holy Mother of God, what have I let myself in for?"

"We thought about going on one of those babymooners when I was pregnant with Emma, but I was so sick the whole time I was living on re-hydration salts and then I had a lot of children very quickly so that kind of . . ." Jennifer caught a look from Sandra and decided she should shut up, except she couldn't quite succeed. "Sandra, when they fingerprint you going through customs, do your fingers end up being all black like you're in the police station?"

"Jesus, it's like talking to someone from Mars! You're frying my brain! Please, would you ever stop talking?"

Jennifer complied – there was no point in making Sandra feel nostalgic for her knicker job and her posse of girls before they even put a toe on the plane.

New York. Jennifer had been in New York only once, a very long time ago, as a stopover en route to Chicago when

124

she'd got to spend a few hours sightseeing. Curiously, first impressions were still the same. The noise, the energy, the feeling that you had just been slapped in the face and told to wake up quick because this is real life and real life can end at any moment. Gazing up at her hotel, Jennifer was filled with admiration. As always Sandra did everything right, booking the right hotel within easy walking distance of everything so that they could get everywhere fast and efficiently, getting it all for a brilliant price too.

As the lift doors opened and they began the long walk down red-plush carpets to their hotel room, they came across a man in uniform dressed like a security guard with a glossy, well-toned dog obediently following at his heels but it was like Sandra had been hit by a truck as with a sharp gasp she collapsed against the wall.

"What's wrong?" Jennifer asked anxiously.

"The dog – the beagle dog!"

"What you mean, the dog? Oh God, you don't think it's a bomb or something?"

"Oh, far worse than that, Jen . . . but then *you* were the one who insisted on coming to New York even though everyone knows the place is crawling in them."

"Crawling in what?"

"Bedbugs! They use beagles to hunt for them, don't you know? Hopefully he's screened our room already and sniffed out any live ones, but I'm just warning you now, if you wake up covered in blood tomorrow it's not me gone rabid – it'll be the critters!"

"You're joking?"

"Yeah, yeah, I'm joking – not!" Sandra snorted as she opened the door.

Inside the room Jennifer collapsed on her firm bed with crisp white sheets and stared at the ceiling, then remembering Sandra's bedbug theory slithered off and sat on the chair.

Passing by the phone and biting her lip – Dan had told her not to ring home straight away – Jennifer slipped into the bathroom and took the most indulgent shower that she'd had in years.

Fifteen minutes later, feeling refreshed and flicking through the channels, anticipating a night of cocktail bars and pizza joints ahead, Jennifer heard the disturbing sound of retching coming from the pristine black-marble bathroom where Sandra had gone to freshen up.

Jennifer knocked politely on the door, then entered to see a wretched-looking Sandra slumped over the toilet bowl. "Jesus, you look like crap!" she said.

"God I don't know what's wrong with me," Sandra wailed before another torrent of sick ensued. Her knees shaking, she sat on the edge of the bath, before fumbling her way to the room, sitting on the edge of the bed and sipping some bottled mineral water in between deep breaths. "Do you think it was something I ate on the plane? I wonder . . ."

Grabbing her mobile, Sandra rang home and her face went green mid-conversation so that Jennifer had to rush for the shiny metal pedal-bin under the table for her to puke into again.

"Gastroenteritis! Joe says the two youngest have got it, would you fecking believe it? I must have it too, my guts are heaving!"

"Come on, you don't know that, let's just get an early night and we'll wait and see."

"Oh, good Jesus, if I could die right now I would,"

Sandra moaned, thumping the pillow restlessly the next morning after a night of hell.

"Do you want me to get a doctor?" Jennifer yawned.

"Sure what can they do? With a bug like this you just have to drink fluids and ride it out."

Sandra's response didn't surprise Jennifer – her friend wasn't one for flinging money away on doctors. Besides, despite the fact that they had health insurance this trip, Sandra would be suspicious that they didn't really, that somewhere in the small print there would be a loophole that the insurance company would exploit if she dared run up any medical bills.

"You take a few hours on your own, Jen. I'll just rest here and drink fluids – maybe we can go out together tonight," Sandra gasped optimistically then bolted for the bathroom once more.

A few hours on her own – what to do? What to do in New York all on your own when you hadn't been let loose on any big city since your honeymoon? Shopping was the obvious answer but Jennifer couldn't be bothered with shopping yet, even though her wardrobe was practically non-existent. People-watching would be much better, she decided, and where better than Central Park – with its joggers, roller-bladers, horse-drawn carriages and ice-skating – to indulge in some amateur anthropological studies?

At Wollman Ice Rink, show-offs doing jumps, young couples hand in hand and geriatric love-birds moving slowly, smiling and remembering days gone by, brought a flash of casual style to the Park and their happy faces were enough to tempt Jennifer into trying on ice skates for the first time in her life.

"What size?" the guy asked her as she leaned over the rink.

"European size six," she said in what she hoped was a firm voice with lots of New York attitude.

He handed her the American equivalent in shoes and she was off, hesitantly creeping around the edges at first, then building up speed. A dozen times she fell on her rear end but the last time she heard the whoosh of skates stopping behind her and then a pair of strong arms lifted her to her feet from underneath her armpits.

"Thanks," she smiled sheepishly at the tall, lean, handsome figure of a man, probably in his late twenties. He smiled at her good-naturedly behind a head of scruffily gorgeous, blond, wavy hair that covered his ears and fell across mischievous blue eyes.

"No problem. It can be difficult to get the hang of," he said magnanimously as Jennifer rubbed some ice dust off her trousers and tried to appear indifferent to his good looks.

"But despite your tumble, today just happens to be your lucky day," he said brightly.

"Why's that?" she said flirtatiously, feeling a delicious little thrill of excitement. "Because a nice strong man like yourself is there to pick me up when I fall?"

"No, because you're lucky enough to get the last of these," he said, reaching into his back pocket and handing her a small pink flyer.

There in big black print were the details of an outrageously sassy Irish comedienne who was playing that night in some pokey club downtown. Of course she'd heard about these small gigs that big names sometimes played to enhance their street cred. Studying the time and venue details Jennifer was racked with a cough, the effects, she presumed, of too much exercise and the cold ice.

"I gave most of these out in Times Square earlier to anyone who looked Irish," he explained.

"So you're saying I look typically Irish?" Jennifer smiled.

"Well, you do actually but since I'm Irish myself I hope you won't take offence. Andrew Devaney, but everyone calls me Andy," he said, holding out a sinewy hand. "My parents are both from County Kerry originally."

"Jen Murphy," she said, suddenly reverting to her maiden name and it felt curiously right and convenient since her wedding ring still didn't fit, months after Adam's birth.

"So, do you want me to give you a few skating tips?"

"You'll be here all afternoon," she laughed, holding out her hand and placing it in his sensitive but well-worn paw. He was a sculptor, she learned, and in between coughing she told him about being in the Big Apple alone.

"That's bad luck, your friend being sick and doing the tourist thing on your own."

"Well, maybe she'll recover. Actually, I should go check on her," she said, glancing at her watch and noting it was after three.

"Well, nice to meet you and maybe you and your friend will make the gig?"

"Well, you never know, she might be up to it," Jennifer agreed, making friendly chat.

"Or you could even come alone," he added playfully.

"You never know," she said, looking at the flyer again and back at Andy's gorgeous eyes.

"You could even come alone." The words rattled around her head and excited her, as she sat in the cab and was

hurled around in her seat while her Eastern European driver shouted on the phone and yelled abuse from his window whenever the urge took him.

It was stupid, she knew, a good-looking guy like Andy, a fat married housewife like herself, worse for wear after having three children, but she had packed some suck-it-all-in pants à la Bridget Jones in her suitcase just in case . . . just in case of what exactly?

Twelve

"We can't go on like this," Mark still had his hand on the kitchen door to make good his escape when he turned and faced his wife, who was drinking tea from her exquisite wedding china, eating low-fat porridge made with de-ionised water and sitting in her beautiful kitchen – surrounded by beautiful things.

"I don't see why not. I'm perfectly content not to talk to you for the rest of my life," Rebecca sniped as she clinked her spoon off the side of her china cup.

They hadn't spoken in days, not since their last disastrous 'baby-making conversation'.

"You're just being silly, Rebecca. Look, it's perfectly okay if things between us need a helping hand . . . I don't see why we can't go and talk to an expert . . . get some advice . . ."

"Pointless, it's all pointless," Rebecca interrupted, her eyes blazing. "They'll only tell you what I've already told you – getting pregnant after the pill can take a while. You might as well save your money for another six months before you start consulting any doctors. Don't push me, Mark, I warn you, I'm standing my ground on this."

"Well, seeing as you're being so blunt, I'll be blunt too. We're not having nearly enough sex for you to get pregnant anyway," Mark said hotly.

"Well, you're the one coming home late most nights, hanging out with your mates or watching TV – not much of a turn-on for me, thanks very much!"

"Well, maybe if you were a little bit nicer now and then I'd be more inclined to hurry home and make love to my wife," Mark defended himself, his voice rising in anger.

"If it's sweet you want, darling, you could always try a few doughnuts – you're getting to have a bit of a middle-aged spread anyway," Rebecca said meanly.

"Screw you, Rebecca!"

"And screw you too," she said as the door slammed.

Finishing her tea, she sighed deeply. Maybe having a baby would be a good thing. Life had become predicable and the child inside Rebecca was sulking at the thought that 'this is it; this is as good as it gets'.

Most Wednesdays, Thursdays and Fridays Rebecca worked at the salon; on Mondays she played tennis with Lou. On Tuesdays, Thursdays and Saturdays she generally got her hair washed and blow-dried and on Fridays she got her nails painted at work. On Saturdays she went out for coffee and read the weekend papers, and on Sunday she power-walked around the town bypass and did the grocery shopping for the week. The monotony of it all was slowly killing her, but still she suspected a baby wouldn't make things any better.

So it was part rebellion, part boredom, a little bit of desperation and a little bit of a spoilt nature that caused Rebecca to reject her daily routine and curt text messages from Marjorie about the club fundraiser and get in her beautiful car and just drive. But it was something to do with the day as well. It was a beautiful clear-skied spring morning with sunshine to rival the Costa del Sol. The day made her feel like she was on holiday and just in case her impromptu drive turned into a real holiday, Rebecca had thrown a selection of clothes into her suitcase and fired the case into the boot of her car.

It had been so long since she had taken her real baby for a serious burn. Opening up the soft-top and sliding her sunglasses onto the bridge of her nose, she let the wind whip her hair into a frenzy and suddenly she laughed, feeling as free and as light as her blown-away tresses. Every now and then she found herself going ten miles over the speed limit, an easy thing to do in a powerful car on a long straight stretch of road and she checked herself – reluctantly.

A guy on a motorbike, his long hair flailing under his yellow helmet, his black-leather jacket fitted snugly to his torso with the leather fringes billowing in the wind – passed by at phenomenal speed. Ahead of her the biker weaved in and out of traffic like an aggressive wasp until he was no more than a speck in the distance. Freedom, real freedom. Rebecca wished she could follow and bit her lip in resignation. It wouldn't do to get points on her licence, it wouldn't do for the local press to get a whiff of her being done for speeding, it wouldn't do for Mark to be embarrassed by an out-of-control wife doing well over a hundred on the motorway, but how lovely to break free of other people's perceptions of her as the sleek, well-behaved businessman's wife.

It was the sound she heard first, and she thought it had something to do with the wind, but then she heard it again, far away but closing in fast. Puzzled, she checked her rear-view mirror and rolled her big brown eyes underneath her designer sunglasses. There it was, the offending object, heading towards her busting its guts with the effort of it all, zipping about like an annoying mosquito at the limit of its 1.4 litre engine. Rebecca had been in this position several times before. Young dumb male, in his first boy-toy tries to race beautiful, young, sophisticated woman in her high-powered motor.

As she watched the motorised roller-skate gasp closer, engine in a high-pitched state of distress, she found her body stiffening. Ordinarily she let the little testosteroned idiots have their thrill and pass her out. Ordinarily she would keep her irritation firmly behind her shades and her eyes focussed on the road, but today she was feeling rebellious. Today she was itching for confrontation and when the little twit was just behind ready to overtake, his pathetic little vehicle plain to see, she put her foot to the floor and roared in front, so far and so fast he didn't know what hit him.

Ten minutes later she heard him again, charging down the motorway loud and intrusive, jumping lanes to get to her, to get a shot at overtaking the woman in her sleek machine. His driving behaviour was ridiculous, like a granny in a Zimmer frame trying to overtake a world-class athlete – it was daft, dangerous and ultimately pointless, but that didn't stop him coming.

As Rebecca overtook him again, it was like life

flashed in front of her, being arrested, being taken to the police station for reckless driving, an appearance in court, the local reporter in a frenzy trying to take down all the juicy details so they could be splashed across the provincial paper in big headlines for everyone to snigger about. *Oh, the country society queen, that's right, married to the local big shot, 200 mph no less, abusive language in the Garda station.* It would all have been awful, dramatic but somehow a great release. Naturally she would come quietly, if a bit sulkily when arrested, but in the end there was no squad car with blue flashing lights to reprimand her so she just kept on driving fast and straight until the annoying boy racer, his speed ambitions choked, disappeared from view, until she was in another stratosphere with her boring old life just a memory and all worries of her future life obliterated.

By the time Rebecca hit Dublin city, the first hint of spring weather was turning into one of those beautiful warm days that made Irish people lose their heads with hopes of a real summer.

The doorman nearly fell over Rebecca in his eagerness to haul her luggage into her four-star hotel of choice. It would be worth his trouble. Rebecca would make it worth his trouble; she always tipped hotel staff big – it made her feel important.

"How will you be paying, Madam?" the receptionist asked in a fluent, heavily accented voice and without a moment's hesitation she handed over her credit card.

"If Madam is interested we have a full range of spa and beauty treatments available in our luxury salon," the receptionist added as the porter took her bags.

"We'll see, I don't want to be tied down to anything

too definite," she said, smiling catlike as she took her room key.

No, Madam would not be interested in any body-pampering opportunities today, she thought as she threw herself on the bed, kicked off her shoes and flicked through the TV channels. Today Madam had too much restless energy contained in her neat little person. Today she needed a proven activity to give her a simultaneous dose of both adrenaline and amnesia. Shopping – she would shop till her arms ached from carrying bags, starting with the city centre and moving out to the suburbs and, after she had seriously burnt Mark's plastic and he had apologised profusely for his recent gruff behaviour, she'd consider whether or not they would still be joined in matrimony. Leaving her wedding ring at home might be a big enough clue for him to realise that she was punishing him for seeing her as a farmer sees a prize heifer – ripe for impregnation.

From her hotel window Rebecca had seen the walled park of St Stephen's Green, and it had whispered to her of distilled memories – the essence of her youth.

Now, tripping over the lazy lunchtime crowd of city workers, she found herself on a bench in front of the stagnant pond waters where an army of aggressive ducks were fighting over crusts of soggy bread.

Unexpectedly, images came back of being young, being nineteen and sitting on this same bench all summer with the man who first broke her heart. Gary – laughing, blond, blue-eyed Gary, a twenty-something music columnist whom she'd met on a night out with the office crowd at a Twisted Steal gig. Gary had been scribbling away in his reporter's notebook when she bumped up against him on the way to the bar and accidentally spilled some drink down his shirt.

"I'm *so* sorry – I've ruined it," she apologised, blushing with embarrassment – she fancied him from the first glance and he knew she was rightly smitten.

"Ah don't worry, Babes, it was headed for the wash anyway," he said magnanimously as he closed the cover on his notebook.

Her cheeks blushed when he called her "Babes", this older sophisticated guy who seemed so confident yet friendly, who seemed knowledgeable about the world – in a different league to the teenage pimply boys of her acquaintance.

"You like this lot?" she'd asked him shyly – personally she thought the band were complete rubbish, but the office crowd had persuaded her into the venue that night.

"Like them? You mad? They're shite! I'm just short a few fillers for this week's column. They're even worse than the last time I saw them," Gary groaned as he took a gulp of cider, rolled up his notebook and stuck it in his back pocket. A little bit of froth clung to stubble around his mouth and Rebecca was tingling with lust as he grinned a huge grin, showing off perfectly straight, white teeth.

They didn't even last an hour before finding a dark corner and beginning to French-kiss and feel each other up against a wall, feeling the heat of each other inside their clothes, knowing that at any minute someone might throw them out for being an exhibition.

"Do you really have to go?" he begged at the taxi

rank as her place in the queue moved on and her car approached. "We could make a night of it, go to Midnight at the Olympia, get a few drinks in – why stop now?"

"I don't know. I don't feel like paying in again somewhere tonight," she hesitated.

He laughed and looked at her with a bemused tenderness. "Who said anything about paying? I'm Gary Larkin, my column is legend. Babes, I don't pay in *anywhere* around town . . ."

Rebecca shut her eyes now and remembered how she had shut them that last day too on this very bench.

"Are you alright, love?" a guy in his forties on his way back to work asked her as she found herself sniffling into her hand and making very undignified snorty noises.

"Shoes!"

"What, love?" he asked, startled, as he leaned over the bench to listen in close.

"A woman can never have too many shoes, don't you think?" she said almost threateningly as she turned to face him full on.

"No, I don't suppose they can," he said, somewhat puzzled as he twisted an empty plastic bottle in his hands.

"And I bet your wife, if you have one, has a ton of the bloody things at home."

"Right enough she does, so many that I reckon most days it kills her that she has only one pair of feet – not that that ever stops her buying more."

"Exactly – shoes are important – I must buy shoes – shoes are a *fabulous* distraction," she heard herself muttering as she hurried away. Regaining her composure she headed for the nearest shoe shop where she instantly bought three identical pairs of shoes but in different colours and the shop assistant bundled them into boxes as fast as she could before the obviously on-the-edge redhead came to her senses and changed her mind.

At the till, as her receipt was printing out, Rebecca's mobile phone beeped and she smiled to herself. It was probably from Mark, saying he was sorry for this morning's behaviour – the stubborn fecker often apologised for his misdeeds by text. It wasn't a perfect culmination to their differences, but it was a satisfactory resolution all the same.

Feeling triumphant, she retrieved her phone from her handbag and as she read the message she let out an involuntary little gasp of horror and just a little fear.

Went home 2 day – forgot my phone. Know UR still on pill U lying bitch – found foil wrapper in en-suite bin!

Reeling from shock, Rebecca gripped the shop counter to steady herself. Thinking the price tag had stunned the customer into sudden frugality, the shop assistant packed up the shoes into enormous swishy bags as fast as her fingers would allow. As the transfer of goods was completed, the shock suddenly left Rebecca and her hard-as-nails genes from her dad kicked in instead. No, shopping in Dublin wasn't going to give her enough satisfaction.

Rebecca booked herself on a flight to Paris.

Thirteen

Sandra was like a dummy from a wax museum when Jennifer got back to the hotel room.

"Want me to get a doctor yet?" Jennifer asked as she threw her handbag on the bed.

"No point, the policy says I'm liable for the first $300 myself and anyway there's no cure for what I have except time," the poor distressed invalid groaned from underneath the bedclothes. "So where did you get to then?"

"Just walked around taking in a few sights then went to Macy's," Jennifer lied.

"Buy anything?"

"Not even a lipstick." There was no point in telling Sandra about the people-watching. Sandra's idea of New York was to shop until the spoils of war could be packed inside empty suitcases and smuggled back home to be shown off with pride, like bringing home the heads of enemies on a plate but at a discount price.

"I might just be able for the smallest bit of pizza later on," Sandra moaned.

Jennifer wasn't at all convinced.

In the evening, with Sandra still moaning, Jennifer glammed herself up and felt vaguely good. Suck-your-guts-in pants were a huge self-esteem booster and the long spangley smock top she was wearing, which was ironically somewhat fashionable, hid her soft dough belly. Her hair was blow-dried – the best style she had achieved herself in years – and she was wearing casual denims, huge gold hoop earrings (borrowed from Sandra) and gold heels with her toes painted a vibrant red.

Then at the last minute Sandra baled out.

"I'm so sorry Jenny, your first hol away in years," she said after another vomiting attack.

"Since my honeymoon," Jennifer clarified.

"Since your honeymoon, and here I am like a wet blanket ruining everything. Look, you go eat alone and I'll join you for a club for definite. I'm pretty sure I could lean against the bar for at least an hour before I collapsed."

"Don't be daft, Sandra, and stop apologising – it's not your fault."

"But what will you do by yourself? What will you do without me?"

What would she do? Probably she'd be too late for a big Broadway production. Of course she could hang around the bar in the hotel, like a lush, or worse still a prostitute or maybe . . . the thought of those blond curls and laughing mouth . . .

"I'll send you a text," she promised as she closed the door and headed for the lobby.

What am I doing? she thought as the driver dropped her off at the comedy club. As it turned out it was really an Irish bar and suddenly things felt awkward, being a woman in a strange place, hitting a bar, meeting a guy who wasn't her husband for a casual drink. Pretend you're somebody else just for the night, she told her panicky self and in her mind she invented a composite ideal from the best of the best. Looks, Charlize Theron; legs, Julia Roberts; personality, Reese Witherspoon; okay, she could do this – just about, maybe.

Inside the place was heaving and she could tell she was surrounded by her own. It seemed anyone who was remotely Irish was here to see the famous Tullamore Sex Tramp Annie McDonagh strut around in her car-bar shoes and behave like an outrageously liberated woman having nothing but laughs and smutty fun. All along the length of the bar and on the floor, staff were working like excitable electrons and after a while Jennifer caught sight of Andy in a corner with a group of other people, leaning up against a chest-high round table. For a moment Jen felt like running; it just seemed ridiculous to be here on her own. Shut up, you can do this, she told herself. It may have been a while but you can do this – you used to be the queen of conversation!

"Andy, how's it going?"

"Hi!" he looked pleased at least.

"Decided to drop by after all – Sandra is still puking rings round herself back in the hotel. What time is your woman due on?" Her delivery was fluid and casual; she was doing okay, she told herself. Keep holding your belly in and stand tall with your shoulders back, her bossy other self ordered.

"Ah, not for a while yet. What will you have to drink?"

Slyly, she had a look at what the two young fashionable girls beside him were drinking: low calorie Lite beer. God, no, she couldn't stand that stuff – it was like weak washing-up liquid so she opted for beer on draught, which was at least worth drinking. Casually, he caught the eye of a waitress working the floor and ordered.

Andy made the introductions. There was Colette married to Irish-American fireman Pete, who spent the night mostly in her own little group talking to two girlfriends; next to Colette was Keira, a gorgeous dark-haired, dark-eyed girl, with an American accent but of obvious Irish extraction whose granny hailed from, "the county of Longford"; and two blokes from Cork who were both trying to impress a Chinese-American girl, Lauren, with their scintillating wit and impossible tales of adventure. Every now and then Andy's friend, Conor, who owned the bar sent over a round of free drinks to thank him for handing out the morning's flyers.

"It's a new club – Conor's real keen to promote it," Andy explained.

"Can I just say I absolutely *love* your jewellery! Is it the new Irish design everyone's raving about?" asked Keira, casting her eye on an engraved silver-dagger necklace and a thick silver bracelet that Jen had bought on her honeymoon in Dubai's gold souk.

"Eh no, sorry, I don't know anything about the new Irish design – this stuff is from the Middle East actually – but there is a resemblance, isn't there?"

"There's actually something to the Irish-Arab connection alright," the Cork guy started. "See, North African pirates had a nasty habit of raiding the West Cork coast at night and hauling the locals away as galley and harem slaves."

"Some connection!" said Lauren drily.

"Not a lot of people know but Cork is a *really* exotic place," the dark-haired guy persisted in telling his bored student. "We were European Capital of Culture a few years back."

Keira was still showing off her jewellery. "I've got loads of Celtic pieces at home – my mom bought me my first Claddagh ring when I was only a little kid!"

Jennifer dutifully admired Keira's Celtic necklace and, with fingers crossed behind her back, told her it would always be a classic piece.

Time flowed as freely as the beer until the black-haired, rosy-cheeked, fast-talking Annie strutted onto the stage in her blood-constricting corset, all mad eyes, fishnet tights and feathers in her hair and expletives exploding out of her mouth with every sentence.

"Not a single fucker from Ireland here – should have known."

The room collapsed in laughter and thunderous applause at Annie's opening comments. For two hours the talented comic reeled them in with her tales of life, spinning her magic, shaking her enormous boobs and generous rear end as if she were the most wonderful goddess, all pure, sassy energy and incredible sex appeal. At the end of the set the whole room erupted in screaming, clapping and ear-shattering wolf-whistles.

"You want to go to a party?" Andy asked easily as people began to drift.

"Sure, where is it?" Jennifer asked, trying to keep the excitement out of her voice.

"My place."

"And where is your place?"

"The Bronx."

Jennifer felt her stomach knotted with fear, but then again it had been so long maybe what she was feeling was just earth-shattering excitement.

When the cab pulled up in front of the six-storey building and shrieked off, Jennifer was sure they'd been dumped at the wrong address.

"It's a factory!" she said in surprise to Andy.

"Was a factory here in the Bronx. Myself, two friends and my sister bought it a few years back – great light, great space – for the same money we would have got a closet in Manhattan, if we were even that lucky."

Jennifer was only in the door when she sensed the vibe and felt excited. A wide hall of solid wood stretched in front of her and at the hall end her eye was drawn by an oak and copper sculpture, its rusted nails battened and bleeding a pleasant rust stain into the timber. Paintings in oil and canvas lined the cool white walls of the hall and upstairs in Andy's loft odd chairs covered the dark-stained wooden floor, and along one wall a homemade bookshelf was lined with books, both fact and fiction. From the ceiling hung an old wooden canoe and rows of roughly hewn box shelves kept jumpers, trousers and bedding neat and tidy in a corner of the room.

All the brickwork was painted a blinding white, but most breathtaking of all along the length of one wall the original factory windows made a beautiful patchwork of glass and steel. In Andy's understated kitchen people were hauling beer out of a giant fridge and a short but powerfully built dog, with a squat head and sharp ears, was being fed meat on a stick by a guest who would pause momentarily, rub his silky fur and coo, "Good boy!" Suddenly, the beast stopped licking his chops and sized up Jen and she immediately froze, imagining the power of those jaws on some tender part of her anatomy.

"Leon, come here, boy," said Andy, seeing Jennifer's anxiety as the canine sniffed her ankles. "It's okay, he's quite safe – he just wants to get to know you. You should feed him – that's a good thing to do with dogs – it shows you want to be one of the pack."

Laughing, Andy placed a small bit of meat into Jen's hand and urged her to put it under the mutt's nostrils. Jennifer wondered how the beast ended up with such a sensual, sensitive name. Judging by his appearance he should be called Spike, Gnasher or some such title denoting latent violence.

"Go on, give him the treat," Andy urged.

Forcing herself to hold her nerve, Jennifer stuck her palm under the brute's nose and was rewarded with one or two big doggy tongue-licks and a wagging tail for her bravery.

"Hey, he likes you!" Andy beamed.

"Thank Christ for that," she smiled. "And thanks for inviting me," she added in shy politeness.

Smiling back, he took her on a quick tour of the open-plan room where she met scarily confident, self-actualising people: actresses, an antique dealer, a gallery owner, a poet called Hugo who ranted off a few of his own lines which Jennifer thought were pretty crap, and a very loud and opinionated lesbian war photographer, Verna, who was having a baby with her equally loud and opinionated interior-design partner, Bernice.

"I'm the one inseminated Verna – I really think I have a right to know whether my child has a vulva or a penis!" Bernice sulked as she played with a ruby-red piercing on her nose then ran her fingers up one ear which was tip to lobe decorated with piercings.

"Oh, Bernice, does the sex of one more child really matter when there are *so* many kids in the world dying every day?" Verna sighed dramatically.

Clearly it mattered to Bernice who stuck her tongue out in temper showing yet another fabulous metal piercing.

At two in the morning the party was still pulsating but the mood had turned mellow. Sinatra was crooning in the background, a down-at-the-heels acrobat called Henri started juggling with shoes, and as Jennifer plugged into the buzz she watched Andy talking to his guests, his body language friendly, his face smiling broadly, his hands outstretched as he made some casual point or other.

"Hey, Jenny," he had taken to calling her Jenny, which she liked, "have you met my man Simon – he's straight in from Vegas – how big was the pot this year, Si?"

Simon told him and Andy whistled low and shook his head. "Man, it's some life you lead, the life of a card shark."

Looking at Simon, Jennifer couldn't visualise him as a card shark. He had a stillness about him, right down to small gestures like picking up a bottle of beer and putting it to his lips. Every sinew seemed at peace as Simon took up an effortless cross-legged position on the floor.

"Simon is a tai-chi and yoga instructor," Andy said, explaining his friend's unnatural flexibility. "He also happens to be a professional poker player."

"Isn't that, I don't know, a contradiction of sorts?" Jennifer queried.

"It's all about the ying and yang, Jenny," Simon explained, holding his beer bottle by the neck so delicately it was almost levitating. "With poker you really have to focus, keep your body calm, not give anything away. In between games I'm chilling in my hotel room, meditating and seeing the big picture. Winning money also puts me in a good place to give back to others as well and that leaves me free to do the work I was born to do."

"Simon does a lot of work with people on welfare," Andy translated. "Guys just out of prison as well as with high-paying Park Avenue Princesses who like to greet the morning sun or visualise the petals of a water lily opening to have a childbirth without pain."

"Pain, pain – I'll tell you about fucking pain," interrupted a very tall, sinewy blonde with big hungry eyes who was towering over Simon in six-inch-high, open-toed, shiny, red stilettos. Then she drawled seductively, "Oh, Simon baby, I'm begging you, do that thing with my feet, they're just killing me!"

"You mean my toe-sucking special, Magda?" Simon teased throatily.

"Jeez Louise, I ain't doing nothing for your pleasure," she said. "It's my pleasure I'm interested in!"

"Oh, you mean *this* special reflexology toe thing," said Simon as he took Magda's foot in his hand and massaged it firmly, ironing out all her cramped little muscles until she *oohed* and *aahed* in ecstasy.

"Ouch, watch my bunion, will ya!"

"Baby doll, you gotta give up those weapons you wear and get some sensible MBTs."

"You shittin' me, Simon, I've only just got my first film project off the ground. You think when I do my interview and photo shoot for *Cosmo* they're gonna want me messing up their magazine wearing some nasty Maasai footwear, maybe giving people the idea that underneath my Gucci dress I'm wearing surgical stockings and old-lady pads? I don't think so, I really don't think so. Keep rubbing, baby. You missed a spot, *ouch,* oh yeah!"

Listening to Magda's purrings of delight shook Andy into sudden action. "Cathy's kittens! Man, I forgot all about them. Their human mom's gone to Yonkers for the weekend. Wanna come feed them upstairs, Jenny?"

He smiled innocently at her but she couldn't help but wonder if this was an invitation to something more.

There are moments in life like this, Jennifer thought as she took a sharp breath inwards, moments that can change your life forever if you read between the lines to the possibilities beyond. But Jennifer chose to let the moment pass, even though a piece of her ached to give in, to be less responsible, to see where life might lead, to break away from the Jennifer of her acquaintance and become a huntress once more.

"It's late, Andy. I should really get back to Sandra. Maybe you could get me a cab?"

"Sure, gotta check on the little guys first," Andy said without skipping a beat.

Jennifer felt relieved and just a little bit disappointed at his nonchalance and easy composure. So there had been no chemistry between them after all; he was only being polite, asking her to the gig, his party, introducing her to his friends. New York women were so well groomed, smart and stylish. Against them she was nothing special, exotic or rare. Thank God she hadn't made an idiot of herself by flirting with a younger man or doing something worse in an empty apartment, something involving innocent kittens.

As Andy disappeared she got up to find her coat but paused as someone put on some Latin music and a big cheer went up. Then several couples melted into each other, moving slowly and deliciously in a closed position, knees slightly bent, facilitating the movement of hips, legs intertwined . . . but at intervals the dancers switched to an open position, turning separately but never truly broken, never letting go of each other's hands.

"It's the merengue," said a tanned stranger with blond, shoulder-length, almost angelic curls. He must have only recently entered the room as she would have remembered such a striking contrast of skin and hair.

"A meringue?" Jennifer asked confused, thinking of her ever-hostile oven.

"The dance you're watching – it's the merengue," he repeated.

Recognition registered on her face.

"Dance?" the man-angel said, but it was more an expectation than a question.

"I . . ."

His sinewy hand took hers and spun her round so that she came within kissing distance of his beautiful, smooth, brown face, dark smiling eyes, his sensual full mouth, his aristocratic nose (most definitely Italian), and his fascinating, sun-bleached, blond-white hair where the occasional streak of grey was the only little clue that he might be older than he seemed. He was tall, but not too tall, about five ten or so, his body lean and dressed simply in faded blue denims, polished black shoes and an open-necked white linen shirt with a woven leather lace at his throat. More than anything he had a natural grace, a way of holding himself in a room that said 'this is me', a magnetism that drew her towards him, a knowingness that only comes with age, experience and perhaps a little sadness, a knowingness that made him instantly more attractive than Andy Devaney and his kittens or any youth half his age.

Horrified, Jennifer realised he was pulling her into the middle of the floor, this man of a sensuality so intense it made her gasp. Her less than perfect body flinched as he slipped his hand to her lower back and held it there firmly, but no more firmly than the dance required, and she swore something happened that had made her flinch, swore his aura merged with hers, that as much as she didn't want it to happen electricity flowed from their touch.

He looked at her with a gentleness that made her want to melt, smiled at her kindly and began to lead and in the end there was no choice but to move with him and suddenly Jennifer was doing the most erotic thing with a man that she had done in years and as the music pounded its ecstatic Latin beat she felt strangely feminine, strangely lost and yet safe as his hand stayed firmly but gently on her back and she resisted the urge to lead and just followed . . . just trusted . . . just gave in.

"You've got good natural rhythm," he complimented and Jennifer felt herself blush.

"Thank you." She couldn't look at him for the embarrassment and pretended she was absorbed in the music as he gripped her to him in a tight embrace from the waist up while below the waist they snaked around each other like two charmed pythons in a basket.

All the while smiling, he turned her, felt the natural movement of her, and when her body became limp because the dance demanded her willingness to yield, he became her natural backbone, he became her strength.

A length of long curl fell in front of his exotic eyes and watching it Jennifer began to blush from her throat to her breast, began to feel that her entire body was betraying her on this dance floor as she engaged in something so innocent but so intimate it was definitely a betrayal of her marriage vows.

"Your cab," Andy interrupted as Jennifer came out of a particularly dizzying spin.

"I . . . I'd better go," Jennifer faltered, not wanting to go, not wanting to leave.

"Stay a while," the rugged angel urged, his beautiful mouth curling into a slow, sexy smile.

"No, honestly, I'd better go," she said more firmly and he held on to her hand for the longest time and just stared.

There are moments like this, Jennifer thought as she rushed through the city in her cab, unexpected moments when something small changes, moments when someone beautiful catches you unawares and rushing in sees the real you and bravely, openly, steals a part of your soul.

Fourteen

The louser had cut off her account and the money she earned from the salon was peanuts; Rebecca had stupidly spent most of it in Paris in a daft attempt to prove to herself that she was an independent woman and to delay her return to confrontation and the realities of married life.

This is just a distraction too, maybe I shouldn't be doing this, she questioned as she pulled up outside the door of the small, boring 1970s bungalow with ugly stone cladding, dusty windows and a rusty pink tricycle parked in the porch. For a while she just sat in her car and stared at the door in a panic but twenty minutes later she rang the bell and steeled herself for the hurricane.

"Hi . . . Dan, it's . . . it's me," she said cautiously to the slightly dazed, thirty-something daddy prototype at the door. Her brother-in-law looked a state. His hair was tousled but not in a sexy way; his eyes hooded from lack of sleep, his trousers rumpled and stained with goo and when Rebecca looked down she saw that he'd forgotten to button his fly. Well, appearances probably weren't too high on Dan's agenda any more; he'd pulled her sister, got married and had kids. His lifecycle wasn't exactly over, but it looked as though it should be, in the interest of humanity.

From around the door two identical little faces appeared to gape at the pretty young woman who was so exotic she wore make-up, fashionable jewellery and an exquisitely embroidered turquoise blouse with cream linen trousers and designer heels.

"I like your shoes, they're pretty," said Emma, smiling from around the doorframe.

"Are you Mammy's friend?" asked the no-fuss, straight-to-the-kill Abby.

For a minute Rebecca didn't know what to say – she'd last seen her niece Emma when she was a few months old and the other two children – she barely knew their names.

"No, this is Mammy's sister, Rebecca," Dan said wearily. "You haven't changed much, Rebecca – guess it's because you don't have kids giving you wrinkles and grey hair. Jen's in New York, want to come in anyway?" He sounded as if he didn't care much either way.

"Well, I came to see Jen but if she's not here . . ."

"Oh, *please* come in," Abby cooed in her most delightful voice, flashing a practised angelic smile which could, when she wanted, light up her entire face. Her greedy little eyes were already on her aunt's designer necklace which she knew she could swipe in a moment of confusion and stash somewhere private like a bold little magpie.

"Well . . . maybe for a few minutes . . . just for tea?"

Rebecca said cautiously, trying to work out if tea might be a little too presumptuous but Dan didn't seem to notice any subtleties in her voice. He was yawning, and the baby was rubbing his eyes and pouting grumpily.

"Tea, tea is good," the dad of three assured her, his tongue nearly stuck to the roof of his mouth with the effort of speaking. Before Rebecca could change her mind he bundled her into the hall and shut the door.

"Pretty shoes, Mammy never buys anything *that* pretty," Emma said in open admiration.

"Here, you can sit here," Dan said as he took a pile of laundry off the couch and flicked away some dried-in crumbs from a deep groove between the broken-in leather seats. "Milk and sugar?"

Rebecca nodded for milk, passed on the sugar and smiled tightly. The house was a mess. There were snagged cobwebs in every corner of the room, bits of mauled-up tissue paper near the TV and even though she could just about peer into the dining room through the double door, she could clearly see toast and blobs of jam stuck to the floor. Christ, she wouldn't want to see the kitchen in case the tea Dan was making poisoned her altogether.

"Jen went to New York with Sandra, you remember Sandra?" Dan said as he handed over the mug, kicked off his slippers and sat with his brew resting on his belly.

"Of course, Jen's friend." It was weird Dan wasn't mad with her. Maybe it was true what Mark always said, that men didn't hold grudges, although she'd get to see if her husband still felt that way once she got a solicitor to sort things out between them. Had it really come to that with Mark? Maybe it had.

"Your ring is pretty. Can I see?" Abby asked, eyeing

up Rebecca's engagement rock, which she was wearing on her right hand.

"It doesn't come off, sweetie," Rebecca lied, feeling uncomfortable at the child's request. Fascinated with her shoes, her nephew was trying to eat them from the end of her toes until she slipped them off, deftly put them on the arm of the chair and curled her heels under her bum.

"Oh, can I try on your shoes, Aunt Becka?" Emma immediately asked.

For God's sake – did these children harass all the guests? Already she could see the baby changing tactics on her shoes as he pulled himself upright and slowly began approaching his target by dragging himself the length of the couch like a fat little slug intent on munching.

"My shoes are very high, honey, you might fall and hurt yourself," Rebecca said firmly to Emma, reaching to put them on top of the bookcase which was bursting with all sorts of kiddie rubbish. Thwarted now in his shoe-munching goal, the baby threw back his head and screamed furiously. Agitated, Rebecca looked at Dan for guidance but Dan was too tired to notice her uncomfortable body language in the presence of icky-sticky children.

Then, as if remembering something vital, Dan sat upright and began to babble excitedly.

"Hey, seeing as you guys are all getting on great, would you mind if I ran to the supermarket? We're low on nappies and it's easier to go on my own than drag the kids. I'll only be fifteen minutes – twenty tops," he promised, seeing a panicked look in Rebecca's eyes.

How could she refuse if he needed her? And, besides, she hadn't seen these kids ever.

"Ehm . . . " she dithered.

"Thanks, really thanks a lot," he gushed as he bolted for the door and scarpered, leaving Rebecca with a nasty feeling that he'd never return.

Ages went by – half an hour, then forty-five minutes. Rebecca spent most of the time anxiously following her nephew around the house in her bare feet as he pulled at stuff and occasionally stuck something small into his mouth. Then the little horror would clamp his jaws and look at her defiantly but eventually he'd spit out whatever he was gnawing and hold it up for her to admire.

"You're to say thank you, Aunt Becka," Abby explained, as Adam held out his latest trophy, a teeny-tiny plastic Princess Ariel Mermaid bra.

"When you say 'thank you' he claps his hands and laughs," Emma explained.

"If you don't take it he'll cry *really, really* loud," warned Abby.

Rebecca definitely didn't want that, she'd heard the wailing earlier on, it was enough to make eardrums bleed. Annoyed, she took the saliva-covered offering and as promised the little rug-rat clapped his paws in delight. Rebecca wasn't sure how much more of this mind-numbing behaviour she could take. Where the hell was their father?

Suddenly, a tremendous banging at the front door startled Rebecca to attention. She was nearly afraid to open the door at all, but then she saw the family car parked on the street and knew the banging had to be Dan. Maybe he'd accidentally let go of the groceries and they'd crashed on the front porch. At least she should be able to escape now. The whole visit had been stupid anyhow – what was she hoping to achieve? Flinging open the door she was met by the sight of a figure hunched in two, breathing heavily, then moaning, then emitting sharp scary '*aagh*' sounds.

"Dan?"

"Oh Christ," the figure whimpered in obvious pain.

"What's wrong? Why are you bent over all funny like that?"

"It's my back, it's gone, my back, I can't move, it's completely locked."

Taking a good look, Rebecca saw that her brother-in-law was virtually wedged in the front porch, bent over like a contortionist, although unlike a contortionist he'd no degree of flexibility. Panic started to build as her instincts told her to run very fast out the door.

"I'll call someone, the physio, who's the local physio?" Desperately she wanted to off the responsibility on some other sensible, selfless adult.

"No point, she's on a half day," her brother-in-law moaned in pain from a geographic position somewhere beneath his bum and through his trouser legs.

"A friend then – I'll call a friend?"

"Collapsed, collapsed to the ground, at the checkout desk, collapsed with one hand in the trolley and the other on the conveyor belt for *five* minutes and nobody even *noticed*, I kept reaching in with one hand and throwing up the groceries and *nobody even* noticed, nobody thought a lone hand firing things up to be scanned was in any way an oddity, can you believe that, *nobody* noticed and I was panting in pain . . . *aagh!*"

"How the hell did you get home?" Rebecca was by now also doubled in two so she could see some portion of Dan's face.

"The cashier *finally* noticed the trolley talking and got up to look, then she packed my bags, took my wallet out of my ass and got customer service to load up the car. My head was wedged into the steering wheel all the way home. Oh fuck the pain . . . *aagh*!"

Rebecca didn't know why exactly, but suddenly she felt absolutely furious.

"So could you maybe help me in and then unload the groceries?" the talking bum continued hopefully.

Fuck, fuck, fuck, fuck, fuck!

"I think it's in spasm, it's happened before, when I get to the see the physio tomorrow, *if* I get to see the physio tomorrow, she'll probably just tell me to spend a day or two in bed and by then Jen will be home anyway."

Rebecca knew what was coming next as she manoeuvred him inch by inch into the house and onwards to the bedroom, helped him get into bed and lie on his side.

"You wouldn't just stay, would you? Just for tonight . . . just until I get to the physio? I'm sure I can survive after that by hobbling around on a crutch or an old walking stick."

Wisely, he took her silence as acquiescence and writhing on the bed left the rookie auntie in sole custody of one miniature Sumo wrestler and two curious little nieces.

Back in the kitchen the baby started to chew Rebecca's leg, but somehow she knew from his mode of chewing that some kind of food was expected and soon.

"Where does Mammy keep the jars, you know, the baby food?" Rebecca asked the most sensible-looking one.

Emma stared back blankly and told her Mom didn't have

any jars but sometimes she froze the baby's dinners and stuck them in the freezer and sometimes the baby just had the same dinner as the rest of the family only mushed up.

Determinedly, Rebecca stared to rummage in the freezer for anything that might resemble infant food, but none of the stuff in bags or frost-furred plastic containers was labelled. How the hell did this lot survive?

"Oh yes, I smell poo!" Abby suddenly shouted at the top of her voice.

"What?"

"Poo, it smells," said the child as she held her nose in disgust.

Quickly, Rebecca picked up the kids' shoes and had a look. Nothing. Dan's shoes from the supermarket were clear too.

"Aunt Becka, it's Adam," said Emma knowledgeably, pointing at his nappy.

Oh Jesus! When Rebecca picked up Adam she could smell his ripeness and thought she might vomit as she held him at arm's length like the most disgusting item in the world.

"I'll show you," said Emma, leading her aunt towards the baby-changing unit, finding the baby wipes, giving Rebecca the nappy and directing her towards the drawers with baby clothes. It was with genuine fear that Rebecca slowly pulled back the tapes and investigated Adam's nether regions. Bloody hell, it looked as if his entire bum had exploded and as soon as his naked skin felt a bit of air his little appendage sprayed a shower of wee that hit Rebecca full in the face while Abby collapsed in laughter around her heels screaming, "So funny, Aunt Becka, so, so funny!"

In battle mode Rebecca started to clean as fast as she could, the baby fighting her every bit of the way, trying to turn from his back onto his tummy to escape this red-haired dragon lady. The power in his hips to turn was terrifying but each time Rebecca pressed him down with enough force to keep him rigid even though big baby screams were percolating in his throat, waiting to explode full throttle.

Having wrestled him into a new nappy (it was on the wrong way but his inexperienced aunt didn't notice), Rebecca released him like a tagged baby crocodile so he was free to patrol his entire habitat gnawing at everything that took his fancy – mostly legs.

Back in the kitchen, she went to check on the fridge and freezer once more but when the cold white giant refused to yield up any of its secrets she decided to fire a yogurt and banana into the baby and groaned as he managed to smear half his supper onto his hair for the split second she took her eyes off him to throw pizza and chips into the oven.

"Oh goody, chips again!" cheered Emma.

"We had chips last night too," said a delighted Abby.

Well, at least someone was happy with her domestic skills.

By the time she had got her nieces into their pyjamas and their teeth brushed, Rebecca was fit to collapse.

"What time does the baby go to bed?" she asked Dan as the two girls busied themselves in the bathroom "doing wees".

Pulling himself onto his elbows with much "*aaghs*" and "Christs", Dan got into a position where he could pant an intelligible response.

"The baby? Oh, Adam kind of goes to bed when he's ready."

"What, but that's ridiculous, doesn't he have a routine?"

"Well, when Jennifer was breastfeeding him she just took him off to bed and let him nod off, you see."

"And now, now that she's clearly not feeding him herself. What does she do now?"

"Well, we're just muddling through now she's in New York. You could try his soother, he likes that, and Michael Flatley's *Lord of the Dance*, for some reason he finds that very relaxing and don't forget to bring his beakers to bed for him to suck."

"Doesn't he have a bottle?" Rebecca asked incredulously.

For a minute there was a silence until it was clear that Dan was building up to a really big "*aaaagh!*" followed by a sort of strangled whimper.

"He doesn't like milk," he finally panted.

For the love of all that was precious – who ever heard of a baby that didn't like milk?

While the girls pretended to get into their beds, Rebecca dimmed the lights in the bedroom (she had seen that on a TV programme once where some nanny doctor came to the house to sort out undisciplined children) and placed the baby in the cot. Mystified, Adam looked at her, sucked his soother rhythmically and then, standing up against the bars, he put his hands straight up in a defiant 'take me out now' gesture.

"What you doing?" Abby asked, puzzled, as she danced through the door in pyjama bottoms that were far too long for her little legs. Emma was right on her heels.

"Putting your baby brother to bed."

"But he doesn't sleep in the cot, Aunt Becka,"

Emma explained. "Mammy just puts him in when she's busy."

"Well, he's sleeping there tonight," Rebecca said in a firm no-nonsense voice and Emma and Abby exchanged knowing looks, shrugged and said goodnight.

Two hours later Adam was still shouting at the top of his lungs like a world-class tenor. Rebecca tried the soothing, the patting, even the dreaded *Lord of the Dance* music which just made the brat dance around the cot in frustration. He threw both his beakers at her, on one occasion hitting her nose with force, and he cried so hard that he just about held on to his soother as he swayed at the wooden bars like a demented chimpanzee.

Wearily, she gave in and decided that if he'd sleep at all it would be worth trying him in the bed. Maybe he'd go out like a light and she could sneak off and watch some television. Still fully dressed, she snuggled under the duvet and the little fecker seemed to like this arrangement a whole lot more. Out of her peripheral vision she saw his eyes shutting slowly, his eyelashes fluttering as they gently brushed his soft plump cheeks.

Slyly, she made to leave, but like a limpet he glued himself to her head and held on tight to her hair, squishing his nappy right into her nose, the nails of his little toes digging into her mouth and chin, affording his little head and warm torso the opportunity to droop over the crown of her head. Every now and then she planned escape, but Adam detected the slightest movement and whimpered threateningly. At one point the demon even sicked up a little bit on her hair and as the minutes passed into hours she could smell her crowning glory begin to curdle, unable to do anything about it until he drifted off and released her. It had to happen soon, she told herself, this little dance between them couldn't last forever.

The light was barely coming in the windows when Rebecca heard the first bloodcurdling scream and wondered where the hell she was. Again came the screaming voice, loud, insistent and strangely patient.

"Aunt Becka, I've done a poo, wipe my bummy! Aunt Becka, Daddy's got a bad back and I've done a poo. Aunt Becka!"

Every bit of Rebecca ached. As she stretched out one foot and one arm (Limpet Boy was attached to the other half of her body) Aunt Becka experienced that yeuchy feeling of waking up in bed wearing yesterday's clothes with a sticky mouth that had gone the night without toothpaste. Her beautiful embroidered turquoise blouse was moist with sweat and her dry-clean-only linen trousers were crumpled badly around the crotch.

"Aunt Becka!"

Dumping the now wailing baby in the cot Rebecca went to investigate the commotion and found Abby perched like a black spider on top of the loo, looking as if her little bum and the rest of her were about to plunge into the bowl at any minute as her fully stretched-out spindly arms clung to the edges for dear life.

Just as Rebecca was finishing the big clean-up, Emma strolled into the bathroom and quietly reminded her aunt that breakfast would have to be made, school lunch packed, Abby dressed, the baby fed and changed and all of them be at the school gates for nine.

"Unless," she started coyly, "unless it's too much

trouble with Daddy being sick. I could stay home and help with Adam, tell you what Mammy docs – you could write a note to my teacher," she finished breathlessly, hopefully even.

Rebecca looked into the big eyes that were pleading and the decision wasn't very hard to make. Besides the kid had the inside track on how everything worked in this mad house and she could tell Abby would be as clueless as a fish in a sandpit.

"I'll tell your teacher it was an *exceptional* morning," said Rebecca, glad that she didn't have to fight the morning traffic, battle with Sumo/Limpet Boy or cajole Abby into doing necessary stuff like putting on shoes.

Twenty minutes later they were all sitting on the couch munching jam and toast and watching kids' TV. Something sharp and sticky kept prodding her face and a dozing Rebecca was vaguely aware that Adam was trying to plug jammy toast up her nose. Every so often she jostled him around while she had the best snooze she could, resting on one elbow, while trying to ignore the shooting pain in her neck – the result of her lying rigid in a contorted position with Adam all night.

As she dozed an awful thought entered her head. Maybe her sister had done a runner and left Dan for a carefree existence, one without children. Maybe the New York shopping expedition with the best friend from the past was all a big ruse. Rebecca's eyes opened for a moment as the terror set it; then she smiled to herself and chuckled. No, Jennifer was far too sensible for any kind of dreams beyond the predictable and homely, she reassured herself as she shut her eyes and snoozed fitfully. Feeling her relax slightly, Limpet Boy also made himself comfortable and re-attached himself to Rebecca's head and shoulders as the TV blared. The urine in his nappy was stale – she would change him in a minute, or maybe ten. God, this mammy lark was hard, she thought as she yawned, rubbed a jammy streak from her cheek, then skilfully ignored the unspeakable pain of rock-hard crusts being poked in her ear in time to the theme song from *Postman Pat*.

Fifteen

"What's your biggest seller anyway with the *Slinky Bunnies* crowd?" Jennifer asked as she picked up a knicker-and-bra set and ran her fingers across the lace. Having made a last-minute miraculous recovery, Sandra had dragged Jennifer shopping round the city and out to Jersey Gardens and made them both buy a ton of unnecessary clothes.

Suddenly Sandra's eyes narrowed suspiciously as if she was in possession of some amazing trade secrets that nobody should ever know.

"I suppose it would be the dress-up nurse and fireman uniforms, the portable poles for pole-dancing, they're doing a storm, and knickers with *Spank Me* written on the back."

"Poles?"

"Between the poles and the fireman uniforms you do wonder all right," Sandra smirked.

"And *Spank Me* knickers?"

"Oh God yeah, we sell so many even grannies must be wearing them."

"Or else every buyer buys several pairs. You could start a range – you know, different-coloured *Spank Me* knickers from Monday to Friday like kids' bibs."

"Jesus, that's a great idea!" Sandra said excitedly.

"Sandra, it was a joke."

"Yeah, yeah, like you being in the Bronx dancing around a meringue with a blond angel."

Sandra still refused to believe that Jennifer had done anything crazy the night she'd fallen into a coma-like sleep and slept until dawn. "You know, we get a bonus if we identify any gaps in the market. God, if your idea floats I'll buy you a pair of Jimmy Choo shoes!"

"My feet are too fat for Jimmy Choo shoes, you daft cow . . . Sandra, are you listening?" She wasn't – the cash-register look had popped up in Sandra's eyes and jammed.

Sandra's entrepreneurial knicker-mood lasted all the way home as she scribbled figures on the in-flight magazine and doodled knicker designs. Jennifer wasn't much on for a chat anyway, not when she had to go home to that madhouse where life had been turned upside down by her husband and his mid-life crisis brought on by unemployment. Now the holiday was over, maybe she'd have to sell her wedding rings on eBay. In New York she felt so free without those bands of gold anyway, almost free enough to contemplate casual sex with a nice young man in a bohemian loft and do the same and more with a kind dancing angel with a Roman nose.

The train journey through the Irish countryside was maddeningly long and the rhythmic rocking of the old train on the tracks was failing to numb Jennifer's troubled head. Suddenly an image of Dan floated by, an image which rapidly became corrupted by the appearance of Andy on Dan's shoulders, then merged with her mysterious Bronx Angel and lastly Pierre the French Weatherman, all such beautiful guys with beautiful Botticelli curls whether bleached, greying or touched with red-gold sunshine. Every time she tried to imagine Dan, one of these Adonises came back determined to be noticed, increasingly wearing fewer and fewer clothes, showing off six-packs, biceps and strong, manly thighs in no particular order.

With determination as strong as any manly thighs, Jennifer forced herself to stare out the window and make mental comments about the scenery to herself as if she was an eager tourist. Lush fields, green hedgerows and, Jesus, was that really the head of a curly-haired angel disguised as a cloud floating by at several thousand feet? Go away, go away, I'm returning to my husband without any need for guilt, she silently roared at the fields, hedges, clouds and some sheep, with, would you believe it, curly fleece like angel hair!

At her front door she realised she had no cash. Her local cabbie told her no matter, he'd pick it up during the week, and she smiled. Such a difference from New York – it felt good to be known and trusted in her own community.

Nobody seemed to be getting the door and Jennifer was impatient to see her babies so she started fumbling for her key, rooting in her bag amongst the tissues, a wad of leftover dollars and old tickets that she had accumulated over the last few days. Head stuck in her bag she became aware of the door opening. It was really getting very shoddy; she should get Dan to varnish it soon. Quickly she raised her head to give him a beaming smile, a hug, a kiss and a thank-you but instead her mouth must have dropped to her knees in shock.

"Hello, Jennifer."

How dare she, how fucking dare she!

"Where's my husband?" Jennifer hissed at the crumpled-looking redhead with fuzzy, un-brushed hair, bloodshot eyes and peanut-butter smeared on a spot above her right cheek.

"In bed lying down."

Indignant, Jennifer snatched her baby son from her sister's hip and legged it down the hall like a woman possessed. Jet lag – like everything else in life would just have to wait.

Dan explained his bad-back predicament and the logical conclusion of asking Rebecca to stay and even though Jennifer ranted it was hard to be too scathing. Still, as she stayed with Dan making chat, she hoped she'd eventually hear the latch of the door being lifted, the door shutting, the clatter of heels on the driveway, the roar of that pretentious motor as its red-haired owner revved the engine and disappeared forever, but deep down Jennifer knew problems are seldom so accommodating, especially ones with red hair.

There was safety in numbers, safety in noise, and her little girls who were playing out the back garden were so effortlessly lovely but noisy that if she was with them no one would notice awkward silences hanging in the air, waiting to be punched. Leaving Dan, she went to find them and pull them into her arms. Three more steps now and she'd be at the door into the kitchen, a few more paces and she'd be into the back garden.

The doorbell rang. It was Yummy Mummy Number One, Vicki.

"Ooh, you're home – isn't it terrible news?" Vicki commiserated.

"What news?"

"Dan and the bad back of course – here're my crutches from walking the wards before I gave birth. Your, er, sister rang and asked could she borrow them, because apparently he can barely move – didn't actually know you had a sister, Jenny."

Then from the door Jennifer saw another car pull up and Sexy Sadie made an entrance.

"Just passing – thought I'd drop by and see if you were back."

Jennifer was just about to close the door when she saw the big four-wheeled drive with the unwashed tyres. It was Helen, laden down with farm produce, including eggs which were so fresh they still had the feathers stuck on them with birdy-bum glue.

"God, isn't it awful about himself? Heard he's crawling to the loo. Brought along some stuff to build him up – isn't it as well your sister was passing and able to give a hand?"

"Will I put the kettle on?" Rebecca asked quietly.

Jennifer shot her a look. Every bit of her wanted to rip into her sister's perfectly tanned skin but, because of the mammy onslaught, she was forced to bare her teeth in a scary grin and nod assent.

There was so much commotion that Dan began stirring and appeared at the end of the corridor, much to the delight of the clucking hens in the kitchen.

"Dan, can you make it on your own? I have crutches here if you want a shot at them!" shouted Vicki, pretending to mow him down as she aimed one at him, rifle-style.

Watched by his Laughter Yoga groupies, who were hanging around the kitchen door, Dan did what could only be described as a 'royal wave'.

"Dan, come and join us for a cup of tea, man!" Helen roared. "I've brought over some lovely brown soda and two of my own pies but I have to tell you now if you were on the rugby team I wouldn't be letting you off with just an old back injury!"

A puffing and groaning Dan hobbled in unaided, looking abashed in his dressing gown and slippers. Recovery was slow but looking certain, he said, adopting the same super-cool hero stance as when he'd been struck down by the dreaded Man Cold.

"There's a mug of tea for you now," said Helen gently. "Did that physio sort you out, because if you're still in pain you could always try Marty Meagher the bonesetter. My mother had back trouble a while ago and he was the *only* fella she'd have any truck with."

"Why, what happened, Helen?" asked Jen, keen to jolly along the conversation, keen to keep her friends in the kitchen for as long as possible, before she savaged Rebecca.

"Well, the parents were celebrating their fortieth wedding anniversary and with a few drinks on them didn't they both lep up on the kids' trampoline for a bounce."

"At least they weren't starkers, like your kids now, Jen," Sadie laughed as she gestured towards the back garden where little orbs of white flesh were bouncing for the stars.

"I'll get them dressed," Rebecca said quickly as she disappeared out the back garden to round up the two budding nudists from the jumbo-sized trampoline.

"Whatever about kids," said Vicki, "can you imagine oldies starkers on a trampoline? All that wrinkly flesh, everything gone south – *aaagh*, it doesn't *bear* thinking about,"

"They weren't naked, only a bit drunk," continued Helen, getting annoyed.

"Sorry, Helen, go on, tell us," said Jennifer, jostling Adam on her hip and looking out the window fleetingly – at least the pair of little streakers were wearing pants now.

"Well, Mammy was crippled afterwards, she was, and she said, 'Helen, Man Meagher got me right once ten years ago and he'll get me right again – you just drive the feckin' car!'"

"Is that the fella where you could have a horse in before you and a dog after you and you take a ticket when you get there and wait your turn?" Sadie asked in her throaty Scottish tones through a big hunk of buttered bread and jam. It was a tough job having sexy curves – they needed constant feeding.

"The very same and all I'm saying is, if the back doesn't work out for Dan going the traditional route, Marty the Man Meagher is always another option."

"Thanks, Helen, I'll remember that," said Dan, giving his wife a discreet hug.

Helen, seeing the small display of affection, chastised herself for being such a poor guest.

"Oh my word, here we are chattering on about stupid stuff and you just back, Jen, and we never asked you did you enjoy yourself!" Helen paused, waiting for the fun-filled details.

"Ah sure, New York's New York, everyone's been – shopping, Central Park – what's there to tell," Jennifer smiled, still eyeing her brood through the window. Rebecca had them in trousers and tops now; that meant her evil presence would be back any minute.

"Starbucks," said Vicki, cradling her coffee, remembering her singleton days.

"Never mind Starbucks – sexy New York policemen!" Sexy Sadie salivated.

"Oh God, yeah – on horseback!" said Vicki.

"Sexy New York firemen," Dan added in for fun.

"New York pizza," said Helen, sticking to the traditional food vein.

Sexy Irish American sculptors and men with winged feet, thought Jenny, closing her eyes for another gorgeous brainwashing moment of lust, desire and Botticelli curls.

"Mammy, Mammy, Mammy!" The girls jumped all over Jen, demanding presents, then kisses and hugs, then presents again.

There was nothing for it, but to pull out everything – clothes, dollies, sweets – and let them charge around the house, and then the friends decided to leave and the mindless chatter and noise that keeps fights at bay dissolved in an instant. Only then did Jennifer realise that she was nearly hyperventilating from rage; she couldn't look at Rebecca but she needed to look at Rebecca; this was her home.

"I want you gone out of my house." The order was mostly directed at the crown of Rebecca's head which was still an annoying foxy colour, not a grey hair in sight.

A slight nod and Rebecca silently left the kitchen and began to gather together her stuff.

"Jennifer," Dan half-soothed, half-pleaded.

Outside the kitchen door Jennifer could hear the pounding of little elephant's feet. It was Abby – the acoustics alone gave the child away. Jennifer could never work out how a kid so slight of frame could be so heavy of foot.

"Mammy, Mammy, Aunt Becka is crying! Mammy, Aunt Becka can still give us hugs and tell us stories, can't she?"

Adam roared and gave Jennifer a look of displeasure as she picked him up. No doubt his fat arms were searching for the new nanny too since she'd abandoned him for New York.

"Jennifer, I'm on my last legs, you're just back – can she at least stay the night?"

"Well, I suppose that red-haired selfish cow might be of some use to me for once, considering that I've never got any value out of her from baby-sitting, but I'm going to bed and, Dan, tomorrow – tomorrow *you* can throw her out!"

It was late, very late. After hours of trying to sleep, Jennifer was still up and she knew Sandra, a predictable insomniac dealing with jet lag, would probably still be awake too.

"Sandra?"

Jennifer could hear the clicking of keys. Jesus, the mad cow was back working already.

"Sandra?"

"Uhm?" The fag-sucking down the end of the phone was followed by a loud gulping noise.

"Having a nightcap to help you sleep, Sandra?"

"Nah, one of the girls is having a hen's soon and I'm just on a drink a night to build up stamina. At my age you have to go into training for these things, Jen."

"Right." God, Sandra had a truly hectic social schedule, Jennifer thought enviously.

"I'm sorry to bother you, Sandra – it's just I've just got a bit of a situation here."

"Yeah, me too, I've only gone and got meself some tapeworms."

"Yeah right, very fashionable, come back from the States with a tapeworm – what are you trying to slim down, you skinny cow? Your boobs?"

"I'm not joking. I've got them tapeworms for sure. I've been on the Internet all evening."

"Sandra, talk sense, would you? Tapeworms are huge – you couldn't have more than one at a time – they're like cuckoos, you know, only one per nest."

"Sorry, did I say tapeworms? I meant those threadworm yokes. I'd say after me not eating for days they were starving. White wiggly little things. I was going to give you a call, just in case you got infested. I was thinking of the baby mostly."

Jennifer could feel the itch building down the phone. Jesus, if it wasn't one thing it was another. It wasn't until she became a parent that she realised children weren't always sugar and spice and all things nice. She'd already been on nit-watch, scabies-watch and now worm-watch – although, they'd been on worm-watch before – just the once.

"I was going to ring you tomorrow anyway to run a few things past you on account of you having the full science degree and me not getting to finish my college education."

Jennifer groaned inwardly to herself – she knew what was coming. In Sandra's mind a science degree equated to a medical degree and maybe a free diagnosis from her friend.

"Says here the little feckers don't like carrots and they hate garlic as much as any vampire. What do you think?"

"I think you should go to the doctor."

"Ah, but Jen, you know, you go there, hand over the cash and leave none the wiser."

"Three little words Sandra: *pay the money!*"

"What about the garlic?"

"Like I keep telling you, three years of a science degree doesn't make me a doctor and in cases like this I'd recommend medical dynamite, not garlic."

"Bloody kids – bring home everything from school except good grades. Do you think if I had a tequila a night that would help? What's it again about tequila and worms?"

"People fight to eat the worm at the end of the bottle."

"Feck that, I've probably got enough of the wiggly freeloaders inside me already!"

They said goodnight and that's when Jen realised she hadn't told Sandra about the Rebecca situation.

Restless and unable to sleep, she walked into the kitchen and switched on her electric cooker. It was a stupid distraction, but she didn't want to think until she saw Rebecca's car round the corner and zoom away for good.

As she waited for the oven to heat up, she fished out her ingredients, her scales, pottery bowl, sieve and the little scrap of paper with the old-fashioned writing and the translucent spots from years of baking grime. This was the dreaded scones recipe that she was driven to crack even if her sanity cracked first.

Working fast, she pulled all the ingredients together, working the mixture from dry powder to buttery crumbs. The sound of the oven fan whirring filled the kitchen and she heard her own heartbeat pound as excitement and dread merged with optimism. The milk was added last, then the blasted mixture all went too soggy. Frantically, in an effort to correct the damage Jennifer added in more flour, then more again and couldn't understand how the flour was being soaked up at a tremendous rate. Her hands sticky from margarine, sugar and milk desperately pounded and shaped, her hair fell in front of her eyes, blurring her vision. Twelve scones, twelve minutes – how could it possibly fail?

Anxiously, she watched as the digital oven display counted backwards from twelve to zero and the timer screamed in alarm. A warm, sweet smell of baking filled her kitchen but on inspection the scones were still raw. Distraught, Jennifer punched five minutes more on the clock but the result was just the same: raw, doughy and useless. Another five minutes and her dough babies were burning around the edges but pale as the moon in the centre. Never again, she raged at the raw, rubbery, burnt rocks and at the dirty little handwritten recipe that had a blob of grease obscuring some of the black spidery letters.

In the girls' front room, where Rebecca was sharing

the double bed with the baby, Adam began to fuss and Jennifer heard Rebecca making soothing noises. Exhausted, Jennifer collapsed alone into the marital bed, not caring one bit that Dan was probably tossing on the uncomfortable futon in the other room. As Jennifer sank into the mattress she drifted into a world where nothing seemed real. In the world of her head giant white worms roamed her front lawn and were fighting to get through her letterbox. Giant worms turned into redheaded demons which tangled around each other in erotic embraces with Hollywood hunks – living and dead.

Images swirled around her head so fast she felt delirious. Inexplicably, one of the worms took on the head of Sylvester Stallone and held hands in a circle with girlie worms in an imaginary erotic dance. Then Jennifer's dream filled with scones – so many scones that they were clogging up the hallway and the stairs – she was wading through them at ferocious speed so she could take up the fight against the giant white worms bursting through the letterbox led by Sly Stallone – now dressed as Rambo.

Abruptly Jennifer opened her eyes. It was early morning, the room was still half-shadow and when she went to take her first breath no breath came. Still calm, she tried again – nothing came. On her hands and knees she crawled to the bathroom and somehow ran the shower, all the time panic building, all the time two voices screaming in her head, one shouting, *You're going to die*, the other imploring her not to panic.

No air, no air, her brain sent the critical message but her voice box remained resolutely shut. In her small suburban bathroom she could hear her heartbeat pounding, her voice fighting to escape from muteness as steam swirled around her and she clung to the side of the bath, staring at mushy washcloths and soggy toddler pants. Please, God, please, God! Then after it seemed death had won with his iron grip on her throat, there came a mute scream, a short rattle and a raspy cry from within as her vocal cords parted and air rushed to her lungs.

"I'm okay, I'm okay," she managed to say over and over, but as Dan burst through the door despite his injuries she knew everything was not okay and that something – everything – was really, really wrong.

Sixteen

The plan was to sneak out of the bungalow in the early morning to avoid an un-sisterly confrontation and then have it out with Mark back home. After all, who the hell did he think he was, freezing the money in their joint account just when she had exhausted her nice little stash of cash from her other account, which was her fun fund for her access only? Outside in the boot of her car, her Paris purchases were still 'resting' – there had been little point in hauling them inside to experience collateral damage should three pairs of grubby little hands stumble upon their earthly beauty. Fortunately, it wouldn't be long before they got to meet their designer brothers and sisters back in her sumptuous walk-in-wardrobe.

All escape plans had been stymied, however, with the strangulated noises coming from the bathroom that morning. Dan had hurtled down the corridor, despite his bad back, jumping over the laundry like he was doing the 100-metre dash just to get to his wife, bundling her into the family wagon and, not sparing the gearbox, disappearing at speed to the local hospital.

Alone in the house Rebecca was thinking she was rapidly turning into a 24-hour nanny when a little voice brought her back out of her agitation.

"Aunt Becka, is Mammy all right?" Emma asked as she stood there in her school polo shirt and trendy red sweatshirt with her school logo emblazoned on the front – in French.

"Your mammy? Yes, of course, she's just a bit . . . you know, tired from being away," Rebecca lied competently. "I'm sure she'll be back home soon."

"Ooh Aunt Becka, I've pooed out a six!" Abby grunted from the open door of the bathroom as she set about her morning business of public bowel evacuation complete with running commentary.

"Yes, so I see," said Rebecca wiping her clean with barely concealed distaste. "You're so smart I don't know why you're not at playschool full-time, Abby."

"Because she bit a little boy on the bum in the toilets through his pants – she's on probation," Emma explained with a sigh as she struggled into a pair of knitted tights.

"I've got teeth!" Abby said in confirmation, proudly, reaffirming her biting reputation.

"Aunt Becka, maybe I shouldn't go to school again today if Mammy and Daddy aren't here. I can show you how to look after Adam," Emma asked hopefully as she struggled to brush a tangle out of her beautiful pale-blonde hair, her eyes needy and intense.

"Now, Emma, we all have to go to school. Stay here a moment and watch Adam in his cot, will you? Aunt Becka just needs to run out to her car for a sec."

The two or three basic tops Rebecca had worn since she'd become the Resident Nanny were filthy and crumpled and her beloved designer jeans, which she'd been forced to wear since her linen trousers were ruined from play-dough, had to be changed soon or she'd be arrested by the hygiene police. Although she winced at the thought of any item from the array of gorgeous designer clothes in the boot of the car getting destroyed, she was running out of clothing options – not helped by Dan. One spare half hour when Dan had managed to hobble around on an old walking stick, Rebecca had found him in the utility room unloading a colours wash, where in amongst the socks and pants she saw her lovely cream linen trousers and gorgeous turquoise blouse.

"Oh God, I'm so sorry, I'll buy you some more," Dan had apologised when she held up her linen trousers, now baby blue, and saw how the legs had shrunk so much the lining was showing. Her gorgeous blouse had bobbled from bits of broken white tissue, courtesy of the kids' unemptied pockets. Dan baulked, though, when she told him how much her clothes would cost to replace.

"That much – really? I wouldn't know – you see, Jen buys all her clothes in the supermarket including the basics."

How awful, Rebecca thought, that something as expressive as your clothes should be deemed "basics" but he was right – Jen did buy *everything* in the supermarket, she'd seen the receipts.

Today, however, Rebecca really had no option but to dip into her brand-new purchases from Paris for something vaguely suitable for drudgery and childminding.

Bolting out, she found herself muttering about

infuriating in-laws who took advantage as soon as you showed your face. God, she really hoped Jennifer wouldn't have to be hospitalised or she'd be imprisoned in this house in the role of drudge forever. No doubt after his Olympian-style sprint to the bathroom, Dan would also be coming home even more incapacitated than before.

Rebecca had hardly taken a few steps out the door when it began to hail and, head down, she ran as fast as she could to her car. Except it wasn't there. Puzzled, she looked up and down the quiet street and then she was gripped with panic: it *really* wasn't there. Sweat was beginning to break on her forehead. Like a lunatic she ran down the road and for some ridiculous reason started looking in the neighbours' driveways as if they were the likely harbourers of stolen vehicles.

Frantically, she ran back into the house and picked up the phone to ring the local Garda Station and, when the phone was finally answered, a jaded country policeman stated his exact global position much to Rebecca's annoyance – she knew bloody well where he was, she'd just rung him!

"My car – I'd like to report that it's been stolen," Rebecca panted down the phone, all the while hearing her annoying nephew screaming for breakfast from the cot.

"Are you the owner of the vayhicle?" the Garda wearily asked.

"Yes, yes, I am."

"When did you last see the vayhicle?"

"I don't know – maybe the day before yesterday – things have been kind of hectic here and I haven't exactly been watching it."

"Haven't – exactly – been – watching – it," the Garda

repeated slowly. "I see. Are you sure it definitely isn't where you last parked it, Madam?"

"No, it definitely is not. It's a bloody big yoke, Guard. Believe me, I'd definitely know if it was still there," Rebecca said with more than a touch of sarcasm.

To his credit, the monotone Garda pretended not to notice her increasing agitation.

"Make, colour, registration? You *do* know the registration?" he continued in his comatose tone.

"Of course I know the registration," Rebecca spat at him down the receiver.

"You'd be surprised the number of people who don't."

Rebecca ranted off the make (sexy), the colour (gorgeous), the price tag (excessive) and waited for the sharp intake of breath, the breathless excitement that would charge up the whole police station in a frantic hunt to find her car before it was crashed in a joyride, used to ram a country post office in an armed raid or broken down for parts to be redistributed to Eastern Europe and beyond. After a few seconds she realised no such excitement was forthcoming.

"Are you the only person who has access to the vayhicle?" The Garda was beginning to sound like a pre-recorded message now, his tone was so flat.

"Yes, well, except for my husband of course – he has keys."

"Would your husband have borrowed your car without telling you, perhaps to go to work if his own vayhicle didn't start?"

His line of questioning was really beginning to annoy Rebecca now. At this rate her car was going to end up in Russia or Central Asia.

As he droned on Rebecca became distracted by events outside the sitting-room window as a manky white van crawled along the kerb and a dishevelled man in dark crumpled clothes and a black-leather biker's jacket jumped out every so often to stuff something into the back of his very suspicious-looking "vayhicle". For some reason she felt the urge to go and investigate his activities.

"I'm sorry, Guard, could you hang on one minute? There's just something I need to do."

"Madam, this is a Garda Station. We're not in the business of hanging on. There could be an incident at any minute."

Somehow she doubted that; she could nearly hear the clink of his metal spoon on his cup as he stirred his morning cup of tea.

"Just one minute, Guard, that's all I need."

And before he could answer either way she legged it out the door just in time to see the thin crumpled man throw some familiar bags into the back of his van. Then she realised they were *her* bags, *her* bags full of lovely ferociously expensive clothes, untouched since their purchase in Paris.

"Stop, stop, they're not for you, they're mine!" she yelled after the van, but the driver seemed to pick up speed. "Stop! There's been a mistake! They're not for collection. Stop!"

Rebecca strained to get a look at the licence plate but, conveniently, it was clogged with mud.

"I've been robbed," she spluttered down the phone to the Garda Station when she got back into the house.

Surprisingly, Mr Excitement was still on the other end.

"You've had quite a morning, haven't you?" he sighed wearily.

He must have been on his second cup of tea by now. From the sound of it he might even be making inroads into some nice buttery toast.

"It's my clothes. My bags of clothes from Paris, several thousand euros' worth, I haven't counted up how much exactly – you see, I kind of went a bit mad."

"Bit mad," the Garda repeated slowly. "I see, and where were these clothes when you last saw them?"

"In my car."

"Oh, so the car has turned up then, has it?" he asked smugly as if he expected as much.

"No, it bloody well has not!" Rebecca spat out. "They were in the boot – the car thief must have taken them out before he stole my car."

"So the clothes thief could make off with them later perhaps?" the Guard suggested.

Rebecca distinctly felt that the copper was giving her a good ribbing, but she couldn't be sure – that monotone voice was quite distracting in its own hypnotic way.

"Now see here, maybe 'clothes thief' is too strong an accusation," she said. "They were snatched by one of those bogus charity collectors, you know the type – they drop leaflets and tell you your clothes are going to overseas charities but it's all a scam and they sell on your stuff to some poor people in developing countries instead."

"Bogus . . . charity . . . collector."

Wearily she waited while the Garda wrote it all down. "Did you happen to get the vayhicle registration?"

Rebecca felt the sigh build up inside her before she

heard the next word's pitiful entrance into the world of sound. "No."

"No. I see, that doesn't leave me with a lot of options then, does it, Madam? Now about the car thief . . ."

Suddenly Rebecca caught sight of the white envelope lying on the floor, lying beside her driver's licence. Both had been posted through the letterbox and her name was scrawled across the front of the envelope in big, jaggedly black-ink letters.

"I'm sorry, Guard, could you hold on a minute," she asked again, not waiting for a reply this time.

Nervously she ripped open the letter and found a sheet of typing paper with more jaggedly black handwriting inside.

Took the car. Bought by me and registered in my name so it's mine, no contest. Left your shopping bags at the gate. Mark.

Rebecca could feel her face burn. Mark – the crafty bastard. Had he got one of his cronies to help him to take the car? How did he even know where she was? She wouldn't stand for this. There'd be retaliations, severe ones, all of them financial.

"Ehm, sorry there, Guard, I think I'll have to ring my husband after all."

Down the phone she could hear a most discontented sigh as her policeman no doubt brushed the breakfast crumbs off his regulation light-blue shirt.

"I'm very sorry to have bothered you," she continued, feeling a bit silly.

"So you've located the car then?"

"Eh yes, but don't worry – I might still be on to you because, although I've located its whereabouts, I think it still has been stolen, technically anyhow."

Rebecca knew she sounded a bit daft and she could tell from the hesitation in the policeman's voice that he was hoping she wouldn't be ringing him back any time soon.

"And the clothes – are they still stolen too?"

"Yes, but as you know I didn't get –"

"The registration. Yes, I know; you wouldn't be the first one to have trouble on that score."

Cheeky bastard.

In the cot her only nephew was crying for Ireland. Frantically Rebecca raced to his cage and jiggled him on her hip while she picked up the phone and dialled Mark's mobile. It was engaged. Her voice full of implied menace, she left him a scathing message threatening to do everything from burning down her own beautiful house with him in it, to having someone plant a bomb under his car.

Fuming, she rang the home phone. It rang out too, but after the beep she threatened more violence from her own hand, while all the time Adam in a soggy nappy bawled in her ear and tried to prise the phone from her grasp. In the background the girls were fighting and screaming over who was to get the last of the coveted Rice Krispies and who had to make do with cardboard Shreddies. It was a nightmare getting them all fed and out the door so that Emma could get to school somewhere roughly on time.

Rebecca rained down her curses on her husband's head, hung up the phone and went to break up the mêlée.

"*Bonjour*," Emma's French-speaking teacher greeted them with frosty friendliness.

Rebecca very quickly got the measure of her. Fortunately her time as an air stewardess came in handy for dealing with snotty-nosed battle-axes, and as the child transfer was completed, Rebecca rattled off a few phrases in a French accent so thick that it sounded like her mouth was crammed with marbles. It did the trick. The frosty teacher, who was used to mammies doing a runner as soon as the first 'marbley' vowels left her own mouth, was temporarily disarmed at the briskness of Rebecca's French-language delivery. Her body language bristling, the teacher closed the door on the weatherworn prefab.

"You made Emma's yeuchy teacher mad," laughed Abby as Rebecca strapped her into her car seat before heading onwards for family supplies.

"I sure did. Okay, Abby, let's do Tesco," Rebecca announced breezily. Getting in, she put her foot to the floor and was surprised when it merely chugged instead of taking off like a rocket as she was used to.

"Aunt Becka, Adam is covered in brown stuff," Abby said matter-of-factly as they rounded a bend.

"What kind of brown stuff?" Rebecca asked, tensing as she looked at Abby in the overhead mirror.

"Smelly brown stuff," said Abby definitively.

Rebecca too got the smell, strong and suffocating, and Adam, who was out of her sight trapped in his car seat, started bawling in distress.

"You drove too fast and gave him icky tummy," said Abby, holding her nose.

Rebecca stopped the car and tried to clean up the pools of sick with a whole packet of baby wipes. Stripping Adam to his woolly tights, she saw an old baby cardigan on the back seat and threw that on her nephew for warmth. Admittedly, he looked a bit odd but he was probably warm enough to go shopping and as he stopped crying Rebecca decided that it was better to persevere with errands than go back home.

"Okay, Abby, let's do *Tesco* – again!"

In the clothes aisles of the shopping chain, Rebecca eyed up the items labelled '*fashion*'. Supermarket chic – the very thought made Rebecca cringe as she remembered her stylish designer casuals, her evening wear, her prized Prada handbags, her precious Karen Millen dresses and tops – all useless, all residing in the wrong house. The memories were enough to make her salivate, then cry, but a little voice brought her back to her current clothing nightmare and so she decided to take the plunge. There was no option really. Her funky new Parisian clothes would be on the backs of some lucky foreigners in the next while and the clothes from her small suitcase from Paris were now shrunk, manky or totally unsuitable for looking after toddlers.

Three pairs of trousers, two T-shirts, two shirts and a cardigan later, all to be stuck on Dan's laser card, and Rebecca was ready to hit the food aisle – but without a parent in tow to advise her she wasn't exactly sure what to buy.

Discreetly she stalked a mammy-type to see what she put in her jumbo-sized trolley and when the mammy disappeared around the corner Rebecca put the same products in her own basket – frozen waffles, frozen pizza, nuggets and chips. Under Abby's dubious direction, she also loaded up on fruit, bickies, buns, bread, yogurts, nappies and wipes (after a few days with this brood she had learnt you could never have enough wipes) and then she made her way to the checkout where her functional clothes were swiped with all the respect due a tin of beans. An awkwardly dressed Adam was still a bit sniffy and the

Eastern European girl at the till looked at Rebecca with obvious distaste as if to say, 'You bad mother. Back in my home country you would be the talk of the village.'

When Rebecca walked into the house Dan and Jennifer were still missing and she was exhausted and it wasn't even eleven. Thank God for that big purple dinosaur with the creepily optimistic outlook on life – both Abby and Adam seemed to love him to bits.

Sprawled out on the coach, Rebecca hovered in that awful 'suspend' state, not fully awake but not able to give in to the lovely caresses of sleep in case the kids stuck knives in their eyes, suffocated on some harmless-looking object or electrocuted themselves while under her very reluctant and very amateur supervision.

Later on that evening, forty miles or so down the road, a well-built man would relax in his sitting room, turn on the telly to watch football on his new giant flat TV screen, rest his steak and side-salad dinner on a cushion and perch his bottle of mineral water on his armrest without any fiddly coaster being foisted on him to save the pristine nature of the furniture. Armed with two phones, the man would entertain himself now and then by playing back his messages on both the landline and his mobile so he could fully appreciate the anger and irritation in his wife's voice. Those kids weren't giving her a moment's peace. Excellent – it was just the kind of stress a spoilt, indulged woman with no children of her own needed.

A few more times he would play the messages, just to get the full effect of all the screaming, wailing and crying and all the while he would thoroughly enjoy the feeling of being the master of his own castle, without a nagging wife in situ bugging him about his mess, his habits and the general state of the place. Not that the house was stinking to high heaven since she'd left. No, funnily enough, since his other half had gone AWOL, Mark Gleeson's house was cleaner than ever Mark Gleeson could remember.

Seventeen

Totally exhausted, but over her attack, Jennifer had waited in Outpatients that morning to see the doctor, feeling vulnerable in her night gear and dressing gown. But every now and then, Dan had shot her a smile and hugged her arm. Such obvious affection meant just one thing – he was worried she was really sick and he was going to end up minding the children.

"You go on in, honey. I'll wait here and read something." Not that there was anything to read in the dingy waiting room with peeling dark-green paint, unless you wanted to read about cystitis, vaccinations or the food pyramid. Still it was no harm to read about the food pyramid so you could alarm yourself about how many fruit, vegetables and pulses the average individual should eat in a week. Getting enough roughage into the system seemed a pretty impossible task.

As the nurse called her name and she shuffled down the seats, Jennifer steeled herself for the examination room.

"Come in, come in, till we have a look at you," the cheery young doctor greeted. "Now what exactly seems to be the problem?"

Damn, Jennifer wasn't at all in the mood for up-beat professional happiness; she would have much preferred somebody grumpier, someone far more economical with words. Nodding his head sympathetically, the doctor listened to her account of the wheezing attack in the bathroom, gave her a thorough examination with the stethoscope and did what any self-respecting medic would do under the circumstances: loaded her up with every possible pharmaceutical missile to nuke all bugs known to the universe, living and dead.

"Right, so there's your anti-histamine for the night, the antibiotics – have you ever been on these before? No. Well, ring me if you have any problems. Now the steroids – best to take them after a meal. And the inhaler is four puffs a day through the spacer device."

"The *what* device?"

"The spacer device – it attaches to the inhaler you'll be getting. Foolproof way to make sure you get all the medicine you need. Don't worry, the pharmacist will show you what to do."

"So what exactly do I have then?" Jennifer asked, feeling somewhat alarmed.

"Ah, that's the thing – too early to say. Probably bronchitis – there's a bad throat infection doing the rounds. Have you been experiencing a nagging cough of late?"

"Yes, now that you mention it. I was away recently and was coughing a bit but I just thought it was the end of a cold, nothing serious."

"Well, there you go then. You're probably just a bit run down," the cheery doctor continued.

But Jennifer wasn't so certain, now he'd put the frighteners on her and got her thinking.

"But what if it's not just something simple, what if it's something else – something worse – adult asthma maybe?" the words tumbled out.

"Is there asthma in the family?"

"Not that I know of."

"Right, then, we won't worry about asthma for the moment. Final question, Jennifer, is there anything worrying you at all?"

Involuntarily Jennifer's chest began to tighten. Well, let's see, her husband had lost his job and was inexplicably deliriously happy, her sister had turned up on her doorstep unannounced after an absence of several years, she was having raunchy sex fantasies about just about every man she met, dreaming about massive white worms with the head of Sylvester Stallone doing erotic dances, and doing erotic chocolate dances herself the minute her husband was out of the house. Clearly she was out of her head. But she didn't tell this to Dr Cheery – she didn't want to worry him, but still . . .

"What would worry have to do with not being able to breathe properly?" she heard her logical self ask indifferently although her mad self was desperate to know the answer.

"Well, if people are stressed, it's not unheard of to get a panic attack but in your case because you have had a cold and a sore throat it's more than likely acute bronchitis."

"And not panic attacks?"

"And not panic attacks." He smiled as if she was a young child and he was indulging her little whims.

"But if I was worried about some things . . ." she said in a whisper, her feet dangling over the end of the examination couch, making her feel like a little child.

He didn't hear her as he had walked across the room to write her prescription, but at the last second he turned and frowned.

"I'm sorry – you said something?"

"No, nothing," she swallowed the words briskly.

"Oh right. Well, seeing as we have you here we might as well get a blood sample out of you as well. Check the old iron levels. A mum like you can't be too careful."

Too right – a mad mammy like her who was on the brink. Before she barely muttered a word of consent, Dr Happy of Face but Evil of Intentions drained her veins and was smiling away to himself contentedly as he held her blood offering aloft.

"So when you get home rest up for a week or two . . ."

"What? What do you mean *rest*? I can't rest – not when I've got kids to look after and my husband's back is in bits . . ."

Dr Happy looked up, stared her in the eyes and spoke slowly as if he was dealing with someone whose first language wasn't English.

"Jennifer, I don't think you understand. You are *ill* and *need* to rest. Bronchitis can turn nasty and end up in pneumonia if you're not careful. Is there no one who can give you a break? Because, if you don't look after yourself, you *will* end up in hospital."

She heard herself mumble something chirpy to appease him, that she would try, that she would make time for rest, something soothing for his benefit. Rolling down her sleeve, taking care not to snag the cotton dressing where her skin was punctured for the blood-letting, she picked up her bag and rejoined Dan. Handing him the prescription, she saw the worried look on his face and sighed. Somehow she felt all the medicine in the world would be useless anyway.

Jennifer knew what kind of prescription she really wanted – a prescription that she could fill at the pharmacist's for one nanny (to be used as needed), a cook (to be used thrice daily), psychologist Dr Phil on tap to discuss the dynamics of her relationships, and a cleaner (to be used four times a week) and for the dose of real help to be reduced as symptoms of house-untidiness and overall madness lessened. Yeah, that's what she really needed – that combined with a ginormous overdose of luxury spa treatment at a remote child-free destination of her choice. God, she was good at this diagnosis business – maybe she had a career ahead of her as a quack doctor.

Parked outside the pharmacist's Jennifer played with the radio until Dan arrived with her filled prescription and in among the antibiotics and steroids was a funny-looking plastic globe.

"That's the spacer thing there – the drug from the inhaler goes into the plastic ball bit so that you can take your time breathing the medicine in – the pharmacist did a demonstration for me."

"Wonderful. It reminds me of that bubble thing people use to get the crack cocaine into themselves faster. Yeah, I think I'll just pretend I'm doing crack cocaine, wouldn't that be fun, a little break from reality?" sighed Jennifer.

Dan looked at her askance for a moment; then continued in a strained up-beat voice. Damn, this cheerfulness, first demonstrated by the young doctor and now being flaunted by Dan, was far too infectious for her liking.

"You just rest, honey, take your time, whatever time it takes to get better," Dan soothed.

"From whatever the hell I have and in the meantime who's going to look after me and the kids, with you going round the house like Long John Silver? That bitch you let in my front door?"

"Now, Jennifer, don't upset yourself, you might –"

It was too late. Her body was already in full attack, wheezing, fighting for air, falling back on the headrest of the car exhausted five minutes later, her heart pounding in her chest.

"I'll get you better, Jenny, I promise."

"I never get sick, Dan, you know that."

"I know, sweetheart, your body just needs a rest."

"What if it's asthma, adult asthma? Adult-onset asthma is a really crappy thing to get."

"It's not asthma – just rest, Jen."

"How do you know it's not asthma? The doctor doesn't even know for certain it's bronchitis. He even said . . . well, he implied it might be panic attacks."

"Just rest . . . stop worrying . . . just rest, okay?"

When Dan got in the front door of the house and the adrenaline had finally stopped pumping, it was clear that Superdad had done himself an injury after the spectacular bathroom heroics of the morning and from driving the car as if he was a Formula One whizz kid. Stiffened from the exertion, Dan immediately got a taxi back to the physio who diagnosed a contorted muscle in his rear end and immediate pummelling was required to release the sprain to the point where Dan didn't know if he was in pain any more or actually enjoying himself.

Back in the sanctuary of her own home, where another sunny unwanted postcard from Spain greeted her, Jennifer had no doubts about whether she was enjoying herself. No, Jennifer O'Malley – lately Murphy, but only in New York – was just about as miserable as one can get.

Eighteen

For the next week Jennifer saw Rebecca flitting in and out of her life, always in the background, playing the reluctant Florence Nightingale. In between resting in bed and sleeping the sleep of the comatose she'd hear Rebecca's low voice, her foot on a squeaky floorboard in the corridor. Occasionally they saw each other but neither made eye contact for long and she knew Dan had probably warned Rebecca to keep confrontation at bay in case Jennifer went into a spasm of coughing and lost her breath. Jennifer hated having the skinny bint around, hated that her kids seemed to like her sister, hated the fact that she needed her. Jennifer hated being indebted to anyone, it was just her way.

Sometimes the kids bounded into her room whenever Dan sanctioned it. Adam loads, of course. Jennifer loved the feel of his squidgy little arms around her neck, loved his toothy smile. The girls would peek their nose in from time to time, Emma knocking politely, Abby scratching outside like a giant mouse until she got the okay. Emma old enough to be worried about her, Abby her normal clueless, noisy self.

"When will you be better?" Abby asked as Jennifer went off on her second trip to the doctor's to be reassessed. "Ah, soon, honey," she assured her.

They still didn't know why she couldn't breathe any better; they still cited bronchitis along with slight anaemia. Sometimes she felt a bit better and other times she felt her voice box about to close over and she'd run for the shower to force her vocal cords apart with hot, steamy, mist.

It was Dan who really solved the problem, re-activating his old work laptop (brand new but already dated by computer standards), searching the internet for a bit of worthy information to lessen her distress.

"I think it's not just bronchitis but vocal-cord dysfunction as well. You have all the symptoms, Jenny – the vocal cords close over and one of the biggest causes is stress. Are you stressed, Jen?"

With huge self-control Jennifer ignored Dan's daft stress question and, eyes down, began to flick through a magazine as she watched her baby son's tiny chest rise and fall in contented sleep beside her on the bed.

"So what's the cure for this vocal-cord dysfunction thing?" asked Jennifer.

"When you're in the middle of an attack, you breathe through your nose and out through your mouth but long-term deep breathing, voice lessons and . . . well, even counselling to get to the root of any psychological problems . . ." Dan's voice trailed off without his meeting her in the eye.

"I like the idea of voice lessons. I've always fancied myself as being a bit of a diva although, being the eldest in my family and always the responsible one, well, there was never really a part in my big sister role for stamping my foot and having a tantrum."

"Jenny, this is serious. I'm worried about you."

"There's a lot to worry about," she shrugged, noticing that Adam was moving now on the pillow. The eye rubbing and wailing was only seconds away.

"Well, why don't we make a big long list of everything that is wrong and how we can fix it? And if I can't do everything the next while until my back is one hundred per cent, well, there's always –"

"Don't say her name. It annoys me no end that *she's* still here."

"Jenny, you're going to have to talk to her some time, sort this thing out."

"I haven't talked to her in years and it hasn't done me any harm. I've just got on with my life, same as her."

"Except you bottle everything up and look where that's got you," Dan said angrily.

"Don't you *dare* raise your voice to me," she said, hitting her pillow in frustration.

Adam's little face was screwing up for a big wail. Jennifer was always amazed how long it took for him to take in air before it came out again in a huge pissed-off-with-the-world scream. Wearily, she picked him up. Oh why did he have to wake up right now? She could sleep for another ten years straight. As her anger built up she felt the iron hand around her throat and tried to shake it off, but it wouldn't move.

'Breathe, breathe, breathe, breathe in through your nose and out through your mouth, you silly woman!' the voice inside her head shouted.

Shutting her eyes she forced herself to focus, focus on opening her throat. Jerking her body up taut, she grabbed the side of the bed with an iron clasp, all the time making that awful barking noise that frightened the hell out of Adam. He was pulling her hair and pawing at her face in fright until Dan took him and then the baby completely lost it, throwing a tantrum in Dan's arms, wanting to get back to his mother.

Five minutes later Jennifer had recovered sufficiently to whisper that Dan could hand over the infant for a hug and when he did the little baby hit her in the face repeatedly, angry that she had frightened him, she supposed. Flustered, Dan ran a hand through his hair while leaning on one crutch for support.

"Jenny, only you can get yourself better. If you need to sleep for a week than sleep for a week, if you need to talk . . ."

Talk, talk about what? He didn't know it but talking would be bad. If she started to talk she would talk for a month. There'd be no talking; silence was in everyone's interest.

"Okay," she smiled tightly and returned to reading her magazine.

Not content but not sure what else to do, Dan took Adam again and shut the bedroom door as quietly as the squeaky door handle would allow.

Outside Adam protested at being removed from his mum once more but Jennifer knew he would stop roaring when he got some lunch – hopefully someone would have the sense to feed him in the next while. He had the appetite of a small elephant, her son. She just knew he was going to grow up to be a rugby player from all the food he got through every day. Helen would probably coach him as soon as he could walk and she'd steer him in the right direction all the way to international matches.

As she drifted into a shaky sleep, Jennifer thought about the strong embrace of her New York dancer, of how good it felt to droop in his arms and allow him to lead, to be her very backbone for those short exciting minutes of fear, desire and confusion. Very close to sleep, she thought about the cool hands of her mum on her forehead, whispering consoling words to Jen the child about resting, sleeping and getting better and as she heard her gentle voice Jennifer wept silently into the pillow. "I miss you," she told her dream mum as she sleepily wrapped herself tight in the duvet so she could remember how it felt to be protected, to be hugged, and more than anything, to be loved.

Nineteen

Rebecca was going mad; there was no other word to describe the total meltdown she was experiencing at taking sole custody of Jennifer's children. Her sister was in an exhausted state and Dan had set his recovery back days in the mad dash to hospital, so he too was also spending long periods of time lying down. Dan wasn't much use in knowing about the basics of family life anyhow and had dissuaded Rebecca from discussing anything with Jennifer – she was just too fragile at the moment. That suited Rebecca fine – she didn't want to talk to her big sister anyway.

Survival was the name of the game and the days were a blur of socks and nappies, lunches to be made and endless driving with no time for herself, her hair or any aspect of her appearance. The sense of never having a minute was terrifying and, in a moment of complete insanity and growing hunger, while both biological parents were resting in bed, the new surrogate mother scooped an enormous spoonful of the kids' yummy peanut-butter straight out of the jar, and then found she couldn't stop eating it until there was little more than a smear around the rim.

When the guilt of looking at the peanut jar became crippling, Rebecca pushed it to the back of the cupboard where she came across real booty – a giant jar of *Nutella*. With an impending sense of danger Rebecca opened the lid and gave in to a total chocolate-hazelnut disaster. The world of crispy salad leaves from the deli and low-fat dressing seemed a million miles away. Family existence was totally crazy, Rebecca thought, as she sucked the *Nutella* spoon clean in the style of Hannibal Lecter after a nice feed of human liver. For her, the constant mind-numbing boredom of being a housekeeper and childminder was bad enough, but the overall atmosphere was made much worse by the feeling of debilitation which hung over everything. Rebecca had always hated any kind of sickness, hated tip-toeing around a house trying to be quiet, talking in hushed voices, hated the sound of doors opening and closing quietly, of lunch trays and cups of tea being ferried back and forth for the infirm.

Mostly, Rebecca just hated calm and the awful feeling of calm before the storm, and in her bones she felt this place was ripe for a hurricane. Static hung in the air and all her instincts told her to run, run before the tension exploded into something truly awful but she couldn't, not while the kids needed her for basic nursemaiding at any rate. Each one of them was unsettled by their parents' physical mishaps and each one of them was trying to find a little bit of deeply buried 'mumsiness' in their by-now favourite aunt. Just one more week, she'd give it one more week, well, maybe two, but that was it, this family would just have to cope and then it would be back to her own home – although there was a big bloody hurricane brewing there too – a big bloody anticyclone coming in from the Atlantic that threatened to consume whatever and whoever was in its way.

Whenever Rebecca got a break from Adam, she scoured her mobile for messages from Mark and an expected grovelling apology, but apologies and messages never came. His silence was both infuriating and enticing and Rebecca knew if she'd had her beautiful car on standby she'd have been home in a flash, demanding explanations about his lack of remorse and general lack of consideration for her feelings.

Her car – God, how she missed it! Her set of wheels was freedom but it was also excitement – her baby stuck to the road like glue and when she put her foot down and passed out annoying white-van drivers and tractors or OAPs doing forty miles an hour, it made her feel powerful and sexy, it made her feel like a rebel in an ultra-safe world of boring people. Sighing, Rebecca looked down at her once-beautiful nails, now tacky with chipped varnish. This morning she'd broken another talon zipping up Emma's school coat so that her fingernails were now all uneven – there'd be nothing for it but to cut them back to stumps.

Never mind, French manicures looked great even on very short nails, she tried to cheer herself up. Not that she could afford a French manicure at the moment. Still, it was dangerous having them look so ragged, because if they weren't kept groomed she knew from experience she'd be tempted to start biting them – first a gentle little nibble then a full-scale chewing attack. She had to get out of this madhouse at least for a while; if her fingernails didn't sucker her, the junk food would succeed in bringing her down – the biscuits were already trying to woo her with promises of a good time.

"Dan, could you get up and take charge? I have to go down town, just for an hour or so, it's important!" she shouted into the office-futon-ironing-cum-junk room where Dan was resting. Quickly, before he could protest, she zoomed into the bathroom to give herself the express 'no make-up look', locked her greasy hair back with some industrial-strength hairspray and a hair band and rubbed off the chipped nail polish and put some oil on her cuticles. At least she still had her high-quality beauty products. Thank God she hadn't left them in her car; she'd better remember to wear them more often. Living in this house was turning her into a slob. Wearing supermarket clothes was turning her into a low achiever and, worst of all, she didn't really care any more, well, not like the Rebecca Gleeson of old.

After a few minutes of walking, Rebecca found herself drawn to the up-market hotel on the edge of town as her dormant inner vamp sought out the soothing familiarity of a salon. Quickening her pace, she followed the directional signs to the luxury spa and, half racing up the richly padded stairs, she came across the wonderful familiar air of contented luxury. Aimlessly walking around the room, she flicked through a few brochures about facials and hot stone massages earning one bored glance from a kooky, blonde, frizzy-haired receptionist, wearing an above-the-knee smock dress and red satin pumps which stuck out the side of her desk. In her hair the twenty-something oversized child wore a fat purple hair band with an enormous black satin bow. It was evident she was trying to cultivate a look that said: 'I'm really too sophisticated for this small country town, I'm just taking a breather before my future relocation to LA, New York, Sydney or Tokyo.' Tokyo would probably be good – she had that mad Japanese youth-look perfected already. Engrossed in a glossy magazine, the girl tapped her fabulously crystal-studded talons on some celebrity image or other, completely ignoring Rebecca until she coughed to signal her presence.

"Are you looking for an appointment?" the zany one said in a monotone, looking up and staring out over awkward trendy glasses with multi-coloured plastic frames.

"Dympna?"

"Rebecca, is that you?"

Rebecca realised she obviously looked as unlike herself as Tranquillity's former beautician, now sitting in front of her. Embarrassed, she tried to smooth her cheap satin blouse over her utilitarian jeans and appear cool and sophisticated, a look she was having difficulty pulling off.

"You've certainly changed your look, Dympna," Rebecca said briskly, pressing herself against the desk, uncomfortably aware of her Tesco attire cramping the style of her designer shoes.

"Was let go from Tranquillity and I decided to go a bit mad, dyed my hair a slutty blonde and bought myself a pair of see-through glasses to look a bit clever. I'm just temping here on reception, kind of like what you used to do in Tranquillity. So . . . how're things?" Dympna was coyly fishing for information about Rebecca's disappearance off the face of the earth.

"Family emergency – my sister and brother-in-law are both ill and needed some hands-on support. I was only part-time in the salon anyway, as you know," Rebecca covered. "So business is down in Carrigmore?" she asked, deliberately changing the subject.

"You could say that again, although it doesn't seem too much better here. People aren't as flush as they used to be of course. There's been a big downturn in massage and, as for waxing, the women of Ireland are either going for the gorilla look or they're doing DIYs. I think DIYs are more likely myself. I've heard stay-in 'waxing parties' are the new cocaine."

Rebecca nodded sympathetically. The days of everyone and their granny having designer gardens, housewives re-mortgaging to get a flashy kitchen and hot tubs replacing standard baths were over, so it was no surprise that the women of Ireland were cutting back on their personal grooming too.

"Worst of all," Dympna whispered in outright horror, "full bushes are now all the go and as for getting manicures done during your lunch hour – old, old news, you can forget about it! I really think the best way to go is mobile beauty work. When people are being careful with the cash, could be the best option, you know."

Rebecca knew all about mobile beauty clinics. When she'd just qualified she'd done a few call-outs and it gave her the chills just remembering. Smelly bedrooms, customers expecting more for their money instead of less – if you left a single hair on a leg they'd nearly expect a discount. That's why she had ditched the one-on-one beauty completely for receptionist work, for a job where contact with the public was more restricted. No, she wasn't interested in mobile beauty clinics – let the tight-fisted clientele stick to their 'wax and whine' parties – she wanted no part of their meanness ever again.

"So are you looking for work here?" Dympna asked sweetly, cocking her head to one side in a funny lapdog manner.

"No, no, just looking at the treatments available. I might get a massage or facial done to treat myself when I can get away from baby-sitting my sister's kids," she lied. Everything cost a fortune, but now that Dympna posed the question, maybe she did need a job after all. Casually, Rebecca said goodbye and walked back into town to make a few enquiries at the handful of beauty salons but they were all spewing the same line: "Business is very competitive at the moment." Translation: 'Please get lost.'

Depressed, Rebecca walked back to Jen's house, her misery intensifying when it began to drizzle as she hadn't an umbrella to shield her from the rain. Before she knew it, her beautiful foxy waves started to go frizzy behind her headband and she knew her brown mascara would be beginning to sludge. Remembering her previous life as a singleton, Rebecca planned revenge on the husband who had reduced her to supermarket basics. Smiling, catlike, she remembered how Mark had annoyed her on a flight to London once and she had brushed against his tea (with milk in it) so that it landed nicely in his crotch and gave him the fright of his life. After feigning professional concern, she took great delight in getting him an icepack and wedging it between his thighs with that sweet fraudulent air-stewardess smile that she could turn on and off like a light. Back then he was hooked no matter what she did, no matter whether she was nasty or nice. Those were the days when he couldn't stop looking at her, when he would have given her anything she wanted for a smile and a kiss. Well, if she wanted her life of luxury and plenty back she'd have to go home and soothe his bruised ego and wiggle out of the contraception deception. She'd need to put on a pretty good performance worthy of her old air stewardess days, but then she remembered how Mark took her car and cut off access to her account. No, there was a game to be played and she needed to win but she didn't know how she would play it – yet.

In the pokey bungalow one of Jen's mum chums had called in with a beef casserole for the invalids and was having a cosy chat with the semi-upright Dan in the kitchen. Rebecca had forgotten which friend it was again, but the firm line the visitor took with Dan was bringing it all back . . . ah yes, she'd taken the same firm line when it came to doing the teas at the mother and toddler group the other day when Rebecca had dropped in . . . the nurse back at work part-time. Recognising Adam, she'd come over for a bit of a chat and as much of a nose into her affairs as Rebecca would allow.

The foil-covered casserole was plonked on the counter top as well as a freshly baked Oxford Lunch. How the hell did Jennifer have so many useful friends? *And this one* . . . Brenda, Barbara, Beatrice, Brona . . . some such heavy-set name to match her heavy-set form . . .

"Want another cup of tea, Betty?" Dan asked.

"No, I'd better run, thanks, Dan. Rebecca, nice to see you again," Betty said kindly as she went to grab her handbag off the counter top. "You're doing a great job here with these kids and you a single woman."

"Do you think?" Rebecca said somewhat coolly, not in the mood to be patronised.

"Absolutely, a mighty job you're doing and . . . well, I don't know your plans or anything but, if you're looking for a job in a caring role, the hospital are looking for some temporary care assistants, mostly in Geriatrics, nothing too regular of course, but God knows, we could do with a few people with sense to look after the patients – the money's not bad either. I brought you an agency form to fill out anyway, just, you know, in case."

Who did this presumptuous woman think she was talking to? It was one thing feeding and cleaning up after a baby . . . but an old, wrinkly, sick person? Ugh, it didn't bear thinking about!

"I suppose Dan told you in a previous life I too used to be a woman in uniform. The life of service – you can never get away from it." Rebecca bared her pointy white teeth in what was a cross between her best air stewardess smile and a 'don't mess with me' grimace.

Betty stared blankly and Dan filled in the details.

"Rebecca used to be an air stewardess," he explained.

Instantly, Betty shot Rebecca an assessing glance, which again annoyed the hell out of her. Okay, so it wasn't the sexy job it was in its heyday but it beat the hell out of looking for dentures or hunting out some patient's smelly old slippers. But she was misjudging Betty's reaction.

"Oh, having trained as an air stewardess will be a great advantage if you apply for that carer job," said Betty, "with your training in first aid, as well as Health & Safety issues."

With the grey-haired nurse gone, Dan helped Rebecca prepare dinner for the rug-rats. God, the tedium of it all!

Dinner was late and she found herself hitting a giant pack of cashew nuts hard. It was impossible to appreciate food in this lunatic asylum. There was no time to sit down and indulge in the ritual of food, savouring the sight of a meal, chewing every morsel delicately – making sure you didn't overeat. Mealtimes here were more like feeding the marines before they went on a suicide mission and worst of all Rebecca's stomach had filled out since she had come to stay – she'd probably put on pounds – how many exactly she didn't know, she was too afraid to step on the scales.

If she didn't get back to her walk-in-wardrobe soon, she wouldn't be able to fit into her lovely clothes at all. Maybe she should borrow Dan's tip of a car some day and grab her belongings while Mark was out of the house. Then she wondered what that action would mean, slinking into her own house to get her own possessions, acting like a burglar on a job. Screw that, she'd wait for the weekend when Mark would be in bed suffering from a hangover, she'd storm in around eleven and act like she owned the place, grab her clothes, rocks both real and fake, tell him that she was bored with their life together and that she was getting a good solicitor to sort things out for good.

Yes, that was more like it. Rebecca Gleeson wasn't a pussycat, she was a wild cat, and if you really annoyed her you'd get to see her claws. Of course, if Mark was remotely sweet to her, she might stay, sulk a bit and make him suffer – it all depended on just how lost he was without her around. Then again, maybe he hadn't missed her at all. Nah, he was missing her, she could nearly feel the desperation travel through the air – he was deliberately playing the stoic, but he definitely missed her and she *would* definitely make him suffer – just for fun.

Frowning from her hostile intentions, Rebecca was running an expensive lipstick around her mouth when her mobile rang. She fumbled for the phone.

The harsh accent at the other end was like a violent slap to the ear that brought her back to unwanted reality. Rebecca nearly choked on her lipstick.

"Is that wee Rebecca?" the voice down the end of the line jarred in a high-pitched sing-song Northern Ireland accent.

"Aunt Birdie?"

"Aye, love – how ya keepin', pet?"

For a moment Rebecca was thrown as she tried to understand why her aunt's number hadn't shown up on her display screen and then realisation dawned that Birdie must be in possession of yet another new phone. Aunt Birdie was a devil for leaving her phones on buses, in cafés, on park benches, once she even sat on a phone cracking it open like an egg and another time she put a phone through the wash – amazingly that one had lived to tell the tale.

"Eh fine, Birdie . . . fine . . ." Rebecca was vaguely aware that her own accent was undergoing a kind of musical metamorphosis as her head tuned into the lyrical inflexions of her aunt's tones and her brain cells were momentarily struggling to translate.

"Didn't I get myself a new phone – again. This one does everything but make tea and it comes with loads of free credit and sure who would I be ringing only my family and I said to myself sure I'll just give wee Rebecca a call."

"Oh lovely." Rebecca's stomach tensed. She hated these conversations where nothing much was said and too much implied.

"And I haven't seen you in *such* a long time, Rebecca. If you don't come and visit soon I'll have to come and see you in that amazing house that smashing man of yours built . . . a mansion, that's what I've told everyone."

"Oh Birdie, you wouldn't be that impressed if you saw it – and, besides, it's filthy at the moment . . . we lost our cleaner." And I'm not sure if I even own my amazing house any more and if the cleaner has run off with my husband.

"Sure if it's cleaning you need just say the word – I'd come and clean the house for you!"

Rebecca felt nauseous – was Birdie really that lonely?

"I could come down for a while and then go off and visit that sister of yours. Getting down south is the problem, though. I really wish I'd learnt to drive when I was a young thing."

Rebecca deliberately said nothing but felt the panic building as she sensed Birdie was working up to something big, as she sensed the family obligations closing in.

"I don't suppose you've got round to rebuilding broken bridges yet?"

Rebecca took a deep breath before letting it all come out in a rush. "I'm actually in Jen's house – she got sick – don't worry she's on the mend now and Dan hurt his back so I told them I'd stay a while – help them out with the kids."

"Ah Rebecca, I'm delighted, it was such a stupid fight to have between sisters –"

"Don't worry, Birdie; nothing's sorted and I'll be disappearing out of here as soon as I get a chance."

217

"Ach, in the end, Rebecca, don't you know there's only family, love?"

Family – that awful word again, that millstone around her neck.

"Well, pet, I'll let you off but you know where we are if you need us."

She knew and she didn't really want to remember. Family – it got her thinking. Since she'd distanced herself from all her support network including Mark and had walked out on her previous job, how was she going to survive? Not in beauty, that was for sure, the market was too slow. Her eye landed on the form Betty had left on the countertop. Looking after old people? No, she'd never be that desperate, she'd never fill out that form.

Twenty

Jennifer was all dressed up in her American clothes and had nowhere to go. Well, when she got right down to it, it turned out she had actually gone a bit mad in America with Sandra and had bought a load of rubbish, except for some nice-ish shoes, an impractical handbag, cheap make-up, a few bits of jewellery and a purse, and after two weeks in bed hyperventilating from bronchitis or stress she'd dropped a few pounds so nothing looked right on her anyway. Worst of all, Dan hadn't commented at all on her new wardrobe and had just trudged off to his new easy-build polytunnel, fretting about the difficulty in getting tomatoes to germinate properly, the tendency of cucumbers to wither prematurely and the fact his boat was developing bigger and bigger holes.

Was this the same man who used to slam her up against the wall and take her knickers off with his teeth, Jennifer pondered as she spied him from the kitchen window turning pots upside down and banging them hard with a trowel? Perhaps it was the iron supplements kicking in, now that she was treating her minor iron deficiency (correctly diagnosed by Dr Cheery). Her libido seemed to be waking up too, now she'd stopped breastfeeding, and all of a sudden she wanted to flaunt her vitality, wanted to own stuff, useless girlie stuff, bags of it, new clothes, new jewellery and maybe even new make-up too. Such a splurge would be expensive, not that she cared. The more perilous her financial existence, the more she just wanted to kick up her heels and suck the marrow out of life. What would be the use of having any money in the bank account if she died without having any fun, living any dreams, behaving just a bit outrageously now and then?

"I'm going shopping for clothes and I won't be back for a *long, long* time," Jennifer hissed at Dan the next morning as she literally left him in the living room holding the baby. He was lucky to be only stuck with Adam as the teeth-baring middle child was on an official trial day at playschool. "And I'm telling you now, I'll be burning plastic so bad it will smell nasty!" she warned as she pulled on some functional shoes that she knew wouldn't flay the skin off her feet after an hour or two of traipsing around.

"Where are you going – down town?"

"I haven't decided yet!"

"But didn't you just buy a load of clothes in America?"

"All of it useless," she snarled. "They don't make clothes for people like me any more, they don't make clothes for real women, you can only get bits of stuff that wouldn't cover a small child's arse, but that won't stop me trying to find something decent – no, strike that

– something *sexy* I can wear, just for fun." And she banged the front door shut.

The clothes in her local backwater rejected her – she took it personally as she ripped garments from the hangers which promised to be plus size, enough to cover her boobs and hips, and which, as she'd predicted, would barely cover a small child's arse.

Right, she'd got that 'What shape is your bum and other bits?' book for Christmas and had been meaning to try out the recommendations for ages now. When uncertain whether one was an apple or a brick or a bell with good legs, one needed some serious shops to test the hypothesis – serious shops that one could only find in a city. But this project needed planning, strategy and goals – help that could only come from a woman who'd be sexy if she was wearing a bin-liner and was a voluptuous size forty.

An hour after she'd first left home Jennifer burst through the door, ignoring a look of puzzlement on Dan's face at her lack of purchases and went off to ring Sadie from the cordless phone, noticing as she went that Dan had invaded her domestic sphere and washed the kitchen floor and window in her absence, a fact which set her teeth on edge.

"What's up?" Sadie asked amidst a din of background noise from her children.

"Sadie, I need your help because in case you haven't noticed I look like a bag lady!" Jennifer felt the tears building and although she tried not to grunt like a depressed pig she snorted loudly down the phone anyway.

"Ach, love, don't cry – just hang on a sec."

Jennifer waited as she heard Sadie let out a roar at her

kids over some misdemeanour or other and then things quietened down again.

"Now we'll have a bit of peace – right, where were we?"

"I'm sorry, Sadie, I just didn't know who else to ring – it's just you always look so fabulous while still . . . you know . . . still looking like a *real* woman."

"While still having a bit of an arse, you mean – it's okay, I know everyone says it. So you're wanting to go shopping for a few new glad rags then?"

"Yes, even though I did all that shopping in America but . . . I don't know, a lot of the stuff I bought looks wrong now . . . to tell you the truth, I must have been on drugs to have bought the half of it."

"Ah yes, that's the problem with bargain shopping – you can get sucked into buying a heap of junk that doesn't suit just because it's cheap. Listen, my sister-in-law is looking after the kids tomorrow to give me a break. Want to come shopping in the city? Bring Adam if you need to."

"Oh Sadie, that would be brill . . . and you know all about that dressing like an apple or a brick stuff to flatter your figure, don't you?"

"I do, pet – to be honest I could have written the book."

"Okay then, you just got yourself a shopping partner and, don't worry, I'll be on my own. Dan's taking some time off from work, so he can take Adam," she lied uncomfortably. "And, Sadie, just promise me you won't let me buy a heap of crap, will you?"

"I promise – I'll be ruthless."

"Thanks, Sadie," Jennifer sniffled.

"I'm burning the plastic *tomorrow* instead," Jennifer snapped at Dan as she passed him in the hall.

Wisely, he kept his silence and just nodded as if he suspected as much all along.

Feeling exuberant, Jennifer hit the trendy high-street shops the next day like a heftier form of Julia Roberts on her Mondeo Drive shopping mission. Today the blasted shops would yield up their treasures, she willed, as she parked her car at the jumbo car park and pulled her keys from the ignition.

"Are you ready?" Sadie asked.

Taking a deep breath, Jennifer nodded. Sexy Sadie had already given her the shopping low-down on the drive in. The rule for apples, Jennifer's most likely fruit size, was V necks to emphasise the boobs, no extra fussy buttons or ties round the tummy, long trousers and high-heeled boots to give the illusion of leg extension.

"I'm ready, I'm definitely ready. Let's do this!" Jennifer announced positively and the two of them jumped out of the car like *Starsky and Hutch*, or at least two special-forces guys on a dangerous but important mission, which of course they were.

Soon, in the solitude of her cubicle, Jennifer began the battle. The first few tops she'd chosen were a disaster, too tight round her midriff emphasising every ripple of fat, pushing her love handles up until she looked like a big lump of jelly.

"Take it off," Sadie commanded instantly as she saw the best of the worst.

"Do you not think it's a nice colour though?" Jennifer pleaded, her self-esteem on the floor along with the first trial and error garments.

"I'm the boss today and you wanted me to be

ruthless. Take it off, keep going and don't take it personally if things don't fit," Sadie said firmly.

So Jennifer soldiered on, determined to complete her mission of identifying items that might make it to the till and at one point was excited when she tried on a top and it seemed to fit her beautifully until she realised it was actually a maternity top. Her bottom lip began to wobble but she took a deep breath and ploughed on.

Tops on, tops off, one discarded, one saved. Hurray, a victory! Tops on – every colour, every texture, any size, any pattern so long as it went over her head – she had no pride, just a desire to look better. What were label sizes anyhow?

"Good girl yourself!" Sadie praised when she saw her friend with a few definite successes.

In the next shop a buoyed-up Jennifer charged at a rail of trendy trousers. Trousers – lord, what a nightmare, her bum looked huge – but Jennifer was past crying. Keep advancing, she told herself, keep advancing. Her thoughts were racing. Who the hell has legs this long, she thought as she picked up a pair of skinny jeans? Hold your nerve . . . you're doing fine . . . go up a size – rats, my crotch looks saggy, although the cut definitely improves around my bum. Janey, I look slim . . . well, slimmer at any rate. What does it look like with that top that makes my boobs look fantastic! My word, I actually have potential. I am still the woman I used to be, just a bit less defined around the edges.

"How ya doin'?" asked Sadie, looking fabulous in a stretchy wraparound blue dress with a V neck that made her boobs look ripe for the groping.

"You know, I think I'm doing okay . . . in fact, I'm

pretty excited . . . I feel like going out there and fighting a few women hand-to-hand-combat-style for stuff off the hangers!"

"Well, you go, girl!" Sadie laughed, but not before checking her own rear end in the full-length mirror – as usual it was looking big and curvy but one hundred per cent fabulous.

Like a lioness Jennifer left the changing room and began to roam the shop floor. Her whole being was overcome by a kind of crazed hunger as she flicked through hangers of clothes so fast it was like someone counting money at the end of a day's takings. The old competitive edge came to the fore as she scanned size labels, grabbing everything remotely decent in case that woman behind had her eyes on the same item. *'Back off, baby – it's mine, I have a greater need . . .'* Jennifer tried to telepathically communicate her raw energy to anything female within a half-mile radius and she swore they all took heed and kept away, especially as she shot some deliberately menacing scowls at any possible renegades.

Having ripped bounty off hangers, Jennifer headed back to the changing rooms with bundles of slimming black basics on her arms and bundles of colour, then more colour, then anything colourful at all and suddenly Jennifer realised that for years her life had been dull and grey both inside and out . . . she would have passed her downtrodden self on the street without a second glance but all her being didn't want to be that unnoticed woman any more. Arms laden down with clothes, so many clothes she couldn't count them, Jennifer waited for the shop assistant to leave her post and then charged into her cubicle, knowing she was well in breach of the store's 'no more than six items' policy. Feeling the strength inside her growing as she caught her new reflection in the mirror, Jennifer thought for the first time in a long time that her physical body might be coming in line with the image in her head.

"Wow, you learn quick!" Sadie was genuinely taken aback when she saw the new Jennifer parade her stuff, in clothes that were on the cutting-edge of fashion but which actually flattered her shape.

"I feel like just leaving my old clothes on the floor and walking out in these," Jennifer beamed as she caught sight of herself in some new bootleg jeans, a trendy blue cotton top, some happening jewellery and a funky jacket which drew the eye away from her midriff. In fact, once she had paid for her items she did race back in and change into her life-giving clothes, stuffing her old possessions into one of the giant shopping bags instead.

Having burnt plastic until it was smoking, they headed for tea and chicken chilli wraps at the cool in-store restaurant and let their bodies collapse into softly padded chairs.

"Well, I'd say folk won't recognise the new you at all, you look so good. Dan won't be able to keep his hands off you either when he sees you dressed in all your finery," Sadie laughed, her brown eyes playful under her pale-green eye shadow.

Dan – Jennifer froze at the mere mention of her husband. Feeling cautious but needing to talk, Jennifer asked the question that was gnawing away inside ever since New York.

"Sadie . . . have you ever thought about having an

affair . . . I mean, not really doing it necessarily, but have you ever just thought about it, you know just for a laugh, seeing as you're Sexy Sadie and all and everybody's doing it, if you believe all the magazines and gossip pages?"

For a moment Sadie stiffened and Jennifer thought she'd overstepped the boundaries of their friendship – after all, this wasn't Sandra, keeper of all her secrets past and present.

Keeping her eyes down, Sadie played with a gold signet ring on her right hand, lost in thought or so it seemed until the corners of her mouth curled into a slow smile.

"I suppose it's like what they say, isn't it . . . it doesn't matter where you get your appetite so long as you get your dinner at home? I know having an affair is no big deal these days but I don't spend the time looking for it to happen if you know what I mean."

Jennifer nodded as the sound of herself munching on crisps nearly burst her eardrums. Hopefully she was conveying the impression that she was of the same mind herself as regards the whetting the sexual appetite for dinner and the looking but not looking stuff.

"Do you know, I heard a beautiful thing once," said Sadie, "that when Paul Newman was married to Joanne Woodward he was asked would he ever be tempted to have a fling and he said, 'Why bother with hamburger when you have steak waiting for you at home?' – that's how much he loved her."

Sexy Sadie smiled and Jennifer felt a sharp stabbing pain in her stomach that she was sure wasn't just indigestion.

"Beautiful, that's really beautiful," she forced herself

to say. Maybe if she said, 'eat steak' over and over again it would become a brain-washing mantra that just might keep her flighty mind and her simmering libido on the right track.

When Jennifer pulled into the front drive and trudged through the house with her paper shopping bags, a quick glance from the kitchen window told her the kids were in the garden – playing in the newly built sandpit with Dan alongside them sorting out spare blocks and old bags of concrete. Bustling into the bedroom, Jennifer shoved all her bags into the bottom of the wardrobe. She kept on her new jeans but sought out her shapeless grey top from her shopping bag and put it on again.

Something in her was turning, a dead part of her cells was switching on again, but for the moment she didn't want Dan to notice the change. Dinner, she'd think about dinner, there was nothing like menu-planning to kill any trace of love, lust or passion. How long was it since they'd had bolognese? Bummer, it was only two nights ago, she'd have to think of something else instead. How she'd love to just run away and be distracted by the possibility of something new for once. Opening her wardrobe door, she went searching for the one piece of new clothing she had coveted more than all the rest – a sensuous all-in-one lace and satin teddy in midnight blue with underwire cups and slimming support panels around the tummy and hips and easy access for . . . well, it didn't matter, she wasn't exactly planning for Dan to get a look at it and Hollywood stars weren't likely to be calling to the house any day soon.

Late in the evening with only herself for company (the despicable sister had disappeared from the house for the night and Dan was gone to the pub), Jennifer re-engaged with her sexy new self, pulling a flouncy midnight-blue skirt over the new lace body suit and slipping on her gold high-heeled shoes from New York, click-clicking along like a precocious little girl in her mother's shoes.

Excitement tingled from her toes to her scalp. Sadie was wrong – variety was the spice of life – life was all about hamburgers *and* steak. Steak was fulfilling, nourishing and special, but hamburgers filled a gap even if they weren't that good for you and made you feel queasy afterwards.

Besides, it wasn't like she was a saddo housewife with a webcam in her bedroom, talking to the world in a satin and lace blue teddy. No, she was just exploring the vastness of the world from the security of her home, just surfing the internet for a little excitement, something to curb her hunger, something once eaten soon forgotten, something to fill a gap for reasons she didn't quite understand and couldn't be bothered judging, at least not tonight.

Twenty-one

Staying a night alone in a local bed and breakfast had helped get things clear in Rebecca's head. Mark was playing with her, and distracted by Jen's brood Rebecca had allowed things to drag on longer than they should – but not for any longer, it was time to set things straight. Pulling up at her home in Dan's car (he hadn't much use for it these days anyhow since the big job went down the toilet), she noticed that Mark's car was missing from its usual spot.

Surprisingly the front door opened on Rebecca's first attempt – her dramatic side had thought Mark might go so far as to change the locks. Sunlight streamed through her hall and the crystal hanging from the ceiling bounced rainbows off the polished wooden floor and her apple-white walls. Instinctively she went to throw her keys on the hall table but as she raised her eyes a fraction her blood began to simmer. In front of her was a massive print of firm young jugs in too-small itsy-bitsy bikini tops – a thing from Mark's bachelor days. Where the hell was her oil painting of wild flowers in a blue vase?

Passing by the open door of the sitting room, Rebecca was horrified to see her mantelpiece bereft of all feminine eye-candy and her favourite landscape painting replaced by a giant, vulgar flat-screen TV. Furious, she stormed into the kitchen/dining area bursting for a fight.

"Mark!" she yelled, threateningly.

Looking out the French doors into the garden, she saw that his car wasn't around the back either. His absence was puzzling – he was normally such a creature of habit and when it came to Saturday mornings he mostly made sure he was home. Then her brain noticed other missing items – her showy ceramic cookie jar containing low-calorie plain biscuits only and her wedding china, usually visible through the glass doors of her cabinets, were nowhere to be seen.

Fretting now, she ran up the stairs, still calling Mark's name abusively and still getting no response. In the bathrooms all her creams, lotions and potions had been removed – all that remained was a bottle of aftershave, a can of shaving foam and a canister of underarm deodorant. In a panic she rushed to her walk-in wardrobe and what she discovered made her sit down until the shock subsided and her breathing slowed.

Rows and rows of hangers, proud bearers of her favourite designers, now lay empty, the wood and metal of the hangers making loud clattery noises as she ran her hand through them at first in desperation and then in anger. Gone – her classic items of cashmere and silk; missing – her satin blouses and trousers and her delicately embroidered woollens; vanished – her almost too beautiful linen skirts, jackets and slacks. Jesus Christ, Mark hadn't offloaded all her stuff on Mariola, had he?

Distraught, Rebecca rummaged through her drawers to find that tops, gloves and scarves were missing too although surprisingly most of her underwear was still intact. Burning with rage, she pulled out a pair of scarlet satin French knickers and a matching padded bra. Luxury – she closed her eyes and breathed it in, savouring what she had left.

At least he hadn't found her pole and precious exhibitionist items, she sighed, as she opened the false back on the lingerie door and was rewarded with her prize booty. Stuff it, when a girl has had all her clothes nicked by foreign-national clothes thieves and by her husband (possibly to supply another foreign national, the Polish cleaner) surely there was nothing left to do but dance?

She quickly undressed and donned her tassels, hot pants and boots. Then, as the first beats of an edgy Lily Allen song belted out, she hauled herself up the dance pole to mid-height, feeling the strain on her arms. Instinctively she gripped on with her thighs, noting with some annoyance that they'd softened a bit since her stay at Dan and Jen's but she was still able to shimmy up the hard metal without too much effort.

It was while hanging upside down that she noticed the door opening and suddenly an inverted image of Mark's feet and legs filled her view. Pulling herself quickly upright she saw that his hair was tousled from exercise, his face sexily stubbled with weekend shadow and his blue T-shirt rolled up past his midriff as he began to strip for the shower while still walking. For a moment Rebecca wondered if he even knew who she was.

He looked momentarily stunned, but then a huge annoying smirk broke across his face. "Hey, don't mind me," he said, recovering quickly from shock and slipping into sarcasm. "You just carry on doing whatever it is you're doing. Music loud enough for you?" His fingers hovered over the volume dial of the stereo, his eyes glinting with a hint of menace and smug satisfaction.

"Screw you, Mark!" she threw at him as she slipped off the pole and tossed her hair, standing topless bar some red tassels, in the skyscraper-heeled boots that always made her feel wonderfully indestructible.

"Ah now, I don't think the lads would be very happy to hear that the firewoman they sent over with her pole was being sarky to the customers. God, the lads are great all the same, chipping in for a surprise exotic dancer! Not to bore you with the details or anything but my wife fucked off, you see – I'm reduced to pay-per-view now. So tell us, do you put out many fires in your line of work or maybe you're more the type that starts them?" He was right beside her now, ripping off his T-shirt and hauling off his exercise shorts.

Rebecca didn't want to look at him because being so close to him was making her feel unexpectedly tingly and he himself was close enough to feel the volatile chemistry between them and was obviously enjoying the sensation. A quick glance told her he'd been working out since she left. Damn, men got fit fast. His stomach was toned and the dark little curls of hair around the waistband of his boxers were enticingly distracting.

"Because I have another pole here you can swivel around when you're ready," Mark said softly and mischievously without a trace of venom.

"I don't think so," Rebecca forced herself to say coolly. For effect she ran her eyes up and down his body and allowed them to hover on his swollen crotch for a millisecond before averting her eyes dismissively.

"Have it your own way," he shrugged but his fingers were fascinated by the tassels on her nipples. Without waiting to be asked he clipped them off and was surprised at how neatly they fell into the palms of his hands, allowing his unprepared thumbs to caress the soft, swollen mounds. Rebecca knew she should stride across the room and get dressed but her feet wouldn't move and, seeing her hesitate, Mark continued his fondlings, his mouth and tongue quickly savouring her raspberry-soft nipples before he saw her stony face.

Bemused, he broke away and threw himself on the bed, his arms folded behind his neck, his eyes moving up and down her body.

Rebecca couldn't resist taunting him, casually swinging out of the pole with her right arm and turning, giving him a look that was somewhere between reproach and coquettish play.

"So what's this all for then, Rebecca? Hmm, what's with the big sex show and the new pole?" Mark grinned. "What are we playing for here: the car, your high-class rags – or maybe you want the whole shebang? Sick of slumming it in the suburbs yet?"

"Jesus Mark, like the song says, '*you're so vain*', maybe this big show isn't for you at all. As it happens I've had this pole for months now and I dance for my own pleasure. But since you've brought it up where the fuck *are* my car and my 'high-class rags'?"

"Ah well, from where I'm at it doesn't look like you

have much need for any clothes, high-class or otherwise, and what do you need a car for when you've no work to go to? You've no friends left at the salon, not after the extended little holiday you've been on."

"My *clothes*, Mark, not to mention my china, my crystal candlesticks and half the bloody house – where's my stuff?"

"Threw it in a skip, the whole shagging lot, and your car is in the garage with a big 'for sale' sticker on it." He peeled off his socks and lay on the bed, linking his hands behind his head. "Most of your 'stuff' was just clutter anyway – now it's gone you wouldn't believe how fast Mariola gets around the house." He shot her a look, fully aware that his remarks were cutting. 'Don't take the bait,' she told herself. For a moment she succeeded in keeping calm – and then, despite her best intentions, she took the bait.

"So you have her back cleaning, do you? Nice. The two of you can spend all the time you want in bed now without any interruptions from your dried-up shrew of a wife!"

"Oh well, if you're feeling a bit neglected, I'll take you to bed right now. As the Yanks say, 'I have a window'."

"Yeah? Go ahead and jump right out of it then – make me a rich widow, why don't you!"

"I swear to God, Rebecca, one of these days . . ."

Determinedly he rolled off the bed, crossed the floor, picking up his T-shirt and shorts en route and sticking them in the laundry basket (it had taken Rebecca five years to train him to do that one manoeuvre), and squared up to her in her tantalising boots, coming as close as he could to touching her, without touching her.

The scent of his still fresh sweat made her woozy and

she tried not to make eye contact – but she was beginning to feel decidedly underdressed, more than a bit silly and worst of all just a little bit interested.

"You're a dark bird, Rebecca Gleeson – you and your pole."

"Rebecca *Murphy* – and what about *you* and *your* Pole?" she glared back at him.

"Rebecca Murphy now, is it? Okay, Rebecca Murphy, how about you dance for me?" he quipped, ignoring her Pole remark. "I'll pay you," he added, his eyes drawn to the top of her black leather boots. Without thinking he placed his hand on her satin-clad rear, pushing the material aside gently until his hand was slyly caressing one soft curvy cheek.

"Hey, Mark, I thought you of all people would know the rules – you can look, but you can't touch," she said haughtily as she pushed his hand away.

"Relax, baby, the heavies are on a break," he said teasingly as he shoved his hand further inside her hot pants until he was cupping one, then both cheeks together.

Half-heartedly she pushed him away but he began to caress the softness of her inner thighs and her pubic mound with fingers that were becoming rougher and more daring, as he kissed her neck. As she felt him pull on the elastic at her waist, feeling his head moving from her throat to her navel and then her lower belly, and knowing that if he went further she was finished, she snapped at him and the hardness in her voice surprised her as much as him.

"How much? How much will you pay me if I dance?"

"Pay you? Come on! I didn't really –"

"How much?" There was no doubt about it – those damn boots gave her an air of superiority that went way beyond reason.

"I . . ."

Her fingertips travelled just underneath the waistband of her pants and she felt the smooth, shiny scar on her hip and shuddered as she remembered the summer in Greece when she went a little wild seducing Theo, the Greek God who helped run the small apartment complex where she was staying. Smiling, she remembered using the infatuated Theo for comfort sex after Gary broke her heart, remembered lounging on his wooden boat on the crystal waters of the Mediterranean, remembered locking her long slim legs around his strong muscley trunk. When, towards the end of her holiday, she came off a motorbike and ran her hip ragged into gravel she didn't even mind the pain – physical pain was nothing compared to excitement and being in control. Pulling her fingers away from the scars of the past, she ground her knuckles into her hip with resolve.

"Forget the dancing. Let's cut to the chase. How much for sex? That's really what you want, isn't it? Let's just get it out of the way right now – how much for sex, Mark?"

It took a lot to floor Mark but she had succeeded. He sprang away from her as if her skin was burning, put a distance between them until his addled brain could make sense of her cryptic female sentences. His newly toned and slimmed-down abs were so tempting that she knew if he told her to get over herself that she'd have sex with him anyway, but heart pounding she chose to play poker, just to see who would flinch first, just for fun.

"Well, I took the pot last night. There's over six hundred in the safe . . . three hundred, yeah, I'd definitely pay you three hundred," he said coolly.

"Only three? You want the boots on, baby, they're three a piece – deal or no deal?"

In a second he lifted her off her feet, put her over his shoulder fireman-style and threw her on to their super-sprung, super-expensive and of late ill-used mattress. Deal.

Pushing him roughly on his back she straddled him, making sure the pointy bits of her heels scraped his knees in the process and gave him a hard dominatrix stare. His hands went up to the small of her back to hold her and squeeze her breasts which were bobbing close to his mouth – and he managed to give them a few playful licks before she grabbed both his wrists and pushed them over his head, pinning him to the pillow. Laughing at her seriousness, he played along with her game as she got off him, removed her pants and straddled him once more.

"Careful," he teased softly, as she sought out her own pleasure. "It's not made of rubber. I don't want you to break it!"

Dismissively she gave him a 'you stay where you are and be quiet' stare but Mark had had enough of her pleasuring herself for her own sake and easily flipped her onto her back, pinning her own wrists to the pillow with one hand, much to her feigned annoyance.

"Let me up," she snapped lazily.

"Not a chance. I know how much you like it on top – easy money and too much fun for you!" His spare hand and mouth moved all over as he first kissed her firmly on the mouth, then planted tiny kisses behind her ear and neck that made her quiver, touching the backs of her knees gently with his fingers, plunging his fingers where they willed until her breathing became rapid and shallow. He waited until she was desperate before he entered her, moving slowly and deeply inside her until her body betrayed her with her passion. Then Mark waited for her to be collapsed like a helpless kitten before he took his own pleasure, rolled off and smiled.

"Feeling better – less stressed now you've died and gone to heaven?" he joked after a few minutes when both of them could breathe again.

"How do you know I have died and gone to heaven? Maybe I faked it."

Sitting up, she unzipped the boots and threw them on the floor. He knelt behind her and started to kiss the back of her neck and the hollows of her collarbone.

"Not likely."

"Oh yeah – how would you know?"

"'Cos, sweetheart, when you come you flush pink from here to here," he slowly traced a finger from her throat to her nipples, "just like you're flushed now!"

"Mark!" Viciously Rebecca elbowed him in the ribs and then fell back into his arms. They lay back on the bed together, side by side. He was so warm and his body hair so soft and downy, her limbs never wanted to move from his warmth and snugly protection. So much for keeping emotion out of her sex life – but then it was always harder to play games with Mark. He never played the games the way she wanted anyhow, she thought as she watched his face sink in the pillow contentedly with only half his nose and a big lopsided grin visible to her eye.

"Jesus, Rebecca, that was *so* good I'll throw in the cash, the car and everything else with it because, believe me, you're worth every fucking penny," he mumbled into the pillow.

Suddenly Rebecca stiffened as though she had been slapped in the face. "What did you say?" she asked with steel in her voice.

"You're worth every penny," he repeated, stroking her arm while not moving an inch.

"Before that?"

"Wha–?"

"You'll *throw in* the car? What car are we talking about exactly? Is this *my* car that you *robbed* from under me and what's this everything else you're talking about? Would that be *my* stuff too, *my* clothes, *my* china, *my* paintings, *my* jewellery?"

"Look, I was only having a bit of fun . . . "

"You are such a shit, Mark. Who the hell do you think you are? Who the hell do you think I am? Do you think I'm dependent on your little crumbs of mercy to survive this world?"

Furious, she jumped off the bed and wriggled back into the old cotton knickers she'd arrived in, then pulled on her cotton mint-green T-shirt which lay at a pile near her feet.

"Why don't you go back to your nice little submissive Polish cleaner? A great little cook I'd say she is too . . . easy on the eye of course and she's probably a real little goer in the sack – every time you screw her you can get her something nice, a gold necklace perhaps, a promise of a new dress!"

"Jesus, why are you so jealous of a lovely girl who just wants to get on a bit in life?"

240

"Lovely girl all right! I see the way you look at her, with that . . . with that look of yours!"

"What look?"

"*That* look, *that* look that was in the photo of you two at Christmas . . . I think it's only now that I've realised what that look was all about, that look that says *you* would be a lovely mother to my children. That look that says I never want to see you out of my kitchen, doing some real cooking and being barefoot and . . . and pregnant!"

Damn, she'd mentioned the P word – and the P word was a real incendiary device.

For a moment neither of them talked – the anger in the air was just too suffocating.

"What you did . . . pretending you were off the pill . . . that was real lousy, Rebecca," he said in a wounded voice.

"Well – yeah." There wasn't much to say in her defence – she knew it was lousy. All she wanted to do was run. She had her jeans on now and was fastening her belt at such a breakneck speed she kept stabbing herself on the metal buckle.

"Rebecca, would it be too much to ask what the hell you're doing here today?"

"It's still my house too," she lashed back at him, pulling on her shoes.

Slowly Mark stood up, moved towards her, took her head in his hands and looked her directly in the eyes.

"You know, I think I was always expecting this time to come," he sighed.

"What are you on about?" Rebecca was in haste to fix her shoes but they weren't going on any easier than her jeans or belt.

"I always knew you were too young to get married, that maybe you didn't have enough experiences behind you, experiences with other guys."

"I had enough to know that most are selfish pricks, if that's what you mean!"

"All I know is that I'm sick of games. I want a grown-up wife by my side, I want children and if that's not what you want then you'll have to tell me because I won't wait forever."

Her insides froze.

"Six months. Take six months to get whatever it is out of your system. Six months to live whatever life you want, to do . . . do whatever it is you need to do, then tell me if we still have a future or not."

"Don't you *dare* issue me with ultimatums – I'll see a solicitor – get everything back, everything I'm entitled to, Mark, and more I swear it!"

"And what will you tell your solicitor? That we're separating, divorcing, that your husband is a sly fox who cut off your cash flow? By the time you sort things out it will take months anyhow and that's the end for me, Rebecca, I won't wait any longer."

He stared at her intensely, then kissed her on the forehead and drew a wisp of hair behind her ear affectionately.

"Six months – and I'm deducting the time you've already been away . . ."

Quickly he headed for the en-suite and as she heard the shower pump into life she felt strangely hollow. There was nothing to take with her except her pole, her boots, her sexy little tassels, and the flurry of bank notes lying on the bed. Resolve grew inside her. It didn't take an ounce of strength to pack up her boots and pole, resist his poker 'payment' and walk straight out of the room into that new exciting life she was planning for those fabulous boots with their useful crushing heels.

Twenty-two

"We need to talk," Jennifer half-choked, half-barked as Rebecca entered the room.

"Well, it'll have to wait because we're going out," Rebecca sighed, eager to avoid confrontation.

"What do you mean *we're* going out?" Jennifer asked, her words sharp as lemon.

"Just that – we're going out."

"We? 'We' as in 'us'?"

"Yes. Us."

"I'm sorry but why would I want to be going out with you? Us sharing the same airspace is just a temporary little arrangement . . . look, I'll be blunt . . . I've heard you've got work lined up and I just want to tell you that if you're planning on working where I live –"

"Okay, okay, I catch your drift but save it till later, we're still going out and I was told to bring you kicking and screaming if I had to."

"Who told you and go where exactly?"

"Just get some of your nice new stuff on," Rebecca answered wearily. "Your time starts . . . now!"

In less than ten minutes the bright lights of the town were eclipsed by darkness as Rebecca negotiated narrow bouncy bog roads flanked by dense fir trees – bandit country. It didn't take Jennifer too long to realise they were en route to Helen's, but conversation with her sister was spared as the radio was turned up conveniently high. Helen's spacious bungalow was lit up like Christmas when they arrived and inside, milling around the kitchen and sitting room, was a gaggle of mothers – all drinking wine like it was diluted kiddie juice and knocking back crisps like they were the latest fat-free invention. There wasn't a man in sight as Helen's husband and her boys had been dispatched to the nearby mother-in-law's till the following afternoon at the earliest.

In front of the heated oven Helen was layering French bread with mozzarella, beef tomatoes and herbs, moving as fast and assured as if she was on the rugby pitch, her normally braided hair swishing around her shoulders in inky black waves making her face seem at least five years younger, and her lithe body snugly fitted into a sexy well-cut top and flattering black satin trousers.

"What's the occasion?" Jennifer asked, plonking wine and a cake on the kitchen island.

"No occasion, just took a notion for us girls to have a bit of a get-together," Helen said lightly and a few people began to giggle.

As the house began to swell Jennifer cracked into the wine to hasten along a nice relaxed feeling, noticing as she did that Rebecca wasn't drinking at all, probably so she could immediately scarper when she'd had enough of mad mothers over-spilling with emotion.

In the background a TV was turned down low and several giddy predators with fishbowls of wine were glued to a concert advertisement and openly salivating over a famous boy band.

"Which one of the 'boys' would you do?" Sexy Sadie started boldly, verbalising what everyone else was thinking.

"God, all of them – even the gay fella," Laura sighed as the boys walked in slow motion in gorgeous fashionable clothes, muscles in all the right places, hair-gel creating the cutest of tufts and designer stubble sending out all the right 'bit of rough but deep down we're still big softies' messages as they mouthed the words to their latest love ballad.

"What about you, Rebecca?" Laura asked, trying to politely draw the only childless woman into the conversation.

Rebecca smiled uneasily and shrugged her shoulders as she nursed a glass of water, clearly not overly relaxed in the company of randy mothers.

"They're getting on a bit though, aren't they?" criticised Sadie.

"Ah, they'd all be only toy boys for me – don't forget I'm forty my next birthday," Helen said with a mock sigh. Her bosoms heaved in her sexy top which was really a bit too revealing and more suited to a woman ten years her junior but it wasn't a night where anyone was admitting that they were up the hill never mind over it.

"What about you, Jennifer? Which one would you do if you had the choice?"

"As if I were ever likely to have that choice! Ah, like Laura says all of them – *especially* the gay guy – and no appointments necessary. Sure don't you know *my* next birthday I'm thirty-five which makes it official I'll be a woman in my prime in need of a man in his prime which would mean he would have to be somewhere around . . ."

"Seventeen – you randy old goat!" laughed Laura.

"Oh, when's your birthday again?" Sadie winked, knowing full well the answer.

"Eh . . . tomorrow actually. Yes, tomorrow I'll be officially on the way to Old Crockdom and I know you're only meant to feel uptight about the birthdays with the zeros in them but the ones with the fives in them can hit pretty hard as well . . . "

"Yep . . . I remember when you turned twenty-five you cried for a week . . ."

Jennifer looked up stunned as Sandra strode through the back door on cue, her blonde hair fluffed like a feathery nest, her permanent kohl-black eyes more smouldering than ever and wearing her party ensemble – an outfit that was very bling and uber-sparkly. This wasn't Sandra the Friend, this was Sandra the Performer, who lost no time giving Helen a few conspiratorial winks through her over-sized pink false eyelashes as she took sole possession of Helen's massive country kitchen.

"And so for one night only to cheer up me old friend and to help her past the big three five, I'm at her complete service – me and my big bag of *Slinky Bunny* tricks!"

Everybody sniggered optimistically.

Boldly, Sandra reached inside her sackful of goodies and there was a big revving sound, like the sound of a drill or a high-powered motorbike and, to much whooping and applause, *Miss Slinky Bunny* for the Greater Leinster region herself pulled out the mysterious device, revealing its identity to be a turbo-charged purple and silver phallic weapon of monumental size and shocking manoeuvrability.

"Holy crap, I wouldn't recommend that fellow for any girl who'd never seen the insides of the labour ward!" said Vicki slyly as she grabbed the vibrator and used it as a toy gun, pretending to mow down the bunch of squealing women.

More applause and schoolgirl giggling followed when Chinese Balls and Sexy Bath Bombs were glimpsed and then pink champagne was popped and everyone threw back the bubbles along with chocolate party willies and waited for the real games to begin.

"Now, ladies, while you're all relaxed but as yet not too drunk, I think we'll play the rude and *sexy* word game," Sandra said, raising an eyebrow suggestively.

"Oh, I'm up for that," said Betty as she swallowed a chocolate willy whole. "Did English and French in College for one year before the nursing and I haven't put it to good use in – I don't know – years!"

"Well, this game won't require any French, just a filthy knowledge of the English language. Let's start with A!" Sandra carried off her circus ringmaster stunt with aplomb. "Any takers for A now, ladies?"

"*Ass . . . asshole . . . asinine . . .*" the normally sensible Betty was on a roll.

"Excuse me!" Laura's hand shot up authoratively. "I'm afraid I'll have to object to *asinine* on the grounds that it is neither rude or sexy but roughly interpreted means 'stubborn or silly.' English and History, darling, and unlike you I finished my degree!" Laura smirked from behind her chardonnay.

"Well, Miss Smarty Pants, would you object to *arse . . . arsehole . . . arse-bandit* then?" said Betty.

"Oh no, not at all, all perfectly allowable within the rules of the game . . . carry on," Laura nodded solemnly.

"Er, moving on to B so," Sandra smiled cautiously, steering away from trouble.

"Oh, that would be *blowjob . . .*" Betty was off again. "*Bastard . . . big bastard . . . biggest bastard of all time –*"

"My word, that one year of the English degree really stood to you!" giggled Sadie. "Way to go, Betty . . . give some other folk a look in now and again, won't you?"

"Okay, let's give C a lash, ha, ha, pardon the pun – well, obviously there's the dirty one that no one can say –" Sandra started.

"Not to mention *cunnilingus* – sorry, sorry, that one just rolled off the tip of my tongue," Betty blurted.

It went on and on, eventually reaching "*testicles*" and finally "*wanker . . .*"

Betty's knowledge of the English language was surprisingly extensive and Sandra wisely drew things to a close as a tipsy Betty spluttered out words that were at best a distant memory in everyone else's brain.

"It's just I was always a bit wordy, I guess." Betty blushed from embarrassment coupled with mild intoxication as she mumbled apologies into her wineglass.

Brushing professionally over the whole spelling orgy, Sandra decided to start a new game and went rummaging in her bag for a couple of pairs of enormous black-cotton granny-pants.

"Now, I think we'll get the hostess and the party girl up first . . . step into your knickers, girls, don't be shy."

Any potential shyness evaporated on the spot as Sandra stuffed two enormous yellow balloons down the front of Helen's and Jennifer's granny-pants.

"Right, on the floor, pick a spot and call it the sexy footballer of your choice and start doing press-ups . . . give it plenty of wellie now, girls . . . the first to burst the balloon gets a prize!"

There was much drunken snorting and laughing as they cheered Helen and Jennifer on for ages. The damn balloons were impenetrable until eventually Helen's rugby-tackling skills shone through and, having annihilated her yellow balloon, she crash-landed on the piece of carpet which she had fondly christened 'George Best'.

"Good girl yourself, Helen!" cheered Sandra. "Now your prize is a choice between Chinese Love Balls and what I call 'the absolute business' – The Panty Pleaser!"

"Oh God, give us a look at himself so," said Helen eagerly as she snatched a scary gel moulded device out of Sandra's hands and tried it on over her trousers, switching it on and getting it to vibrate to screams of laughter from her friends.

"Wasn't there a story about some woman wearing one of those Pleasers to the supermarket and getting such an intense orgasm she collapsed into the frozen-food section?" Laura piped up, putting Helen right off the ferocious jelly monster.

Instead the rugby woman stuck to balls – Chinese Love Balls, although she eyed the orbs up suspiciously as if doubtful that anything so small could be in any way useful in the G-spot department.

"Okay, girls, ready for tonight's main feature then?" Sandra asked wickedly, delving into her Mary Poppins' bag for noisy, shiny Big Boy Booty.

Out they came one by one – 'plastic love' – vibrators of amazing size and flexibility, their motors screaming like racing cars, just as sleek and shiny and causing twice the excitement.

"Oh my God, if I brought this lad home my man would leave me for sure! I mean, look at the size of it!" Vicki gasped, her jaw on the floor.

"Let's switch this big fecker on and see what he does . . . oh my God . . . does this bit move as well?" Laura giggled as the monster shook in her hand, lit up and swivelled.

Knickers – bras – sexy nun and schoolgirl outfits – out they came and volunteers ran to the bathroom in herds and the catwalk display afterwards was nothing short of vicious as mums with bums and tums stuck out their chests, strutted their stuff and gave the imaginary paparazzi the finger as they fell off their equally imaginary six-inch heels.

"Now just to *really* get you in the mood, ladies, I have a very special piece of equipment in my other bag and a whole rake of sexy club songs. Helen assures me she has just the right size woofer for the job too."

"I do – well, it's the boys' woofer actually but the sound system is all set up in the dining room just like you asked."

"Excellent job . . . right so, girls, follow me!"

Sandra's dextrous fingers were working at breakneck speed, screwing together three pieces of chrome, fixing the base to the floor and the top to the ceiling without bolts or screws, and like an excitable magnet Rebecca was immediately drawn to the metal construction site.

"I give you the latest addition to the *Slinky Bunny* Range. Dance-poles, ladies! I ask you now, is there a secret stripper in you?"

"Oh yeah, definitely . . . just let me at it . . . let me at it," they all began to hustle.

"Are you *all* ready for some bump and grind then?" said Sandra, mischievously pumping up the volume on the club mix.

The head-flicking went into overdrive . . . the practice hip-wiggling and bum-jerking started almost unconsciously as they all turned into vicious vixens ready to stomp over each other to get to the pole first.

"This is *Slinky Bunnies* finest fully portable dance-pole. Available to buy or to rent . . . I'll just pop the instruction DVD on and you can have a look yourselves."

Immediately there was a stampede in front of the telly.

"Ah yeah, I could do that alright," nodded Laura.

"Yeah, but look at that now – your back would be in bits," Vicki pointed out.

"More advanced . . . doesn't mean you have to go for it though. My fella would be happy if I just pranced around a bit and threw him the eye now and then," winked Sadie.

The DVD voiceover had them pumped up full of notions about how pole-dancing would give their body great definition: "toning their full body frame especially arms and abs."

"*Toned* abs . . . can you imagine . . . I've forgotten where my abs are!" moaned Betty.

"Wow, this is fantastic! You could get a great

workout and turn on your fella as well – think of the time you'd save!" said a neighbour of Helen's, really getting into the idea.

"Now, ladies, remember the DVD and don't get too carried away," said Sandra as an eager Helen slipped slowly down the pole until her bum banged off the floor. Notwithstanding her pain, she was pushed out of the way by the next willing and able victim.

Jennifer laughed as she tried a bit of a wiggle, then after a few minutes abandoned the pole for a safe Black Russian instead.

"Sandra, I can't believe Helen put you up to this! Thanks for coming all this way," she said to her friend when she got a quiet moment.

"Ah, don't say another word, I'm having loads of fun too," Sandra assured her, giving her a big friendly hug. "And it's a total freebie as well because . . . well, you won't believe it," Sandra lowered her voice to an excited hush, "I ran your Monday to Sunday spanking knickers idea past the top brass and they're wild for it – they're going into production with them right now and I'm getting a nice little bonus for floating the idea!"

"Oh, that's great!" Jennifer smiled lamely. Sandra never let a business opportunity go by.

"And there's a little gift for you in there as well from myself to say thanks . . . it's a nice little basque . . . end of the line and maybe a size too small but still gorgeous and sure aren't you planning to lose some weight anyway?"

"Oh thanks, that's very . . . eh . . . thoughtful. Sure if it's a bit too tight I can always get myself a few worms. You're looking a bit slimmer yourself. Is that anything to do with your recent unexpected visitors?"

"Ah, the little fellas! Not a bother there, got myself sorted at the chemist's, there was no need to go to the doctors after all," Sandra chirped.

There was no doubt about it, Sandra always had an eye for a bargain, whether it be cheating the doctors by getting free advice from the pharmacist, stealing your friend's business ideas or buying end-of-the-line products for presents. Still, it was impossible to be cross with her. Their temporary love-in was busted up, however, as Rebecca, unable to contain herself, started twirling around the pole, holding positions with thighs as strong as the bar itself, causing gasps of admiration all around. As she turned upside down, the back of one knee holding onto the metal, the other leg extended wide, hair sweeping off the ground, the wannabe mammy dancers burst into a round of applause and Jennifer was annoyed that her little sister – a veteran showstopper – was stealing the show in front of her friends, at *her* birthday bash.

"You'd have to be very fit to do something like that – I don't suppose you'd ever think of taking up rugby," Helen asked the upside-down Rebecca to uproarious laughter.

Rebecca righted herself and shimmied back up the pole using her curled toes, then legs and arms.

A knock on the back porch diverted their attention from the closet contortionist and Helen ushered a formidable, slightly grumpy-looking middle-aged woman into the room.

"Girls, I just thought we might get our nails manicured and painted for the laugh. This is my neighbour from up the road – Keelin."

From up the pole Rebecca saw her former co-worker from Tranquillity and froze, as did Keelin, but both of them averted their eyes and as a little crowd formed around the manicurist, Rebecca, not wanting to look an oddball, took a deep breath and waited her turn for finger-pampering.

"Hi," Rebecca said coolly, splaying her fingers in front of the no-nonsense beautician. On a good day she wouldn't trust Keelin with her body bits, but a manicure was probably safe enough territory.

"I forgot you lived out these parts, Keelin – bit of a commute every day into the salon?"

"Never took me more than thirty minutes, since I live halfway between Carrigmore and Bannestown. How about you, are you enjoying your little break away?" Keelin asked coolly but obviously burning with curiosity.

"Yes," Rebecca, smiled tersely and wondered how much she knew about her situation.

"The salon has a new receptionist covering – your friend Lou, in fact, but then I expect she told you that herself."

Rebecca fumed inwardly – no such contact had been made.

"She did a great job with the tennis-club fashion show, compèring it on the night – it got a great write-up in the paper," Keelin continued in an off-hand mildly sarcastic manner.

"Yes, Lou always had lots of hidden talent." Rebecca gritted her teeth as Keelin buffed.

"Your husband is looking great too – never used to see him in the gym but he seems to be there all the time now." Keelin looked Rebecca in the eye, waiting for her to comment on this choice bit of information but Rebecca bit her lip and fumed silently instead.

"Thanks, nice job, how much do I owe you?" Rebecca said finally, examining her hands.

"Nothing," Keelin said briskly. "Helen paid me already – very decent that way, Helen, very kind, thinking of me for extra work."

"Okay, well, thanks again."

"No bother, they looked like they were well overdue for a manicure anyway."

Cow!

The rest of the night Rebecca blazed and Jennifer drank. Somewhere in the small hours of the morning a very sozzled Jennifer was shoved into her car by a furious driver who drove too fast over bouncy country roads and who swore violently about bitchy friends, bitchy sisters, sneaky co-workers, bastard husbands and something totally mystifying about "a job being a job at the end of the day".

Twenty-three

The nurses were sitting down, talking low, filling each other in on how the previous night had gone on the geriatric ward. Mr Daly had apparently taken a swig of his urine bottle again, thinking he was drinking beer, and some poor old codger by the name of Mr Hudson didn't make it through – but then he wasn't for resuscitation.

"Poor old sod – he was one of the sweeties." One of the nurses shook her head sympathetically.

An uncertain Rebecca, her eyelashes almost glued together from lack of sleep, her hair tied back in a tight ponytail which emphasised her chalk-white face, overheard their concerned mumblings as she waited for instruction.

She'd been barely in the bed from the previous night when it was time to leave her still hung-over, snoring sister and salute Dan who was up early making breakfasts before school. Still, it was good that her brain was numb

– it was the only way she could make it through this, for even though she'd applied for the job the day the local beauticians had blown off her beauty aspirations, she hadn't really thought she'd end up working here, not for real.

"Ehm, excuse me . . ." Rebecca tried to interrupt the ward sister who was on the phone deep in conversation with someone about patients and theatre. Short-haired, tubby and serious, the nurse was writing furiously on a chart, tapping her pen every now and again in irritation.

"I just wanted . . ." Rebecca began again.

A frown wrinkled the nurse's forehead as Rebecca tried to communicate her needs but an anxious voice began calling from a nearby ward and the nurse, who Rebecca could now see from her badge was called Grace Fogarty, began to sigh deeply.

"Nurse . . . nurse . . . toilet, nurse . . . nurse!" came the plaintive cry.

"Could you please see to Mrs Kinsella," Bossy Nurse Fogarty snapped at Rebecca, keeping the phone stuck to her head.

"Who?"

"Nurse . . . nurse . . . the toilet . . . I need the toilet now!"

Nurse Fogarty turned away from Rebecca.

The nurses were still in their coven and Mrs Kinsella unfortunately had a very demanding voice – and worse, a very pressing need. Uncertain, Rebecca walked towards the nearest ward and was beckoned to a distressed old lady with snow-white hair, sunken eyes and crinkled shaking hands.

"Thank God, nurse!" The old woman in the bed,

blue cotton blankets and starched white sheets around her throat, grabbed a hold of Rebecca with her papery hands. "Me slippers, nurse, me slippers!" the woman continued urgently and Rebecca helped her ease some grotty mauve slippers onto her veiny crumpled feet. "Me frame, nurse . . . oh God, me frame!"

The Zimmer frame squashed between the metal hospital bed and a small painted locker was loosened into life and Rebecca helped Mrs Kinsella swing her bird-like legs off the mattress to get into position for walking.

As the little old lady shuffled forward, Rebecca noticed with distaste that the geriatric section was ancient, dark and cramped – not at all like the new general hospital with its brightly coloured doors, wide corridors and fresh paint. The ward toilet seemed miles away, especially as Rebecca and Mrs Kinsella continued their journey at a rate of one inch per hour.

"I'll leave you here so," Rebecca said as she opened the heavy door for the frail humped-back Mrs Kinsella but the woman looked at her, confused – frightened even.

"You'll have to sit me on the potty, nurse." The face was very worried now.

A tight feeling began to build up from the middle of Rebecca's stomach as she slowly eased the old woman onto the raised disabled toilet seat and tried to avoid any kind of personal contact, looking around the room instead . . . scratchy toilet rolls . . . boxes of bleached white tissues . . . industrial-looking soap . . . surgical gloves . . .

"I'll just wait for you outside," Rebecca told the old lady.

Mrs Kinsella looked alarmed again. "The other nurses don't do that. I might fall, nurse."

"Oh . . . right . . ." Rebecca, who was already wedged halfway outside the heavy swing door, returned and waited with a tight smile on her face, which got tighter as Mrs Kinsella started to grunt.

"Nurse!"

Oh God, they never mentioned this on the application form. Rebecca had thought she'd be helping the nurses to fluff up pillows, making a few beds, doing a bit of dusting round the lockers, getting the patients some water but not this . . . how the hell had she missed this . . . there must be someone else whose job it was to do this.

"Nurse!"

Oh, sweet Jesus.

"Mrs Kinsella, could you just stay there and I'll get back to you in one second."

The years of experience as an air stewardess came flooding back as Rebecca spoke with an authority in her voice that she didn't actually feel and went to seek out someone who could tell her who did the serious hygiene stuff around here. Bossy Nurse Fogarty was nowhere to be seen, but Rebecca came across a blonde one who looked a bit friendlier but who was in an awful rush pushing the heavy metal drugs trolley at speed.

"Hi there, I'm Rebecca . . ."

She chased after the blonde but the nurse was storming ahead, her navy legs and sensible shoes rounding the corner from the nurses' station into the ward and straight for the bed where Mrs Kinsella should have been. The nurse looked up in surprise as she realised there was no mouth to receive the collection of pretty coloured pills that she'd prepared in a see-through plastic container.

"Where is she?" she asked.

"That's what I wanted to talk to you about . . . see, I took her to the toilet . . ."

"Where is she now?" the nurse interrupted urgently.

"She's still in the toilet, but I told her I'd be back in a minute."

"You left her in the toilet . . . alone?"

"Yes, but –"

"Oh my God!"

Five seconds later, when they both came upon Mrs Kinsella, the poor old lady was in an awful state as she'd tried to wipe herself unaided and had messed up her nightwear, the toilet, her slippers and even her socks. Rebecca thought she was going to pass out but the nurse had only concern for the old lady as she snapped on some surgical gloves and told Rebecca to get some drawstring bags from the sluice room.

"Er . . . where's that?"

"Good God, do you not know anything? It's next door with all the bed pans and urine bottles," the nurse barked impatiently.

"It's my first day here." Rebecca was hoping for a little understanding.

The nurse rolled her eyes – she didn't say it but it was plain what she was thinking: 'A rookie – that's all we need!'

When she returned Rebecca snapped on surgical gloves herself and did things she'd never dreamed of while all the time Nurse Roberts, as it turned out she was called, talked to the old lady soothingly and gave Rebecca withering looks as if she was just one more thing to wear her down, one more annoying responsibility.

Well, when it came right down to it, Rebecca didn't give a damn. With this job she was definitely just passing through.

It was a walking, running, confused nightmare. So many of these withered bodies to change and wash, some of them immobile and in nappies, some of them with cushions between their knees to prevent bed sores, some of them as light as dried wishbones, others the size of small boulders being shuffled up the bed, turned and washed. It was disturbing, but the work was urgent so that within the first hour of being on the ward even Rebecca was lost in another world, another world where she didn't have to think and where nobody cared if she had lipstick on or not so long as she could strip beds at lightning speed and throw soiled draw sheets into a waiting laundry bag.

"We're miles behind this morning, Paddy, and no thanks to you," Nurse Roberts snapped at the young male care assistant as he sauntered in just in time to give out some breakfasts. "And we still haven't got the hoist from Ward 2 to give Lizzie her wash."

"Ah sure we'll get there, we'll get there, isn't that right, Donald?" the six-foot-two smiling hunk of young twenty-something flesh, with tousled dirty-blond hair and brown eyes, joked as he began spoon-feeding plain yogurt to an old man with vacant eyes who was drooling from the side of his lips. Paddy's tanned forearms moved backwards and forwards as he spooned in the bland meal and caught the dribbles with the spoon to feed back into the motionless mouth.

Nurse Roberts was frantically shovelling sugar into porridge until one old man with watery eyes shouted at her loudly.

"Salt!"

"What?"

"Take salt on the porridge – salt, not sugar."

Momentarily stunned, Nurse Roberts tore open a paper sachet and promptly poured salt onto the already sweetened porridge, then moved on to the next person. Rebecca's stomach churned – that has got to taste disgusting, she thought, salt and sugar, but nobody seemed to care as the old man ate his meal slowly and without complaint.

All day there was no time to think – just to do and do badly.

"Rebecca, can you do the drinks trolley?"

"The what?"

The drinks trolley turned out to be a fiddly fecking thing with chunky buttons and too much hot chocolate – everyone wanted soup. Pushing it along the ward was one of the better tasks of the day. It put her in mind of being an air stewardess again, not that pushing the trolley was a particularly desirable task on a plane either.

"Rebecca, can you give out the crofts?"

What in God's name were *crofts*? It turned out *crofts* was funny-nursey-speak for glass carafes – of water.

"Rebecca, can you wipe round the lockers?"

"Rebecca, can you please lift everything out of the way first and then clean round the lockers?"

Impossible task – especially as these old people had their whole lives crammed into these tiny bedside spaces.

"Rebecca, Rebecca!"

Twelve bloody hours of it and when the time came to

finish, Rebecca's back was tortured and her hands were chafed from the dust of surgical gloves being snapped on and off a hundred million times.

Just as she was about to walk out the door at the end of a crucifying first day's work Mrs Anderson, an inoffensive little former dolly-bird in bed number five, had a little moan about something that was bothering her and Rebecca tried not to hear but Mrs Anderson was very loud and very persistent.

"Nurse, nurse, I need my glass eye cleaned!"

Oh God, well, she definitely hadn't a clue how to do that – it probably involved some special cleaning fluid and maybe the skill of a consultant.

"Can you wait a minute till I ask someone how to do that," Rebecca answered hoarsely – the dry air was making her throat and nose feel hot and itchy on the inside.

"*Ask* someone? I don't need you to *ask* someone," Mrs Anderson said derisively. With a snort of contempt Mrs Anderson took the glass sphere from its eye socket, stuck it in her mouth, sucked it and swirled it around on her tongue and stuck it back where it belonged.

Rebecca wondered if she had just seen what she had seen and if she had, it counted as one of the worst things that she had ever seen in her entire life.

"Don't say anything – she's just trying to shock you," Paddy whispered in her ear and Rebecca was glad enough to find a strong male presence at her back just in case she hit the floor with a bang.

"See you tomorrow – that is *if* you're still coming in?" he teased, grinning broadly, and Rebecca was struck by his youthful certainty and his easy, alluring manner.

She found herself wondering what the hell was such

a young, good-looking guy doing working in a madhouse like this? Although the same question probably applied to herself and throughout the day she had been planning ways to quit, deciding that a phone call early in the morning would probably be the best bet.

"Yeah, see you tomorrow," she said blithely, surprising even herself with her job commitment as she let loose her red mane from its scrunchie and grabbed her coat.

On the way out one of the nurses, who was finishing up her shift, made some harmless banter with her as they both walked towards the entrance.

"You'd want to be careful with that Paddy Morrissey – he's young and a bit dangerous, if you know what I mean?" the nurse laughed, raising an eyebrow.

"No, I'm afraid I don't know what you mean," Rebecca answered in a disinterested voice.

"Oh, only that he likes his fun – bit of a ladies' man, I gather . . . Have you seen the Scooby Doo Van?"

"The Scooby Doo Van?"

"Oh *yes*, the Scooby Doo Van, and it's not for nothing that his nickname is Shaggy," the nurse said with a wink as she left Rebecca at the door and headed in search of her car.

Almost immediately Rebecca thought of her last meeting with Mark, his outrageous ultimatums and his implied hint that she might have as much fun as she liked in her life in the next few months without a twinge of marital remorse. The cheek of him! Would he really feel so gracious if she actually took him at his word, she wondered as a smile began to curl about her lips. A ladies' man . . . a little bit dangerous . . . Paddy Morrissey?

Sure he was only a child and no match for a real woman with fire in her veins and a hardened head to keep her steady. Still, a little bit of delicious danger with someone who had so much to learn about life and love? Tempting? Oh absolutely, no question there, as tempting as a fast car with the keys left in it and the engine just raring to go.

Twenty-four

Dan was giving the kids a bath when an exhausted Rebecca fell through the door sometime after eight. Their aunt could hear her nieces screaming for Dan to send in Mr Shark to stage a surprise attack under the bubbles but a minute or so later the excited screams turned to wails and Rebecca knew Abby had probably disappeared under the water, swallowed a cupful of bubbles, and with eyes stinging, ears blocked and throat searing, had caused her daddy to pull the plug on the night-time fun. Loud gurgling noises rattled through the hallway and padded feet scampered for the bedroom where a freshly woken up Adam was now also screaming his lungs off waiting for Dan's shushes and words of comfort.

A washed-out Jennifer stopped Rebecca in the hall. "As I said last night we need to talk," Their eyes met and Rebecca's body language indicated her hesitancy but she started for the messy living room for the long overdue 'compulsory chat'.

"No, not here, not in the house," Jennifer told her sister firmly. "In the garage."

"The *garage*?" Rebecca protested, her tired limbs aching for the softness of the couch.

"I don't intend to lose my temper and I don't think I will lose my temper but just in case I do, I don't want to upset my children – the garage is more private, nobody will hear."

Shaking her head, Rebecca followed her out.

It was cold in the garage and between the cooler air and Jennifer's unnerving calmness Rebecca forgot the weariness of work and became alert like a cornered wild animal.

"First things first. You being around when Dan hurt his back and when I was sick . . . well, I suppose I should thank you for it."

"Go on then – thank me for it," Rebecca said, her words burning.

"Okay . . . *thank you* . . ." Jennifer drew the words out, trying to act like an adult and keep the peace but she couldn't make direct eye contact with her sister, preferring to focus her words on the top of her head instead.

"Look, Jennifer, I'll save you the trouble . . . I couldn't be bothered freezing my ass off out here . . . I'll be gone in a few days . . . obviously it would be better for me if it wasn't as soon as tomorrow . . . and I'd like to say goodbye to the kids . . . but I know I'm cramping your style so I'll be out of here asap."

"Who said anything about leaving?"

"Well, you don't exactly need to be psychic –"

"Nobody said anything about you leaving. As it happens I don't want you to leave, not yet anyway."

Rebecca was floored.

"I *am* wondering why you're not at home with your loving husband and why you're at the hospital doing work that must be beneath you, but since you are here slumming it and working a crappy job, I think I'd be right in assuming there must be trouble in paradise?"

Rebecca said nothing but her anger sat within her like a sleeping volcano.

"And naturally I have been wondering why my little sister, who has always seen herself as being so much above me, is camped on *my* doorstep – but then it dawned on me last night when you were surrounded by *my* friends that you don't know anyone else, do you? You don't know anyone else who could help you if there is trouble in paradise?"

"I don't have to take any crap from you, Jennifer – I'll go now if you want."

"Go where – who do you know – after all these years being Miss Perfect on the outside, who exactly are your friends, Rebecca?"

For a few seconds Jennifer stared at Rebecca and her sister stared back just as hard. If they'd been children again both of them would be screaming by now, kicking each other's shins and pulling each other's hair out but, now that they were adults, both could only seethe and it wasn't half as satisfying as intense physical childish rage.

"There's something about you, do you know that, Rebecca?" Jennifer exploded, not able to help herself any longer. "You're just made wrong – you're so bloody selfish – that's why you don't have any friends, never had any real friends!"

"Stuff you, you self-righteous cow! Who are *your*

friends that they would allow you to turn into a bitter old bitch, a woman who's let herself go to hell since having babies? Jesus, with the exception of last night, where I admit you made a bit of an effort, you don't ever dress like a woman who's in love with her man any more and, as for Dan, you've cut the balls off that guy completely with your need to control everything! So don't talk to *me* about 'trouble in paradise' – put your own house in order first!"

They were standing close enough now to breathe each other's breath, close enough to see rage and hurt mirrored in each other's faces. The tension in the air was suffocating. They had slapped each other with their angry words and each was in shock at the other's perception of their lives.

In the male-dominated environment of the garage Jennifer could hardly bear to look at all the useful, manly things that belonged to the husband whose balls she'd apparently cut off. Dan's tools, well-used and cared-for lay on his orderly work surfaces, and there was his broken boat that reminded him he had Newfoundland sea-water in his veins, that broken shell that he was trying to repair bit by bit, with glue and strips of glass bandage so slowly it was beyond painstaking. Jennifer hated that broken, rotten, blistered craft that Dan had taken to loving like it was a piece of his soul, along with his greenhouse and his new kids' sandpit. With irritation she noticed he had even bought a small child's Lego set and was building it on a shelf by the wall.

Things to make, things to grow, dig up or explore were things little boys were allowed to do, but not grown-up educated men. The only muscle they needed to flex was their brain and, because she had consistently encouraged Dan to work his way up the executive chain, Rebecca thought she'd cut his balls off? God, she'd love to do in that smug, sanctimonious, selfish, spoiled cow right here and now. Her angry eyes took in a row of hammers positioned on a shelf near Rebecca's head. No, maybe the garage wasn't the best place to conduct an argument after all – if either of them went ballistic it could all easily end in bloodshed.

"This isn't the way I wanted it to be," she said, her voice shaking. "I didn't want there to be any shouting."

"Yeah, right, that's why you wanted me in the garage!"

"Look, I'll get to the point – you can stay as long as you want and I won't charge you any rent just so long as you mostly buy your own food and help out a bit round the house and maybe do a bit of baby-sitting now and then. Put simply, I have plans for myself and having you around might actually help me accomplish them."

"What kind of plans?"

"Nothing you need know about . . . I certainly don't need *you* to psychoanalyse my marriage. So if it suits you can stay. I presume it won't be for more than a few weeks?"

"No, I've got some decisions to make myself – I'll only be here until I make them," Rebecca faltered.

"Fine, a few more weeks are all I need too and, after that, well, let's say we don't have to reinstate each other on the Christmas-card list."

Numb with nothingness, the two women traipsed back into the living room. Jennifer curled up on the rocking chair. Rebecca collapsed on the couch, vying for space with Barney, a pile of books and about a dozen Barbie dolls.

Finding the remote control under a filthy cushion, Rebecca switched on the TV and kept it on mute as she stared at the screen. Mindlessly she flicked through the stations, listening to the creaking of the rocking chair. She badly wanted to say something but the words kept getting choked in her throat so she just began somewhere.

"Did you know Birdie rings me sometimes? Such daft conversations about nothing you wouldn't believe," she laughed nervously.

"Yeah, she rings me too, frying my ear with whatever free minutes she has." Jennifer actually smiled for a moment and Rebecca allowed herself another little laugh too while still staring at the TV screen.

"Have you . . . I was just wondering . . . have you, you know?"

Jennifer shook her head. "Have you?" she asked the TV set.

"I keep meaning to . . . it's just such a long drive . . ."

"Yeah, I know what you mean . . . I can't bear to do it either."

Rebecca bit her lower lip at Jennifer's frankness. "And have you heard . . ." she began cautiously.

"Let's not talk about him, okay?"

"Yeah, well, he doesn't contact me anyway. I suppose he also thinks I'm a cold-hearted bitch not made right, as you say."

"Look, I'm sorry about the 'not made right' comment – it was a bit low," Jennifer said quietly.

"Yeah – well, they say the truth will out, but it doesn't matter anyhow because for the next while we're not going to discuss anything deep and meaningful, are we?" Rebecca said bluntly. "It's all 'pass the sugar' from here on in and that's fine with me too." Her retort was like cold sleet on warm skin and the silence that filled the room stung with the old hurts of sisterhood.

Unusually, the whole house was completely still. Dan had the baby asleep and was probably now reading princess stories to his freshly bathed daughters. Such silence was hard to take, the noiseless flicking of the remote control excruciating, so much so that Jennifer made an excuse for Rebecca to turn up the sound on the television.

"That . . . that there . . . stop on that . . . turn it up!"

"The weather – in *French*?" Rebecca asked incredulously.

"That's how I try to stay on top of the French thing for Emma – I try to at least hear this."

"She doesn't like that mad French school, you know." Rebecca addressed the television screen. "Did you know some kid went in there last week with a fluffy bunny rabbit and they went ballistic because it wasn't a toy made out of wood?"

"I know."

"Which bit do you know; that she doesn't like school or the bunny-rabbit incident?"

"Everything, I know everything, okay?"

"Well, if you know everything, why do you send her?"

"Because it'll give her an edge, it's the best, everyone says it's the best, that's why."

"Best for who – you or her?"

Rebecca was looking at her sister directly now and Jennifer felt uncomfortable and started to gaze at her chipped and dirty nails, broken and worn by housework.

"Turn it up, Rebecca, stop jabbering and let me watch the weather in Japanese if I want. If you must know I fancy yer man, okay! He's nice, he's safe and he's always smiling whatever the weather – pardon the pun."

"How the hell did you get her into that school anyhow with your total lack of French-speaking ability?"

"New school, they needed the numbers. Besides, we got extra points because I told them Dan's granny was French Canadian, not that she was of course. After that they couldn't get us in fast enough, especially when I told them Dan is shit hot with wood, could make anything out of wood – developmental toys, a dolls' house – I would have told them he could have made a whole log cabin out of wood if it had helped get Emma in."

"Sounds like hard work if you ask me, and you're always baking for some fundraising thing or other for that school too. I saw the recipe for the scones, by the way – it fell out of a cookery book in the kitchen – it's kind of hard to read, isn't it?"

Jennifer flashed her sister a deliberately ferocious glare. Rebecca was spoiling her vibe and Pierre the Weatherman was doing a lot of lovely smiling tonight, talking in that soft fluttery French voice that would whisper silken words into her ear if she was ever caught alone with him in a lift, or possibly an airing cupboard. In her imagination Jennifer knew Pierre would be a gentle lover, a sweet lover, the kind of man who is forever a romantic and who would cover her in little kisses, maybe a few tender love nibbles . . . the kind of man who would never want to skip foreplay, the kind of man who would *always* know her correct bra size, even after several years of marriage.

As Pierre whispered on beautifully about the spell of continental weather to follow in the next few days, all the while smiling, Jennifer felt resolve building. Nothing was sorted between herself and Rebecca but right now she wouldn't be asking Rebecca to leave because right now she was a woman on the verge of something and a woman on the verge of something needs backup and it might as well be an irritating sister who got on alright with her kids as anyone else. No, nothing was sorted – but everything was understood as they both engaged in the game of watching mindless TV to fill the silence. A perfect way to kill time – sure hadn't their own parents partaken in the mindless-TV-viewing game for years so conversation wouldn't be necessary?

"Jennifer?" Rebecca's broke the daydream and Jennifer was surprised to hear determination in her sister's voice.

"What?"

"Just one thing – you don't have a monopoly on your friends, you know."

"What do you mean?"

"Helen thinks I'd be good at rugby and has asked me to come and try out any time and Sandra thinks I'm ace at pole-dancing – she might even have a job for me, in fact – and some of your mammy friends thought I was dead funny at the party and couldn't stop laughing at my beauty salon and air stewardess stories."

"So, what's your point?"

"Only that you don't have any power over me and my life – I make my own choices and I'll make my own friends too."

And with that Rebecca went to bed.

Twenty-five

The alarm clock bleated out seven o'clock. Rebecca's bones ached deep inside and her muscles were contracted in fear all along her chest and back. Groaning, she hit the alarm clock so as not to wake the girls, banged the pillows on her bed and went into a panic as she thought about the twelve-hour shift ahead. What in blaze's name was she doing? Was she only showing up for work because that young hunk Paddy had practically dared her?

The power shower nearly deafened her but it didn't wake her up, the hauling on of drab navy work-clothes and black practical shoes pulled her down like lead and she only really woke up when she reached the kitchen and burnt some breakfast toast.

Walking down that hospital corridor to do the mundane work of handling people who were fragile, grumpy and alone against the outside world, she already felt she was part of the fabric of the place. Day two and she was already an institution in this institution.

"Nurse, nurse, toilet, nurse, toilet!"

Rebecca's spoilt inner child winced as the toilet mantra started as soon as she rounded the corner. This time the call came from Marjorie – an eight-and-a-half-stone, dry-as-paper skeleton with sleek black hair who was going through an obsessive "wee-wee" stage. Permanently worried about having a wee she told everyone that came within earshot that she needed to be taken to the bathroom and then, after sitting for five minutes, would shout, "Nothing, nurse, sorry, nurse, there's nothing there!"

"Do you not think she'd be better off in nappies?" Rebecca asked Jen's friend Betty, who'd started on the ward that day.

"No, you'll just have to keep taking her," Betty insisted.

"But why? She never has anything to do – it's such a waste of time, Betty!"

"Because the one time you don't take her is the time she might have an accident and then she'll be distressed. Dignity – it's all matter of dignity," Betty said, banging a pillow.

Rebecca set her jaw tight. Dignity cost time and there was so much to do and not enough people to do it but bit by bit she advanced, getting patients ready for breakfast, changing nappies of grown-ups still sleeping like babies, bringing basins for washing, fishing out false teeth and then she was right in front of Alice, the sharp-as-a-knife, nearly thirty-stone granny. Alice – one of the ward favourites.

Full of life, with twinkling eyes and beautiful translucent skin, Alice would normally chat away when anyone came within earshot but this morning she was still snoring contentedly. Rebecca's brain was switched off, her limbs working like a robot, when she pulled back the aerated cotton blankets and crisp white hospital sheets and stared at horror at Alice lying in a soft, brown, gooey mess.

Nurse Bossy Knickers Fogarty had gone for the drugs trolley, another nurse was on the phone and Rebecca was alone waiting for Paddy, late again, to come and give a hand. Suddenly, the clatter of the drugs trolley entering the ward sounded and Bossy Knickers, seeing Rebecca rooted to the floor doing nothing, immediately goose-stepped over to investigate. Rebecca, on the verge of retching, pointed to Alice's bed covers. Elbowing her way past the rookie, Bossy Knickers began to assess the situation and sighed as she addressed the by now fully awake Alice.

"Alice, haven't I told you before that eating chocolate in the bed before you go asleep is not acceptable? Now we'll have to wait for the hoist from the other ward before we can lift you up and clean you properly."

"It's chocolate?" Rebecca squeaked in relief.

"Of course it's chocolate – we've been here before, haven't we, Alice?" the bossy nurse continued.

"Yes, nurse, I'm sorry, nurse, it's just me visitors like to bring something nice when they come and sometimes I have just a few bites and I forget about it," Alice beamed.

Rebecca had nearly been flattened the day before by an avalanche of cakes and biscuits that the elderly lady's family had squashed into her beside locker.

"I know I shouldn't have so many sweets but it's not like I have to worry about me teeth," Alice said, trying to cajole Bossy, and that much was true – her teeth sat in a glass on her locker waiting to be put to good use for breakfast. "And don't worry about me, nurse – I'll wait for the hoist to lift me up, and sure I'm nice and warm here anyway."

Alice's lovely soft plump hands reached to pull the blankets up to her neck and Rebecca smiled. It was impossible to be cross with her.

As Paddy finally sauntered onto the ward, late again, a chocolate-covered Alice popped in her teeth and shot the boy-babe suggestive looks from under her naturally long, dark lashes.

"Would you like to bounce a granny like me on your knee, gorgeous?" she roared at him as he faced the food avalanche in the locker to hand her a hairbrush.

"Ah Alice, would you stop! You'll get me fired with that kind of talk," he laughed.

"Paddy, I'm only eighteen on the inside – that's the trouble – I never went past eighteen on the inside!" More little suggestive looks were shot at him as Alice let the blanket fall from her chin and wiggled about on the sheets, her enormous breasts bouncing around like excitable puppies.

The hoist was found, the bed was stripped and bedding stuffed into big bags. Rebecca hauled the bags into the sluice room followed by Paddy who was looking for a bedpan.

"I want to talk to you," Rebecca said as he was about to leave.

A huge smile broke out on Paddy's face as if he was expecting as much. Rebecca almost swore he swaggered backwards and forwards on the spot where she was standing.

"Yeah?" he inquired brightly, leaning towards her as

much as he could without having a sexual-harassment case on his hands.

"Just to let you know I might only have been here a few days but don't think you can take advantage of me," she said evenly, staring him in the eyes.

"Sorry?" he asked, genuinely puzzled.

"You . . . being late two days running, putting extra work on me until you saunter in. I've met your type before, you know –" she had – the male trolley-dollies were the worst for gassing with the passengers on the plane and doing no real work, "and I'm too old to let anybody walk all over me. Do you understand?"

For a moment he said nothing as if females never reacted to him like this in ordinary circumstances. Rebecca imagined he was the kind of guy who swanned across a nightclub and melted the knickers off twenty-somethings if he half-smiled in their direction but his gorgeous mouth and almond-shaped brown eyes weren't going to work on her – well, not that quickly.

Confused at his current knicker-melting deficiencies, Paddy flashed Rebecca his best turbo-charged grin, Mach 4, for maximum dazzling effect and still the corners of her mouth didn't budge from her scowl and, not knowing what more to do, he laughed as if she was nothing more than a bitter old crone who'd lost her sense of humour.

"Yeah, I understand," he said, his eyes narrowing.

"Good," Rebecca said authoritatively, ready to brush past him, but he was blocking the door. For a split second their eyes met in challenge and then he moved away slowly and, as she walked along the corridor back past the nurses' station, she knew he was sweeping her up and down with his eyes. Sexual allure – god damn, she still had it and she felt a powerful surge of pleasure that thrilled her to her very toes.

It was a baptism-of-fire kind of day, a day where one thing more revolting than the next happened in quick succession. After breakfast Rebecca helped Betty irrigate the ears of Johnny the Gent – a handsome man of eighty-five who was very proud of his neat and tidy appearance. Every morning Paddy was accosted by Johnny to dickey him up with some nice "young-fella" hair gel and to shave him properly with the razor – Rebecca had taken a few slices out of Johnny that morning when Paddy was late and sensible Betty, used to Johnny's ways, had rescued Rebecca from a possible punch. Despite his age, Johnny's strength and temper were legendary.

Now alone with the Gent and Betty, Rebecca eyed him up warily as she held a metal emesis basin which contained the fruits of the irrigation: the biggest, greenest, furriest wads of ear-wax that Rebecca had ever seen. A trolley clattered down the corridor and Rebecca found herself gazing longingly in the direction of the room where she could have her lunch and some time alone. Her dream was broken when from alongside she heard a marbley "Thank you!" and a scream of "*No!*" from Betty as Johnny popped both bits of ear wax into his mouth and started chewing them as if they were the finest toffee. Neither of them were going to try and wrestle the wax from Johnny's mouth – they didn't want him to think he was Muhammad Ali again.

"I suppose it won't kill him!" Betty rolled her eyes as Rebecca held her hand to her mouth to stop herself from gagging.

Worse incidents were to follow. Rebecca tried hard to forget.

By the time break arrived Rebecca could hardly look at her food. She watched in awe as Betty the veteran nurse munched through sandwiches, yogurt and an apple without a moment's revulsion. Looking up from a bridal magazine, Betty noticed Rebecca's pale face and smiled as she bit her apple to the core, then started on tea and slimming crackers.

"You're not hungry?" Betty inquired, seeing Rebecca hug her lunchbox tight.

"It's just I'm a bit queasy after this morning."

"Yeah, you had a bit of a run of it today . . . it was some morning."

"I suppose . . . I don't know how you do this job every day, Betty, to tell you the truth."

Betty's grey pony-tail shook as she laughed and her double chin wobbled as she brought her left hand up to her face to brush away cracker crumbs. "Ah sure, you'd get used to anything after a while. Besides, it's the kind of job you can do whatever your situation . . . you know, especially if you're married and have a few kids."

Kids. Of course, eventually having kids had to be factored into everything – where you worked, what kind of car you drove, how you filled up your house. Rebecca thought of her own empty big house and winced inwardly.

"And it's better working in a small country hospital than in the city where there's too many unfamiliar faces – you never know who you're working with from one day to the next or even what language they speak. And it's not always like this, you know – this crazy. What was the worst of it for you today?"

"Probably Alice. I nearly died when I pulled back the bedcovers and saw all the mess. Not that it bothered her in the least – she was flirting with Paddy like mad as if being covered in chocolate made her all the more irresistible."

"Ah, Paddy . . . we could *all* be flirting with Paddy like mad," Betty purred. "Except, you know, I'm married and unfortunately my cousin expects me to be the Maid of Honour at her wedding this summer so I'm resisting all candy at the moment, eye-candy as much as the real stuff, but if I were single what I wouldn't give for one go at that firm, young body!"

Rebecca laughed. "How old is he anyway? Twenty-two, twenty-three?"

"Old enough to know what to do . . . sure you can tell by looking at him he could go all night. You could have a go at him, Rebecca, tell us *all* what he's like!"

Rebecca gazed at her ring finger – the fine lines from her wedding bands had been there for a surprising length of time after she had removed all traces of her marriage.

"Actually, Betty, I'm not exactly single myself," she smiled.

"I know, sweetheart, not that your sister said anything. I just kind of guessed."

"Do you know what he's doing here – Paddy? I would have thought a fella like that –"

"Wouldn't be bothered working in this place? Well, I think he likes the steady income and he never works weekends for a start . . . that's when he does his music stuff and some surfing too if he gets a chance . . . of course, you'd know all that if you'd seen the van – have you seen the van?

Ah yes, the van again, the special Shaggy/Scooby Doo Van.

Rebecca shook her head as she started to take her first tentative bites of lunch.

"Oh Rebecca – you've *got* to see the van!" Betty laughed heartily.

On the way back to the ward, Rebecca passed Bossy Nurse Fogarty with Paddy, partly screened by curtains around Johnny the Gent's cubicle.

"When I say 'now', Paddy, you're to give it your best shot – all right?"

The concentration was intense as they bent over Paddy's chest with their surgical gloves on and Nurse Bossy with her needle poised ready for attack.

"Now, Paddy, now!" Bossy Fogarty ordered.

As Rebecca watched something hard and sloppy hit her with force on her right cheek and when she reached up she found white goo was running down past her nostrils towards her lips and chin. Paddy and Bossy were standing looking at her mesmerised for what seemed like ages and then Johnny lost the run of himself and started screaming and beating Paddy on the head until Paddy got the Gent under control, whispered something soothing in his ear and got the old fella to relax on his pillows with a smile on his face.

"What . . . what *is* it, for Christ's sake?" Rebecca asked as a grinning Paddy offered her a piece of blue paper roll to wipe away the fluid.

"Infected cyst . . . about the size of a plug . . . been on Johnny's chest for a while now but he was never in the mood for us to have a go at him before. I didn't think it would all come out so hard and in the one go. Sure I don't know my own strength!" He grinned as he flexed his arm playfully in front of Rebecca's eyes and winked.

Caught between fury and tears, Rebecca momentarily hid her eyes in the blue paper rag and, even though she tried to suck in her emotions by clamping her jaw shut, squeezing her fists and staring at a spot on the floor, she knew her eyes were brimming and she could bawl at any second. Such indignity – what the hell was she thinking of working here at all? Tomorrow she'd ring and hand in her notice. After all she was Rebecca Gleeson née Murphy, she didn't need this job at all, she used to be somebody and, despite Mark's lack of faith in her, she sure as hell was somebody still.

With her jacket buttoned tight, Rebecca strode out of the ward into the car park and began to walk briskly back to Jen and Dan's. Her legs ached from standing for hours – ached as badly as if she had done three aerobic classes back to back with a spinning class added in just for fun. From her knees down to her heels were lead and the hot balls of her feet throbbed with pain as she walked. Her head was muddled and her umbrella was wilful.

Then she heard the sound of pounding music and the teasing voice of Paddy shouting loudly: "Rebecca – can I give you a lift?"

Wow, was that really the van? Her eyes took in the eye-catching Toyota Hiace, a blast from the seventies with gold and orange daggers of fire chasing down the sides.

Paddy's friendly almond eyes were smiling, he'd changed into a soft cotton red hoodie and his hair was gelled back up into perfectly soft and sexy spikes.

Inside – where it would be warm and dry or outside where puddles of water were already extending halfway up the calves of her trousers? Even without Paddy sweetening the deal with his good looks, the inside of his Scooby Doo Van was preferable to puddles.

Pulling herself through the door, she saw it was all worn brown suede and velvet, and she had a vision of the Bee Gees serenading her while their giant medallions rattled, and she began to giggle.

"I know, I know," he said as he saw the mesmerised look on her face. "Everyone says it's a seventies time-warp although the van is really an early eighties job. I was thinking of ripping everything out and putting in gold and black seats, a leather gold and black wheel and a new sound system but . . . well, the cash ran out and then me and my mates, we kind of got used to the retro look – in fact it kind of became my trademark."

"Yeah, it's kind of funky in its own way," smiled Rebecca. There was no way she was going to offend him by telling him it was grotty, not with the rain battering away outside.

"I ripped the back seats out because, well, you know, I do a bit of DJ-ing?" he said proudly.

DJ-ing was probably a big hit with the young ones Shaggy Morrissey hung around with, Rebecca surmised.

"Yeah, I heard you were into music." Rebecca's head swivelled backwards for a minute and she took in the barren interior, where the equipment would be stored, she supposed. Almost obscured by fuzzy dice she caught sight of him taking a sneaky peek at her and she felt playful and a little bit wicked as she smelt his freshly sprayed deodorant mix with his natural musk.

"So, where exactly do you live?"

"Oh, up here through the lights then second left."

As they moved off and went over a ramp, the van shuddered then wobbled and Rebecca began to laugh uncontrollably.

"Sorry, it's not the best of movers," Paddy apologised, blushing deeply, obviously aware that he was losing valuable street cred by the minute.

As traffic lights changed, the van took ages to move from stop to drive, Paddy's wheels acting like a big old dinosaur or a half-dead donkey in no mood to do anything much except amble along and maybe eventually lie down and die.

"This it?" he asked when they finally got to the entrance of Jen's housing estate.

"Yeah, thanks, no need to drive me to the door – I can take it from here," she said as she unfastened her seatbelt.

Suddenly, he caught her by the elbow and held her gaze a fraction too long.

"About this morning and yesterday, I'm sorry I was late. I had to call in to see my gran, she's got no one else to help her with her groceries, you see."

"Okay," she said evenly, not wanting to be hostile since he'd given her a lift but not wanting to appear like an idiot either. His granny excuse was probably just a ploy in the sympathy stakes. Paddy wasn't much more than a teenager in Rebecca's eyes and he probably loved his sleep just as much as he loved his action on the dance floor.

"I just wanted you to know that it's not a regular thing, me being late – I'm not a total shit or anything."

He smiled at her and suddenly she felt a genuine

surge of interest, the interest of the older woman who always has a bit of her inside that is 'just eighteen'. Rebecca could have sworn he felt the seismic shift too because suddenly he beamed as if relieved that his knicker-melting ability had just been restored. It had, but Rebecca was playing it cool – no need for him to think that he was going to have the upper hand in whatever it was that she might start and maybe never finish.

"So will you be back to work tomorrow?"

"Suppose so," she smiled again.

Waving goodbye and stepping out of the time-warp van she noticed for the first time his friendly warning to the world attached to his back window: *If my van's a rockin', don't come knockin'*, a giant sticker in happy psychedelic colours announced. As she watched Shaggy and the Scooby Doo Van disappear around the corner Rebecca thought she might be tempted, just for fun, to see if the boy really could live up to his sexually suggestive nickname.

Twenty-six

Jennifer sat on her bed in her nightie with a mini-fortune's worth of self-help books spread out on the duvet. Seeing them fan out in front of her she got a flashback to her organic chocolate-bar breakout at her wedding anniversary and felt a wave of self-loathing – again. When she was sixteen Jennifer hadn't needed any self-help books and chocolate bars were never dangerous – everything seemed certain and safe – but now, nearly twenty years on, nothing was certain and Jennifer O'Malley was a total enigma to the Jennifer Murphy of the past and strangely Jennifer Murphy O'Malley had no idea why.

Lying still on her bed should have been a moment of quiet contemplation – Rebecca was on a day off from hard labour at the hospital and had voluntarily taken the kids for a walk – but outside Jen's bedroom door Dan was battling hard with the vacuum cleaner as part of his newly devised 'cleaning strategy' for their home. From experience Jennifer knew he would be loading the dishwasher next and mopping down the kitchen floor in a fraction of the time and in far better humour than his wife had ever managed it. Such tasks were also part of the home 'cleaning strategy' which had been developed and implemented with executive-style efficiency over the last while. A non-actualised part of Jennifer's brain half-hoped that Dan's back would go into painful spasm soon so domestic disorganisation and familiar chaos could once again reign.

The questions in the books she was flicking through were scaring the life out of her but seeing Rebecca pole-dancing that night in Helen's with an army of admirers around her feet had shaken something in Jennifer – a desire to shed her old persona and morph into something more beautiful, interesting and alive – but what exactly she didn't quite know.

What do you want people saying at your funeral? one book asked threateningly. *If you died today what would people actually say at your funeral? If you could do anything knowing that you would be successful what would it be? What do you do every day that gives you joy? Make a list of ten things you would like to do before you die.*

Jennifer sat with a pad in her hand, doodling and panicking. Nothing would come into her head. How the hell was she so clueless about her own life? It was enough to make her want to suck on a nice instant latte, except the lattes weren't exactly hitting the spot lately. Okay, she'd give this pseudo psychology one more shot.

You're at the end of your life, sitting in a wheelchair looking back over all your decisions – what do you regret most in your life?

These questions were far too scary.

Outside the vacuuming was getting increasingly violent. Jennifer distinctly heard the sound of metal getting sucked up into the machine and she rolled her eyes. That was the thing about Dan's brutally efficient 'cleaning strategy' – every task was strictly timed so if anything got sucked into the cleaner he didn't give a damn so long as he met his deadline. He hadn't really left the corporate world behind at all – he'd merely diversified. Why couldn't he be a conscientious slow cleaner like her? *Bang, bang, thump* went the body of the vacuum cleaner on the floor. Oh hell, back to the self-analysis.

What are you most afraid of? Another book demanded.

Cripes, maybe she should just go to a fortune-teller and find out her destiny over a crystal ball or hopefully a long life-line. Sandra was bound to know someone in the fuzzy semi-entertainment world of predictions. Sitting beside some kind of mystic called Psychic Zara or Madame Miranda would be so much easier than having to answer these hard questions. For now she would settle for a joy fix every day (not including chocolate) and the promise of clearing some of her mental fog from between her ears. If she ever reached a point where yogic flying was a possibility, well, that would be a bonus. As she decided on a more detailed plan she realised that her ears hadn't been subjected to vacuum abuse for at least forty minutes and just as she felt a nice calm descend, there was a sharp rap on the door and when she opened it Dan was standing there with a big smile on his face and an aura of childlike eagerness about his body.

"Come on, I want to show you," he gushed, leading

her by the hand past her freshly vacuumed floors and into the kitchen which smelt beautifully of pine floor liquid and all-purpose gentle cleaning cream in nose-irritating citrus.

"Now, I know you've been meaning to do this yourself for months and just couldn't get round to it, so I devised a logical strategy for maximum effectiveness and ease of user clarity," beamed Dan.

What the hell was he talking about?

"Da *da*!" he said with a flourish as he flung open her kitchen cupboards and showed her how everything was beautifully arranged, tins small and large stacked precisely with all their labels facing out, flours, sugars and similar items stacked together, old jam jars and sauce bottles identified and culled from the shelves ready for soapy sudsy hot water in the sink and future disposal at the recycling plant.

"So what do you think?" he asked as he snapped on some oversized brand-new yellow cleaning gloves and began an assault on the old jars and sauce bottles in the sink with his trademark violently aggressive no-nonsense managerial style.

When she didn't answer, he turned and looked at her.

"What's the matter, honey, did I do something wrong?" he asked.

Suddenly Jennifer burst into tears, big scary sobs that racked her body and then she fell on her knees, her face in her hands, rocking back and forth, not wanting to see him, wishing she could cover her eyes and ears together so she could block out the whole world and her feelings of inadequacy.

"Jennifer!"

"It's just you're so bloody good at being a domestic goddess just as you're so bloody good at everything else and here is me fighting with the house, with routine, with everything for years, not thinking it possible to get on top of anything and here is you turning everything around, being a happy homemaker too . . . How do you think it makes me feel that I could barely cope, especially when you were away and here is you . . . easy as pie running the whole fucking shebang, happy as bloody Larry?"

"Jeeze, Jennifer, I never meant to upset you, I thought I was helping."

"Well, you're not helping – you're just making me feel like a total fucking retard!" Big bubbles of snot were escaping from Jennifer's nose now and her face was blotchy and red, then she began to feel uncomfortable around the hindquarters as she realised her kitchen floor was still wet and so too was her nightdress.

"I never really thought about it that way," said Dan, a bit subdued. It was clear that all the bubbly joy had gone out of his jam-jar washing as he realised his wife's distress.

As Jennifer got off her knees and leant on her sparkling kitchen work surface for support, her nose still streaming and bits of loose hair falling into her eyes and mouth, Dan slowly came up behind her and put his arms around her while she sobbed. His yellow gloves were still on and it created a surreal moment as she saw them interlocking in front of her nose.

"How about we go to bed?" Dan asked in his most seductive voice while nuzzling her shoulder.

Oh God, not that, anything but that.

"Rebecca might be home with the kids any moment,"

said Jennifer to her smudge-free microwave which smelt of irritating detergent-enriched lime something-or-other.

"No, she won't. I told her to take the kids on a nice long walk and it's a beautiful day outside," Dan continued determinedly as he licked the back of her neck.

Turning sideways Jennifer noticed the sun streaming through her gleaming windows and glared ferociously. Damn the sunshine – why couldn't it rain in typical Irish fashion? Then the kids would be home and sex deferred for another month at least.

"Plenty of time for some afternoon delight with my *gorgeous* baby," Dan continued, running his by-now-gloveless hands up her sides in a mad rush for her breasts.

As he circled her nipple with his finger, a trick he'd been performing for the last ten years at least, Jennifer realised he wasn't going to be deterred and braced herself for what she knew was coming – the sexy knickers request.

"Maybe you might have a look through your lingerie drawer, see if you have any of those sexy stockings from the old days – I think you might be getting thinner too – maybe that bra and knickers I bought you would fit you now – what do you think?" Dan asked her other shoulder excitedly, nuzzling it a little too eagerly, causing a shiver of dread to chase down her spine.

If he had a job, if he was at work she wouldn't have to endure this doubt about herself, doubt about their relationship. They could disappear into routine, maybe avoid asking important questions about themselves for years, forever.

Turning her around Dan grinned with lust and anticipation and Jennifer forced herself to grimace back. I don't want to do this, she told herself, but his erection was growing and if she didn't look perky he'd sulk and she'd end up having to do it anyway in about a day's time to placate him. Besides, it had been at least a month since he'd demanded his conjugal rights – so it was true what they said, that a pack of twelve condoms was a year's supply for an old married couple. Time to break in another rubber so, for a bit of marital entertainment. Gossamer . . . ribbed . . . super-sensitive? Now that she thought about it, they had about three years' supply of condoms in the bathroom, which really was a case of oversupply and definitely not demand.

"Jennifer?"

"Uhm – oh right." Reality was calling and reality was crushing.

"You on for this?"

Her lingerie drawer, what was left of it in between housing industrial mammy knickers for the time of the month, kids' rattles and some indigestion tablets left over from when she was pregnant with Adam, contained as usual nothing in the way of seductive items of clothing, except some singleton knickers which she kept to taunt herself into slimness – it never worked. Of course she knew how deficient in drawers her drawers were before she started the search but Dan seemed nevertheless certain that like a magician she'd pull something out of the bag – a bunny suit perhaps, complete with ears and cutesy fluffy tail. Unless he really expected her to wear the red bra and knickers from his trip away . . . she wouldn't, of course, they did nothing for her self-esteem.

"There's nothing, nothing at all that you can put on?" he asked, disappointed.

"Nothing," she sang back happily, hoping the lack of visuals would kill his itch and she could use the unexpected child-free time doing something useful like sorting laundry or maybe doing something wildly decadent like waxing her legs. All she knew was there was no way in hell she was pulling out her new midnight-blue teddy from her shopping spree with Sadie – that was for her eyes only for reasons she didn't quite understand.

"Oh, okay, we won't worry about it." He stripped to his boxers and knelt on the bed extending one hand towards her in invitation.

But his disappointment was too much to bear. She couldn't have sex with a man so quietly but so obviously disappointed in her.

"Wait, I do have this!" she called triumphantly, fishing out Sandra's too-tight birthday basque, pulling it on and watching the immediate effect it had on Dan, and "I also have these," she smiled broadly as she went rummaging in the wardrobe and pulled out a pair of useless, sparkly sling-backs that Sandra made her buy in America. "Unfortunately I don't have any sexy knickers so you'll just have to pretend I was wearing edible ones and you've just chewed them off, okay?" she rattled on as she pushed out one hip, put a hand on what was actually now a waist, courtesy of the corset, and then nearly fell off her heels from lack of practice.

A primitive desire lit in Dan's eyes as he tugged her onto the bed and ripped off his own underpants in two seconds flat.

"Honey, I'm going to fuck you sideways," he told her happily as he threw her on her back and she smiled at him as she tried to hide the queasy feeling of dread.

Pump, pump, pump – on it went forever. Every now and then she thought he would come but there was no big release just frustration as another position was tried and pumping began again. Eventually Jennifer knew she would have to intervene or she'd burst. In her brain she switched on the movies. First up was Steve McQueen circa 1962 – what a guy, what a sex symbol – her toes began to curl and her back began to arch.

Dan noticed the subtlest of changes in her and changed the tempo to match the tilting of her hips, then it was back to a few more movie stars, all of them living, then a hot but unsuitable boyfriend from her early working days, and then her lips began to part and her tongue sought out the wetness of his mouth. As she kissed him urgently Pierre the Weatherman came into focus and she pulled up her knees scraping Dan with her shoes and then it was Andy from New York, Andy whom she could have tossed around in bed all night to the mewings of his little kittens and she nipped Dan's shoulder catlike as she remembered, then lastly that beautiful man, her Bronx angel, his tanned face, earnest eyes and sun-bleached curls, and she could feel the orgasm rising, taking over, making her spasm in joy and relief.

Dan collapsed on top of her panting, then rolled off and covered his face with his forearm – happy, spent, triumphant.

"That was sensational – you *really* got into it in the end," he praised when he could talk without losing his breath.

Yes, but I wasn't with you, I was with everybody but you. She let her thoughts hang silently and they were like poison making her feel like an awful wife as she sometimes felt like an awful mother.

"You know, I saw this article in one of your magazines how it's all the rage to have sex with your partner every day for one month solid – no interruptions, no excuses – the more sex you have, apparently the more you want – what do you think?" he asked, still on his back, his chest glistening with a sheen of sweat.

Jennifer felt nauseous. Sex every day for thirty days? That was three years' worth of condoms at their present rate of sexual consummation.

"I'm going to take a shower," she said noncommittally as she watched him slip his underpants back on, his breathing deepening as he snored.

As she washed her body, washed and conditioned her hair and let the water run over her skin repeatedly, not caring for the scald marks that were burning into her flesh, one thought kept returning to her mind again and again. I'm going to have an affair – it is only a matter of time, it's only a matter of choosing the lucky guy.

Dan was still dozing when she began searching for her hairdryer and dressing gown. Looking for a brush, she was padding down the corridor when she noticed a pile of paper from the letterbox, bills for the most part, takeaway leaflets, another annoying postcard from bloody Spain, all of them fodder for the bin, and buried underneath the lot, so small she almost missed it, a small pink sheet with a svelte ink-drawn figure down the side. *Learn to Dance Latin with a Professional Instructor – Salsa and Merengue,* the leaflet coaxed. The merengue, the sexy dance from New York, Latin dancing – sex without sex – oh, who was she kidding? She dropped the entire pile back at her feet and went into her disturbingly sparkling kitchen to make a nice cup of instant latte even though she couldn't stand the taste of latte these days and was dying for a vodka or, better still, cocktails complete with umbrellas, cherries and anything else wild or pretty.

The kids were in bed, Rebecca was called in for nights at the last minute and Jennifer was enjoying a glass of wine while her husband did boy things in the garage that would last for hours. For the second time that day she hauled out Sandra's birthday basque from its paper bag. This time she tried it on for herself alone in front of the mirror and gasped as the boning flattened all her bits and pushed her boobs into another stratosphere. Wow, who would have known? She looked like Jessica Rabbit, or even better a prostitute – she was, as Sandra promised, a real Mammy Von Tease in a too-tight burlesque corset – no wonder Dan had gone ballistic.

In the bedroom she took out the girls' other birthday gifts to her – a pair of fluffy handcuffs, silky black stockings and a kinky suspender belt – then she threw them into a junk drawer with some stationery, bits of ribbon and some old baby bibs and socks. Trancelike and still dressed to thrill, she drifted to the computer and flicked it on. It sang its greeting and bubbled in its eagerness to take her into all sorts of exciting worlds. You want to meet someone not so special? You want to have a discreet on-line affair?

What was her desire? Where to tonight for Jennifer Murphy? The answer surprised even herself as she keyed in the word *salsa* and read about the exotic world of

South American dance. South America – funny how things came full circle, she thought as she read until her eyelids began to droop from tiredness and her eyeballs felt scratchy and dry.

Twenty-seven

It was Rebecca's third shift in a row on nights – she was the most obliging care assistant the hospital had ever employed – working days and nights on call – working as much as possible now because it was only when she was working that she could forget – forget that her life had no direction, forget that inside she was as hollow as a cracked chestnut on a drenched autumn path. No, it was better not to have a spare minute, it was better that Jen's kids wore her down whenever she wasn't working and filled her head with noise because noise was good, noise was always a useful distraction.

But working nights, time went by so slowly that sometimes in the darkness Rebecca's brain defied her 'forget everything' instructions and tonight her brain refused to concentrate on the dog-eared newspaper supplement left by a visitor earlier in the day.

Looking up, she noticed a light flashing and sighed. Mrs Redmond needed attention – again.

"A glass of water, please, nurse, I can't quite reach it," Mrs Redmond apologised in a whisper as Rebecca rounded the corner, her rubber-soled shoes squeaking on the floor.

The old lady's limbs were stiff from inactivity and Rebecca could see the pain on her face as she tried to hunch forward from the pillows to make ready for the drink.

Silently, Rebecca switched on the overhead light and poured water from the see-through jug, then held the glass to Mrs Redmond's saggy lips while she took two or three tiny sips.

"My pillows, nurse, could you fix my pillows? My neck hurts – I have arthritis in it, see."

Rebecca smiled a small smile and stayed silent, not wanting to give too much attention, not wanting to engage in any conversation, just wanting to get back to reading her boring supplement. Banging the pillows her face came quite close to Mrs Redmond's and she could see the old lady staring back intensely.

"I used to be like you – I used to be a great beauty, you know," Mrs Redmond said very clearly.

Stunned, Rebecca's fingers stopped fluffing pillows as she took in the crumpled face before her, the earnest green eyes, the loose skin around the mouth and cheeks and for a moment she saw it, she saw the beauty from long ago and felt panicked.

The old lady reached a gnarled veined paw over and grabbed Rebecca's smooth young hand with a surprising strength. "You don't see the time going by, you see, nurse. So much I wanted to do but you never get the time to do it all, you see." The effort of trying to explain her life, or lack of it, to a complete stranger took its toll and

Mrs Redmond collapsed back on the bed, her grey-white hair outstretched like an open concertina on the newly plumped pillows.

In the bed alongside her, patients were stirring and Rebecca left quickly before there were any more irksome demands for her attention.

The awful nothingness of nights played with your brain, Rebecca thought as she heard the squeak of her own shoes on the polished floors, as she heard the clatter of trolleys on distant corridors, as she listened to raspy breathing and coughing and little moans and groans throughout the night from passengers whose only goal now was to catch a plane to another realm, to that final destination in the sky.

At two in the morning a patient went into cardiac arrest and an inexperienced Rebecca didn't know what to do but stand by his dated flower-patterned curtains. The nurse, however, moved faster than a juggernaut – a doctor appeared, a crash trolley pushed Rebecca out of the way, everything happened so fast, hands everywhere, voices raised as instructions were called out and acknowledged in a terse but professional manner, but it was all useless, all meaningless as life just suddenly stopped.

"Why didn't you pull out the bed – make it easier for us to get around to treat him?" the nurse asked, exasperated, as she pulled the curtains around the dead patient while other patients were momentarily consoled with "There, there, go back to sleep" hushes.

"Nobody told me – I didn't know. How could I know? I'm only new to this!"

For hours she waited for daybreak, feeling that once there was brightness there was safety. Leaving the hospital, her hands itchy from surgical gloves, her mouth dry from dehydration, her brain worrying and fretting, all she could think of was buying a huge frothy coffee and a massive Danish from the corner shop.

Then she ran into Paddy, himself getting off nights from an adjoining ward.

"Hey, Rebecca!"

"Patient died last night," she told him plainly, not wanting to engage in any conversation.

"Oh yeah, that happened to me the last two times I was on nights with the geriatrics. I guess the patients hate to see me coming in case I jinx them or something," he joked.

"It's not funny, Paddy," she snapped, feeling the tension in her shoulders and tears filling behind her eyes.

Chastened, he shoved his hands in his pockets and looked a bit sheepish, then tried out his special sunshine grin again.

"It's always rough – the first death." He moved closer, hands out of his pockets as if to give her a big hug but then, remembering the frosty reception he got the last time he tried to invade her personal space in the sluice room, he stayed frozen to the spot.

Instead Rebecca bear-hugged him and sobbed, collapsing her face into the shoulder of his soft red hoodie.

"And the nurse was a complete bitch about it . . . said I didn't move fast enough or something . . . but nobody told me what to do . . . maybe if I'd known, that poor old man would be alive today!"

Paddy's shoulder was warm and comforting, she could have stayed there all day except at some point she realised she was probably embarrassing the poor guy. Her eyes were red from sniffling, her face blotchy and her nose running.

"I'm sorry. I guess I'm just tired, hungry and emotional. I could do with some breakfast – I'm starving but all I want is coffee, orange juice and some kind of junk."

"Come with me, baby, I know just the place!" Paddy cajoled, walking slowly to his Shaggy Love Mobile.

Following him lamb-like, Rebecca pulled her coat tighter against the morning chill, the cold air penetrating after the dry hospital environment. Jumping in the door, she breathed deeply as high-energy breakfast radio thudded round the van, making all her worries disappear as the bubbly presenters with their silly jokes and pranks returned some comforting noise to the space between her ears.

"What you want?" he asked as he parallel-parked his van outside the local fast-food joint.

"I'll come with you," she said.

"Don't bother, it's cold – why don't you just stay, enjoy the music and keep warm."

Rebecca was too tired and too worn out to argue. "Just get me whatever you're getting – as long as there's coffee and a chocolate something or other tagged on, I really don't care."

She bounced back on the seat and took in the early-morning activity from her tacky, brown, interior vantage point. From her window she could see Paddy slowly move up the queue until he was at the counter putting in an order, then paying.

He appeared back at the van with oversized bags.

"I'm sorry – I forgot to give you money. How much is it?" Rebecca fumbled for her purse.

"It's okay – don't worry about it," he said dismissively.

"But I can't let you pay," she laughed.

"Why not?"

"Because . . . well, because you're . . . "

"What?"

"Because you're younger than me – you probably need every penny."

"Jesus, I'm twenty-four, legally an adult, I have my own bank account and the last time I checked there was real fecking money in it and all." He bit into his egg muffin and fired her a look that wasn't quite a put-down, but it was enough for her to put away her purse in embarrassment.

Egg muffin disposed of, he started up the engine and put on the wipers – it had started to drizzle. "Now I hope you don't mind but I need to stop a minute on the way and check on something," he said.

"The granny again?" Rebecca asked playfully between munches and slurps of hot coffee.

"No, not the granny," he laughed.

Rebecca shrugged her shoulders nonchalantly. What did she care if he took her on a detour trip to the moon? She was only heading back to a madhouse full of kids where it would be impossible to get any decent shut-eye anyhow.

"Thanks – I won't be long," he smiled.

After a few wobbles and a slow chug onwards, Paddy stopped the Scooby Doo Van further downtown, parked, fed change into a meter and headed for some old buildings off the road. He didn't ask for her company but Rebecca followed anyway.

"I suppose it's a bit too late to ask, but you're not a serial killer, are you, Paddy?" Rebecca put a mock-petrified look on her face as they came right up alongside a lock-up.

"If I was going to kill you I would hardly have fed you first," he joked, shaking his head.

The door made a clatter as he undid the heavy-duty lock and pulled the metal sheeting upwards. Then he hit the light switch and she saw a paint-spattered white sheet covering an object which nearly filled the entire space. With one hand Paddy whipped off the sheet and for a moment Rebecca's breath stopped.

"Do you like it? It's a 1984 –"

"Black Porsche 924," Rebecca finished.

"Yeah . . . how'd you know?"

Rebecca walked around the beauty, drawing the palm of her hand along the metal, smoothing its flank tenderly the way one might put a hand on some prize horseflesh. The paintwork was faded almost to a grey but Rebecca knew it would only require a bit of elbow grease to shine it back up to a gleaming black.

"Rebecca!"

"Uhm?"

Ignoring him, she headed for the driver's side. The beauty was up on ramps but she opened the door nonetheless and, in a trance, peered in. She got in. The door was so heavy it made a clunk when it shut behind her, the leather seats were cool then warm as they hugged her body shape. Inside was incredibly masculine and angular, the black carpet a bit dated but strangely sexy, the chunky gear-box to her left, the square buttons on the dash exciting for not being one bit girlie or feminine. It was a car that made no apologies for being a timeless jolt of screaming testosterone and she loved it, every single bit.

In her snug driver's seat Rebecca grabbed the steering wheel and squeezed hard – the leather was warm and springy, the stitching a little rough and torn around the edge. "Hello, baby," she whispered softly. "Do you remember me? I sure remember you!"

"So you approve?" Paddy said, breaking into her reverie.

She looked out at him. "You really like *old* things, don't you, Paddy?"

"It's not old – it's a classic – a timeless beauty," he said, looking her in the eyes, and he began to blush and stammer. "I-it was my dad's but – he doesn't have time to fix her up – so he's giving her to me for my birthday and is paying the insurance for a year. I'm going to have to sell the van – it drinks petrol anyway and it's slow as fuck. The car needs a bit of work though before I can drive her – nothing major. Hey, while you're there maybe you can help me out. I'm bleeding the brakes at the moment and I need someone to press on them – hard."

He was whipping off his hoodie and rolling up his sleeves now and she noticed that long golden hairs covered his young muscular forearms. As he bent over she caught a glimpse of his taut stomach and was doubly aroused not only because he was hot but because he hadn't a clue she was watching him.

"Okay, I'll help. What do I need to do?" she called through the wound-down window.

"When I say press, I want you to press in the brake, and when I say release I want you to take your foot off the brake. Do you think you can do that?" he asked as he came right up to her rolled-down window.

"Yeah, I think I can do that," she smirked condescendingly.

"Thanks, it'll only take a few minutes but you're really doing me a favour." He walked off excitedly to do his bleeding but turned for a moment as if he'd just remembered something of vital importance. "And, Rebecca, when I say 'press' I really mean pump. I want you to pump the brake real hard. Do you think you can do that – pump real hard?"

As Rebecca's mischievous brain thought of the sexual meaning of his questions, her eye caught sight of herself in the car mirror. Were those the beginnings of permanent creases around her mouth? Mrs Redmond's words came back to haunt her, "I used to be a great beauty – I used to be like you – you don't see the time going, nurse."

"Yes, Paddy, I can do that," she assured him. "I can pump as hard as you want."

For twenty minutes she pumped super-hard until he stopped fiddling around the wheels, stood up and wiped his hands on an old rag.

"If we're done now, Paddy, could you drop me home?" she called through the wound-down window, ready to leave this beauty of a car for the moment.

"Would you look after Adam for me for half an hour?" Jennifer demanded more than asked as Rebecca, dreaming naughty thoughts, floated into the hall.

"Bloody hell, I'm just finished work. Can't Dan do it?"

"He's got a job interview."

"Oh, well, that's something, I suppose."

"And Abby's at playschool – they're giving her more mornings now, if she can keep her teeth to herself – the baby's fed, he's changed – you just have to play with him." Without waiting for an answer, Jennifer took off.

An exhausted Rebecca wanted to collapse into bed and she tried to put on Barney to distract her nephew but the contrary child would have none of the purple dinosaur and pulled himself to the patio window, standing up and banging with his little fists leaving Rebecca in no doubt that he wanted out to the garden and to the small patio area beyond where the sandpit was in full use – whatever the weather.

"Okay – come on!" Rebecca gave in, tucking the little roll of squidginess under her arm.

Eagerly he plonked his well-padded little behind in the pit and started to play with cups and buckets. Then he began to chew a yellow scratched plastic spade and started to cry, pointing intently at an empty red bucket.

"Oh you want me to *fill* it!" Rebecca interpreted the little wails and helped him make a sand castle until Adam, screaming with delight, tried to catch the grains between his fingers and ended up falling on his tummy. Laughing, Rebecca remembered how she too loved digging as a child – sandpits, the beach, mud. When she was little she told people she was going to be an archaeologist – she'd forgotten that. Everybody had laughed. Her mother told her she was so pretty she'd probably never have to get her hands dirty – yes, she'd forgotten that, forgotten how easy it is to kill a childish dream.

Adam cried a bit for no reason and to pacify him Rebecca put sand on his fat feet and he wiggled them about, taking pleasure in the sensation of soft grains trickling between his toes. He was so happy that she kicked off her own shoes and socks and placed her feet in the sand too while sitting on a wooden chair beside the pit. Closing her eyes for a minute she felt the wind on her face, the breeze tickling her wet hair as she ran over sand – soft sand first then the hard, wet, ripply kind nearer the breaking waves. Her mind played the special movie in her head where she was in a green swimsuit, searching through rock pools, clambering over slimy boulders to get to tiny pink crustaceans and sometimes little fish, digging until she reached the water line below, then making elaborate sandcastles with swollen moats. Her lids danced with the intensity of colour and then unexpectedly she saw him – her father – half-buried on the beach with screaming children all around, piling sand up to his chin, the little soft-grained crystals caught in the trim marmalade beard that was his trademark – that and his gorgeous red-brown hair that he'd bestowed on her alone.

Adam's fat little paws were cold and Rebecca badly needed sleep or coffee to remain functional so she picked the little boy up and carried him into the house. She heard the postman drop off the morning's letters, the same old junk – bills – flyers – free trial offers from this or that business and another sunny postcard. God, but Jimmy was tenacious. Turning the card over she read the inane message from a distant father, then placed the card back on the floor with the other mail and went to watch TV.

Ten minutes later when Jennifer stomped through the door, Rebecca heard the explosive bang of the kitchen bin opening and closing and knew that matters from Spain had been disposed of with the anger that they deserved. Such was life, she thought as she turned up the volume of a kiddie programme that had Adam dancing around like a clockwork toy.

Twenty-eight

"I'm here for my private Core Stability class with Zac," Jennifer told the receptionist, feeling delightfully wicked as Zac's funky name rolled off her tongue. The receptionist nodded towards the gym and Jennifer walked into the mirrored dance studio, laid out her foam mat and found herself a blue rubber ball of planet proportions which she was dying to shove under her bum, her tum or wherever Zac said was its natural home.

"Eh . . . the ball is for more advanced work . . . we won't bother with it yet," Zac, the twenty-something, tanned, toned and track-suited Adonis with blond spiky hair told her gently, implying that she was definitely in the granny league for now.

The fitness-assessment session, which she'd run off to a few days ago while Rebecca baby-sat Adam, had told her not to expect great things at the start of her body transformation, but still Jennifer couldn't help but hope.

Gorgeous Zac started on about this elusive big

tummy muscle straddling her blubber which had to be trained back into tautness through discipline and exercise and by "switching it on" when she was in the "neutral position", a position which defied her own internal global tracking system until Zac got her to rock her pelvis backwards and forwards, then hold it in a strained position.

"There, that's neutral, hold it just there," Zac commanded in a very authoritative manner for a twenty-something Adonis, and Jennifer willingly obeyed even though her back was aching and her thighs were wobbling from the pressure.

"Now start to pull in your inner core muscle like you're pulling up a zipper but try to breathe out at the same time."

What the hell, how could anyone breathe and suck their blubber in at the same time? It was physically impossible.

"Breathe Jennifer, breathe – no need to turn blue."

"It's just it's hard to think and do the pulling-in stuff at the same time," she puffed.

"You're thinking too much – you'll have to try and think less."

Well, what do you know? The beautiful people in the world didn't do thinking – what a relief!

"Don't think – just feel," Zac implored.

Something told her she was going to enjoy this 'don't-think-just-feel' class as she laid back and toned up around her pelvis much to its bewilderment and shock.

"See you next week," Zac said pleasantly as their session came to an end.

"Oh, I'm not going anywhere yet, Zac," she told him

breezily as she headed for one of the giant metal monsters in the gym and switched it on.

Physically wrecked but feeling invincible, she started the walker and increased the speed, keeping the gradient at zero – there was no need to bulk up her thighs – not when she was going for the slender legs of Cameron Diaz. After two minutes of gasping she was close to passing out and all that kept her going was her jealousy and the flirtations of a blonde twenty-something lovely who was gyrating her lycra-clad bum in front of two weight-lifting young bucks.

I *will* re-invent myself like the bionic woman, she scolded herself as the sweat began to drip. The blonde temptress was laughing now and bringing a bottle of mineral water to her lips as the guys competed for her attention by popping their muscles in a not-too-subtle fashion. Jennifer didn't think the bimbo had done any workout at all as her make-up was still perfect and she didn't show any signs of being swept away by a river of sweat. Damn youth and damn the naturally high metabolic rate of all those just past their teens.

I *will* be beautiful, she told her panicked body, as to hell with Cameron Diaz' legs, she changed the gradient to steep and forced her limbs to scramble up the rubber slope. Somewhere past the first awful moments of shaky legs, Jennifer gained a second wind, burning unused resources hopefully from her bum and thighs and then her energy began to surge for a full ten minutes – maybe even eleven. On the way home her calves ached as she extended her feet for the car pedals but pain was irrelevant. She was finally shaking her body into action, shaking up her life.

"From now on I have an exercise programme," Jennifer haughtily told Dan as she slammed the front door and saw him doing Tai Chi in the kitchen with Adam hanging out of his shins. He'd learned the basics from YouTube in an effort to maintain a calm focus while he waited for the outcome of his job interview.

"That's great, honey, I'm pleased for you," the Zen-like husband assured her.

"And I'm going back out later this evening."

"Jesus, Jennifer, you don't think you're overdoing it?" The Zen was beginning to fizzle out as Dan temporarily lost his focus and shook the baby off his trousers.

"I am *not* overdoing it, I'm catching up on lost time and anyway I'm going out to have fun, not kill myself."

"But Rebecca has plans for this evening too."

"God, Dan, I think you're getting far too fond of the new nanny – surely you can cope on your own for just one hour?"

"Well, of course I can."

"Good."

"So, where are you going later on?" he asked sheepishly.

"I'm going to learn to do the merengue."

"Oh God, Jennifer, a baking class! I wish you'd give up on all that baking stuff – it drives you crazy and frightens the rest of us."

"Don't even go there. And Dan . . ."

He saw the mad glint in her eye and smiled cautiously.

"The merengue is a dance!"

In the evening, still feeling a bit stiff, Jennifer entered the dance class in the local parochial hall and immediately wanted to run. What was she thinking? There were four couples, maybe five in attendance, although it was hard to see who exactly was with whom, and two women like herself seemed to be on their own. Now captured in the hall, the other partnerless ladies looked bashful and restless as reality set in.

"Come in, come in," the bubbly forty-something dance instructress beckoned with a flourish, a purple and green scarf damming a mass of black shoulder-length wavy curls.

Her huge brown eyes were framed by false eyelashes fluttering like a peacock's tail and from time to time that tail would flatten, displaying shiny lids painted aquamarine. There was not an ounce of flesh on the dancer's tall frame – to Jennifer's eyes she seemed to be all floaty trousers and top and very nimble, very fast, small black feet.

"People, people, don't be shy, stop hiding in corners, come into the light!" the dance instructress trilled, gesturing to the middle of the floor, playfully skipping across the room for effect as she shepherded her trainees together, her yellow top gliding over her red floaty trousers, adding another layer of drama to what was already a very dramatic persona. "My name is Cassandra and I will be your teacher for the next few weeks. In this dance class be prepared to undertake a South American journey of passion as I lead you through salsa and the merengue and I guarantee by the end of the course you will not only be dancing Latin, but you'll be thinking Latin and *feeling* Latin to your very veins!"

One of the 'singles', a mumsy-looking woman three stone overweight with a bad perm that gave her the head of a sheep, was already backing for the door and Jennifer also began to feel weak at all the talk of Latin passion.

"But for now I must get to grips with my music . . . now, let me see, salsa or the merengue to start?"

For a few minutes Cassandra was bent double over her CD player, skimming through CDs in a leather flip-pocket, hovering on a plastic case once or twice and then changing her mind, flicking through at speed until she found the tracks she needed.

"Ah yes, let's begin with the salsa. Okay, ladies, make one row, men opposite in another row. We begin on the right foot – men on your left foot – up, up, high arches now – now move to the left, tap, tap, that's right . . . now forward and back . . . loosen those hips and side to side. Right, come together, take your partner . . ." She paused, surveying the three partnerless women. "I see I will have *two* ladies to dance with tonight, not a problem, but you . . . you, my sweet, will get to dance with my sexy Irish Latin. He'll be back any moment."

And she gestured towards a stunned Jennifer.

"Come along now, darling!" She pulled Jennifer firmly by the hand – pulled her into the dreaded light. "A lot of the dancing is in lines opposite each other but, for the dancing with partners, you'll need to watch me then practise by yourself."

Jennifer nodded and as she prepared to dance with her shadow, she saw Cassandra commandeer the two partnerless ladies, taking each by a hand and throwing them around for a few synchronised twirls with a force that belied her slight frame.

"Sorry, ladies, if you found that a bit forceful, but I

need to be *firm* with you two, I can tell . . . to push you and pull you despite your resistance . . . but it is so hard . . . so hard for me to dance the role of the man because this is salsa and salsa speaks to my soul and my soul is *all* woman!"

She sighed theatrically, throwing one of the mums into a violent spin that nearly demolished a table holding decanters of water and glasses stacked high.

"No, no, no!" she roared abruptly mid-twirl, startling her fillies as she left them and strode across the room to a nervous young man with two left feet who along with his fiancée, as it later emerged, was trying to learn a few sexy moves for their wedding.

"I'm sorry, darling, do you mind if I borrow him for a moment?" she asked the giggling bride-to-be who gestured with her hand that she would have no problem allowing complete access to her klutzy boyfriend.

"Now, this move you've got completely wrong – it's not like that – it's like this – hand down, now draw me towards you firmly – I said firmly, man! – now hold me back for one moment – steady, steady, now wait for it – now pull me – pull me hard – don't be gentle, I won't break! – pull me and turn me and again – do it again!"

Cassandra's instructions were fired out at the husband-to-be as if from a tennis-ball machine and he sweated under the pressure.

Watching Cassandra take control of the young man, Jennifer was amazed that she could be so forceful, be so assured of her physical body, in her walking, in her dancing, in her very posture. Cassandra didn't just move – every movement was an art form and every movement had tiny little flourishes built into it so that weirdly the eye was attracted to the spot Cassandra was in at any one moment as well as the spot where she was planning to move next.

"Now, let's take it from the very beginning," she said, relinquishing control of her male victim. "I'm going to take one lady partner at a time from here on in, so, my dear, you will have to practise alone until I'm ready to take you *all* to myself!" Cassandra spoke throatily in what was almost a flirtation to the blushing mum with the bad perm who joined Jennifer in the bizarre ritual of dancing with one's shadow.

As the music became fun and loose, the back of the woman Cassandra had chosen for dancing was rigid with fear. Looseness and sensuality, the essence of Latin, didn't come easily to people who had spent their whole lives keeping their passions in check, spent their whole lives developing stiff backs for Irish dancing. Now when invited to let rip they couldn't do it – not quite yet, not even with Cassandra barking commands in their ears.

"Very good, very good, one more time from the top as a group and I think we will begin the merengue – a few steps, nothing too confusing."

The group stood motionless in the centre of the floor, waiting for Cassandra to make her music selection. Glasses of water were poured and downed as a means of combating the shyness they felt doing something ridiculously sexy with terrified strangers.

"Ah yes, here we go, the merengue . . . oh, this puts me in mind of South America, dancing the summer away as a girl when all I lived for was dancing and wine and men . . . but enough of that!" Cassandra giggled. "Feel the music, people, feel the sensuality!" And she was gone, her body swaying hypnotically to the beat, swaying to the memories that made her silly as a schoolgirl. "Now, let's all move to this side of the hall, we're aiming for a kind of slow sensual shuffle forward and back. Ah yes, that's right. Now, ladies, I must warn you, if you are ever in a club and someone asks you to dance the merengue, be warned the man will try and wrap his legs around you like *this*."

A graphic demonstration ensued as Cassandra dramatically hooked a leg around a nearby pillar. The young couple giggled, the middle-aged lovebirds coughed and shuffled and the partnerless women looked horrified at their dance teacher's ostentatiousness and sexual prowess.

"So will we begin? Oh, what do you know, here's my Irish Latin back just in time!"

Horrified, Jennifer realised she was being partnered with a man, a real man wearing faded blue denims, a faded blue shirt and a black kerchief, a man with dark brown eyes. A real man of smooth tanned skin and soft shoulder-length sun-bleached hair streaked with the occasional grey. It couldn't be. It must be an apparition. No, it was – it was definitely him – her Bronx Angel in the flesh.

The music started and a wiggling Cassandra was roaring orders for all to merge. As instructed, her Bronx Angel moved close and the electricity jolted through Jennifer from the first touch as they embraced, circled and bounced deliciously off each other's knees.

"Andy's party . . . the Bronx . . . we've met before," she stammered, doing her best to make conversation in between steps and ignore the outrageous sexiness of their movements.

"Yes, I remember," a wayward blond curl brushed her cheek and Jennifer thought it was as well he had his hand on the small of her back – it would serve as support when she collapsed to the floor.

"You're very good, you must be doing this for years," Jennifer rabbited on like a teenager, not looking at her Angel directly, but slyly through her lashes.

"Years and years," he smiled back, turning her, feeling the natural movement of her, allowing her to gradually loosen in response to the sexy music.

Just as she was ready to ask what he was doing on her home soil, Cassandra cut in and abruptly stole her away.

"Sorry, darling, I haven't given you much individual attention tonight but brace yourself, now's your chance to dance with a *real* master."

For the next fifteen minutes Jennifer became Cassandra's reluctant victim as she was swirled, pushed, pulled and swayed, while the overweight bad-hair mum was partnered with her Angel and began to melt under his quiet physical charms. Jennifer watched enviously as he supported the woman's complete unravelling, keeping his hand delicately but firmly on the small of her back.

"So, people," Cassandra strode across the room and snapped off her CD player, her waves of hair jostling under her vibrant scarf, her layers of clothing jumping upwards as she did another little skip across the floor, "next week, same time . . . , practise, practise, practise . . . and next week I will have a CD for all of you to help you all in your Latin Journey. So, until next week, feel Latin, breathe Latin, dance Latin, *be* Latin!"

The last part was directed to Jennifer who blushed to the back of her neck at Cassandra's instructions. In front of her eyes the Bronx Angel floated towards the door. For a split second she thought he was hesitating as if he wanted to exchange some words with her but having lost the naturalness of the moment, decided instead to leave. Still, before he left she witnessed him smile a smile in her direction, a smile that lit up the entire room. In response all she could do was give a self-conscious, stupid little wave and in the car park she sat for ten minutes listening to her heart pounding in her chest before she had the wherewithal to drive back home.

Once inside the front door, Jennifer leaned against the hardwood and took a very deep breath. Closing her eyes she pulled in the deep-core muscle that her Pilates instructor had revealed to her earlier that day and marvelled as her inner corset tightened around her abdomen, marvelled at her stomach's inner strength and gasped as the movement sent a wave of energy through her pelvis that felt both powerful and sexual.

Startled, she heard a small creak and as the kitchen door opened she watched Rebecca watching her until guilt made her look away but not before Rebecca had registered the flustered look on her older sister's face.

Rebecca had seen that look countless times before and, like women everywhere, she recognised it instantly. Lust, excitement, obsession and love – no one could mistake that excited glow for anything else. Quietly Rebecca shut the kitchen door.

And Jennifer bolted for the shower to scrub the scent of something fresh and exciting from her tingly, newly sensitive skin.

Twenty-nine

The floodlights were dazzling when the van wobbled up to the cold, mucky pitch where the rugby girls were practising, the steam from their breath clear to see. It was drizzling and there was a little wind. Hell, why had she told Helen she'd do this? Maybe it was because rugby was free exercise, and her curves were in need of taming now she didn't have the luxury of a gym three days a week, and in Jen's house there wasn't enough room to swing a cat, never mind swing out of a sexy dance-pole.

"Thanks for the lift, Paddy – you don't have to stay though – I'm sure someone will give me a ride back when it's over," Rebecca said as she made to get out of the Scooby Doo Van.

"Sure, I'll stay a while anyhow," Paddy said as Rebecca headed for the field where Helen and the other rugby girls were already in the thick of it, passing worn training balls between them as they sprinted in threes down the field and back, occasionally slipping or letting the ball fall from their arms and roaring with laughter as a team-mate skidded in mud.

"Come on now, girls, come on, no slacking!" she heard Helen roar when a bit of playacting and tussling broke out in the middle of the field.

Instantly Rebecca regretted coming. She was more than likely going to be worse than useless and she never got on great with big groups of girls. Before long jealousy always reared its ugly head – it had been like that with her all her life, especially in school. Besides, she'd only really come to get out of the house because Dan and Jen were having a row about him getting a job and Paddy was eager as a love-struck pup to give her a lift anywhere she wanted to go.

"You don't mind if I watch, do you?" Paddy asked gingerly, his hands ploughed into his pockets, his nose buried in his scarf and his hood up against the damp drizzle. The particles of rain were illuminated like dust in the floodlights, giving a ghostly feel to the pitch, making her feel like this wasn't real, that this was another Rebecca doing strange things in this place.

"No, of course not – stick around if you want a laugh." Rebecca wondered if she was blushing – it would be hard to tell anyway, as the wind and rain slapped her cheeks.

On the sidelines, a well-built man in his fifties with green wellies and a head of burnt-copper-red curls escaping out of a black beanie hat; was roaring at the girls to sprint hard and pivot around traffic cones on the sodden grass.

"Keep up the speed now, Derval! Chase her tail now, Breda!" the man yelled.

Abruptly he turned and his face creased into a huge

smile when he saw Rebecca hiding behind him, rubbing her cold hands nervously and peering out at the mêlée with a sense of excitement but mostly immense fear.

"New recruit?" he asked, raising his chin a fraction and looking at her with playful eyes from under his mop of unruly copper corkscrews.

"Well, I don't know . . . maybe . . . Helen told me if I ever had a chance to turn up at training."

He handed her a shovel-like hand and she shook it firmly.

"I'm the coach . . . Declan, Declan Lennon," he said in a friendly voice.

"Rebecca . . . Rebecca Murphy."

"Know anything about rugby, Rebecca?"

"A little . . . seen a few games on telly and a few in the flesh . . . not sure exactly what happens . . . you know, in rucks and scrums and things . . . I'll probably be worse than useless, you'll probably run me off the pitch by the end of this!"

"Ah now, you don't need to know much in the beginning – all you need is passion – if you have passion everything else will come to you in spades," he said kindly, his eyes twinkling again.

There was no introduction to the nine others on the pitch; they were far too busy following the shouted instructions of Declan or Helen who as captain was motivating and manipulating as much as she could and at times just roaring like the devil himself. Helen gave Rebecca a quick nod of the head in acknowledgment but a fraction later she was gone, shoving her girls up and down the pitch, physically pushing them in their backs to increase their speed.

Rebecca watched all of them flash by, in shorts despite the biting cold and rain, Helen with her shapeless socks in a heap around her shins, the elastic gone completely, athletic types moving fast, ponytails bobbing, shorter more rotund figures grabbing girls around the knees in tackles that ended in a mud bath. Rebecca self-consciously wriggled out of her tracksuit bottoms, wondering if Paddy was watching as she peeled off to her shorts – but nobody noticed and nobody commented as her knock-out, long, shapely legs went on view.

"Right, Rebecca, sure we'll just throw you in at the deep end and see how you'll get on – the main thing is to remember in rugby the ball gets passed to the back," said Declan briskly.

Nodding enthusiastically, she tried to ignore the fear that she was going to make a complete twit of herself and that all these proper sportswomen would then treat her with disdain.

"We'll line up in threes again, passing the ball to the left, and make sure you keep moving straight ahead after the pass is thrown, got it?" Declan commanded.

Rebecca felt like she'd just been asked to secure a post against enemy attack and had no idea how to do it – but she was in the thick of things now so she tried hard not to be paralysed by the fear in her limbs. Suddenly she was sprinting, and someone was throwing a ball at her hard. Catching it she threw it to her left, and sprinted straight down the field just as she was told. Then the girls began looping, throwing the ball fast and constantly moving and chasing and she strove to keep up until she was dizzy. More than once she dropped the ball but there was no time for embarrassment as it was scooped up instantly like it was something precious – something worth dying for – while screams and laughter rang out in the air.

"Run! Run!" Declan urged if he spotted the slightest attempt by any of the pack to slow down. "Run in pairs now, push your partner, drag your partner, keep up the speed, run, run!"

A big hand pushed Rebecca firmly in the back to increase her speed. It was Helen, ploughing into her like a tank as they both sprinted to the opposite end of the field. Then it was Rebecca's turn to push Helen back across the mucky pitch. Then all was repeated with another team member until Rebecca's arms ached and the small of her back felt bruised.

Out came some tackling bags then and Declan was holding them aloft and suddenly girls were belting into the sacks full force as if they were training for the army.

"I don't think I can do that," Rebecca gasped at a five-foot-two well-built girlie-girlie blonde who waited beside her for a turn to charge at the sack.

"Course you can – watch."

The diminutive player ran at Declan like a bull and his green wellies skidded from underneath him as he landed on his rear and all the girls high-fived, and then bent at the waist from laughing so hard.

"See, what you need to remember is the bigger they are the harder they fall," the blonde told Rebecca with a wink and a little wiggle of her hips as she came back to her original spot. "Go on, go for it, show him no mercy now, hit him with everything you've got, woman!"

Psyching herself up, Rebecca took a deep breath and headed for the bag like a warrior, even letting out a great big '*Yaaagh*' as the target came into sight. All of a sudden she was spinning in air as she hit the spot with such force she tumbled and landed on her back. The place erupted in raucous laughter and any first-night niceness that might have been extended to her was well and truly over, but in a good way. A blushing Rebecca took a bow and then did a playful girlie curtsy to a round of applause. Immediately she knew she would be accepted as one of the pack, if she wanted, and something deep inside wanted very much to belong to this bunch of women whose energy and lust for life was enormous.

Time disappeared – the drizzle fell through the floodlit darkness like dust. Rebecca had no idea about strategy or tactics and she just muddled through as best she could and followed as many instructions as she could, getting herself up when she fell, tackling when she was told and passing when she was roared at loudly.

Without warning, or so it seemed, all of them even Declan were in a huddle, following each other closely, trying to get the ball and every now and then someone would fire the leather prize backwards between their legs and there would be a scramble for possession.

"Is this still rugby?" a breathless Rebecca asked a fired-up Helen when both of them came shoulder to shoulder.

"Tag – for practice," Helen said quickly, never diverting her eyes from the ball.

"Tag what?" Rebecca asked confused.

"Tag rugby," said Helen, herself momentarily confused that she was being asked to explain, and then she was gone, chasing the ball, gaining possession and doing a little war dance as she got one over on Declan, although he was still trying to catch her, his green wellies wobbling dangerously around the ankles.

"So will we be seeing you again?" Declan asked mischievously as Rebecca collapsed down beside him on the sidelines with a bottle of water after training, her heart bursting not just from exercise but from excitement.

"If you think I could be of any use to you," she smiled back a little shyly.

"Indeed you could," said Helen as she plonked her rear end beside Rebecca's.

"What'll we name her?" the coach asked the captain nonchalantly.

"What?" asked Rebecca, looking up and wiping a clump of sodden hair from her forehead.

"Your nickname, you have to have a nickname," explained Helen.

"Well, we can't call her Red, that's my name," Declan said as he ran his hand over his curls.

"I have it – 'Legs'," Helen said decisively. "Her legs are useful – she could turn out to have the fastest legs among the lot of them, if we train her up good."

"'Legs' it is so," said Declan, beginning to stir.

"And if we ever do that fundraising calendar that you're always bullshitting on about, Declan, those legs would be more than an asset for the sales," Helen guffawed.

"What calendar?" asked Rebecca, confused.

"Tits and arses and rugby balls just in time for next January – ah, don't worry, Rebecca, there's no chance of me ever allowing that kind of malarkey, I wouldn't let my troops have that much fun in their shorts – it's pain they need if we're to move up a division for next year!"

"See you next week so, Legs!" Declan saluted Rebecca military style and walked off the pitch to his car, threw his muddy gear bag into his filthy four-by-four and got it to splutter into life.

"What's your nickname then?" Rebecca quizzed Helen as she watched the girls organise the gear to be put away.

"The Antichrist," Helen said matter of factly.

"For obvious reasons?"

"For obvious reasons but for now I'm off to gentler pursuits – have to make some buns for tomorrow's school fundraiser – how're you fixed for a lift?"

"Well . . ." Looking behind, Rebecca realised that Paddy was still there – had been there the entire time.

"Don't worry," Rebecca said, deciding at once, "my lift's sorted."

"See you next week so, Legs." Helen gave her a wink and took off with a training rugby ball under her arm.

Gradually, the rest of the group trickled away, someone sorting out the washing for the next game, and Rebecca waved at them not knowing all of their names but feeling something like gratitude for their generosity of spirit and camaraderie.

A bit confused and a bit bruised and tender, she walked back to Paddy's van with giggles in her stomach. Immediately he went to open the passenger door and she shook her head, indicating the back of the van instead.

"I'm covered in mud – well, I'm not that bad, I suppose, but I wouldn't want to ruin your seats, Paddy – I'll sit in the back," she told him breathlessly.

"Okay – if that's what you want," he shrugged.

"Guess what, I've got a new nickname," she said as she sat in the open door of the van, full of excitement for the game. "In fact, now that I think about it, it's the only nickname I've ever had! Legs, Paddy, they're calling me Legs – isn't that just wonderful?"

"Well, I can see why, they're a fine set of legs – nice and toned," he said admiringly, looking down at her cold and reddened calves which were dangling out the door.

"Ah, that's probably because I pole-dance." She watched the flash of lust in his eyes and smiled to herself for her badness. "No, you don't understand – they're calling me Legs because they're *useful*, my legs are *useful*, Paddy. I don't think anyone has ever thought my legs useful before – you don't know how wonderful it is that my legs are suddenly useful." Laughing, Rebecca jumped up and embraced him in a bear-hug and, taking his face in her hands, gave him a big happy kiss full on the mouth and then just as quickly stopped, drew a breath and looked at him with a mixture of shock and surprise.

Neither of them spoke. It was like a pin had been pulled on a grenade and the thing between them was now live and dangerous, a thing that must either explode or be quickly thrown away.

Paddy's instincts were heightened as he pulled her into the back of the van with him, banging the door shut behind them, and in the half-darkness fell on top of her, his hands reaching for her breasts as he squeezed them so hard he nearly separated them from her ribcage. The warmth of his body on top of her was electric, especially as her cold legs and face were now tingling from the extra heat. Roughly he pulled her hair back from her face so he could kiss her hard on the mouth and nuzzle her slender mud-streaked throat. Without losing a moment, his hand dashed up her back and she jumped as she felt the coldness of his fingers first on her spine and then inside her bra cups while another hand rubbed her taut stomach hard, then briskly begin to dive for the curve of her hips, his fingers digging into the little silver scar which always made her wince, the scar which was meant to remind her to stay aloof with the male species. Damn, when would she learn? Arching her back, she allowed him to pull her shorts and underwear down past her cold mud-splattered thighs and gasped as he caressed her pubic mound first gently and then with a gorgeous roughness that made her feel animal and raw.

His erection was digging into her through his jeans and deftly she undid his fly. Feeling his member spring out proud, she stopped kissing him and gasped.

"Jesus Christ," she said in shock.

"Yeah, I know it's a bit on the large size" he joked, a bit self-consciously.

"You're not one of those super-enhanced porn stars, are you?"

"What?" he laughed in embarrassment. "No, it's all mine – all a natural gift."

"Well, I suppose if we're going to go any further we'd better put a cap on it," she told Paddy's penis and for once she understood what top-heavy girls meant when they said men only talked to their chests.

"Uhm, the thing is, Rebecca, I didn't actually see this happening, not here, and I don't have a rubber on me –

they're not exactly the regular size that they sell at the chemist's," Paddy apologised, blushing boyishly.

Their awkwardness broke the spell of lust and Rebecca began to feel self-conscious and a bit stupid and, pulling her shorts back up and jumping into her tracksuit bottoms, she tried to normalise the situation as quickly as possible and make a bit of a joke.

"I always thought that was just a gag – you know, man goes into a chemist and asks for condoms and the pharmacist says 'What size – large, extra large or liar?' I didn't think there really were guys as . . . well, as big as you out there!"

"It's not a joke," he said, leaning his back against the side of the van and trying to get comfortable.

"Well, maybe it's just as well nothing happened – I'm not sure if – if all this was just the rugby talking – you know, the excitement." Rebecca smoothed back her muddy hair as a sort of distraction technique. Although if she were honest; she'd played this kind of raunchy scenario with Paddy in her head quite a few times of late.

"Or maybe there's someone else on the scene?" Paddy tried to tease out, his face in shadow as he reached out for her hand and tentatively caught a few fingers.

"How'd you figure that?" she laughed as he moved from brushing her fingers to squeezing her whole hand firmly.

"You're a good-looking woman and after tonight I know you're definitely not frigid," he said. "Not that I ever thought you were anyway," he added quickly.

"Okay, there is someone else but we're kind of on a break at the moment," Rebecca said quietly, pulling her hand back and interlacing it with its sister on her lap.

"Okay – enough said," Paddy nodded solemnly.

"But tonight – bringing me here – it was good of you, Paddy. I really needed to get out and find a distraction."

"Sure, aren't we work-mates and you might have been a bit scary at first but I think you're sound now, Rebecca, I really do."

"And you're a nice guy too, Paddy, but you understand at the moment while I'm trying to work things out . . ." Her face searched his for understanding but all she saw was desire and youthful good looks.

Suddenly they were tearing each other's clothes off again in a mad frenzy.

"Oh bloody hell, what am I like?" Rebecca laughed as she hauled off her top.

"Gorgeous, that's what you're like," he groaned and then he ceased to talk as he kissed her muddy cheeks and tugged her muddy hair back so she could fully surrender to his kisses.

She laughed so much he stopped and asked her what was the matter.

"God, I was just thinking you'd pay big money for this at the salon," Rebecca giggled as Paddy pushed up her sports bra and began teasing her nipples with his teeth.

Confused, he broke away from her once more. "You'd pay big money for what at the salon – sex?"

"No, you twit, an all-over body wrap! You'd pay big money to look the way I do now, covered in mud from head to toe. Hey, don't stop kissing and don't forget we're not actually having sex – not until we get a raincoat to fit that weapon!" She laughed as she reached up to find his mouth once more, then pulled him back to the floor to continue their wrestling. "Oh, and Paddy?" She broke away from his maulings again for one minute of sense.

"What?" he asked, frustrated at her constant stopping and starting.

"Next time bring that beautiful car of yours, okay?"

"The old Porsche – why?"

"You don't need to understand, Paddy, just make me happy." She felt the delicious young strength of him all over her and was reminded that the best sex is often where the deed itself is delayed until desire is a feverous inferno.

Her desire was lit like a candle, the flame burning slow and bright, and she knew as she flirted with the first sparks of infidelity that she flirted with destruction itself. Not caring, she kissed Paddy deeply, recklessly, with burning lips and with a gladness in her heart that she hadn't felt in such a long time and best of all, most surprisingly of all – it felt fun.

Thirty

All week Jennifer felt giddy as she thought about her next dance class with that outrageously passionate woman and her Bronx Angel, whose name she still didn't know because she was too tongue-tied and too overwhelmed to act like a fully functioning adult in his presence. All week she ate less and felt nervous energy coursing through her frame, but it was good for her figure; so too was buying salsa CDs in the supermarket instead of calorie-laden chocolate. In the kitchen in the morning, doing the dishes, with the girls in school and Adam sleeping, she practised holding her body tight, keeping her upper frame rigid while everything below moved snakelike as her CD player belted out crazy Latin music. Tap, tap, tap, twirl and back to basics again. At one stage she even snatched a silk flower from a vase in the living room and put it between her teeth like a she-devil intent on seduction but then she heard Dan come in and mid-twirl she started to tidy things out of the dishwasher.

"You're enjoying the dance classes?" Dan began cautiously.

"It's something to do." She set her lips in a line which passed as a semi-friendly smile but not a smile so friendly that he'd be tempted to place any daytime sexual demands on her, with or without washing-up gloves on.

"They say Latin music is great for increasing sexual desire," he said, testing the water, and she immediately felt like drowning.

"Do they?" Out of a sense of nervousness she switched on her inner-core muscle at the sink and went into Pilates overdrive – in out, in out, went her belly secretly. Then she started to do her pelvic-floor exercises – up, hold, pulse, pulse. Pulsing all her body bits was turning into a kind of nervous little tic, the mechanics of it all made her feel tight inside and strangely sensual.

"And if you keep on dancing, you'll be fitting into some lovely sexy little outfits before long," he continued, extremely cautiously now.

"Do you think?" Jennifer deliberately didn't smile. The thought of sexy little outfits for anyone's pleasure but her own made her feel panicky.

"So keep it up – having fun," Dan encouraged somewhat clumsily.

"Oh, okay then, I will."

There was an awkward pause, an awkward pause that never existed in the early days of their relationship, the days of trailing long-stemmed daisies across her lovely, young stomach.

"Right, well, just to let you know I'm really getting going on the vegetables in the polytunnel now as well," he spluttered, just looking to make conversation.

"That's nice."

"It is nice growing vegetables. It's a kind of trendy too, you know?"

"Yeah?" Her body language told anybody within an ass's roar that she didn't care about the answer.

He knew it too as he hovered half-in, half-out of the door that led to the garden.

"So any idea what's for dinner tonight?"

"Haven't decided yet," she said in a restrained friendly way as she placed a bowl on a shelf.

"Oh – oh, okay."

He took the hint and left and Jennifer automatically released her core muscle to complete slackness. When had this awful distance begun, this wanting to flee each other's company but yearning to be close? Determined to exorcise any thoughts of doubt, Jennifer switched her CD player on again and pranced to the beats of salsa and merengue. Closing her eyes she thought of her Angel, his smile, his curls unknowingly brushing her cheek as they danced and she knew that the longing she was feeling was dangerous and more than a little wild.

In a panic Jennifer noticed time had sneaked away from her and it was time to pick up Abby from playschool. Grabbing her handbag, she ran out back to where Dan was having an intimate moment with a juvenile tomato plant.

"Dan, I'm getting Abby now and Emma's off early – staff meeting – will you keep an ear out for Adam if he cries?"

"Yeah – sure – would you stop en route and get some –"

"No time – gotta go."

"I'll ring you!" he shouted after her.

"No point," she yelled back, "phone's not powered up – I think the battery's on its last legs and I've no phone credit left!"

Alone with his seedlings, with empty pots and bits of earth to one side, Dan looked towards the house and felt puzzled. It wasn't like his wife to let her phone credit or her battery run low – she was so organised that way, dealing with the family finances, taxing the cars on line, paying the TV licence. He knew it was ironic that here was he, the computer graduate, and he never got on the home computer when he didn't have to – he wasn't even into games and since he'd been made redundant he'd almost stayed away from computers altogether out of indifference really.

Wearily he put down his earth-sodden trowel, left his muddy green garden boots at the back door and slowly tiptoed past the bedroom where Adam was snoozing. Hearing nothing, he walked into the home-office-cum-everything-else, stared at the computer screen and smiled to himself. He'd get onto the internet and put twenty euro into her phone account. Maybe he should be doing more of the bill-paying and on-line shopping. Jennifer always looked so stressed but he didn't want to drive her mad either. Look where doing a few chores around the house had got him! She'd completely exploded at the thought of anyone in the kitchen interfering with her cupboards.

Still standing, but bent over the keyboard, he put money into her phone account then mindlessly began to look up something on greenfly. As he activated the search engine he came across Jennifer's recent history and smiled – salsa dancing, the merengue, the tango, origins of Latin music,

Venezuela, Brazil and South America – recent interests for her and memories of what could have been for both of them if things had turned out differently.

Distracted by his thoughts, he didn't notice the long list of words on the search engine's recent history but when he did he was so stunned he had to sit down for a moment. The words flew off the screen and attacked him with their directness, fun sex games . . . erotica . . . low sex drives . . . high sex drives . . . how to know if you're on the verge of an affair . . . on and on it went. Was this his Jennifer, who since the birth of Adam had virtually turned into a nun, who made him feel guilty whenever he asked for sex, the Jennifer who pushed him away and reduced the physical sharing between them to some kind of obligation, a chore that must be endured?

Maybe she didn't think he'd noticed her withdrawal from him, but he had noticed. He knew she was tired – but did she want something else, someone else, was she already having an affair? Confused, he began to click on sites his wife had been visiting, then switched the computer off and felt his body numb from his fingertips to his skull. A second later the phone rang and Dan answered in a stupefied daze. He should have felt warmly excited, but as he answered, "Yes . . . thanks . . . great . . ." all he felt was traumatised, confused and inexplicably sad.

Abby's playschool teacher was delighted with her new angelic, non-tooth-snapping behaviour and couldn't resist gushing when Jennifer turned up to collect the reformed little devil.

"A lovely child, so kind and aware, she's been helping me get the juice and bickies ready all week and she's especially lovely to the younger toddlers." The teacher lowered her voice, "In fact she's a different little girl completely – you know, some children just don't settle the first time round at playschool – maybe it was just as well she took a little break until, you know, the biting thing subsided." She touched Jen's arm gently.

"Yes, maybe it was."

"Goodbye, Abby!" The teacher gave Abby a friendly smile and gave Jen a look of approval as if to say, 'Today you get one tick for being a good parent!'

Driving the car, Jennifer kept squinting in the rear-view mirror, trying to subtly extract information from her suspiciously well-behaved middle child but Abby wasn't forthcoming and seemed irritated by her mother's constant little enquiries.

"Good day, pet?"

A little growl followed by a reluctant nodding of the head.

"Good that you're getting on so well at playschool now."

A disinterested little grunt followed and then Jennifer thought she saw her second-born shove something whole into her mouth.

"Are you eating something, Abby?"

A ferocious shake of the head and bulging cheeks followed. Jennifer's eyes narrowed and her mother's instinct switched on to 'suspicious'.

At the school gate Emma hung back and kept staring at her mother from under lowered lids, then hanging her head and looking at her shoes in a practised, '*see no evil, hear no evil, speak no evil*' way.

"*Bonjour*," Miss Fitzpatrick got the mandatory

French greeting out of the way and then launched into the attack proper in English. "I'm not sure if you're aware, Mrs O'Malley, but all the children were sent home a note recently to say French lessons for parents re-commence in the next week and I know you missed the previous two classes so I'm just informing you in person that they are starting again."

"What night?" Jennifer asked snappily and a little bit defiantly.

"Wednesday – for the next twelve weeks."

"Sorry, I couldn't possibly attend. Wednesday is the night I dance."

For a moment Miss Fitz was speechless. It was evident she'd counted on complete parental compliance on the matter. "But it's important that parents improve their language skills so they can support their children in their education!"

Emma looked like she was about to burst into tears as she recognised the restrained hostility in her teacher's voice and the resistance in her mother's.

"As it happens I *am* doing everything I can to improve my language skills."

"Oh, are you doing a course somewhere else then?" The teacher dropped her guard momentarily.

Jennifer glared dangerously. "No, but every night I'm watching that sexy weatherman Pierre doing the day's forecast and sure it's not even a chore – he's *such* a ride."

Miss Fitz's firm young bosoms heaved angrily as she now recognised blatant resistance.

"Like I said, I *do* think it's more important to support your child in language development than to dance," she insisted.

A very bold Jennifer couldn't resist going for the kill. "You don't have children, do you, Miss Fitzpatrick, because if you did you'd realise that actually it is far more important to dance than to do *anything* else. Emma, sweetheart, come on, we're going home and we're stopping at the burger shop for lunch." Yes, that's right, she aimed a telepathic dagger at the teacher – sometimes my children eat nutritionally deficient food and I'm completely over feeling guilty about it.

"Are we really going to get a burger?" Emma asked as she kept pushing away her small sister who was jumping all over her like an over-excitable pup.

"No, sweetheart, I don't have enough money for burgers today, but we'll *definitely* go soon."

"But why did you tell teacher we were going now?"

"One day you'll understand why grown-ups do all sort of things that don't make sense," Jennifer assured a doubtful Emma and a powerful feeling came over the young mother as she took her daughter's hand and squeezed it tight. As she did she noticed Abby was walking with her head down and feeding something surreptitiously into her mouth.

"Abby!"

The child's face was all crumbs but she played dumb for as long as possible and clutched the pockets of her little skirt possessively and a little guiltily.

"What have you got in there?" Jen delved into the pockets. "Good grief – there's loads of biscuits in your pockets! If you eat them all you won't have a tooth left in your head!"

No wonder the kid was behaving so well at playschool. Being an angel was a ruse to help her steal biscuits, probably from the little kids she was being so lovely to. Jennifer felt like exploding but then she began to sigh. Stealing biscuits was probably ten times better than sticking her teeth into the tender flesh of her classmates. All things considered, stealing biscuits was probably *progress*, she thought as she drove home practising what was now turning into an all-over body-toning regime. First it was some facial toning exercises in the rear-view mirror she'd recently learnt off the computer – it was all squeeze, squeeze, flash the eyebrows, jut the jaw out, pulse the cheeks, squint through eyelids and pretend to drink through a straw. Then she practised her Pilates, pulling in her inner-core muscles around her abdomen, then squeezing her butt-cheeks together, doing a few pelvic-floor exercises with a few thigh-toning exercises thrown in as well.

Just as she was returning to a few more eyebrow flashes, she caught sight of Perfect Yummy Mammy Madeline and her brood tailgating in their shiny people-carrier. Madeline was so high up she must have seen every eyebrow flash, knee-squeezing and thigh-toning exercise, but it was impossible to be certain as per usual Madeline was wearing sunglasses on her perfectly formed button nose. Caught out in the muscle-popping and squeezing, Jennifer decided to act overly friendly and wave casually at Madeline who gave a half-salute back before quickly turning a corner, concerned perhaps that anyone would see her acknowledging this obviously lunatic woman.

"Hi, Dan, is he still asleep?" Jennifer asked as she collapsed through the door with lunch bags, coats and a ton of kiddie art – bits of paper, plastic bottles and toilet-roll cylinders that were heading for the recycling pronto.

A still dazed Dan nodded.

"Great. Will you give Abby some lunch, although she's full of bickies and she probably won't eat anything, and will you fix Emma a snack – don't let her watch too much TV and help her with any homework. Thanks. The new 'me' is big into looking after her appearance – I'm off to the bedroom to lift a few freestyle weights!"

Dan let his wife go without a word and wondered when exactly he had been installed as the Resident Nanny but it would be better to keep Jennifer happy for now than to look for a fight. Something told him she wouldn't be too pleased if she thought he was snooping out her computer habits. Something also told him she wouldn't be at all pleased when she found out his new job involved working in a hardware shop amongst wood and nails and paint and everything that the non-intellectual part of his brain and his puzzled little-boy head had been craving as much as life itself.

Thirty-one

"So you don't think that my hair looks really thick and bushy now you've cut all those layers in it?" a quietly hysterical Jennifer asked her hairdresser who was putting the final touches to the new hairdo, fluffing, preening, desperately trying to hasten her client along to the all-important spraying and paying.

The hair sadist looked in the huge mirror in front of Jen for a minute, still stroking the savaged hair, a practised look of puzzlement on her face. Jennifer was also looking in the mirror. They were both looking in the mirror waiting to see who would cry chicken first, waiting to see would anyone be brave enough to shout, 'Okay you're right, your hair looks crap and only a hat will fix it!'

"Sure how could it look thicker when I've cut so much out of it? Cutting so much out of it could *only* make it look thinner, not thicker," the scissors artiste said, this time with a practised air of innocence and just a touch of courtroom cunning.

348

"See the thing is, when I said I wanted layers I meant *long* layers not short layers – remember I said I wanted a casual, fluffy kind of look?" a near-hyperventilating Jennifer continued, drawing out every word. Actually, what she really meant was dangerous, sexy *and* alluring, but she was to shy to be that ridiculously specific. Now, however, she was devastated. How the hell had her instructions led her to look like a sheared sheep? Cutting her hair had seemed so important. When a woman cuts her hair it's a signal to the world that she's changing in some important way. Now she'd have to run from everyone she knew for the next six months at least.

Sighing, as if she was really, really trying to see Jennifer's point, the hairdresser tried a confused look and for the first time Jennifer realised that her hairdresser's own hair was a disaster zone, her roots were an inch overdue and her greasy locks were scraped back in a tight ponytail. Obviously this woman had no interest in cutting hair at all. The cow was pulling off Jennifer's cape now in a firm manner, a giant can of hairspray in one hand. Yes, she was definitely trying to advance things along to the all-important spraying and paying.

Handing over her credit card, so she could be legitimately robbed, Jennifer held back the tears and endured some infuriating hair-care advice while the till printed out her receipt.

"Every hairstyle takes a few weeks to settle – mousse is good but hairspray is best of all," the robber consoled.

Jennifer smiled so much in pretend-appreciation that her cheek muscles ached, and taking her coat she charged out the door and allowed the first tears to explode down her face. Outside her tears merged with the rain. She could have walked home and wrecked the new hair, it was not like it would have mattered, but she'd already texted Dan to tell him she was finishing up and asked him to pick her up in the car park.

Head down, umbrella like a shield, she raced towards the familiar vehicle, opened the passenger door and dived into the seat, not wanting to see Dan's gawk of horror, but when she looked up Rebecca was staring back instead.

"What are *you* doing here?" she hissed at her gorgeous sister, gorgeous whether her hair was back or down, styled or greasy, whether she'd a scrap of make-up on or was in full war-paint.

"Adam threw up all over Dan just as he was heading out the door so he asked me to get you instead. What *did* you do to your hair?" said Rebecca, reversing the car, one eye on the mirror and the other on Jen's butchered locks.

"Isn't it obvious? I got a dangerous *and* sexy new look. At the very least, it was meant to be casual and sexy. Now tell me the truth, do you think she hit the mark on any of my requirements?"

"Uhm . . ."

"I'll answer for you. Like hell she did, the stupid cow! She needs her eyes tested and her brain examined. Robbed me blind, she did, and she thinks *hairspray* will fix it and that my hair will eventually relax into an ideal state. Did you ever hear such rubbish?"

"It's not that bad. At least you have a style now whereas before it kind of just hung there."

"Are you saying I'm boring, Rebecca?" Jennifer's eyes narrowed dangerously.

"No, of course not – just your hair lacked a bit of excitement, that's all."

"Well, thanks, thanks for being so condescending. So you think I'm not exciting either. I'm just your predictable, sensible, boring older sister, amn't I? Pull over the car, here at the corner, pull over the car!" Jennifer was shouting like a madwoman.

Rebecca pulled over at the kerbside of a small building with a tiny, dirty window and a freshly painted sign announcing *Tattoos and Piercings* to the world.

"You're not going in *there*, are you?" Rebecca asked, appalled.

"Watch me!"

Alarmed, Rebecca struggled out of her seatbelt, locked the door and ran into the dirty-looking den of iniquity where Jennifer was already shaking her umbrella fiercely with a murderous look on her face.

"I'm here to get something pierced," Jennifer announced to the bloated guy behind the counter, who was wearing a too-small yellow T-shirt which rode up his fat belly, Hawaiian shorts to the knee and pink flip-flops. Straight away she noticed he'd pierced every available flap of skin and was heavily tattooed – so, unlike the hairdresser, he took his work seriously.

"Specifics?" he asked with a practised air of boredom.

"What?"

"What specifically would you like pierced?"

Jennifer ran a few scenarios through her head: tongue pierced – no, it might swell up and she wouldn't be able to talk for a week; belly button pierced – no, her tummy was too big for that, she'd look like mutton dressed as lamb and she was sheep enough looking as it was. Then

351

she remembered New York and Bernice the lesbian's piercings, wall-to-wall metal in her ears and a red-ruby stud on her nose. God, she'd love to turn up at the school gates looking a bit like a female Sid Vicious – nobody would ever try to foist language lessons on her again. Then again, yes, definitely, the best option would be . . .

"Nose. I want my nose pierced."

"You do not," Rebecca gasped. "I'm sorry, my sister is a bit upset about her hair, she's just had it done today and she's a bit freaked out about it."

"Very brave look – puts me in mind of the eighties," said Tattoo Man. "A bit Limahl, a bit Cyndi Lauperish. Now that I think of it – even a bit Rod Stewart. You probably don't remember the eighties, do you?" He smiled at Rebecca and Rebecca smiled back sweetly.

Jennifer gritted her teeth. Right, that was that, she was definitely getting her nose pierced.

"Like I said, I want my nose pierced – now how do we go about it?"

"A lady in a hurry! Lucky for you, I'm free right now. Hop in the chair and we'll get you started. But, first things first, what kind of jewellery do you want?"

"One of those silver balls will do just fine," Jennifer said firmly, gesturing at Malcolm's (for that was his name) tray of silvery delights and off he went to scrub up in the corner sink like a surgeon before the big op.

"Jennifer, I think you're being very rash." Rebecca folded her arms firmly but her voice was very shaky.

"Why, because this is out of character for sensible, boring old me? Oh, I know you think I'm not a very exciting person, Rebecca, that's why you didn't want me at your flash wedding, isn't it, because I wasn't sophisticated enough to impress your new friends down the country, because you were embarrassed by the very sight of me!"

"That's not true!"

"Isn't it? How am I supposed to feel when my sister is getting married and tells me I can't bring my only baby to the wedding because it's adults only – and Emma, your own goddaughter, banned as if she was something awful that jumped-up snobby people shouldn't have to look at!"

"Now I'm just going to disinfect your nose and mark the spot where the piercing is going to be," said Malcolm, disregarding this heated exchange.

The spotlight beside the chair was switched on and adjusted. Out came a cotton bud dipped in some sort of fluid and Malcolm rubbed inside Jennifer's nostril, and then the outside of her nose was rubbed vigorously with some sort of wipe.

"And as if that wasn't bad enough you had to make it worse by making it black tie as well, evening wear compulsory for *all* your guests when I was still as big as a house and feeling really fat and ugly after having Emma!"

"Now, I think the dot should be here. What do you think?" Malcolm held a mirror up to Jennifer's face.

"Perfect, go for it," Jennifer said assertively, all the while staring at Rebecca.

"So what kind of wedding did you have in the end, considering none of your family turned up? Not your wayward brother, your embarrassing sister or either of your parents, but then of course you were mad to make a statement and walk down the aisle yourself like a modern woman who doesn't even need her da to give her away anyway!"

"You're a real bitch, do you know that?" Rebecca hissed as Jennifer wiggled back on the blue leather seat which was like a dentist's or barber-shop chair and Malcolm pumped it up to the right height with his foot until she was at the perfect angle for piercing.

"Okay, I need you to relax – no more talking," Malcolm insisted as he approached, snapped on some blue surgical gloves and, having worked out that a cat fight was escalating, decided to complete the job fast. "First I'm going to clamp your nose with a forceps and that will feel a bit funny, but the pressure will cut down on pain and bleeding, after that I'll be sticking the needle in and we'll loop through the jewellery, okay?"

"Don't worry, I've had three babies, I've seen bigger forceps than that – do your worst," Jennifer sanctioned with a malignant smirk in Rebecca's direction. But when she saw the size of the needle she gulped hard. It was more like a slim nail than a needle but it was too late to back out now.

"Okay, relax, breathe in, breathe out, breathe in, breathe . . ." before Malcolm got to say the word *out* a second time, it was done. Jennifer gasped and her eyes began to water from the assault.

"So who's boring now?" Jennifer lashed out as she caught sight of her new look in the mirror and listened to Malcolm's cleaning instructions for her nose. "Maybe I am a shabby mum of three who wouldn't look good at any of your posh do's about town, but you know what, at least I've done a few things with my life to justify looking this crap. What have you done, Rebecca, you who always looks so bloody perfect even when you should be looking crap? You know what I think, I think people who look perfect all the time are boring – really, really boring!"

"Yeah?" Rebecca unfolded her arms, ripped off her coat and rolled up her top to expose her gorgeously flat midriff. "Malcolm, you got time to do me? My sister here wouldn't have the stomach for this, in any sense of the word, but I do and I want it pierced – now! Get out of the chair!"

A startled Jennifer scrambled down, applying pressure to the inside and outside of her nose with a tissue paper to stem bleeding.

"Wow, you girls don't hang around, do you?" Malcolm said admiringly as he disposed of Jennifer's needle, ripped off his gloves, adjusted the leather seat to recline and fetched a new tray of equipment.

"So what, really nice stuff you got for me then?" Rebecca asked snottily, flashing contemptuous looks at her older sister.

Out came the jewellery and, although Jennifer's vision was obscured by a large paper tissue which was blotted red, she could still see the gorgeous little adornments and twinged with envy.

"A simple one to start – easier to clean," said Malcolm, indicating a plain metal ring and Rebecca nodded assent.

"And anyhow, you bitch, it was *my* wedding! I was entitled to have it any way I wanted, and surely you could have left Emma with someone for the day?" Rebecca tossed her flame locks and got comfortable as

Malcolm washed his hands a second time and snapped on some new gloves.

"You inconsiderate cow, she was only tiny and I was breastfeeding her at the time!" Jennifer retaliated fiercely, wiggling her nose cautiously before deciding to pull away the bloodied tissue.

"Well, maybe you should have bottle-fed her then," Rebecca said with a derogatory little laugh and an annoying smirk as Malcolm sterilised her stomach with an alcohol wipe.

"How *dare* you tell me what I should or shouldn't have done – breastfeeding was *my* choice!" shouted Jennifer, boiling with rage, crumpling the bloodstained paper hanky in her fist.

"And everything about the wedding was *my* choice – it was my big day not yours," Rebecca glowered.

There was a cracking noise as the plastic and paper case containing the needle was torn apart.

"Okay, Miss, you'll need to relax, take a few breaths," Malcolm instructed. Out came a new nail-sized needle and Jennifer saw Rebecca turn pale.

"Want me to hold your hand?" Jennifer asked mockingly but also in earnest – being the big sister was not something she could dismiss lightly.

"No way!" Rebecca gave a short, hard, dismissive laugh like a cat hacking up a fur ball.

Suddenly Malcolm pierced through and Rebecca drew a sharp breath. Her eyes closed, her head lolled to one side and Jennifer screamed and ran across the room.

When Rebecca awoke Jennifer was standing over her, stroking her hair, squeezing her hand and crying.

"What . . . what happened?" Rebecca's tongue was stuck to the roof of her mouth and she felt groggy.

"You fainted."

"Happens sometimes," Malcolm concurred.

"Your stomach looks great though," Jennifer piped up in a small voice.

"Yeah?"

"Yeah."

Rebecca took the hand-mirror and angled it to her torso with a kind of puzzlement.

"Can't believe I did that," she said, shaking her head.

"Sure I practically dared you," Jennifer laughed, helping her to sit upright.

"Guess we're really blood sisters now," Rebecca smiled as she looked at Jennifer's nose piercing.

"Oh yeah, and blood's thicker than water," Jennifer added without a thought.

One look and they were both in tears, bawling, hugging and saying sorry over and over.

"Ladies, ladies, please, you've really put me through the mill today – could you *please* get it together?" Malcolm sighed.

"Don't go away anywhere, Malcolm," Jennifer said, plonking her plastic down on the counter and as was the custom paying for her little sister as well.

"Don't worry, I won't," he promised.

"Good, because next week, the way I'm feeling, I might want to get my clit pierced." Jennifer cackled nervously.

"And if you do I'll ensure your piercing is in *exactly* the right place because, believe me, Madam, when it comes to ladies I've seen as much as your average gynaecologist," Malcolm said wearily as he handed back Jennifer's card then stuck his nose back into his comic, waiting like a spider for his next customer to enter his lair and endure his measured little bites.

Thirty-two

A sex bomb exploded from the bathroom later that evening as a flawlessly made-up Rebecca, her hair bouncy and glossy, her clothes casual but edgy stormed through the door. A denim miniskirt, bought in the supermarket, barely skimming fake-tanned thighs, looked amazing and was set off by black knee-high designer boots. Rebecca looked young, much younger than her thirty years and Jennifer, despite her newly acquired nose-piercing, felt much older than a meagre thirty-five.

"It's all yours!" Rebecca swished past, ready for a hot date with her new toy boy, a tight blue T-shirt riding up slightly in the front to reveal the freshly pierced belly button.

"Thanks." Seeing the sexual power of her younger sister breeze past, Jennifer's belief in her own sensuality and joyous anticipation of her dance class evaporated. In the bathroom, wearily, her hands opened her make-up box and she sighed as she saw the contents were a mess of sludge, dust and crumbly bits of blusher. Her newest lipstick had been savaged by the girls only last week with a tweezers and her gloopy brown foundation was at the end of the tube.

Suddenly, the door closed and she realised the sex bomb was on the wrong side of it – with her.

"You can borrow anything you want," Rebecca said cautiously, after handing over her own make-up.

"No point, I wouldn't know what goes where," shrugged Jennifer.

"I could always make you up?"

"Like when you were a teenager and I used to come in from work or college and would let you practise on my face?"

"I used to think you were so cool to let me do that . . . I-I used to think you were so cool anyway," Rebecca stammered.

"Well, there's been a whole heap of damage done since then and I don't really think make-up is going to fix it." Jennifer deliberately steered the conversation back to basics.

"But I'd like to . . . I have the time . . . can I do it any way I want like when we were kids?"

"Don't care – just so long as I don't look like Frankenstein," Jennifer sighed as she plonked her bum down on the toilet seat, shut her eyes and held her face aloft.

Eagerly Rebecca swept Jennifer's hair back in a big band and cleansed and toned and buffed away dead skin until Jennifer's face was glowing. Lightly, with her fingertips, she applied a sheen of moisturiser, then hid any flaws with a liquid foundation pen. Brushes, big, round, small and busy attacked Jennifer's pale palette of skin, her eye sockets and brows.

"God damn, but I still have the make-up artist touch – you look fab," Rebecca said approvingly as her sister admired her handiwork in Dan's shaving mirror.

Fifteen minutes later, a tarted-up Jennifer was released from the bathroom and her little sister bounded out the front door with plans to bewitch Mr Wonderful Willy in his amazing automobile.

The hall was nearly empty when Jennifer arrived, except for the last of the stragglers from Cassandra's earlier waltz class and the soon-to-be-married salsa couple. Sitting thigh to thigh, the duo waited for Cassandra to announce the start of class, their hands interlinked – occasionally they would stroke each other's wrists and smile or whisper and the girl would cover her mouth and stifle a giggle, then look up sweetly from beneath mascara-plumped eyelashes. It was a sickening display of courtship but fascinating all the same. Two minutes later, the older middle-aged couple arrived.

Cassandra fiddled around with some music, trying one track then discarding it for another, jostling her hips back and forth, moving her weight from foot to foot as her hands fiddled with CD covers looking for the perfect number for tonight's little rumble.

The second couple might have been past the first flush of love but they were still affectionate in a wearily familiar kind of way. Feeling like a gooseberry, Jennifer's eyes kept darting towards the door. There was no sign of the mum with the bad perm from the week before, or the other woman – she knew they couldn't take all that fluid passion – and most disappointingly of all, no sign of her Bronx Angel.

"This looks like all we're going to get tonight – so everyone please take your positions!" Cassandra clapped her hands, did a little skip across the floor and pulled Jennifer in a tight embrace while shouting instructions to the other couples. "Now, my little flower, it looks like it will be just you and me *all* night . . . ooh la la, I like your hair and your *nose*, very Bohemian," she said with a dramatic arch of the eyebrow and a toss of her curls. Cassandra's joie de vivre was very unsettling. The Irish weren't at all good at in-your-face dramatic passion, but Cassandra didn't seem to notice – at least not with Jennifer.

"So, darling, good week, did you get to practise the steps much?" Cassandra started as she shoved Jennifer around the floor and fired her into a few bewildering spins.

"Ehm . . ." Jennifer wished Cassandra would stop talking, so she could concentrate on counting the steps in her head.

"Perhaps a bit in the kitchen doing the dishes or when the children were in bed at night?" Cassandra queried in her caressing voice.

Was that one, two, three, four, tap, or one two, three, tap, then turn then four tap? Jennifer was getting flustered and she worried about stamping on those dainty little toes at the end of Cassandra's pencil-long legs.

"Eh, yes, a bit . . . not that much though . . . I'm probably not very good actually . . . sorry!"

"Oh, sweetie, don't run yourself down, you're just a beginner and you've got good rhythm, something that can't be learned . . . technique now, technique can always be improved."

"That man who was here last week . . . blond hair to his shoulders, tanned, Roman nose . . . I was wondering what he was doing coming to class . . . he didn't seem like a beginner," Jennifer suddenly blustered.

"Oh, my Irish American Latin – lovely man, I could eat him up with a spoon – so sad, such tragedy surrounds him!" Cassandra sighed dramatically.

Jennifer was very interested now – tragedy was *very* Latin.

Pupil and teacher were side to side, their hands raised as they slipped arms over each other's shoulders, then slowly and sexily, yes, definitely sexily let their arms slither away until they broke at the fingertips.

"Does he come here a lot . . . perhaps with his wife?" Damn, that wasn't subtle at all – she'd more or less screamed out her lusty intentions.

"A wife? God no, darling, a man like that is a free spirit, a man of the moment, like air through your fingers!"

Cassandra was back in fantasy world again and Jennifer's voice was almost snappy as she urged her to focus on reality for just half a minute.

"Yes, but he must have been married once or in a relationship . . . he strikes me as someone who would be . . . I mean like you said . . . all that tragedy . . ." In the excitement Jennifer was forgetting to count, though it was hardly necessary anyhow as Cassandra was such a forceful lead.

"Separated, two teenage daughters, marriage broke down only last year and now his girls are grown he's bought a camper van to tour the Old Sod. Well, it's the

Old Sod on his father's side, I understand. So now our lovely Latin goes where he wants, does what he wants and he lives for dance, a gypsy on the landscape, dancing anywhere all along the western seaboard."

"Really . . . so tonight he'd be . . . ?"

Cassandra's concentration snapped and she physically broke from Jennifer and strode across the floor like a terrifyingly cross catwalk model.

"No, no, no you're *mauling* the poor child! Keep that up and she'll never marry you. Like this, watch – observe first, *then* do," she berated the sheepish husband-to-be.

Cassandra took the poor giggly girl-child in her arms and, assuming the role of dominant male, twirled the bride-to-be, once, twice, three times, until the young woman staggered from dizziness and another fit of the giggles.

"Now, Fred Astaire, your turn – don't forget what I've shown you!" Cassandra stabbed her finger and scowled in a half-forceful, half-friendly way that reduced the husband-to-be to a heap of jelly and had the bride-to-be giggling away as if to say 'He's a big feckin eejit, isn't he?'

Gasping they all broke for water after five more minutes of intense dancing.

"Now, class, just letting you know that there are still places left for the annual Salsa Festival. Where would you think that would be?"

Cassandra pointed at Husband-to-Be who turned a shade of beetroot, plunged his hands into his pockets, guffawed a little and after a little cough finally suggested, "Longford?"

"Longford . . . *Longford*? In the *middle* of the country? Let me tell you there is *nothing* remotely Latin about

Longford!" Cassandra shot a look of pity at Bride-to-Be who threw back her head in a hearty laugh as if to say, 'You're right, he's a terrible feckin' eejit altogether but he's still mine and by God I'm going to marry him, hell or high water!'

"Have a guess, darling!" Cassandra tenderly prodded Jennifer who felt awkward at the singled-out attention – she was squeezing her glass so tight she was afraid it might shatter.

"Galway, I suppose it would have to be Galway, the Spanish city," Jennifer said, blushing.

"Galway it is, sweetheart," Cassandra smiled prettily. "Yes, the only real place for salsa is South America but we'll make do with Galway – a weekend of dance in two weeks' time with all my dance classes in attendance –"

Jennifer cleared her voice. "But Cassandra, do you really think we're ready . . . I mean we've only just started dancing . . . won't others there be much more experienced?"

"Ah Jennifer, let me tell you how I learned to dance . . . a summer-time of dance . . . me not more than a girl . . . men of all ages . . . moving until the movement was instinct. There is only one way to dance, do you know what it is?"

Jennifer shook her head, embarrassed that she was still in the spotlight.

"The only way to dance is to *dance*! Two weeks . . . several hundred people . . . will you be there, Jennifer?" Cassandra handed out a practice CD. "No time for the merengue tonight, people, but no matter, that means our salsa is all the better." Turning with a flourish, Cassandra clapped her hands authoritatively, announcing the end of class.

Will I be there? Jennifer questioned herself as she pulled the car out of its driving spot. Will I be there? Two minutes later she slowed to a halt as a stooped-over elderly woman took forever at the zebra crossing. As she looked closer she saw a pair of funky boots she recognised and saw that their owner seemed to be displaying a funny, twitchy walk and was at times almost bent in two. It was Rebecca. What was she doing all alone?

"Rebecca, where are you going and why are you walking so funny?" Jennifer shouted out the car window as the 'elderly' Rebecca just about reached the centre of the road. "Is it your belly, your piercing, are you in pain?"

"You, you . . ." the flame-haired beauty raged.

"What about me?"

"Just get me home, would you?" Rebecca collapsed into the passenger seat.

All the way back in the car Rebecca refused to speak, just crossed her legs tightly and cursed under her breath, and as Jennifer parked she shot out like a demented wasp from under a glass and ran for the front door.

A minute later Jennifer could hear a screech and a fit of cursing from the bathroom.

"What's wrong with her?" Dan asked, emerging from the bedroom bleary-eyed from dealing with Adam who was running a temperature, but was now asleep. Skilfully Dan averted his eyes from Jennifer's slightly mad hair and dubious nose-piercing.

"Don't know. I'll go ask."

Sensibly Dan didn't wait for any answers but beat a path to his garage.

Jennifer knocked on the door and called softly, "Rebecca, are you okay?"

Inside the bathroom, the wailing, cursing and histrionics continued.

Suddenly the door opened and a wild-eyed, hysterical woman shook and shouted.

"I was with a man who has to specially order in johnny bags because he has such a big willy and we were nearly doing it in his Sex God of a car, with both of us trying not to rub off my belly button, when I nearly jumped out of my skin . . . oh my God, I don't want to even think about it . . ."

"What?"

"I've got worms and your *beautiful* children must have given them to me!"

Jennifer held the doorframe of the bathroom for support as she bent double with laughter. She laughed so hard her belly shook and tears fell down her cheeks, and then Rebecca stomped her foot in frustration and Jennifer was nearly on the floor again from convulsions.

"Laugh! Is that all you can do?"

"Oh for God's sake, you're not the first ever to be afflicted! Sandra got a dose of them too a while back – they must be doing the rounds of the schools – either that or maybe you caught them from the hospital. Take a few deep breaths and wait here, Princess . . . I'll be back."

Two minutes later a still giggling Jennifer reappeared with a tablet and a glass of water.

"Here, take this. Why don't you pretend it's an ecstasy tablet – it kind of adds to the fun and lessens the horror?"

"You are one twisted individual, do you know that? I can't believe I nearly started to like you again," Rebecca snarled as she grabbed the tablet and knocked it back.

"Oh don't be such a condescending cow and anyhow

you kind of have to be a bit warped when you're a parent. I remember when we had the scabies scare Dan had to paint me all over with vile liquid and I joked that we could pretend it was chocolate body paint and –"

"Bet you don't pretend that much any more." Rebecca gave an irritating little smirk.

"What's that supposed to mean?" Jennifer asked, suddenly sobering up from her giggles.

"You tell me!"

"Yeah, well, you tell me what a married woman is doing in a car with a man who isn't her husband?" Jennifer hissed back, hand on hip.

"With a man with a giant willy – you forgot that bit."

"Stuff his willy – are you having an affair?"

"Trying to . . . well, at least I'm up front about it unlike you and some guy at your dance class."

"There's nothing going on with me and *any* man at my class," Jennifer snapped.

"Really, that's funny because I saw the way you looked the night you came home from your first class and I know that look and it's a 'man look' alright."

Jennifer could feel her cheeks burning but Rebecca had disappeared and came back five minutes later wearing a pair of skin-tight supermarket trousers and a silver bomber jacket.

"One of the rugby girls is kicking off her twenty-first tonight with tapas in the wine bar down town and I'm dropping in for a bottle of plonk, maybe two if the worms hate the vino. Don't wait up, sis – the slaughter might take quite a while!" Rebecca tore out of the house like an angry inferno, leaving an angry Jennifer looking after her longingly.

Rugby girls – Helen would be there, no doubt. Trust Rebecca to muscle in on her friends, just as she predicted that night they started roaring at each other in the garage, then watched TV silently and angrily like an old married couple.

In the kitchen Jennifer's thoughts brewed along with her coffee. Men with giant willies who needed to order in their condoms didn't really exist, did they? Could Rebecca really be that lucky? As she stirred in the milk Jennifer set her jaw in a tight line. No, it was just Rebecca trying to wind her up.

Jennifer snapped a mini Kit Kat in two, stirred her coffee with one half of broken biscuit then sucked hard. Feck it, she had to hear more about this sex-god guy with the massive appendage. Besides, what was it Cassandra said, she had to *think* Latin, *feel* Latin, *be* Latin and in rural Ireland a tapas and wine bar was as close to Latin as she was likely to get. Leaving Dan in charge, Jennifer touched up her new trendy make-up look and, to hell with any notion of shame or embarrassment, decided to gatecrash a twenty-first, letting loose a bagful of childish giggles as she shut the front door behind her and clattered off expertly on high-heeled shoes without the slightest trace of a wobble.

Thirty-three

"You're playing a friendly next Sunday fortnight," Helen told Rebecca as she finished training and left the pitch, exhausted, wet and muddy.

"What, but I'm an amateur, I'm nowhere near ready," she stammered.

"Well, if you don't play soon it'll be the end of the season – the end of April and it'll be all over for the rugby. You need to get out there and do it for real now, Legs, and I don't want you slacking because your interest is waning – a match now, a match will help you keep your eyes on the prize."

"But Helen –"

"It's not Helen any more, Legs – it's the Antichrist from here on in and you *are* playing a match. Practice is over, it's time to do it for real," the General told the terrified new recruit.

College student, eighteen-year-old Adele Roche sidled up to a flustered Rebecca as they left the pitch. It was the second weekend in a row that the fit young thing had made it home from her studies and partying for practice, much to Helen's delight as the teenager was a cunning and fearless asset on the pitch. As she walked Adele wiggled her hips like a catwalk model, her stride long, her expression slightly jaded. Already she carried herself like a woman aware of her brash sexiness but weary of the ways of the world.

"You didn't tell her about the belly button, did you?" Adele asked as she caught up with the still stunned Rebecca.

Rebecca shook her head.

"You're better off – she hates anything like that, you know, hates the thought that you might get sick from an infection or that you'd get injured from having the piercing pulled out during a game. She takes the health of her troops real seriously, does Helen."

"I taped over it just like you said," Rebecca said, smiling appreciatively.

"Yeah, taping is the business alright and don't worry about the match next weekend. Carrigmore are a decent bunch – they'll give us a good workout too – we've trained with them the odd time to make up numbers."

Rebecca went white at the mention of her hometown.

"You alright?" asked Adele innocently, taking a swig of water.

"I'm fine – it's just I didn't expect to be playing so close to home, my home."

"Oh, you're from Carrigmore originally, aren't you – well, sure, can't you get your local mates in to cheer you on – it will be great *craic*. Come on, I'll give you a lift back into town."

After Adele dropped Rebecca to the door in her pink girly motor, Rebecca ran up the stairs frisky with energy and texted Paddy. Still on 4 tnite – give me I hour. In the shower, the hot water bit into her shoulders and the pain forced her to think about the Carrigmore match. It was okay, she convinced herself, nobody was likely to be there to see her play. It was only a friendly, Mark's crowd played soccer or Gaelic, and besides nobody would expect her of all people to get her hands dirty. She'd escape unnoticed, it would even be exciting.

Just like tonight. Tonight Paddy wouldn't know what hit him. Tonight he was going to think he was one lucky guy.

"Hi!" She stepped out to the front door dressed in a belt of a skirt, her favourite knee-high boots, a pink low-cut fitted sparkly top and a black fitted leather jacket with zips running up the inside arm (she'd bought it for next to nothing in the local charity shop). Her hair was fluffed and cascading down her back and for her eyes she'd gone heavy on the eyeliner and glitter to create an alluring Asian style.

"Jesus," Paddy said, gulping hard when he took her all in.

"Remember what I said, that I wanted to go somewhere *exciting* this Friday night?" she flirted.

"I remembered – I think you'll like what I've lined up – and, Rebecca, I'm glad you texted – I thought something was wrong after the last time – when you took off."

Remembering the night of her affliction, Rebecca shuddered.

"Just had a short-term problem that needed sorting but tonight . . . everything's fine tonight." She looked at him hard, leaving him in no doubt as to her brazen intentions.

As the chemistry between them sizzled, Jennifer,

passing by the door on purpose, couldn't resist taking on the role of the annoyingly overly friendly Irish mother.

"Rebecca, is *this* your new young squeeze – are you going to bring him in?" she trilled.

"Hello, Mrs . . . ehm . . ." Paddy melted with embarrassment. Then, recovering himself somewhat, flashed Jennifer a special beaming smile, not quite Mach 4 – which was far too sexual – but Mach 3 point 5 or thereabouts.

Rebecca fumed as the inane questioning continued but Jennifer ignored her evil glares.

"And is that your *lovely* car out there . . . you must have a great part-time job . . . but it's good to have some fun time at the weekend, isn't it . . . I suppose you're busy studying for the Leaving Certificate?"

Rebecca turned round and mouthed the word 'cow' silently to her sister at she sashayed out the door and into the night, full of hope for her boots, her skirt and ultimately for herself.

It was getting quite dark. The car rumbled and stuck to the road like glue as they rounded corners and played hide and seek with the moon which was ducking in and out of wispy grey cloud. Gradually, they climbed upwards, leaving the twinkling lights of the town behind them.

"Where are we going?" Rebecca asked excitedly.

"Sshh!" Paddy turned on the radio and touched her knee from time to time as they drove.

Eventually he turned into a clearing in a wooded area out of town, which was a beauty spot by day and at night a blanket of blackness.

Rebecca watched the lights of the town below and was touched at Paddy's romantic nature, touched that he wanted to be alone with her surrounded by the beauty of the night.

"Wow, the view is magical and this place has a real special feel to it, a secret feel, it's *so* romantic," Rebecca gushed and Paddy nodded somewhat sheepishly.

The radio was still thumping in their ears as Paddy pushed his car seat back almost to the back seats and Rebecca scrambled over to him, straddling him, her hair in his face and his hands underneath her top which was pushed up to her bra. Her desire was so strong she was oblivious to the pain of her back being jammed up against the steering wheel.

Suddenly there were lights and another car, a hatchback, pulled up and parked at the other side of the clearing. Then another car zoomed up and pulled in beside the first car.

Rebecca, completely disconcerted, stared out at the newcomers. Then she saw there were two sets of legs dangling out of the back of the hatchback.

"Paddy, what the . . ."

As she sat bolt upright in Paddy's lap another car came by and a man and a woman got out. The woman bent over the bonnet in a short skirt and then the man commenced pummelling her from behind. Out of nowhere another two men appeared and squashed their noses up against the window of Paddy's car and Rebecca looked at Paddy with a murderous look on her face.

"Paddy, is this one of these places where people go to have sex in public – a dogging spot?"

Two more faces were squinting in the window now, waiting for some serious action to start.

"You said you wanted to go somewhere exciting and I didn't want to let you down," Paddy blustered.

"Jesus Christ, start the car now and get me out of here, you idiot – I'm Rebecca Murphy and nobody gets to see Rebecca Murphy's naked ass for free! Did you really think I would show off my assets for anybody, you numbskull? What the hell is wrong with you?"

Rebecca flung herself onto the passenger seat and, checking the door was locked, made wild 'go, go, go' signals with her hands. Thankfully the horny masses let them go unmolested as they reversed at speed out of the seedy beauty spot and Rebecca made Paddy drive like a lunatic so she could put the vile, cheap place out of her mind as soon as possible.

"I'm sorry, Rebecca, really I am," he apologised for the twentieth time as they reached Bannestown. "I thought you'd enjoy it – I mean, you're a girl who likes to pole-dance and play rugby and I thought you'd be up to doing something *really* exciting,"

"Like having sex with different men in public or letting them watching me and you having sex instead? Is this something you do on a regular basis, Paddy?"

He shook his head and she gave him a dig in the arm and stared at him disbelievingly.

"Okay, once then, maybe twice, I had a girlfriend who was kind of into it."

He parked the car at the fast-food joint downtown and looked at her sadly.

"Does this mean we . . . we won't be doing it now? Only I've got a great selection of condoms." He went to open the glove compartment and she shook her head resolutely and a little frown fluttered around his gorgeous boy-man lips as he sighed.

"Yeah, okay, I understand – totally – only with me going to Australia and all, it would have been a nice little goodbye, a reminder of you, a special memory."

"You're going to Australia?" Rebecca asked incredulously.

"Just for a year – I always wanted to but when my granddad got sick two years ago I hung around to help Gran and then when he died I kind of missed him – that's probably why I ended up working with the aul fellas in the hospital, they kind of reminded me of him – especially Johnny with his bow ties and his fussy habits, Granddad was a bit like that too. Anyway, Gran is going to move in with my mum – living on her own is a bit dangerous and Mum could do with the company."

"Oh." The switch on Rebecca's toy-boy fantasies had been thrown for good and she felt like a schoolteacher who'd been trying to seduce a student. Squirming, she wished her belt of a skirt could be pulled down to her shins and that she was wearing some kind of sensible footwear instead of inappropriate kinky black boots.

"It was kind of a last outing for the car as well. I'm going to have to flog it along with the van to scrape together as much as I can – I mean, I don't know if I'll get any work over there but if I don't I'm going to have a bloody good holiday anyway!"

"That's great, Paddy, sure you might as well – you only live once." Rebecca was impatient to get home now and leave the kid with his dreams.

"But tonight, Rebecca, I really didn't mean anything by it – didn't mean to offend you." He was gazing at her like a bashful little boy who was looking for a hug after being scolded and Rebecca surrendered herself to a hearty laugh and rubbed his arm affectionately.

"It's okay, Paddy, don't sweat it. I mean, like you said, I pole-dance *and* play rugby," she teased gently. "I could see how you'd get the wrong idea about me being a complete exhibitionist."

"Really?"

"No, you twerp!"

Relieved that her good humour had returned Paddy threw her the Mach 4 grin and just for her benefit smiled a tiny crease more to set a new record, definitely a Mach 4 point 5. Quietly, he leaned in and kissed her softly on the mouth.

"I think you're a cracking girl, Rebecca Murphy. I'll never forget you, and whoever he is, he's a fecking eejit to let you out of his sight!"

"I'll tell him that, Paddy – when I divorce him."

"Oh – well, don't tell him until I've left for Oz, will you, because I wouldn't want us to get in a fight over you only for me to hurt him, what with him being middle-aged and me being young and fit."

"Don't worry, Paddy. I'll make sure you're on the plane first!" Rebecca smiled as she punched him playfully in the shoulder and got him to drive her home.

When Rebecca arrived in the door, she smelt baking. In the kitchen Jennifer looked like she'd been dipped in flour – her nose was furry, white powder greyed her hair and her eyebrows and her fingers were covered in a gloopy mess that looked like the kind of grotesque fungus that attaches to dead woodland bark.

"For Jesus sake, it's Friday night! Is baking the best you can do?" Rebecca asked incredulously.

"It's just someone told me that I should try cream of tartar, that maybe that was the missing ingredient from my scones so I'm giving it a go." In front of her on a floured board were misshapen sticky blobs, which she was handling and moulding and trying to make smooth and plump before firing them into the oven. "What are you doing here anyway?"

Rebecca watched uneasily as her sister ran the hot tap and peeled the glutinous mess off her fingers.

"The baby-faced angel hung like a horse, why aren't you with him?" Jennifer continued as she dried her fingers on the kitchen towel.

Rebecca shook her head and smiled, then laughed out loud. "Turns out men with super-big willies are overrated! Anyhow he's going to Australia – all the men in my life end up in Australia as far away as they can get from me!"

"Like that guy when you were younger – what was his name?"

"Gary Larkin."

"Ah yes, he really swept you off your feet, you thought him something special," Jennifer nodded as she casually dried in between her fingers with a towel.

"To tell you the truth, I never knew him at all. Gary liked to pretend he was from some decent working-class suburb, could put on the proletariat act when it suited him, but really he was from Snobsville. That's why he never wanted to take me home that summer of love. Told me it was because he had annoying younger brothers and sisters. Turns out he had an older brother too, a banker with a Porsche 944, basically the same car as Paddy's only the next model up. It was white."

"This Gary fellow was the first to break your heart – naturally you'd kind of hate him, even if his brother did have a nice car," Jennifer said sagely while still watching her oven.

"Yeah, all he cared about was taking my virginity. Then he dumped me."

"Rebecca, don't be so dramatic," Jennifer laughed.

"Well, that's what happened. He used me and one day when he must have been dying for sex he phoned me up and, knowing what a pathetic mess I was after we first broke up in St Stephen's Green, he offered to meet me for a friendly drive along the coast. It was a gorgeous summer's day – we could have been anywhere – Monte Carlo, the Adriatic. He knew I'd have sex with him in that bloody car, he knew I still adored him. I cringe when I think how needy I was . . ." Rebecca sighed, rubbing her temples.

"So is that what Paddy was all about – his car and you trying to change or somehow recreate the past?" Jennifer asked as she switched the kettle on to boil. Oh, the scones smelt gorgeous!

"Maybe – maybe I wanted to be the one in control of how things worked out – I do that sometimes."

"Rebecca, don't beat yourself up. We all give ourselves too freely when we're young."

"He was such a shit. I promised myself I'd never be that naïve with a guy again. 'Bigshot Journo Mr Gary Larkin I don't pay in anywhere around town'! I found out years later he was getting all his expenses paid for by the paper – taxis, the lot, but he'd still let me cough up for half of everything and me in my first job! Turns out his nickname was 'Crime'. Do you know why?"

Jennifer shook her head.

"Because 'Crime never pays', and by God, he didn't, not if there was ever anyone else to foot the bill! You're so lucky, Jennifer. Lucky that you met Dan young, lucky to have a one true love and to have met him again after all those years. It really was fate."

Jennifer sighed. It was summertime, she was twenty-four and herself and Sandra were out for a drink at a Dublin hotel, matching blonde bobs intact, boobs pushed out front and dirty laughter in abundance when they were spotted by a Canadian marine and invited to a party "on board ship", actually a submarine, down by the docks.

They'd boarded the sub as a foursome – Jen, Sandra and two of Jen's college friends, sniggering like schoolgirls as some gorgeous guy saluted when they crossed the water into that mysterious silver metal cigar. The plan had been formulated before they ever stepped inside: they would eat and drink all round, especially as free Canadian beer and platters of delicious seafood were on offer, flirt as if a ride might be on the agenda and at the last minute rush off as fast as a torpedo. Inside the tin can, surrounded by charming, fit and handsome men, some putting on French Canadian accents for maximum sexiness, they nearly forgot the 'plan' when to her astonishment Jen spotted another stowaway – Dan.

Boats were in his family, his brother was in the Canadian navy and Dan had come to work in Ireland for a while in the computer industry. He was planning on calling her parents the next day to see if he could track her down or so he said. They munched on seafood, got drunk and later tore each other's clothes off in a cheap city-centre hotel. Fate, people would say it again and again, when they heard how the transatlantic couple had started the second phase of their love affair. Jen wished everyone would just call it what it was: coincidence, nothing more, nothing less.

"And Dan is such a nice guy. I never went for nice

guys myself, I have a weakness for charming bastards – but I don't let them come even close to hurting me, not any more. I don't ever want to be vulnerable again like I was with Gary Larkin, like I was with . . . Dad. When he left when I was sixteen, I think he took all my love with him. I lost a part of myself when he walked out the door, lost all of my trust."

Rebecca began to shake and Jennifer got up to put her arms around her little sister.

"I know his leaving hit you the hardest, Rebecca. You were the youngest and, besides, you were always Jimmy Murphy's little pet!"

"You know, I think marrying Mark was about finding Dad again in a way, him being eight years older than me, older just like Gary was older too. I wanted to prove to myself that I could be the one to call the shots in a relationship, that I had all the power. But now Mark wants a baby and that terrifies me. I'll be fat, I'll be ugly, I'll be vulnerable and I'll have to trust him to love me, and I can't take that chance. I don't have that kind of trust in me, Jennifer, I don't think I ever will!"

"Oh Rebecca," Jennifer hugged her sister tight as the tears streamed down both their faces.

"Men, they're all just a distraction from my fucked-up life," Rebecca wailed.

"Like baking is a distraction for me," Jennifer laughed and cried.

"Why do you bake or try to bake?" Rebecca sniffed, looking nervously toward the oven that was poised to ping at any moment. "It really is important to you, isn't it?"

"Yeah, it is."

"Why?"

"It makes me feel safe – stupid answer, but it's the truth."

The beeper pinged, the scones looked peaky and the merry dance began as always, two minutes extra here, two minutes there, heat turned up, heat turned down until Jennifer's baking became a race against time, like a doctor racing to deliver a struggling baby.

"Cream of tartar didn't do it then?" Rebecca accurately surmised as Jennifer tipped the lot into the bin without a second glance.

"I think I've tried it all now. I've even tried to bake by instinct, got that tip off Helen, but nothing seems to work," Jennifer sighed.

"Why don't you just pick a recipe from a book, make scones from scratch instead of this guessing game you're playing with a dirty piece of paper with grease spots on it?"

"Because then they wouldn't be proper scones, they wouldn't be perfect, would they?" Jennifer smiled sardonically.

Rebecca laughed a cackling laugh. "And you accused *me* of being too perfect that day in Malcolm's Tattoo and Piercing Parlour! You're the one who's driving yourself demented trying to be perfect, perfect on the inside. Oh to hell with scones! Let's stuff ourselves silly with shop-bought rubbish with extra additives and artificial flavourings. Got anything like that in your cupboards?"

Jennifer came back loaded down with certified adult junk and a few extra bits of kiddie rubbish thrown in for extra bulk and flicked on the radio.

"Friday night and I'm stuck in a kitchen having tea with my sister and listening to the radio – Jesus, I'm getting old," sighed Rebecca as she sat at the counter-top on a high stool and tried to wiggle her belt of a skirt at least down to mid-thigh. "What is that awful music on the radio anyway? Sounds like someone's killing a cat!"

"You must remember how I've always loved traditional music!"

"I remember your wedding reception in a pub when we were all forced to listen to some young fellas playing pipes and the fiddle. It was a lovely wedding all the same. You were the first person I ever knew to get married in a registry office, in a pink dress with flowers in your hair, having a buffet and drinks just for a laugh – you and Dan were the most chilled-out couple in the world. I remember Sandra trying to light a fag and nearly setting her hair on fire she'd so much hairspray locking everything in. They were gorgeous dresses Mum made for me and Sandra all the same . . . I miss Mum sometimes."

"I miss her too," Jennifer answered plainly as she took a first bite of a fun-size Bounty.

"It was a simple wedding – everyone could see the love between you and Dan," Rebecca sighed.

"We didn't have the money for anything flash, that's why it was simple," Jennifer smiled.

"Well, take it from me, flash doesn't always mean until death do us part," Rebecca smashed through a chocolate HobNob with furious teeth.

"Well, nobody's dead yet and, I may be sitting here having tea with my little sis on a Friday night, but at least I know I'm not always this dead boring. With my new Rod Stewart hair and scary pierced nose I might do something completely wild yet."

"Oh, I think you will and very soon too!"

"What does that mean?"

"I'm not allowed say, only you've got a really lovely husband. Oh crap, I've already said too much!" and Rebecca fired a mini Mars bar into herself and smiled away her tears.

Thirty-four

Sadie was at the front door of her house, waving and directing cars into parking spots when Jennifer pulled up for the mother and toddler committee meeting. It was a gorgeous spring day, and everyone arrived wearing sunglasses and things that were vaguely summery, before it was back to wellies and umbrellas for the deluge of rain that Pierre the Weatherman said was coming Western Europe's way.

"Well, I've made it this time!" Fiona the Pram puffed as she jiggled her pram right up to the front door, her skin glistening pink, her baby whimpering softly – from happiness, no doubt.

"And you're more than welcome," said Sadie brightly and Jennifer suppressed a grin. Friendliness was essential if you were planning to off-load your committee position and Jennifer knew this was indeed the plan.

Another new member, Trish, drove up with her young baby and her one-year-old and was in a bit of a panic as her baby had fallen asleep in the car and she didn't want to disturb him.

"I brought my battery-operated listening device. Would you mind saying something so I know I'm picking up," Trish asked Betty. Then it was all *"Angels, this is Charlie, can you hear me?"* until Trish was assured that communications between the car and the house were functioning to her satisfaction.

Back in Sadie's spotless kitchen a large pot of coffee was making vaguely rude noises, the kettle was put on for tea and, as it was dry, all children who could walk, run or toddle were released into the back garden like greyhounds from their traps.

"Okay, ladies, will we begin?" said Sadie. "The annual day out for kids – everyone okay with the Pet Farm again?"

There was a chorus of assent.

"Now, sadly Helen is relinquishing her position as secretary, tea lady, meet-and-greet hostess for new mums and general dogsbody."

"I need more time to go into the schools to recruit young ones for rugby before they get too interested in make-up and boys," Helen explained somewhat guiltily.

"Yes, so this is an opportunity for someone else to step into her big old rugby boots. Anyone interested in the position of secretary?"

Immediately Fiona the Pram stuck her hand in the air like an eager schoolgirl and sealed her fate.

"All in favour of seconding Fiona for secretary?" Sadie asked.

Every hand in the room shot up from the old guard, and victim number one was quite happily snared.

"Now, unfortunately, I too won't be able to be so

involved in the group when I go back to work full-time and I'd like to propose new mum Trish for the chair."

Trish, whose ear was pressed against the baby monitor listening for unusual gurgling or deep breathing, was aghast.

"Oh no, I couldn't, I wouldn't know what to do!" she stammered.

"You'll be fine and you can phone any of us any time for back up," Vicki assured her firmly.

"But I only came to the group for the first time last week," Trish wailed.

"Ach, you'll be fine!" Sadie blustered. "All in favour of Trish taking over for chair?"

Again, all the seasoned mums stuck their hands in the air, releasing Sadie and capturing the new recruit. Trish, looking very agitated, reached for a scone to ease the tension of her new-found responsibilities.

"Okay, before we let you know where we're heading for the night away, I'd just like to ask Jennifer if there's anything she'd like to tell us," Vicki said suddenly, a bemused little smile on her face.

All eyes roamed to Jennifer and she blushed deeply.

"What? I'm not pregnant if that's what you mean. If I'm looking any fatter it must mean I really am fatter, then again Dan is doing a lot of clothes-washing these days and shrinking everything."

"Your hair . . . your nose stud?"

"Oh that, I'm just trying out a new look, that's all." Jennifer tried to flatten down the front of her hair which was taking on a slightly less mullet appearance these days.

"Yes, *where* did you get your hair done?" Sadie asked seriously.

"Feck off, Sadie, you only want to know so you can avoid it like the plague but, if you must know, it was that new place Hairport beside Bookstop."

A low mumbling began and a bit of tut-tutting and head-shaking.

"What – oh, let me guess, you all knew it was crap and never told me!"

"Well, there has been a bit of talk – know someone who got their hair done there recently – shell-shocked is the only word," said Vicki, lapsing into army-speak.

"Sure, does it matter?" said Helen. "It's not like it's an injury that will set you back months – won't it grow out soon enough? It's the piercings I'd be more worried about. Did you get anything else done?"

"Yeah, anything we *can't* see," asked Sadie salaciously.

"Oh yeah, everything you can think of – I'm doing a photo-spread for Sandra for next month's *Slinky Bunnies*. It's called the 'Everything Metal Special'," Jennifer smirked.

"Sandra! Janey, that party night of hers was hilarious and who would have known Betty was so wordy when it came to the English language!" laughed Laura and Betty blushed.

"English, don't talk to me about English," said Fiona the Pram, her face burning in agitation. Looking at Dara, who had gone asleep in the pram, now that he had a break from all the jogging, Fiona's lower lip began to tremble. "I only hope I haven't confused Dara's ear and ruined his chances for school."

"Why, what's up?" Helen celebrated her resignation by munching on a biscuit.

"Didn't I put his name down for the new crèche, where they were meant to be speaking French and doing the baby sign language, only to find out that the two care workers they got were from *Belgium* – it was Flemish they were speaking – and, worse again, that baby sign language they were doing to promote speech – it was to help babies talk early in *English*!" Fiona's big black fat curls began to bounce with agitation at the thought of the wrongs she might have inflicted on Dara's clean-as-a-slate brain.

"Ah pet, don't cry, English is a pretty useful language too, you know," Betty consoled her, rubbing her arm.

"Yeah, listen to Betty, she knows what she's talking about – her English ability came in pretty useful the night of Jen's birthday – *ass, asshole asinine*!" snorted Vicki, her hair shaking as she remembered.

"I guess the only good thing to come out of having Dara at the crèche three mornings a week was the baby massage," Fiona said, perking up. "If you have any olive or corn oil I could show you what we did – we'd have to strip off the babies to their nappies, tune the radio into a classical station – you know, for the ambience – and let them kick on some clean towels."

All the seasoned mammies looked horrified at the thought of unnecessary interference with cranky babies and defiant toddlers.

"Ah no, I don't think so," said Vicki, munching on a bit of biscuit that her youngest hadn't finished. "You know what they say, let sleeping babies lie and all that. What you need, sweetheart, is a break from worrying about how he'll turn out. Why don't you come on our mums' night away?"

"Where are we going?" Jennifer asked wearily as she plugged Adam with a soother. He was sleepy and trying to pull fistfuls of her hair, not such an easy task any more since she had got lots of it shorn off.

"Galway – in two weeks," said Vicki. "It's kind of a bit last-minute, I know, but there was a great deal on offer and we said, sure what the hell, we'd take the plunge. Main activity planned is shopping, although I was hoping I could get some of the girls to do a bit of paintball or something!"

"I'm not sure I can go – we'll be playing a match that weekend," said Helen.

Galway in two weeks? Jennifer's mind was awhirl. Galway in two weeks was Salsa Festival.

"So, Jen, are you coming?" asked Laura, fiddling with the Velcro strap of her black canvas sandals and admiring her new henna tattoo of a flying eagle on her inner left shin.

"I'll have to check with Dan – he sometimes works weekends now."

"Yeah? How come?"

Jennifer took a deep breath. She might as well tell them; they were going to find out anyway.

"He's got a new job."

"Really, I didn't know there was anything wrong with the old one," said Laura, fiddling now with a silver toe-ring on her little piggy.

"Totally new job – he's working in one of the local hardware shops a few hours every week."

There were puzzled expressions as cups, destined for mouths, froze just below chins in confusion.

"He left his job, well, he sort of left it and he was sort of made redundant."

"Jesus, that's terrible!" said Helen with concern.

"Anyway, he's always wanted to have some kind of practical job, says his brain is tired from years of thinking. This hardware job, it's kind of, you know, a middle step before he does something professional again," she lied as she fought back the tears. "I think he'll be doing something more professional in a while, maybe setting up his own computer-repair business or something like that."

"Well, you let us know when the computer thing is up and running and I'll organise for a few computers to get busted – I'll even bust my own so he can fix it," Helen promised.

"Thanks, Helen, that's very good of you." Jennifer couldn't help smiling.

"Would it help if we went into the shop and bought some paint or a few nails," asked Laura seriously.

"I don't think he gets commission for the number of nails he sells, Laura. This job is just something he needs to do, like that fella from *American Beauty*, you know, where he leaves the stressful job behind and goes flipping burgers – I'm sure it's just a phase," Jennifer said with a brightness she didn't feel.

All of them murmured sympathetic noises; Jennifer knew she'd soon be the talk of the town.

After the meeting, feeling vulnerable, but relieved that Dan's redundancy was out in the open, Jennifer pulled up in front of her house, wrestled Adam out of the car seat and nearly collided into Dan who was standing at the door with a look between excitement and agitation on his face.

"Come on, we're going out," he said briskly as Adam was transferred into Rebecca's arms.

"What . . . where are we going?" she asked as he steered her to his car.

Five minutes later Dan pulled up in front of the local hotel.

"Are you taking me for lunch?"

"No more questions, you always ask far too many questions," he told her wearily as he unloaded a bag from the boot and marched her through the front entrance and up to the reception desk.

"Dan O'Malley, I confirmed the junior suite earlier this morning."

"Of course, Mr O'Malley, down the hall, turn left and it's on the third floor."

Firmly he grabbed Jennifer by the hand, pulled her past the luxurious patterned carpets, the heavy gilt mirrors and mock portraits of the gentry, pushed her into the lift and brought her to the suite door, keeping an eye on her as he swiped the card in the lock, in case she bolted like a frightened rabbit.

"Dan, what the . . . this is ridiculous, this is our hometown hotel, what are we doing here?"

"I told you, no more questions." He threw the bag on the floor, flopped down on a chair beside the bed, put a hand under his chin and stared. "Now take off all your clothes," he said briskly like some kind of health professional expecting complete compliance.

"What? Get out of here. Are you mad? I'm not taking anything off!" she laughed.

"Take off all your clothes!"

"What about Abby, who's picking her up from play-school? And Emma has a crafts project she needs to have done for school tomorrow – I told her I'd help her with it."

"Rebecca is looking after them – it's all arranged."

"This is daft, Dan, I'm going home," she told him, feeling suddenly angry.

"Baby, you're not going anywhere – we're staying the night. I knew there'd be no point in booking somewhere two or three hours' drive away – one hotel is like the next when you're only there to fuck."

The panic was overwhelming. There was nowhere to run and nowhere to hide and no children to distract her with all their wails, and screams and sibling rivalry. A night away on your own, with the love of your life, isn't that what every married parent dreams of?

Feeling her throat might spasm for the first time since her nasty bronchitis, Jennifer bolted for the bathroom. "I'm taking a shower!" she called.

Leaving her clothes in a heap on the floor-tiles, she ran the water until it pounded in her ears. All of her being wished she could stay in that hot shower forever but she knew he would be in soon to claim her, rubbing her down with a towel like an owner would a big, panicky dog. In fact, determinedly he pulled her, towel and all, into the bedroom and she noticed that he'd pulled the drapes, opened his brown leather zipper bag and had placed things around the room: a tube of something, a burner and a tea-light, some other things thrown on a locker.

"Turn around – I want your back to me," he instructed as he led her near the bed.

"Dan, for God's sake, this is silly!"

"Turn around, look straight ahead. Do you trust me?"

"What? Of course I trust you," she tried to say to him over her shoulder but he gently turned her back.

"We'll soon find out," he said as he placed his hands gently on her shoulders.

Out of the corner of her eye she saw the soft, black material and then it was in front of her eyes, blacking out all her vision. She could feel the ends being tied fast from behind and his fingers adjusting the cloth around the bridge of her nose. His jeans hit the floor with a thud and she felt him lift her towel and push against her with an erection that was straining against silky boxers.

"Dan?" Her voice was husky, excited and a little bit fearful as the towel fell around her feet.

"Put your arms up," he commanded.

This time she didn't even bother to ask why but did as she was instructed. Soft material brushed her fingertips then fell lightly past her forearms, tickling her shoulders and falling sheer to the tops of her thighs. Swaying slightly she felt the silky material swish and she placed a hand to the blindfold to take a peek, but Dan pulled her fingers away.

"What colour is it?" she asked curiously as she felt the garment's lightness once more.

"Any colour you like," he said as he led her to the bed by the hand and helped her lie down on her back with her head resting on the pillows.

Cautiously, he brushed his lips to hers and she felt his breath. Her throat was dry and she licked her lips but instead of kissing her he took his hot breath to her ear and whispered seductively.

"Jenny, always trying to get away from me with something that needs to be done or someone who needs looking after, but not this time, this time you're all mine, and I'm going to enjoy every single bit of you!"

Slowly he pulled her arms back over her head and then she felt the soft silk scarves around her wrists, felt the delicious stretch and tension as he looped the scarf ends around the headboard, until she was like a spider caught in her own web – waiting. She heard him strike a match, smelt the pungent smell of sulphur, heard the tinkle of a tea-light on pottery and then there was the tickle of Sandalwood, it's woody, seductive character hitting her nostrils with a jolt, a smell imbued with memories of their courting days, a smell she'd never forget.

"Dan?"

A sharp popping noise puzzled her, and she heard him curse.

"Damn thing exploded on me," he yelped and her mouth twitched into a smile.

He took her feet in his lap as a delicate, exotic scent curled around her. It was the rose and bergamot body cream he'd bought her for Christmas and which she'd never used – until now, as he rubbed her toes, heels and shins, a little too briskly, the rubbing of skin making a soothing noise, like the sound of the sea. Then his hands, warm from touching, explored upwards, past her knees up towards her thighs and the bits of her that she would normally try to hide: her stretch-marks, her sagging bits, her cellulite and crinkled fat.

Lifting the soft floaty material on her abdomen, he was soon massaging her breasts, rubbing her nipples until they stood rigid, rubbing her shoulders and outstretched arms. Then, he took her feet in his lap once more and she heard an opening squeak and smelt the sharp acrid smell of nail polish as he painted her toes slowly and blew on them too loudly, with a child's awkwardness.

"*Now*, you look beautiful, *now* you are good enough to eat," he said admiringly and she tensed her arms as he began to prey upon her, starting with her lovely, painted toes. First, he sucked her big toe – it was not something he ever did, it would have made her laugh out loud if he'd tried – but he sucked one toe and then the other and a surprising thrill of pleasure chased to the back of her knees, causing her to gasp. Slowly and lightly his tongue flicked its way all the way to her inner thighs, licking to the edges of her pubic hair until she tilted her hips and strained on the velvet scarves with desire.

"Oh God – Dan!"

Stopping, he moved slightly and anxiously she waited. His satin boxers felt so delicious, their softness a whispery breath around her delicate folds of skin. Quickly, his hips lifted and she felt him pull his underwear past his knees, wiggling until he was free to kick them off onto the floor.

Every movement was a surprise to her as he cupped her breasts roughly, then held them gently. His scent was gorgeous as he moved his tongue between her lips and his hand between her legs. Teasingly he moved the tip of his erection around the edge of her soft inner folds, keeping her tense with anticipation and stoking her desire.

"Do you want me, baby?" he whispered in her ear.

"Yes," she answered hoarsely as he plunged inside.

Her hands wanted to hold his head as she kissed him, to caress his soft hair, but they were locked fast, and frustrated she put all her energy into pushing up towards him, matching his every urgent movement for minutes on end until suddenly his chest hair prickled against her breasts as he stretched above her hands to release the scarves.

"I want to see you," she said, as her hands were free at last to hug him.

"No, not yet." He was dragging pillows down the bed – she could feel their soft forms pile up in the middle of the bed. He pushed her down on the pillows on her stomach, then locked in her arms with his arms, locked in her legs with his and she enjoyed the masculine strength of him all around her as he moved fast and spasmed inside her while she stifled a scream in a pillow. Spent, they lay side by side. Outside it was raining, she could hear the fast drum on the concrete outside – it was as the weatherman had predicted – goodbye to the sandals and fake tan for another few days at least.

Ravenous, Jennifer awoke hours later to the noise of a tapping on the door and felt Dan putting something heavy and rigid on the duvet. Ordering her to keep the blindfold on still, he sat on the bed and she heard the grate of metal on metal and it was then Jennifer could feel the warm, seductive smells of a meal tickling her nostrils.

Piece by piece, Dan cut up her meal and fed it to her: onion gravy, buttery potatoes whipped soft as cream, carrots and turnips, their texture harder and seasoned with pepper and salt, and steak, tender, tasty meat made mouth-watering with a dressing of sharp French mustard then softened with butter and cream.

"Steak!" she laughed as she felt the soft bits of meat on her tongue.

"Steak's okay?" he queried.

"Why, steak's lovely – everyone knows steak's the best."

He held a glass of red wine to her lips to sip. She

could smell the traces of blackcurrant, mint and chocolate hitting her nose and meandering to her brain.

Together they shared the meal, she enjoying every morsel fed to her slowly, Dan feeding himself in between her bites. Chocolate cake was next. Dan's fingers fed morsels of dry crumb and cold chocolate icing into her mouth, sometimes combined with a spoonful of fat cream or a trickle of tangy raspberry coulis and every so often she'd take a sip of wine and hold the chocolate and alcohol in her mouth for a moment before they melted to nothingness on her tongue. Every little morsel of food gave acute pleasure and suddenly Jennifer began to sob.

Concerned, Dan's hands went up to release the blindfold but she brushed his fingers away. "Don't take it off," she begged. How could she tell him that now she was blind all she could see was him, not men from her past or fantasy men from her mind, but just him, the Dan that made her heart race, the romantic Dan, the Dan of old, the Dan who was everything.

Once before he had fed her little morsels of food at the Taste of Chicago Festival where they'd wandered down stalls in the park beside the great lake in summertime and filled up little plastic tubs with exotic bits of things from all around the world before taking shelter against the showers of afternoon rain. Then Kentucky came to mind, their love holiday, lying on her back, her eyes shut tight against the blinding sun, her fingers pressed to her eyelids to further blacken the light and those daisies that Dan trailed up her bare sun-tanned legs to the edge of her shorts, to her taut stomach, past the valley of her breasts, up the line of her throat, down one cheek and behind her ear. In the soft green grass outside Mammoth Cave, Kentucky, shielding her eyes from the sun, a Ferris wheel turned in her stomach when he first whispered, "I love you, Jen."

"What are you thinking?" he asked carefully, cradling her head.

"The Taste of Chicago . . . Kentucky . . . do you remember Kentucky, Dan?"

"Kentucky . . . holed up in that rundown motel . . . the boat trip up the Green River . . . you terrified of snakes . . . yeah, I remember Kentucky, Jen . . . I knew everything there was to know about that Jen in Kentucky, the Jen who trusted me with her life."

"I trust you now," she said, ripping the blindfold away decisively.

"Do you?" he asked, his earnest eyes staring back hard.

Unconsciously her hands cupped together and rested in the soft satin of her lap. It was raspberry pink, this floaty baby-doll camisole she was wearing. Crushed raspberry pink with embroidery all around the top and dark pink and green rosebuds all along the edges, not overtly sexy, but exquisitely pretty and it fitted her to perfection. Her eyes asked him the question and he answered wearily.

"I knew Sandra would know your size and would have something nice. I got it from her and all the rest," he said, gesturing at the velvety arm restraints.

"But you would never bring yourself to ring Sandra. You can't stand Sandra!"

"I'd do anything for the one I love."

And at that moment she was certain that he had come across her trail of embarrassingly secret desires on her computer and at that moment she knew she had probably left the evidence there deliberately for him to find and never speak about.

Kissing the top of her head, he went to take a shower, and started that insanely optimistic whistling again, the whistling that had become such a part of their lives in recent weeks. Curled up on the duvet with her legs under her tailor-style, Jennifer caught sight of her toes for the first time, painted a vibrant ruby red. One of the big toes was painted crudely and both little toes were smudged with paint around the cuticles and outer skin. Dan had tried hard to get the paint-job right – he had tried lovingly but despite his best efforts he had messed up quite a bit.

Turning her head, she noticed for the first time that Dan had had fresh daisies sent to the room, the big kind, the expensive kind. Sighing, she thought of the first days of their love when they'd been happy with a rundown motel and didn't need a junior suite, when the daisies that had brought her pleasure were natural and free. It seemed the more two people stayed together the more effort had to be made to keep a relationship viable, the more money had to be spent to keep things fresh, interesting and alive.

Confused, Jennifer sat up on the pillows for a full ten minutes, pondering her badly painted toes, before sighing and collapsing wearily into her luxuriously crisp hotel sheets and switching on the TV.

Thirty-five

"Down the corridor, to the left, you can help her with her tea – Rosemary doesn't eat much, but try and get something into her if you can. She's a bit confused, but nothing that will faze you. Good luck!"

Rebecca nodded to the nurse, passed the day room where a few old souls in dressing gowns and slippers were huddled around a blaring TV that none of them were watching. Mostly they were all just staring straight ahead with eyes dead to the world and nodding heads full of memories.

The white-painted wooden door to the room was open. In the corner a small television mounted high on brackets was flashing out silent images and a vase of wilted flowers near the window needed changing. The old lady lay elevated on her hospital bed, her violet eyes a surprise oasis of life in her worn-out face.

Rebecca noted that Rosemary had make-up on but her brown pencil eyebrows were drawn badly, no doubt by a frazzled nurse or a pressed-for-time care assistant who couldn't see how perfect eyebrows would matter that much to someone at the end of their days. But it mattered. Dignity – isn't that what Betty had said to her that day she had worked on the ward and suggested Marjorie should maybe wear a pad instead of pestering the nurses to take her to the toilet for the non-existent wee-wee? Dignity, it made sense now as Rebecca realised the careless make-up bothered her more than she would have thought possible.

"And how are you today?" Rebecca asked pleasantly as she busied herself about the bed. The plate of white bread and pats of jam and butter and strawberry yogurt were undisturbed. "Will you eat a small bit of something, Rosemary – the nurses all think you should?" she pressed, buttering the bread and pulling back the silver foil on the jam, allowing the lid to flop back to one side.

"Can't face it, nurse, no appetite – just a drink, please, nurse – a drink of water." Rosemary's gnarled hand shook as she pointed towards the glass carafe on the metal tray near her bed.

"You're new here, aren't you, nurse?" she asked after she had wetted her lips. "Beautiful hair, you've beautiful hair, you don't see too many redheads these days. Puts me in mind of . . . Rita Hayworth . . . have you ever been told that you're her double?"

Smiling, Rebecca shook her head and smeared the bread with jam, feeling compelled to at least try and get food into the frail body. Rosemary looked like she might melt into the very sheets of the bed and disappear at any moment.

"I married a redhead myself. People think redheaded

men aren't so good-looking, but my husband is very handsome – dark red hair, you see, not the colour of carrots, never liked carrot-tops myself – he always had skin like an Arab, no pasty face or freckles . . . beautiful skin, my Jimmy."

"Mum, it's me, Rebecca – don't you remember? Rebecca your daughter?" she asked suddenly, not giving a damn about the bread or jam, just needing some recognition of her blood.

The little old lady laughed and her eyes crinkled into a million little wrinkles. "*Rebecca*? Sure my Rebecca is only a child!"

"No, Mum, I'm not. I'm all grown up now, I'm married – don't you remember?"

"Ah, you can't catch me out there. I never went to my Rebecca's wedding and I would have if she was married. I'd have made her dress too – I'm a dressmaker, see?" Rosemary's lips flickered into a smile again and she waved a frail finger triumphantly to prove her point. Gulping hard, Rebecca tried to hold back the tears. It was true, her mother wasn't well enough to be at her wedding; even then she was confused and needed minding. What a wedding! No mother, no sister, a brother not willing to pay the plane fare home for her big day and a father cut off for his brutal selfishness. Worst of all perhaps, no hand-made dress, no one-off piece made by her gifted mother to treasure, to take out of a box every so many years, to remember the love put in with every stitch.

"Ah there, pet, don't cry!"

Rosemary reached out to pat her on the head and Rebecca thought she would give the earth to snuggle into the bed with her and be remembered, feel the warmth of her like when she was a little child, maybe sick, or being bullied at school, or just needing a hug.

"Is he a nice fella this man you're married to, then? Does he know how lucky he is to have a lovely girl like you, a lovely girl like Rita Hayworth?"

Despite her sadness, Rebecca laughed. "We're probably headed for the divorce courts actually. Not an easy thing, marriage, Rosemary – men aren't that easy to live with, are they?"

"Turn up the TV, would you, nurse? I don't like the pictures on like that without sound – turn it up, please. What was that you said?"

"That men aren't easy to live with – not worth the trouble."

"Husbands are . . . I can't think . . . sometimes the words just go . . . my husband now, he's younger than me, much younger," Rosemary said, dropping her voice to a whisper.

"I know, eight years younger," Rebecca nodded wearily.

"That's right, nurse, eight years exactly." Rosemary perked up, looking somewhat amazed that this redheaded fortune-teller seemed to know details from her life. "Lucky to have him, I am too . . . lovely man, my Jimmy . . . works on the buses . . . very friendly, everybody says so."

"Mum, Dad hasn't worked on the buses for years. He's in Spain, don't you remember?"

Another incredulous little look followed and then there was a polite knock on the door and a tall, stylishly turned-out, well-built old lady with a large head and a hooked nose stood in the doorframe.

"How's it going then?" the woman asked quietly, her bright eyes sparkling behind rounded spectacles, her bright pink nails pulling a well-cut tailored jacket over a fitted skirt.

Rebecca got up from the bed and crossed the room, shrugging her shoulders as she stood in front of her mother's younger sister, Aunt Birdie. Standing beside her, she thought again how her aunt's name was somewhat ridiculous. Birdie: it conjured up images of delicate little robins or starlings but Aunt Birdie was more like an immaculately turned-out ostrich, a vulture even, but a gentle one of course.

"She doesn't know me, Birdie – doesn't even seem to remember anything about Dad, thinks he's a lovely man who still works on the buses."

"Ach, love, don't take it too hard – there's good days and there's bad days – sometimes she's very confused and other days you'd think she was right as rain, right enough to take home."

"Nurse, the thing for turning it up – I like this programme!" Rosemary called out.

It was a wildlife programme about gorillas of all things. Rebecca never thought her mother would be one for nature programmes but, as Birdie had already said, she wasn't really her mother.

"Let's leave her for a bit – come and have a chat – tell me how you are," Birdie coaxed, pulling Rebecca by the arm for a stroll down the dreary corridor where large gold-framed pictures of dogs and Victorian children hung from the walls.

Reluctantly Rebecca followed, looking behind her as she left. All day she'd been travelling to get here, first on the train from Bannestown to Dublin then straight to Belfast from Connolly Station and lastly getting a taxi to meet Birdie at the nursing home. And for what? For nothing?

"How are you, how is Jennifer?" Birdie asked soothingly as they sat on green mock-leather chairs with chunky armrests at the end of the corridor, beside a half-dead potted geranium plant and an old-fashioned wrought-iron radiator. The paint had peeled off and the radiator was re-painted a zillion times so that little chips were showing through here and there, green paint on top of white and black on top of green all nicked away in pieces, like the time itself, like all the years gone by.

"What's there to tell? I've been a nanny to Jennifer's children the last while, the way you were the nanny to all of us those years we lived up North before the move South. All those bowls of popcorn you'd make for us when we came home from school and Mum needed us out from under her feet, if she was getting dinner ready or had someone in for a fitting and Milo your cat hogging the fire and chasing my ball of wool for the doll's scarf I was knitting – he's not still around, I suppose?"

"No, it's Milo Number Three now – I like a cat around the place – some people say they're not friendly, just selfish buggers only interested in their comforts, but I like them all the same . . . but what about you, Rebecca, what about that fine man you married and that grand house you built? Always sorry I didn't get to your wedding, couldn't manage it of course, not with your mother the way she was."

"Dementia – it isn't fair, is it?" Rebecca said, her voice quietly breaking.

"No, pet, it isn't, and it's nobody's fault," Birdie sighed, watching an old woman dawdle down the corridor in her dressing gown and slippers, her Zimmer-frame acting as a second strength to her spine.

Birdie's eyes followed the slow shuffling steps. Perhaps she was wondering when her own time would come to be dressed in slippers and gown in the middle of the day, but Birdie was still agile of body and brain for a woman of her years and deliberately did mad things to keep her mind intact, like line-dancing, playing the bongos at her weekly drumming workshop for old-timers and surfing the web with students at the drop-in community-support centre. Not for Birdie old-time dancing or endless cups of tea, knitting and jigsaws. Birdie was, as she'd always been, young at heart, young enough to keep abreast of the young people themselves even if it meant she was a slave to fashion, and the latest incomprehensible mobile phone.

"We were useless daughters, weren't we, me and Jen? Not around for her when she needed us."

"You were at opposite ends of the country with your own lives to lead. Every mother understands that her children grow up and have their own responsibilities. Besides, I didn't mind her coming to live with me when Jimmy was gone and you and Jennifer grown. It was company, far better company than poor old Milo, and it didn't dawn on me to mind when she first got confused but it was too much in the end, she could have wandered off on her own, take a bus to somewhere she'd never been, walked under a bus even. I didn't want to see her put here any more than I expect you do yourself, but there was no other way, not if we were to keep her well, not if we were to keep her safe."

Safe – Rebecca hated that word, to her *safe* meant dying or already half-dead and she'd played safe herself in many ways. Safe was conforming, safe was being the respectable wife with the beautiful home. Safe was not driving too fast, pole-dancing or wooing good-looking toy boys with return tickets to Australia, but safe or reckless it was all useless in the end, death would find her anyway, death would rob her of her looks and maybe even erase her memory too just like her mother.

"I work with people like Mum, old people in the hospital near to where Jen lives – did I tell you?"

"Do you, dear? Didn't think that would be your kind of thing," Birdie said cheerfully.

"I thought I just drifted into it, the work, but I wonder now if it was for a reason, so that I could feel close to her, feel ready to see her again . . . Rosemary. And maybe to punish myself, remind myself that I wasn't born with a silver spoon in my mouth. I never really felt comfortable with lots of nice things, not when Dad left us struggling when he took off with that slapper barmaid to Spain, leaving us to figure things out by ourselves, Mum doing alterations and making dresses for people till she was nearly going blind, struggling to help Jennifer through college. It's an awful thing to say, Birdie – I love Mum, always did – but when she wasn't well enough to come to my wedding I was kind of relieved. I didn't want the people I married into to know that we came from a small council-built house, to know that I came from a broken home at a time when everyone I knew had parents who were still married."

"Rebecca Murphy, you're as good as any and better than most and, as my mother used to say, God rest her, all the landed gentry there was in this country got out long ago and all those left behind who act above everyone else aren't more than a generation or two removed from the bog!"

Rebecca started to laugh as a nurse walked past, pushing a wheelchair.

"What's so funny?" Birdie queried, fiddling with the ring-tone of her mobile.

"Just thinking of my mother-in-law – she has a fondness for the bog herself – seven toilets she has in her gaudy palace and she never thought me worthy of her precious son, nor ever will. I must remember my auntie's advice that I'm good as any and better than most. I'll remember it every time I use the bog in my mother-in-law's home from now on!"

"So does that mean you might be willing to give things another go with your husband?" Birdie asked quietly.

"I don't know. Marriage is hard. I see it with my sister and I don't know if she's doing any better than myself."

"How is she then? I wish I could drive and see how she's doing for myself."

"She's coping, but I don't know how she's coping with this. She never talks about Mum. I couldn't even tell her I was coming here today, it would upset her too much and she has a lot to upset her already. Dan is throwing her some challenges these days – he lost his job and he's more worried about finding himself than finding a new one."

"Well, I wouldn't know about marriage, never having been married myself but I do know when you kids spent a few hours with me, sometimes it was just to give your mum and dad a break. It's easier without kids around – kids put pressure on a relationship, even the good ones."

Children was all Rosemary had ever wanted though

and she'd delayed her life while looking after her own widowed father, while Birdie was off studying to be a primary teacher and later working, going to dances. Rosemary thought it proper that her younger sister have more fun. Like many older siblings pushed into the role of surrogate mother and surrogate wife, she put her own pleasure last. Until Rosemary's father died when she was thirty-six and she began to go to dances herself, began to look after herself, began to look for a man who'd be a father to her future family and Jimmy Murphy, a smooth-talking philanderer, caught her eye or maybe he caught hers and saw the want in them.

Rosemary was an easy catch and a lucrative one as her father had left a sizable amount of cash in his will. For the times, Rebecca's mother was old starting a family, but she had her longed-for babies and maybe they were the cause of the breakdown of the marriage over time – maybe Rosemary had loved them, all her children, too much and had neglected the needs of her husband. Jimmy was a man who was never going to be comfortable in a marriage anyway, not when he always had an eye for a good-looking woman of independent means. Thinking of her own difficult relationship with Mark, Rebecca knew the last thing it could take was any kind of added pressure, the last thing it needed was kids. Why couldn't he see that as clearly as she?

"Will we go?" asked Birdie. "The nurses will settle her down for the night and there's always tomorrow – we can come back tomorrow."

Rebecca nodded and Birdie waited while she went in to say goodbye and kissed her mother on her papery cheek while Rosemary's eyes remained locked on the TV screen ahead, seeing without seeing, hibernating in her broken memories.

"Leave the dishes, I'll do them later," Rosemary said matter-of-factly as Rebecca tidied the small white plate, bowl and cup into a pile away from her mother's elbows.

"The dishes?"

"If you want put them in the scullery, but you go do something nice . . . go dancing . . . a girl like you should be off enjoying herself." Rosemary smiled, putting her hand on Rebecca's arm and Rebecca was shaken, shaken that her mum still thought they lived in a poky pebble-dashed house with tiny rooms and an outside yard, a house where her mother's tendency to collect garden gnomes and dwarf angels and figures of animals was a passionate hobby but a constant source of embarrassment to her socially ambitious daughter.

"The house is gone, Mum – it was sold, don't you remember?"

"Is it, oh, what harm! I could have always done with a bigger kitchen anyway." Rosemary sighed happily as she continued to watch the television, her neck craning to see the screen as it flashed at her from its elevated angle.

"I have a house – a fine big house, five bedrooms, everything nice. You'd like it, I wish you could see it . . . see how well I've done," Rebecca faltered.

"Big houses aren't so great – more to clean," Rosemary said drily, looking straight ahead, her eyes never off the TV screen.

Back in the corridor Birdie was answering a text message when Rebecca re-emerged. It had been a long day, a day that had drained her of all her energy.

"The same one since you rang me last?" Rebecca smiled wearily, gesturing at Birdie's hand-held gadget.

"Aye, it's just difficult to figure out the half of it, but the young ones down the drop-in centre who help me with the Internet are always doing their best for me with it. Wish I had my first ever phone back. It was heavy with big chunky buttons but it was good. When you're my age, sometimes the easiest things to remember are the things from your past."

"One second, Birdie – I can't go away yet. I know it's stupid and nobody will notice but I have to fix her eyebrows. The mother I know would be appalled if she thought she was meeting the world with shaky pencil eyebrows. If there's one thing Mum always loved it was her war paint – I just need to draw her eyebrows on right, it won't take but a moment."

"You're tired – come away home with me – there's always tomorrow."

"I'll just be a minute. Besides, there's something I want to ask her. Just one minute – I promise that's all I'll be."

Rebecca hurried back into the room and went searching in the bedside locker. It made her draw a breath to think that these bits and pieces were her mother's life now: a hairbrush, some nylons, a spare nightdress, some rosary beads, a black and white photo of the three of them, her, Jennifer and Lee on a sunny summer afternoon in the back garden in dresses and shorts that Rosemary had made herself and a little plastic zipper bag of make-up, smudged with greasy fingertips on the outside. Inside was a lipstick and an eyebrow pencil, some pads and a cleanser.

"What's that you're doing, nurse?" Rosemary asked, smiling away and for a moment Rebecca saw a glimpse of the mother from her past that made her heart ache.

"Just your make-up, I want to fix it."

"Oh, the other nurse did it earlier on – my daughter Rebecca is coming to see me, you see – she's just a little girl."

It was a gentle little remark that stuck in her heart like a splinter but Rebecca brushed away all emotion and switched mode, became the professional people-pleaser she'd always been, put on the pleasant face of air stewardess, beautician or care assistant, became the patient helper who never gets annoyed or talks in loud tones, the helper who is always there to soothe troubled nerves.

"Is she, that's lovely? We must have you looking lovely for her then and your eyebrows aren't quite right – don't worry, it won't take a sec," Rebecca soothed her as she cleansed away the charcoal marks and painted the semi-circles afresh.

Afterwards, she brushed her mother's grey-white hair, as soft as sable. "Do you remember everything about your little girl and all your little children?"

Rosemary's eyes widened at the strangeness of the question. "Well, of course I do . . . I remember everything!"

"Then perhaps you can answer me one question?"

Rosemary smiled and nodded and Rebecca whispered in her ear.

Thirty-six

"Now I have here all the names of who's sharing with who for our Wild Mammy Weekend away in Galway!" Vicki announced, peering at a computer printout in one fist and holding a mug of stone-cold coffee in the other. A huge mound of clothes was dumped at the top of the large, brightly painted double room – it was all part of a cheap and cheerful clothes swap the mums and tots were having, a sort of combined spring-cleaning session and morale booster for group members.

"Okay, let's see, the hotel," Vicki prattled on. "I'm sharing with Sadie – Jen, you're bunking in with Laura, Helen's staying for one night on account of the rugby match on Sunday and she's sharing with . . ."

Jennifer was in a dream and in the dream she went to Galway but did none of the above. In her dream she went salsa dancing for the weekend with a man who definitely wasn't her husband, a man she'd been trying to put out of her mind ever since her real husband had made a monumental effort to woo her with a mixture of nostalgia, eroticism and just the right amount of sexual athleticism. Musing over her strange sex life where she imagined a lot but mostly did very little, Jennifer barely heard her name being called until it was called repeatedly.

"This top, Jen, what do you think?" Vicki asked over the din as she held a bright red summer cotton top aloft. "Helen says it would look good on you, do you want it?"

"Nah, it's not my colour – it would suit Sadie's colouring more – and it's a good shape for a pear."

"Wow, this is great fun, reminds me of being in my twenties and sharing clothes with friends and flatmates before taking off for the night," Betty laughed as she grabbed a bracelet that caught her eye.

Meanwhile, Fiona the Pram was eyeing up a skirt, a big change from her usual trackies.

"That skirt would be perfect for a column like yourself," Jennifer said dreamily.

"Do you think?" and the human bouncing ball swiped the garment into her hands greedily.

"Yeah, run out to the loos and try it on if you want, we'll keep an eye on the baby," Vicki suggested.

"Hey, Jen, you're good at this," laughed Laura as Jennifer urged her to try on a figure-hugging patterned dress. "Pity I don't own a decent pair of heels to go with the glam rags, though."

"Oh, you want shoes? We got shoes. Betty, bring on the shoes!" Vicki yelled and Betty dumped a pile on the floor from a black refuse sack and there was much strutting up and down as mums and toddlers vied for the highest and coolest pair of footwear.

"This is hilarious," giggled a newly returned Fiona as she too had a go at a pair of high strappy sandals. "So what do you think? Do you think they look good on me with the skirt?"

"I don't know – I'd say you'd have to ask the expert," Vicki joked, pointing at Jennifer. "Well, Jen?" asked Fiona.

An expert? Jennifer had never thought of herself as a fashion expert before – if that was anyone's job it had always been Rebecca's. Of course for years she'd watched her mother run up a dress or put darts in a jacket for a neighbour. Sometimes Jennifer had even sewn a panel together herself or taken up a hem if Rosemary was under pressure – she'd felt obliged to help out as so much of the money earned went towards her science degree which never brought much joy in the real world of work. Jennifer felt guilty just thinking about it – her mother's tired eyes, sore fingers and stiff back – all the casualties of war in the battle to give her an education.

"The shoes, the shoes are lovely, Fiona, you should wear them on our trip away to Galway," Jennifer decreed and the whole room agreed.

The April sunshine gave the small city of Galway a dazzling, almost exotic feel. At times like this it was obvious why the city on the Atlantic coastline was called the Spanish city – its Latin character just sizzled to the surface along with the sunshine and the bonhomie of its citizens. Trading with Spain over the centuries, harbouring Spanish fishing fleets, had left its mark on the city's architecture, music and people.

Feeling vaguely reckless, Jennifer tossed her car keys

to the valet, an eager young man in his twenties, and allowed him to reverse her car into a spot so tight it would have given her a coronary. Surrendering the keys made her feel like a big shot who only had to snap her fingers for things to happen.

Being the last to arrive, she found everybody else already in their sparkle and bling, drinking at the bar, high heels crushing into the carpet, jewellery rattling and war paint threatening, all signals to any who cared to notice that a path of destruction would soon be beaten by mums on a mission. On the street, festivities began when a samba band, all heavy drums and whistles, had Helen whooping in delight and doing something that looked surprisingly like the Hakka – with Sadie, Vicki, Laura and Fiona the Pram joining in, jumping up and down to the rhythm and laughing like happy little kids.

In a steakhouse they ate like women who had never seen food before, *oohing* and *aahing* over every morsel because a break from cooking for even a night was a prize worth more than diamonds and at half past ten they spilled onto the city streets splitting into two groups, some searching out the scent of a trendy night club, some content to find a pub with outside seating so they could persevere in the myth that Galway really was exotic as they sipped cocktails, smoked social cigarettes and huddled underneath coats while seriously sexy young things sashayed by almost naked.

"Just got a text from Sadie," laughed Vicki, "saying her gang have lassoed men in a club up the street and are thinking of moving on to handcuffs and would we like to join them for fun and games?"

"Nothing is parting me from my vodka and lime right

now," said Betty matter-of-factly as she puffed on a fag and began to rip a beer mat apart with cold fingers and steady determination.

"Okay, let's head back to the hotel and get a few more into us before bedtime and shopping tomorrow," Vicki decided, getting up from her seat and smoothing down a crumpled new swap-shop skirt.

Back at the hotel Jennifer couldn't keep up with the pace and left the hotel lovelies drinking in their snug red-velvet couches with soft orange glowing lights making them appear as girlish as they felt.

Unable to sleep, Jennifer found herself lying motionless, her eyes wide and dry, listening to doors opening and shutting and drunks careening down the corridor roaring, cursing and screaming friendly abuse. Close to three she awoke, feeling sure she'd only recently dozed off, to witness a tipsy Laura fall over her suitcase and curse loudly. Within minutes Laura had stripped to her knickers and bra and collapsed into bed, and with plenty of drink on her she snored like an electric saw for hours – every now and then, just for a bit of variety, doing a great impression of a petrol lawnmower. After a few hours of snores worse than oil-drilling, her breathing softened to snorts but then a fly warmed by the first rays of light began to whine close to Jennifer's face, landing on her nose or toes, keeping up its incessant racket until, totally exhausted, she got up and showered. By the time she got back, Laura had rolled out of bed for breakfast and Jennifer slipped on a long powder-blue linen skirt with flared panels, a white linen bustier and low heels and hurried down to meet her friends.

"Great night we had last night," an unbelievably

refreshed Laura held court in the dining room as a grouchy Jennifer tried to wake up by consuming as much coffee and sugary fare as possible. "How old do you think that fella was that I was slow-dancing with last night, Sadie?"

"Just about legal," snorted Helen, buttering a croissant.

"So, are you coming shopping, Jen," Betty asked, placing her hand on the top of a silver teapot to pour out a brew thick as Texas oil.

"Been doing a lot of shopping and swapping lately, Betty, might give it a miss . . . have half a notion to drive out towards the coast and get some fresh sea air – clear the cobwebs for the day."

"Meet us for coffee later before I head back home this afternoon?" Helen asked as she guillotined a sausage and bloodied it some more with tomato ketchup.

"Sure maybe I will," but in her heart Jennifer knew her girlie weekend was over. Upstairs her suitcase, which she'd hardly unpacked, was ready to be fired into the boot of her car. Smiling brightly as the sugar and caffeine kicked in and woke her up, Jennifer ate a hearty breakfast like a condemned woman who knew exactly what she was condemning herself to and couldn't wait to get started.

Jennifer always thought the idea of driving aimlessly and just seeing where you would end up was complete rubbish. Everyone, if pressed, could tell you exactly where they were going, could tell you which way their brain was thinking at any moment, however illogical. It was that way with her when she decided to drive her car out towards the coast. Her fuzzy woolly-headed self might have pleaded that her brain was dull from lack of sleep or that the Saharan heat of the day, promised by the Met Office and surprisingly present by eleven o'clock, was causing out-of-character behaviour, but she knew the truth. She knew exactly what she was doing when she parked her car outside the main hotel in the little fishing village, walked around for an hour, tried to talk herself out of staying, then heard the music seducing from within and decided to take just one quick little peek.

Willingly entranced, she pushed open the heavy oak doors of the ballroom and saw dancers move across the floor, amateurs as heavy as steamrollers, semi-professionals as light and wispy as bits of air. Here and there some male dancers were nervously trampling feet, sometimes their partners bearing the pain with laughs and sometimes with scowls and winces. Out of the corner of her eye she saw a sudden flash of blue colour and movement as Cassandra flitted about the room like a long-tailed butterfly making the most of a warm spring before summer is already a memory.

"Jennifer, what a surprise!" There was a little affected wave and a slightly too loud greeting and Cassandra excused herself from dancing with her partner and came to greet Jennifer like an old friend.

"I'm sorry, I didn't mean to distract you from your dancing," Jennifer apologised.

"Dancing? Is that what you thought it was? Darling, he was pulverising my poor feet – I was only looking for an excuse to get away! So, last-minute decision you coming here? Maybe I could organise for you to share a room with someone for the night?"

"No, friends of mine are staying in Galway city – I'm just dropping by so I could see –"

"What you're missing?" Cassandra finished, smiling knowingly, and Jennifer felt herself blush.

"I'm not here to dance, just to watch, I don't want some man whinging that *I'm* stepping on *his* feet!"

"Nonsense – if a man is a strong lead and the lady follows, no damage should ever befall either party. Now let's see, who here would make a good partner? Ah yes, Frank, from my Limerick class, a good solid dancer. Come with me." Cassandra clamped her arm like a vice.

"I'm from one of Cassandra's country classes," Jennifer explained, blushing when Cassandra led her to Frank like a mare being offered as a mounting possibility to a has-been donkey. Frank nodded shortly, his balding head glistening with sweat as he snared Jennifer with his huge hands and pulled her around the room, dancing to order, giving her nothing to complain about, but giving her no real pleasure either and nauseating her with the sweet skunk-like odour which escaped from his armpits down his short sleeves and wafted uninvited straight to her brain.

"Have you been dancing since last night and again this morning?" Jennifer asked, leaning towards politeness, and Frank just nodded again, not caring to speak a word. It was stupid to come, she berated herself, but she couldn't help herself either. This music lured her and it made her sad. This music might have been part of her life; she might have been living in South America right now, with her children speaking Spanish, sunshine in her life in every way imaginable – if things had been different.

The air felt thick and heavy, partly because of the day, partly because of the number of bodies dancing in close proximity. Jennifer heard a passing couple ask if the air-conditioning was working and saw the look of disbelief when they were told it was – someone had to faint soon.

It was that kind of day, that kind of environment

where nothing felt real but everything felt charged with possibility. Her feet ached as she passed the hours, dancing with men, or with women, afraid to stay and afraid to leave, scouring the floor and the door, looking for one face only, and in the early evening he walked in dressed in chinos and a white shirt rolled up at the sleeves and every woman noticed and pretended not to be moved by his presence – all except Cassandra.

Cassandra's strappy little dance shoes found their way to him in an instant and, taking her beautiful Irish American Latin by the arm, she paraded him to the centre of the room. They made a mesmerising couple as they whizzed around the floor. He was such a good dancer that Cassandra got to show off lovely little flourishes that were never worth while showing before a class. Eventually Cassandra flitted off, an overheated butterfly in search of some other nectar, and somehow Jennifer felt herself beside her Angel and willed herself to say something coherent and maybe even half-sensible. The floor was cleared as the dancers made way for some professional entertainment to watch Ivan and Lily, two lithe things in skintight costumes, snake around each other in positions that defied normal human flexibility.

"Hello, again, haven't seen you at classes in a while," Jennifer began tentatively, holding a glass of water as a prop, for if she had a free hand she might have done something reckless like seek to hold his just to see if that electricity she'd felt before was still present, still live and dangerous.

"I'm not taking classes. I just travel to Cassandra's sometimes if the mood takes me," he smiled and she got butterflies in her stomach from the inflexions in his voice.

I'm too old for all this nonsense, she thought, and far too married.

"You look different," he said, puzzled, studying her face intently.

"It's probably my hair, I got it layered – you should have seen it when I first came from the hairdresser's!" she ranted. "I looked a state – I've had it reshaped since then to look more normal."

"No, it's not your hair – it's something else – your nose!"

"Oh, my piercing? I guess I was inspired by that girl in New York in Andy's apartment, Bernice I think her name was . . . you know, I've only just realised I don't even know your name. I'm Jennifer by the way, but my friends call me Jen or Jenny."

"Angelo, my name is Angelo Devaney – I'm Andy's cousin," he smiled and his whole face lit up.

"You can't be . . ." she said, mesmerised and confused. Of course, now that she studied him, he looked like Andy, the same beautiful wavy hair, the relaxed manner, the gorgeous smile. "You can't be an Angelo," she laughed.

"Why not?"

His smile melted right through her as he stepped so close that she was enveloped by his warmth and she shook her head and laughed some more. He was right, why shouldn't her Bronx Angel be called Angelo? Just then Lily the dancer did a flip backwards into Ivan's waiting arms, signalling the end of their routine and the whole room clapped wildly.

Spontaneously Angelo extended his hand to lead her towards the dance floor and when he touched her it was still there, that spark, that spark that only happens a few times in a lifetime and for some never at all. As they danced in the stultifying heat, her throat to the tops of her breasts blushed pink, the panels in her long blue skirt opened like a flower and swirled around her thighs and she thought again that there are no accidents in life, no unexpected moments except the moments caused by people wanting change, people like herself.

"I'm hungry, fancy a late supper?" he whispered in her ear and with just a nod she walked off the floor, still holding his hand, still willing an accident of her making to happen.

They passed every restaurant and pub on the road as they walked and she was puzzled, until he led her to a white camper van parked near to the water's edge, with a little grey-metal table and a veranda waiting outside.

"Have you ever watched the sun go down over the Atlantic?" he asked as he pulled out a silver chair.

Her cynical self didn't even care that it was a cliché – she shook her head and ran her fingers through her hair in one shy movement.

"Well, I've been doing it for the last few days. Funny, I came here to forget but every night all I can think about is all I've left behind on the other side of that ocean."

"Why, what have you left behind?" she asked, a lump forming in her throat.

"Oh hey, I don't want to bore you – just memories. Two daughters who are growing up – without me. They've a new dad now who watches them eat cereal in the morning and who takes them to their games – their mom got married again last year – blended families." He shrugged his shoulders.

"I'm sure they still see you as their dad," she

stammered, watching his lovely face as it registered pain and sadness and something else, acceptance maybe.

"So here we are in the best restaurant in town – what will you have, señora?" he asked jocularly, deliberately changing the mood.

"Surprise me, I eat most things." Jennifer smiled back as she pulled her cardigan around her shoulders and settled back to watch the sun fall like an orange from its tree, careening into the cool ocean bowl below.

"Then I'll start you on some wine while you're waiting," he said, returning with chilled chardonnay and cheap glass goblets.

Her eyes ran up and down the metal step of the camper van a few times, hoping to catch a glimpse of him as he worked but she saw nothing, only hearing occasional muffled sounds that made little sense. A delicious aroma of olive oil and garlic began to waft out to her. Relaxing into the chair, Jennifer watched as young couples passed by in summer clothes, girls in strappy tops and flip-flops, sunglasses in their hair, girlie tattoos on their shoulders, joined hip to hip with their sandalled lovers as they walked, enjoying the spring sunshine as hot as any summer, some disappearing into the doorways of cosy pubs, others off for a stroll down by the sea. Smiling, she watched as a beautiful couple sauntered by, both smoking in the casual manner that young people do when problems are fleeting and the life you take for granted stretches on forever.

Her idle hands would have loved a cigarette at that moment as she remembered her own youth, herself and Sandra, no money in their bank accounts and no real worries. How was it that the happiest days were the days when the hole-in-the-wall machine spat out the plastic card with contempt, when the best parties were the ones you crashed, where the most admired pieces of clothes came from the charity shop, altered perhaps by herself or her mother? From inside the van she heard a sassy salsa music beat and Angelo reappeared with a large bowl of Greek salad in the palm of each hand.

"It's only very simple," he apologised as he placed cutlery and paper napkins on the table.

"Simple is good," she assured, watching him chase up the steps again to bring out slices of thick white bread, pan-fried in olive oil with garlic.

"Goes great with the salad," he said.

Jennifer revelled in the simplicity of her meal – salty lumps of goats' cheese melting in her mouth, cucumber pieces as fragrant as melon, juicy baby tomatoes and shrivelled black olives hulled of their stones softening the bite of raw red onion. All the while, as she ate daintily, she couldn't stop watching him, couldn't stop focussing on his dark eyes which were either full of merriment or far, far away.

It became a game to make him laugh and see his mouth crease into a gorgeous smile, see lightness in his eyes, see his hand shake with laughter as he held his glass of wine. Her eyes traced from his hands to his wrist, where a pale-blue rubber bracelet contrasted with the tan of his arms, to the throat of his shirt where underneath she knew he'd be tanned and toned and she realised what she'd known from the first moment he'd smiled and touched her hand to lead her in dance – she could fall in love with this man – in an instant.

A salsa song came through the doors which Jennifer recognised from Cassandra's class and she cringed in embarrassment then started to laugh out loud. "Oh God, there's a bit in this I can never get right – it's the twirl – I can never do it fast enough and I can never remember if it is one twirl or two."

Immediately, Angelo got up, reached out his hand and drew her to her feet. "The secret is it's as many twirls as you can fit in. You must trust the man who is leading to feel the position of your body in space – trust him to protect you from a fall and search for his eyes after each twirl and that's really all there is to it." He looked at her intently and she held his gaze. "Listen – wait for the beat, then follow," he whispered as he drew her close and she hardly dared breathe as he twirled her fast three times in all, as she held his eyes with trust, as she didn't stumble, as they said nothing for a moment but felt each other tense, felt each other's heartbeat.

"It's getting cold here, let's go inside," he coaxed after the music finished.

Taking her hand, he led her to a settee beside the window which doubled as a small night-time berth. But the space was very cramped and, with a slight hesitation, he led her past the compact kitchen into the back of his mobile home, where a blue and white cotton duvet was draped over a pullout double bed.

"Stay with me, I know you want to," he whispered as they stood there, and she closed her eyes and let the future fast forward in front of her.

There are moments like this, she told herself, moments that can never be rewound and there are no accidents only those which are chosen. Keeping her eyes shut, perhaps to pretend it was an accident, she felt him kiss her and her body tingled, the nervous anticipation of what he would do next making her skin super-sensitive to his touch. She felt his hands on her bare shoulders. Opening her eyes, she allowed him to unbutton her summer top, then un-zip her skirt, letting it slither to the floor. His evening beard scratched her face as she kissed his jaw and then he led her to the bed and she knelt on the mattress in gorgeous underwear and he squeezed her hand affectionately.

Immediately she froze, thinking of Dan, their little code, their way of speaking without words, this innocuous little hand-gesture reminding her of all the times her husband was her friend, her confidante, her lover. She tried to push the memories away but they would not go and she knelt there, oblivious to Angelo, oblivious to her surroundings, as she remembered. And she began to cry.

"Jennifer," he whispered. "Don't . . . don't cry."

"I'm sorry, Angelo, I'm such a fool, I've made a mistake," she said, wiping away her tears.

"I understand," he said, shrugging his shoulders sadly.

Stuck in a cramped space, with spotlights above the double bed and wooden cupboards at their heads, Jennifer felt ridiculous, but she wanted him to not think badly of her either.

"I'm sorry," she said again. "What I want . . . it's not about sex . . . it's not even about men, any man . . . I think it's just about being free . . . yes, I just want to feel free again . . ."

Sighing, Angelo sat on the bed beside her and patted her thigh. "I guess I just wanted to be with a woman again and not feel angry, maybe like you said feel free, free as a little kid naked on a beach."

"When do little kids lose that sense of freedom, do you think, become inhibited?" she sniffled.

"Five, six maybe – my girls are well past that – we all feel awkward round each other now," he said, his mind gone across the ocean again.

Looking at him, Jennifer felt compassion and tenderness.

"Stay with me anyhow, no sex, no strings attached, just lie beside me," he implored as he took her hand. "I just want to know that there's something or someone out there waiting for me, something good."

It was an improper request, but she didn't feel danger or guilt. Slipping beneath the duvet Jennifer lay back on the pillows, her body open as he came beside her and slipped an arm around her waist, smoothing her hair out of her face and eyes, resting his chin on her shoulder.

"Why did you come to Ireland?" she asked softly as he snuggled in close.

"My dad's people are from the west and southwest and when my marriage fell apart I needed somewhere new to think and the Atlantic Coast is a good place to paraglide, no people, just space and all the time in the world to be in it."

"I've seen paragliding – it's like you have a parachute but it's shaped like a wing to catch the wind?"

"Well, that's what I do, a few hours outside New York I teach people to paraglide as an instructor."

"But how do you do that, how do you have the nerve to hurtle downwards and fly?" she asked excitedly as she turned on her elbow to look down on his face.

"You have to jump to fly, Jenny, and once you fly jumping never holds the same fear," he smiled.

They slept like innocent children and in the morning he kissed her cheek and thanked her and Jennifer realised that being happy had nothing to do with Dan or any other man. She had to learn to fly all by herself and to do that all she had to do was work up the nerve to take a huge jump, to make a leap of faith.

Thirty-seven

"This isn't a good sign," sighed Helen when they opened the car door on the way to the match and Adele vomited for the third time in ten miles. "Young ones – why do they have to drink so much the night before a match? Me now – the night before a big game it's no drink, no sex and a spot of meditation before a good night's sleep."

Rebecca threw Helen a disbelieving look as Adele got down to dry retching and hobbled round the back of the car, hoping some fresh country air and the smell of good cow manure would aid in the revival of the flesh.

"Actually the no-sex, no-drink thing is just a speech to rally the baby-faced troops," Helen whispered conspiratorially. "Personally I find a bit of sex the night before can really get my blood up for the fight ahead the next day."

Rebecca really, really didn't want to know.

"I'm grand, Helen, sure there's nothing left now

431

anyway – let's head off again," the pale-faced Adele insisted five minutes later.

Rolling her eyes Helen started off again past the familiar fields of Carrigmore.

As her hometown came into view, Rebecca was a mass of nerves in case anyone recognised her, even though she was set to walk onto the pitch wearing her leather rugby hat and had practised directing her eyes to the ground on the slim chance that anyone from the local paper would show up and think a women's team worth photographing.

In minutes, she forgot the fear of discovery as adrenaline took over and she chased the ball down the pitch for almost an hour and a half and when the whistle blew they'd won, her team were victorious. Not that the victory had much to do with Rebecca. Bizarrely, despite her inexperience, Helen had stuck her on for almost an entire match and it had been tough – Rebecca noticed that for a friendly game the other team weren't that bloody friendly either. They'd been only warming up doing the line-outs, reaching for the ball, trying to get the possession when the code-talking and the slagging began. Half the time Rebecca had no idea what she was doing on the pitch anyway, but they'd won and Helen would be insane with delight.

Helen was furious as hell.

"Well, I hope you're proud of yourselves because you all played like little girls," Helen seethed.

For the first time Rebecca got to see the Antichrist persona up close and all the seasoned girls who really understood the game shifted their eyes around guiltily. A very abashed Adele was wearing a big hole in the grass with her boot. Some were listening to Helen while drinking water, others were lying down on the ground on their stomachs, pulling their head backs into a cat position, or doing leg stretches, trying to loosen up tense muscles and aching tendons.

"I don't understand – we won – why is everybody so pissed off?" Rebecca asked, puzzled.

"We just about won," glared Helen. "Jesus, did you see that winger they had? Moved like lightning, she did. Did you see how they played like they were all fronts, always on the attack – hungry, they were, they *wanted* it, not like ye lot who played like a load of old grannies!"

"Well, it's not like it's a match that mattered anyway. It was just a friendly," Rebecca shrugged as she pulled off her leather rugby hat and shook out her red plaited hair.

Helen looked at Rebecca like she had just suggested roasting children over spits or something far worse like posing for the unmentionable semi-naked rugby calendar.

"Let me tell you, Legs, the only thing that saved them was their inexperience and the only thing that saved us was we actually have people on our team who know how to score when they *finally* get the ball. But if we'd been up against a better team today we'd have been hammered. So yes, we won, but we didn't really deserve to win, they had far more heart! And, Legs . . . look at me now . . . every match matters, *even* the friendlies . . . every game has to be played with heart, or there's no point in even lacing up our boots," hissed Helen, clenching her fist to emphasise her point.

Adele flashed her brows and shook her head slowly as a warning to Rebecca to stop engaging the Antichrist on the post-match analysis.

Rubbing her aching inner thighs (some savage cow had danced all over them with her boots), Rebecca walked into the clubhouse as the other team clapped them off, with sincere cheers of well done and some hearty backslaps because when the battle was over it seemed these two teams, as Adele had originally told her, really did get on after all.

Carrigmore's clubhouse looked like a cattle-shed but was in every other way similar to Bannestown's home ground. The cement floor was smeared with mud from a score of boots and Rebecca followed the chatter and laughing, walking straight past the changing room and the basic cowshed showers. Never in her wildest dreams had Rebecca ever thought she would be scrubbing herself down in a cold draughty room with a plain, drippy showerhead, a cement floor and basic, cracked tiles under her feet and she had decided to forgo the shower for the moment until she'd eaten – her blood sugar was at an all-time low.

In the main hall, Rebecca walked right past the high vaulted wooden ceilings, the club shields and trophies, pictures of rugby teams and colourful flags. Then from behind she heard laughing and suddenly felt herself being lifted from underneath her armpits and then her bum by Declan and Helen and hung off one of the overhead beams, her feet dangling, her voice trying to sound cool but eventually escalating to an outraged whine of protest.

"Ah sure, we'll let her down now," her coach decreed after five minutes when the onlookers got bored with Rebecca's flailing about from the ceiling.

"Thanks a mill, Declan," Rebecca said sarcastically as her feet touched the worn wooden floor.

"Don't mention it! We suspend all the new recruits from the rafters after the first game," Declan laughed.

"You played well, Legs – even if as a team we played crap, you played well," and Helen, thumping her so hard on the back Rebecca could already feel the bruise ripening.

Everyone was ravenous and nobody gave a damn if every bit of food contained a million calories – they weren't those kind of girls. On a table spread out at the top of the hall was a feast fit for an army. The Carrigmore girls had laid on freshly made ham, salad and egg sandwiches all dripping with mayonnaise, silver pots of tea and coffee, buttery brown bread and vegetable soup with a mighty chilli kick in it to fire up the blood and half a ton of home-made scones with butter and jam.

As she stood by the serving table, Rebecca had already decided she was going to eat everything in sight – hang it, she was an athlete now and eating heartily was an unselfish act – her team mates were depending on her to do something vaguely sensible with the ball when she was let loose on the pitch.

"Rebecca?"

Hearing the familiar condescending nasal voice from behind, Rebecca paused just as she was about to take a big bite out of a calorie-laden egg-mayonnaise sandwich which was so slippery with butter and dressing the eggs nearly slid out of their opening onto her shirt.

"Rebecca, is that really you?"

Steeling herself Rebecca turned around and took in the smug countenance of Mark's sister Linda, standing beside her pubescent son Peter, who was looking as shifty as a car thief caught with a screwdriver in front of an undercover detective.

"Peter has taken up rugby, under fourteens, and I was picking him up from practice when I saw the ladies were playing. We caught the very end of the match. God, Rebecca, I would never have taken you for being such a physical girl! Rugby is a world away from Mulberry silk blouses!" Linda's mouth was twitching in triumph at having caught her sister-in-law looking muddy and sweaty and as unglamorous as any woman could possibly be. Even Rebecca's socks were crumpled around her ankles.

The blood rushed to Rebecca's cheeks and she knew she was blushing beetroot underneath all the grit and muck.

"Oh Linda, nice to see you too and you're right – rugby *is* a world away from Mulberry silk but it's great fun *and* brilliant exercise," Rebecca said snappily, pulling a sham confidence from deep inside her rugby boots as she gobbled down some slippery sandwich in one go.

"Well, I suppose it's cheaper than joining the gym," Linda continued snidely. "Membership in the hotels is sky-high – I doubt very much you could afford it."

"Oh gyms are so boring anyway, they just don't compare to fresh air and they're so solitary. Exercising with a team is much more exciting, but I guess for some boring people having fun is never a priority."

"Well, I'll tell Mark I saw you so and that you're, as you say yourself, *definitely* having fun – that is, of course, when he gets back from his trip abroad," Linda said cryptically.

Rebecca's head told her not to take the bait, but her internal 'wife itch' was activated and she just had to know the answer.

"Back from where?"

"Oh, haven't you heard, he's in Poland," Linda said gleefully. "He was on the phone to Dee only last night saying what a lovely country it is, how friendly the people are . . ."

Brushing a bit of muddy hair behind her ears, Rebecca tried to look indifferent as she shook her long red plait and shifted her weight about on her feet. "Oh Poland, yes, I think he mentioned something about that a while back."

"Did he? I understood it was all quite last minute, but obviously you know your husband *far* better than me. Come along, Peter, we're meeting Granny for lunch. I'm sure she'd love to hear how Auntie Rebecca now prefers mud-wrestling to going to the gym. Goodbye, Rebecca." Linda's face broke into a huge smile of genuine joy as she turned on her heel and took off as fast as her pseudo-designer wellies and jeans would allow.

In Linda's wake Rebecca burned – she could imagine her rugby-playing would be the day's entertainment for the bitchy Gleeson women – but what was far worse was Mark's apparent ability to cope without her. Poland, what the hell was he doing in Poland? There'd always been something there with that Polish cow – she knew she should have trusted her female instincts all along. No wonder he'd suggested a break, telling her to get everything out of her system – the bastard had just wanted a break himself – from her.

Scrubbing herself raw in the shower Rebecca let the tears flow with the water and felt her stomach contort. It might be her turn this time to tell Helen to pull over the car so she could throw up in the ditch. Mark had set her free to re-evaluate their relationship – it just never entered her head that he might be applying the same rules to himself.

In the car park Helen was having a chat with the other team captain, telling her Carrigmore would be a fearsome side when they got a bit more experience, when Fiona the Pram, who had come to watch the match with Sadie, excitedly thumped her on the back. Rebecca could see the shining obsession in Fiona's eyes and knew Helen had nailed a new recruit.

Not wanting to interrupt the gang of rabid mums, Rebecca loitered until her eyes were caught by an electric-blue modified Honda Civic in the corner, buffed and shined to perfection, 'For Sale' stickers printed on the smoked back and side windows.

"You interested in buying the car, it's for sale," a sexy young guy wearing a flipped-around baseball hat, casual blue denims and a well-ironed grey T-shirt asked warmly. His blue eyes were large for a guy, like aquamarine rock pools buried in his soft handsome face.

When he smiled a gorgeous smile Rebecca's imagination began to run away with her – this primal interest of hers in younger guys was getting ridiculous and probably would get her into trouble some day if she wasn't careful.

"Is it really for sale, or is it, you know, *for sale*," Rebecca emphasised, raising her eyebrows, letting him know that she knew 'for sale' was sometimes was a code for 'up for a race'.

He laughed uncomfortably and started to pull the peak of his hat over his eyes. "No, it really is for sale. I just got some new spots and all."

"Why are you selling?" she asked, walking over and tracing her finger along the chrome.

"Can't afford her no more. So are you interested?"

"Nice car, but I don't think so," Rebecca said, stroking the wing tenderly.

"If it's the price I can go lower." A little bit of desperation flickered in the rock-pool eyes.

"No, it's not the price – it's just I should probably go for something older, a bit more classic."

"Old will only cause you trouble, older cars are nothing but trouble," the sexy youth argued.

"You're probably right, but still that's the way my mind's heading," she said as she wished the young lad luck and headed towards Helen who was waving at her to get in the car.

"Not to turn your head or anything – I never usually praise more than once if at all – but just want to say that you're a born rugby player," Helen said as two miles down the road she pulled over to let Adele puke – this time the egg sandwiches weren't to her stomach's liking.

"Do you think?" Rebecca asked distractedly, her thoughts far away, Poland-far-away.

"Definitely, you're a natural – you played a great game, just to let you know."

Well, what kind of game would she play now? What kind of game was possible? Up to this Rebecca had thought *she* was playing the game and that Mark would just calmly hang around until she decided who'd won.

"You're still not so hot on the rules of course, but experience will fix that," Helen added as a shaky Adele steadied herself against the bonnet and cautiously gave the thumbs-up sign.

Helen had that sussed right. Rebecca was never so hot on rules and, contrary to Helen's belief, experience only seemed to make the rules less certain. On the way home with every newly built house she saw she thought of Mark, Mark the doer, buying his first property in the UK and doing it up himself with a few mates and selling it on at profit while still only in his twenties, then moving on and doing the same again somewhere else.

Smiling, she remembered the summer when he built the bones of their home brick by brick from the foundation up, only getting in some mates and the professionals when he was really stuck for time and felt winter was on his heels. He didn't have to be so involved; he just wanted to say with pride that he was the creator of his own home. Fascinated, she'd watch as his tanned forearms lifted bricks, with the cement-mixer thumping in the background and the dust from the day stuck to his forehead, and was overcome with lust for the man she wanted, really, really wanted to spend the rest of her life with. Sometimes, as Mark worked, he saw the glint of longing in her eye and reached to kiss her or swat her playfully on her rear end, but he rarely stopped for long. "Got to keep going – you can never tell when the weather will change," he would tell her and she'd bite her lip until she could get him to halt around sundown and tussle him into bed, sometimes not even waiting for him to shower.

The first flush of passion, nothing could compare to it, and now that he was acting like a free agent in Poland, her ego wanted him back, her ego wanted to know that she was the only woman who could hold him even if her head told her that their union was tempestuous at best. Mark Gleeson was exciting, he'd always been exciting, but they fought like children and if she was honest children didn't deserve to be born to two people so selfish. Maybe tomorrow her head would win out and tell her to bring it all to an end, and if it ended her pride insisted *she* be the one to do it, not Mark, not Mark off in Poland doing . . .

"Turn the music up, will you, Helen?"

No, she really didn't want to think about whatever Mark Gleeson was doing, not if she wasn't around to see.

Thirty-eight

"Has Rebecca gone already?" Jennifer asked as she fell into the kitchen after a session in the gym.

Dan was running a diagnostic check on a strange laptop at the table, keying in commands, his eyes firmly fixed on the screen. He was unresponsive and Jennifer felt her stomach knot. All the goodness from their wild sex in the hotel had dissipated and they were back to being boring husband and wife again, to being distant but wanting to be close.

"Dan – Rebecca?" she tried again.

"Yeah, she's gone off in that Porsche she bought from her toy boy," he grunted.

"God, I hope she doesn't kill herself in that old thing. I worry about her and what she's doing." Jennifer sighed as she fiddled with a hangnail on her forefinger.

"Yeah, well, you're not her mother," Dan said a little bit acidly, knocking back some bitter black coffee with his words.

His reply stung and she felt that was its intention.

Showering and walking into her bedroom to dry her hair, Jennifer found a note in Rebecca's hand taped to Rebecca's ridiculously sexy boots.

"*A pressie for you for the weekend – sometimes a little danger is healthy! Try not to break your neck in them. PS check beside the phone for Message 2.*"

In her bathrobe Jennifer scooted off to find the second part of Rebecca's note and her heart thumped wildly as if an animal was trying to break out from her caged ribs.

"I don't believe it! Dan, you'll never guess!"

"Save it for later – I'm going down town to my office," he said, finishing his coffee and hauling on a jacket like a condemned man.

"Your what?"

"My office, my computer-repairs business, isn't that what you wanted? Half of your girlfriends have already asked me when I'd be up and running. It should make you happy; it's something respectable, something more professional than the few hours I'd lined up at the hardware shop. I'm sharing rooms with an accountant so rent is for nothing."

"Oh Dan!"

"Don't bother, Jen, I don't really want to hear right now," he said as he walked out of the house and clanged the gate shut behind him.

Chewing her lip she watched him disappear and wanted to follow but she wanted to savour Rebecca's note too. Her hands shook as she read.

Mum says put the oven on high as it goes and don't open the door for at least eight minutes. Also, it's sultanas not raisins for your scones, and scrap the butter

– she always used marge. Reduce sugar by an ounce and forget about the plain flour, cream of tartar and baking powder stuff – Rosemary says self-raising is the way to go – she fiddled with the recipe over the years but never bothered writing the changes down on that scrap of paper you have. It was all in her head still as clear as anything when I talked to her in the home. I kept it from you until now because I wanted to leave you with something nice. Good luck. Personally I think you're cracked but I know it's important to you – R

It's an awful feeling to think you've glimpsed perfection and to still wonder, but looking through the oven door Jennifer was forced to feel optimistic. They looked right, these scones, and they smelt divine. Coming out of the oven, still hot, she dared not hope but then she cut one in half, the steam rising like tropical rain from the pavement, placed one in her mouth and took a bite. Closing her eyes she remembered all the times she came home from school and was wrapped in this smell, her mother's smell; scones cooling on wire racks, a warm scone in her hand and a glass of milk, doing her homework at the kitchen table, her mother smiling at her, telling her she was a bright one, everything perfect, the days before Jimmy left, the days when marriages were meant to last. They'd have such conversations, herself and her mother, the oldest always the confidante, the one to rely on, but now everything was fading. Her mother's head was a broken sieve with memories dropping through it by the day, but the scones were right, as right as when she was little, and for reasons she didn't fully understand Jennifer began to cry as she remembered a time of happiness when her father might put his arms around her mother's waist or give her a peck on the cheek coming or going from work.

"The only man I ever wanted, the only man I ever loved," her mother had said right up till the day he left.

And then, when he left, she had a new mournful theme. "I should have let him have his dreams, but I got caught up with the family. If you don't tell a man his dreams are important, he'll move away from you, so one day he'll be a stranger across the table," she had told her young daughters, but they, angry at their father's selfishness, had thought her opinions pitiful. "If you love someone you tell them their dreams are important."

Now the words haunted Jennifer and, agitated, she rang Sadie to ask a favour so she could make a leap of faith.

Dan was sitting awkwardly in his office when she arrived at half past six, his head down, cursing, doing some sort of check on a computer plonked on his desk.

"Dan," she said softly, trying to get his attention, placing her portable CD player on the floor.

"Oh, it's you," he said wearily. "Where are the kids?"

"Sadie's watching them for a while – I dropped them at her house."

"Yeah?" He was preoccupied, tapping away at the computer, issuing it with incomprehensible commands, a stressed-out look on his face. "Damn that notice I put in the paper – seems everyone wants to fix their computers now instead of buying the latest model off the manufacturers," he sighed and she noticed he'd two more laptops on the floor awaiting his service.

"Would you rather be at your hardware store instead?" she asked warily.

"I'd love to *own* a hardware shop. If I could just live by my hands I'd be a happy man, but unfortunately I have a brain too and everyone tells you when you have a smart brain you have to use it doing mental stuff. A hardware shop – that's just a dream. But 'real work' has got to be like a millstone round your neck," he said with a touch of sadness and sarcasm.

"Oh Dan!"

"What do you mean 'oh Dan'? Isn't that what you wanted? Clearly you want to be some kind of executive's wife and I won't let you or my family down. I won't bother you with my stupid dreams – they only seem to annoy you or make you anxious."

"Do you blame me for ruining your life? Because I kept you from going to South America when you wanted to volunteer your computer skills to help developing communities? That surprise pregnancy, then the miscarriage when everyone said I should get pregnant again to get over it. It changed everything, didn't it? Got us thinking about marriage, maybe before we were ready and then the girls born close together . . . I made you forget your dreams and I often wondered did you resent me for that, did you resent us having kids before you got to do everything you wanted to do with your life."

Crying, Jennifer plonked herself in front of his desk, grabbed a tissue, scrunching it into a dense ball, and tried to dab her watering eyes.

Dan looked amazed. "Jesus, Jen, have you been carrying this with you all these years?"

Nodding and sobbing, she continued to divest herself of her feelings. "See, *I* don't regret it – the children, even though they're often an inconvenience. I thought of that today when I finally made my mother's scones and felt such a connection, but seeing you the last few months trying to do different things, trying to be someone else, it seemed sometimes like you wanted to be free of me, of our family, of Emma, Abby and Adam . . ."

"But that's mad, Jen. Emma and Abby, my lovely girls, and Adam, my son . . . I wouldn't wish any of them away and I don't regret a thing about not going to South America to work on some project because our family started earlier than we expected!"

"But you always said you wanted to explore your home continent, Canada, the States, South America, and I feel like I've deprived you of your dream . . ."

"But I've done some of that dream and I'm still young. I admit I have thought about South America from time to time but South America was only one dream – I've got plenty of dreams, Jen, and mostly you're in them, you and the kids."

"But when I started salsa dancing I couldn't get it out of my head that things could have been different – we could have had a much more Latin way of life, a life of fun, a life of –"

"A life of passion perhaps?" he teased.

Abruptly he left his desk to come around to her and scrunched his eyes up in amazement when he registered the way she was dressed.

"Jennifer, why are you wearing a mac and where the hell did you get those boots?"

"A present from Rebecca – our feet are the only part of our anatomy that are the same size. As for the mac – it's what I've got underneath it that matters."

"Why? What have you got planned?" His crotch was already bulging out its optimistic intentions.

"Well, I had this daft idea that I would seduce you, prance around in my boots, you know like Julia Roberts in *Pretty Woman* and my handbag is even stuffed full of dollars that I didn't spend in New York. So I was going to do that Julia Roberts line, where she tells Richard Gere she got no clothes when she went shopping because everyone was mean to her and she still has all his money and then I was going to whip off my coat and show you I had no clothes on except for a G-string and then I was going to play some sexy songs on the CD player and get you to place dollars down my thong like in the movies . . . but it all seems so pointless and contrived now . . ."

Dan's face was expressionless. Then she heard him gulp and saw him go a little pale.

"God damn it, woman, that's the best idea you've had in a long time! Do it!"

"But don't you think it's a bit ridiculous and I've blown the whole element of surprise now?"

Dan put his hands on her legs, felt the top of her boots and the softness of her thighs and whistled. "Take it from me, baby, men don't give a shit about surprises – men just want to *see*."

"Dan, I just want you to know that me being naked in full daylight with – with all the jaded bits on display – it's a big thing for me and I know in recent months my libido fell through the floor what with breastfeeding and not getting any sleep and maybe – maybe I was letting my head run away with me to try and get my sexy feelings back, but, well, I think I'm beginning to realise that sexiness comes from me, from me feeling good about me."

"Christ, woman, will you stop talking and start dancing sexy! And do everything else that you've promised and tell me again . . . Miss . . . ?"

"Miss Murphy?"

"Tell me again, Miss Murphy, why you think you'll make an excellent secretary for this firm."

Smiling, she handed over a fistful of crumpled dollars, hit the play button on the CD player, let her coat crash to the floor, shook back her imperfect Cyndi Lauperish hair and strutted her stuff in borrowed boots, and all the time her husband watched entranced like a child who has just met Santa Claus in the flesh and genuinely, genuinely can't believe his luck.

That night in bed, with Adam snuggled up with his sisters, Jennifer and Dan relaxed in each other's arms. A gentle orange light gave a soft glow to the room and to their skin and Jennifer finally felt able to share her blue satin and lace teddy with the man she loved. His fingers were even now alternating between the soft tops of her thighs and the softness of the material. The feeling of oneness between them as they lay side by side, breathing contentedly, feeling accepted, was nothing short of wonderful.

Wiggling on the sheets and sighing, she attracted his attention and instinctively he moved closer, holding her around the waist to steady her restlessness.

"You okay?" he asked softly.

"Stuff on my mind, that's all – been thinking a lot since things changed with your job, been thinking it might be time for me to start doing things again for myself, earning some money, not letting it all fall on you."

"What kind of stuff?"

"Not stuff like I did before – I never want to work in a lab again and – don't get mad or anything but I've been talking with Sandra about running a business to redesign mums who've had a few kids and who haven't a clue where things are at any more. Sandra could help in the sourcing of pretty but flattering underwear for larger ladies and the whole thing would be a consultancy service. I was thinking maybe I could dip into your redundancy money to get me started. If I could earn some money maybe you won't have to give up your dreams – even the mad ones like owning a shop some day."

"I don't know what to say. I didn't know you were that interested in nice underwear, Jen – I've been trying to get you into them for years!"

"That's the point. I would have if I could have found stuff that was nice, fitted well, didn't cost the earth and just landed in my lap without me having to look for it."

"Okay, so you want to run a knicker business. What do you want me to say?" Dan laughed.

"Just tell me I'm smart and you believe in me."

"I think you're smart and I believe in you."

"Good, because there's more. Now don't laugh, I know this might sound surprising, but I . . . I think I want to invent something, something for kids, baby things. Do you know some of the best baby inventions were invented by real mums from high chairs to feeding spoons, but very few of them get things into production big time? How many times have you seen me struggling with a car seat, a high chair, a cot, and curse the man who designed it?"

"Loads."

"Well, I'm going to invent something, use my science degree to do something creative instead of something mundane – although I think it's really more an engineering area I'll be involved in. I've already got a few ideas running through my head that I've sketched out and I'm going to do a 'start your own business' course, maybe get a mentor to help me, see what I can do with my baby ideas or my larger ladies' service for mums. Then I'll have to research patents for my baby products. So what do you think?"

"Fabulous."

"I'm being serious, Dan!"

"So am I. Your ideas are fabulous, you're fabulous, you always have been, you are still."

Placing her face so close to his that their lips almost touched she told him what was in her heart. "The thing is, I don't want you to give up on your dreams, I don't want you to go back to any job that you see as the grindstone, but I want to find my dreams too . . . maybe we can make what we're doing the dream, both working, both looking after the kids, maybe having less cash but more time to find the things in life that will make us happy."

"I'm happy right now, I'm happy just to be here with the girl of my dreams knowing that she's come back to me with her head and her heart as well as her body," he said softly, cupping her face in his hands and kissing her cheek.

Placing her head on his chest Jennifer shut her eyes and remembered the days when being with Dan was a dream, a dream enveloped in the protective bubble of their love and, lying there with her lover, her life, their life, unwound in front of her eyes in all its vivid colour. The days in the Chicago kitchens serving rich and unhappy Americans, sneaking chocolate-chip biscuits and warm decaf coffee when the last of the punters had gone home and the kitchens were empty, the silver surfaces all wiped down, kissing and whispering dreams to each other. Her fired-up brain remembered driving Dan's beat-up American car, not caring what anyone thought of it, the days before becoming respectably middle class and keeping up with the Joneses, and then her brain threw out images rapid-fire from anywhere and in any order, meeting again in their mid-twenties on that Canadian submarine, weekends away trampling the purple and pink landscape of Sligo or Mayo, dashing into little west of Ireland pubs when the damp winter days were drawing to a close. Those dreams cost very little, those days when possessions were scarce and the hole-in-the-wall machine often ran empty. Lights danced under Jennifer's eyelids and she remembered the sunlight of the Southern States in early fall, the days of Kentucky, always Kentucky and those long-stemmed daisies traced from her ankles to the tops of her thighs, to her tense stomach and the valley of her breasts, her throat and behind her ear, she thought of that now as her lover, her friend, her soul mate traced his fingers the same route and kissed her deeply with warmth and absolute love.

Thirty-nine

The sun was sulking behind wispy white clouds, when Rebecca drove off in Paddy's Porsche. Well, it was actually her Porsche now since she had willingly paid a small amount of cash for it and sent Paddy off with good wishes to Oz. Driving along country roads, the peek-a-boo sun warming her face, music blaring, Rebecca felt the power of the car on the tarmac and was smugly satisfied. Let Mark keep her old car if he wanted – she wasn't dependent on him any more, least of all for a set of wheels. No, she'd developed a backbone, she thought as she wiggled around in the deep leather car seat, feeling somewhat uncomfortable as she was wearing Jennifer's Skinny-Mini underwear from her pre-mammy days. Rebecca had put on a wash of her smalls before she went to work in the hospital for the last time but nobody had hung them up in her absence despite her note and, totally bereft of knickers, she'd wiggled into a pair of cotton pants from Jen's past instead. In a day or

453

two she'd go back to her sister's for all of her possessions, including her drying knickers, just as soon as she knew . . . well, she wasn't quite sure what she wanted to know as she allowed her new motor to purr across the familiar road home.

The pretty flowerbeds outside her house were parched, battered from wind and rain and choked with weeds. Obviously Mark didn't give a damn about appearances since she'd left; having the grass on the lawn mowed, allowing it to ferment where it lay in the spring sunshine – sunshine which was turning out to be hot as summer.

Swinging her long legs out of the car, made longer by the laced-up wedge sandals she was wearing, she pulled down her flared denim miniskirt just a smidgen past her thighs. Supermarket chic looked good on Rebecca and was far cheaper too, she'd discovered since her time away but then she'd the kind of frame that could carry off nearly any garment – always had. Checking her appearance in the car wing-mirror, she smoothed back her eyebrows with a finger and reapplied some lip gloss. Over the weeks she'd developed a more casual look that didn't take an hour to put on in the bathroom, an impossible task in Jen's tiny bungalow anyway as someone was always banging on the door every two minutes to take a shower, brush their teeth or do endless 'wee-wees'.

Walking up to the front door, Rebecca took a long deep breath. It had been so long since she'd seen Mark that she felt the bond between them was already hanging by a thread. Vengefully perhaps, all of her desperately wanted him to have gone to seed in her absence like the outside of her home, but she knew from her last visit that wasn't likely. If Mark was anything it was a survivor, she thought, as she noticed with distaste that his vulgar busty bikini print from his bachelor days was still hanging in the hall. Angrily, she ground her car keys into the palm of her hand and went on a mad search of her house.

The sitting-room door was slightly ajar and when she pushed it open fully she was momentarily rewarded with what she wanted to see – domestic disarray, unsorted magazines and newspapers just lying around and empty cups and dirty plates but then, worst of all, she was assaulted by the presence of a new couch, a nasty, dark-brown chunky piece of male presence with bulky arms and strong backs on the couch and matching armchairs. Where was her beloved cream couch with its leather soft as puppy-dog cheeks? Rebecca loved that couch – it had caressed her with its warmth many a night when Mark was out and she was alone watching some mindless TV show for company.

"Mark, Mark Gleeson, where are you?"

Her kitchen was a mess of pots and pans and goo on the floor and on her once-shining virgin cooker and she was slightly euphoric at the sight. Aha, he had turned into a slob after all!

A minute later she heard an unfamiliar hard clinking noise and she turned towards her conservatory and pushed open the doors.

Inside she was startled by the sight of a full-size snooker table and Mark leaning over the wooden edges, his eye skimming down the cue to the ball.

"Mark!"

As he straightened up, she saw the tautness of his stomach. He was lean, leaner than she'd remembered.

Dressed in denims and a white cotton shirt, his eyes signalled his irritation at her presence and momentarily distracted he ran a hand through his dark just-out-of-bed messy hair. For a man whom she supposed should be on the beer since she left, his complexion was clear. In fact, her husband looked annoyingly vibrant, at least five years younger than his actual age. For the briefest of moments Rebecca thought he might smile at her, but his sensual mouth was hard and she could sense his anger as he pulled the cue towards him, standing it tall, like a weapon.

"What are you doing here? The deadline to find yourself is hardly up already."

"I told you before, Mark, I don't do ultimatums, I suit myself," she scowled back, her eyes roaming round the room. Jesus, he'd one of those miniature football tables for child-men installed as well. What were they called again? Subbuteo.

"Well, you're looking well on suiting yourself, I'll give you that," he growled. "Hair's different, more natural – softer," he added with a kind of clinical indifference.

"Didn't have the money to be running to the hairdresser's whenever I wanted, like I used to," she explained with a put-on expression of martyrdom.

"Ah, poor baby – it must have been hard not having money on tap the way you did when you were living with me – never thinking twice before you bought a pair of shoes or a flashy designer dress!"

"I survived!" she bristled, wishing she had worn a pair of spiky heels now as an extra defence-mechanism for her ego instead of her slightly ditzy wedges.

"Sure you did, you survived well enough before I met

you too – I wouldn't have married you if I thought you were a weakling," he smirked.

"Thought I had good genes for the next generation, did you?" she spat at him and then she almost regretted it as she saw his steel-blue eyes harden.

"Well, seems like we'll never get to know now. Maybe it's just as well you stayed on the pill. You're too selfish to be a mother." Looking away from her, he eyed up his next shot.

"Well, you're too bloody selfish and childish to be a father. You seem to have suited yourself since I left, with your snooker table and heap-of-shite couch, and while I'm at it since we're splitting up I'll be wanting my cream couch back – where have you put it?"

"Ah, so you've decided we're breaking up then? But you forget that I might have decided as much myself, Rebecca . . . your precious couch is gone and since we *are* splitting up, it's as well I gave it to Mariola for her new place in town."

"That Polish cow again with her soft ways and her put-on gentleness! I should have known all along you couldn't keep your hands off her!"

"You're fucking unreal, do you know that?" he said, shaking his head.

"Don't 'unreal' me – I know all about Poland, Mark – that sister of yours lost no time in telling me at the rugby grounds!"

"Yeah, I heard about that. I'm beginning to wonder if I know the woman I married at all, between pole-dancing and having a fondness for mud. Anything else I should know about you, Rebecca?"

"Don't avoid the issue, Mark. What happened in

457

Poland? Did you finally declare your love, and get to meet her folks back home? Well, I don't really care what you did but if you gave her my couch you can fucking ring her up now and tell her your wife wants it back!" She walked to the table, deliberately getting in the way of his next shot. The anger she felt was enormous as she met his gaze and directed her hatred at him like a missile.

He placed his hand on her bare arm and roughly pushed her aside, all the time eyeing up the ball as if she wasn't there. He was quiet, furiously quiet, and she knew she should leave him alone, but she just couldn't help herself ranting.

"And this, this snooker table – what's this monstrosity doing in my conservatory anyway? It's great to know you were splashing out big-time on every little toy for yourself while I was off slumming it in the next town!"

"Get out of the way, Rebecca, you're ruining my shot," he spat through gritted teeth.

"So are you going to call that Polish Princess you're riding to get my couch back or am I going to have to do it myself?" she fumed as she pulled her mobile from her bag and started to look up the contact details for their cleaner.

In a white-hot temper Mark uncurled her fingers from her phone and hurled it across the room.

"Let's get a few things straight here, Rebecca. You're the one who shagged off – with, I might add, my very fucking generous blessing – and whoever I give my property to, and that shagging couch was *my* property as I paid for it, is my business – and to tell you the truth,

I never liked that heap of shite anyhow – a man shouldn't be afraid to plonk his arse on his own sofa in his own home without having to listen to whingeing about whether the damn thing is getting dirty or creased. In any case, since you're shagging off I'll be suiting myself from now on. As for Mariola, don't you dare ring her and demand anything from that lovely girl who's out of her own country and only trying to do the best for herself and –"

"Who you screwed!" Rebecca screamed, hysterical with rage.

"Yeah, right, I should be so lucky. She's young, she's beautiful and too respectful to make a spectacle of herself having an affair with a married man, but then again maybe when I'm free . . ." He deliberately let the sentence hang and Rebecca, true to form, took the bait.

"Free, what'll you do when you're free? And that cow respectful of herself? Give me a break! What are you inferring, anyway, that I'm a slut and a spoilt little bitch who's likely to make a spectacle of herself at any moment? Well, maybe you're right, because when I was away I had an affair, what do you think of that?"

Her remark made him flinch, ever so slightly, but he recovered well and took another shot with such force that Rebecca thought he would break the cue.

"Congratulations – hope you enjoyed yourself," he said, pulling himself to his full height in front of her.

Despite her long legs Rebecca felt like an insignificant speck. His indifference threw her. She expected him to be incandescent with rage, not coolly congratulating her about her sexual experiences outside of their marriage.

"So how was it then?" he continued mildly, not

looking at her and making an exaggerated show of positioning the cue between his tensed fingers.

"Nice – it was nice. As it happens we didn't go all the way but we certainly groped," she answered hotly and her own words said out loud made her cringe.

"Wow, nice, earth-shattering stuff! And you got round to groping, did you? How old was this guy anyway that you didn't get past being felt up?" Mark laid the sarcasm on thick.

"Stuff you, Mark, I don't have to hang around and listen to your sniping. I'm leaving. Just to let you know I'll be contacting a solicitor and sending any papers to your solicitor, who just happens to be your dorky boring-as-hell brother. What a relief that I'll never have to talk to him or any of your rotten family again!"

Rebecca knew she shouldn't pour petrol on the flames but she couldn't resist and with her car keys she quickly gutted the soft green belly of his precious games table and threw him a look that could burn the house down.

It was as if she'd tripped a switch as she saw his brows crease and his eyes narrow.

"You're such a little bitch. You think nothing of that, do you? Think nothing of the fact that it's my work that has paid for that table and everything else in this house. Well, take a good hard look at what your temper has ruined and hazard a guess at how much it will cost to repair it!"

Rebecca gasped as he lifted her off his feet and pushed her face close to the rip so she could appreciate her vandalism up close. Cursing him, she squirmed to be free but she could feel the tense anger in his arms and knew escape was unlikely and then suddenly he began to laugh.

"Well, I don't mind if I do!"

Without warning he unleashed a flurry of sharp, hard smacks to her rear end and Rebecca yelped in disbelief.

"What the *hell* do you think you're doing?" she yelled over her shoulder as he released his grip and wiped away his tears of laughter.

"What am *I* doing? Sure you know me, I'm like most husbands – I don't do anything unless I'm told. Buy this couch, Mark, put in this kitchen, Mark, sign these separation papers, Mark – I'm *always* only acting on your instruction. But still, I'm dying to know, since when has my wife being going around with *Spank Me* written on the back of her knickers?"

"What?"

Rebecca sprang off the table like a traumatised cat and began to tug at her underwear but not being able to see anything and distrusting every word from his mouth she stepped out of Jennifer's flowery girlie knickers and turned them over in her hands. There in spidery writing on the back were the words *Spank Me*. Sandra! These wretched knickers couldn't have been bought years ago by her sister – they had to have originated from that nympho Sandra! Probably they were an ill-fitting present for her sister – a one-off sample or the scraps from the end of a line – that was Sandra's usual form.

"Just to let you know, they're the wrong day of the week as well," said Mark, his eyes crinkling mischievously. "They say Monday. Jesus, you don't have a pair for *every* day, do you?"

Stunned and blushing Rebecca noted the tiny *Monday*

writing printed underneath *Spank Me*. How the hell had she missed such a message? All she saw when she put on this underwear, admittedly in a hurry, was a pretty little flower pattern.

"This has nothing to do with me, they're actually borrowed knickers," she said a trifle haughtily as if that should be enough to settle the matter.

Mark raised his eyebrows in surprise. "*Borrowed* knickers? Jesus Christ, what *have* you been doing since I set you loose on the world, Rebecca?"

"Oh you know me, Mark, I've always been a spontaneous little thing!" For dramatic effect she threw up her hands and the front of her top rode up and he saw her belly piercing and instinctively he went to touch her lovely taut stomach.

"Lovely, reminds me of the wild little thing I married – she used to be spontaneous but she got a bit predictable over the years. I'd never get to see her without the perfect hair and the full-on make-up and the stylishly safe little outfits that made her look older than she really was."

"You should thank me for always looking so well groomed. Of course, I never wanted to let you down – always wanted to be the *respectfully* well-turned-out wife, especially in front of your family!" she said with a little sarcasm to cover the plaintive honesty.

"Nobody ever said you had to be any way except the way you were," he said softly, picking her up again and sitting her on his precious snooker table. Her hands fell together on the lap of her cheap supermarket-bought skirt and, knickerless, and without her usual expensively defensive high heels Rebecca began to cry and hated herself for her weakness.

"Rebecca, just say the word and I'll let you go," Mark whispered. "You can be free to have all the nice sex you want with whoever you want. Just say the word, Rebecca, and I'll let you go. But I want you to go knowing that I love you. I always have."

"But you don't love me, you can't love me because I'm not the person you think I am, Mark. Right now outside the house is my car, *my* car I paid for, an old Porsche, a real beauty that goes like a rocket . . . and what you don't know is sometimes I drive too fast and do other stupid things . . . and then there's the pole-dancing . . . I *love* it, love it so much that I'd like to run classes here in Carrigmore and shock the stupid fogies in this town with my fabulous moves and my even more fabulous pierced belly button . . . and I'd like to tell that dried-up old biddy from the tennis club to shove her unpaid position as secretary, I'd gladly leave the boring fashion shows to Lou in future, because . . . well, because it's not me, it's far too bloody ladylike . . . and then there's the rugby . . . I'm good at it, Mark . . . if I stayed in Carrigmore I might even join the local club. How would you feel about that, how would you feel about your wife never being as respectful as your Polish cleaner, never wanting to be dignified or nice? How would you feel about me being able to score a try in our marital bed every night? Do you think you could handle a Rebecca *that* spontaneous?"

"Oh God, yeah!"

He moved in to devour her but she pushed him away and sighed wearily.

"Wait, there's more – spending time with Jen's kids made me realise the things I enjoyed doing when I was a little kid. Even being in the sandpit with her baby switched something on in my brain, a memory perhaps, and I know this sounds crazy, but I like to dig, I like to stick my hands in the earth, to clear weeds or build a sandcastle – it's – what's the word? – therapeutic, yeah, that's it, it's therapeutic and somewhere along the line I remembered, remembered that when I was a kid I always wanted to be an archaeologist but everyone would laugh in school or at home. See *I* was the pretty one, everyone expected me to do something girlie, like being a beautician or an air stewardess and Jen was the one with the brains, Jen was always the one who was going to college –"

"What are you saying? You like to dig? Baby, if you want to dig, go ahead and dig, sure digging is in the family. Maybe I could get you a job driving a dumper truck on a building site if you find digging that therapeutic!"

"Mark, this isn't a joke – all these things I want to do take time, discovering the new Rebecca takes time, and so I still can't answer your question, the one question that's important to you, the make or break question for our marriage, the 'are we having a baby question', I just don't have an answer right now!"

For a second he broke from her gaze and stared towards the door, concentrating, mulling things over, and then he spoke with a considered carefulness.

"What I want more than anything is a happy wife and I've always known your happiness couldn't come from me, it had to come from you . . . and I hear you, I hear the excitement in your voice when you talk about this stuff. So, I guess I'm willing to take the journey with you. Yes, I want kids, you know I want kids, and I hope you'll want them too but damn it, woman, there's no getting away from it, I love you, even though it drives me crazy, and if I'm not meant to be with you I don't know who else I'm meant to be with and that's the truth."

"But what about Poland? What were you doing in Poland if *I'm* the only one you love?" she asked acidly.

Squeezing her arm reassuringly, he smiled at her jealousy. "Mariola – she got married and naturally as her esteemed employer I was invited to her wedding, Inspector Know It All!" he said, slipping her hand up her skirt and onto her bare skin, making her jump. Then remembering their earlier fight he frowned. "This guy you groped . . . you really didn't actually do it with him, did you?"

Rebecca shook her head. She thought now wasn't the time to mention that the impediments to a full-blown extra-marital affair were big willies of porn-film proportions, uninvited worms and al-fresco sex that went beyond even her exhibitionist standards.

"No, I told you that already."

"And will your solicitor still be getting in touch with . . . what did you call him again, oh yes, my dorky brother?"

Rebecca sighed and looked towards the ceiling, then taking a deep breath she locked on to his eyes and despite herself smiled, then laughed out loud like a child.

"No – because much as it pains me to say it, I can't leave you either, you're part of who I am. I don't think I realised that until I went away. You were always in my thoughts, Mark, even if half the time I was planning your murder."

Taking her hands in his, Mark gently stroked her fingers, then reached into the pocket of his jeans and Rebecca felt something hard and cold touch her left hand.

Seeing her wedding band, her eyes began to mist.

"When you left it behind I didn't know what to do with it, so I kept it in my pocket so it would always be there if you came back home to stay."

"Put it on, Mark," she whispered and he slipped her wedding ring upon her finger and looked at her with all the tenderness that had been between them in the early days of love.

"I'm sorry about . . . well, it was a very short skirt and it was kind of a funny message," he laughed as he kissed her playfully and toyed with her hair.

"It's alright, the new Rebecca isn't made of glass, never was in fact," she smiled back.

"Don't think that I'm not still pissed off with you for ripping my snooker table though – I'm going to make you pay for it out of your shoe money," he joked.

"Oh, I think you'll find that the new Rebecca cares very little for shoes, except some nice sturdy rugby boots or some slapper high heels for dancing around poles. What a pity my pole is at this very minute stashed in the boot of my car," she sighed dramatically, giving him sly looks.

"Oh I'm sure we can find some equally attractive activity for you to engage in instead. Now that I think of it, I haven't seen you wear that old air stewardess uniform of yours in a while – maybe you can put it on and invite me to join the mile-high club from the comfort of my bed?"

"Why, Mr Gleeson, I would have thought a guy like you would be in the mile-high club already," Rebecca winked.

"A valid assumption, but I kind of need to renew my membership," he whispered teasingly in her ear.

In the end she didn't get to dress up or do any kind of imaginative air stewardess role play for as soon as Mark dragged her through the bedroom door he was all over her, like a possessive animal, marking out his territory again, scenting out his woman with his maleness and, surrendering to his desires, Rebecca felt wanted, felt loved, felt absolutely bloody wonderful and home again in her heart.

Forty

The telephone rang and answering promptly Rebecca could hear the exaggerated clearing of a voice down the phone.

"Hello, I'm ringing about the ad in the paper . . . the pole-dancing classes?" the booming male voice inquired in a slightly grand but haughty way. "I was wondering if it will be ladies only or whether you would be receptive to men joining as well – it's just I rather like shoes and wouldn't mind the dancing bit either!"

Rebecca froze. When she placed the ad in the paper about classes she was only doing some basic market research, testing the waters to see what kind of interest there would be if she went ahead and completed an instructor class in pole-dancing and were to give lessons locally. So far a few local women had rung in response to the ad, some genuinely interested, others obvious busybodies, but to date there had been no inquiries from men. No, this phonecall was unique and just a bit bizarre for sleepy old Carrigmore.

"Ehm . . . well . . ." Something about the voice freaked her out – she knew it from somewhere, it was very distinctive, but she just couldn't put a face to the voice at the other end of the line.

"Perhaps if it's ladies only you might consider private lessons? Have you a private rate?"

Wait, she had it. Of course, without his usual side-kick in tow she hadn't been able to place him, but she knew who he was now. It was Herbert, stuffy brother of that shrill-voiced sergeant major from the tennis club, Audrey. Jesus, whenever the fossilised fecker had looked at her feet before she'd always thought he was checking out her legs starting with her ankles, but maybe he was really more interested in her footwear than her shapely calves and rock-hard thighs.

"So for private lessons, what would your rate be?" he asked again, this time more impatiently.

Rebecca began to bristle, thinking of all the times the tennis club elite had treated her like an outsider, a complete and utter nothing, a dogsbody to do all the thankless work. And that cow, his sister Audrey, couldn't even remember her name, calling her Rachel, perhaps just to annoy her and keep her in her place. How had she put up with these awful, ignorant people before, how had she such lack of confidence that she even cared what these rude and stuffy people thought about her? To think she'd lived in hope of the day Bert Boy and his crowd might be willing to bestow an apple or a summer cucumber, fruit of their greenhouses, upon her, this single gesture a definitive signal that she might be worthy of being included into the club's inner circle. Private rate, the audacity of the man! Private rate indeed – whatever her private rate might be it would have to be something substantial. If Brother Bert wanted a course of dance lessons, and enjoyed shoes that much, he could bloody well sell some of the family silver to pay for the enjoyment of his little fetishes for big feet.

"I'm afraid the classes will of course be ladies only and, as for a private rate, well, yours is an unusual request and not one I'd thought of before, but per class privately I would have to say my rate would be a minimum of 150 per hour, that is, if I were to do private classes at all and I'm not saying that I will," Rebecca said breezily and with as much indifference as she could muster. Down the phone line she could smell interest, meanness and a little bit of desperation and it made her feel delightfully predatory.

"Bit steep though, what?"

Mean, tight-fisted fecker, did he think she would condescend to teach him for a few friggin' tomatoes and a punnet of strawberries instead?

"Well, as I said, that is just my provisional rate, it might even be higher. I am a very busy woman and my time is extremely valuable, you see!"

"Oh, well . . . and your name, I don't see it written down here . . . what is your name should I need to contact you again?"

He was definitely hooked, he had a pressing need to parade about in some stilettos, she could tell. Herbert had probably been waiting his whole life for this opportunity and she was undoubtedly his only outlet for shoe-fetish expression in this sleepy backwater. She could more than likely charge him whatever she wanted for the experience – and she would, that is, if she could be bothered.

"Gleeson, my name is Gleeson, *Rebecca* Gleeson," she

added a touch maliciously. Maybe now she had something he wanted it might concentrate his and Audrey's stuffy minds into remembering her real name in future.

Laughing, she banged down the phone, just as Mark was walking through the door with an awkwardly shaped item, bound in colourful wrapping paper and topped with a huge yellow bow.

"What's this?" she asked, hand on hip but grinning from ear to ear. Herself and Mark hadn't stopped having sex since she'd been back in the house and if they hadn't fallen in love again, they had at least fallen in lust which was just as good.

"Present, open it!"

"What's the occasion? It's not my birthday. What have you done wrong?"

"Does a man need a reason to buy his wife a present? Go on, open it."

"I will if I can wrestle it out of all this paper," she said, tugging at the wrapping with ferocity but not getting very far in its destruction. "What is it anyway? It seems to have a very long pole and a roundy bit at the end. Could it be something for dancing? I swear, Mark, if it's some kind of mop or cleaning brush I'll throw it right back at you."

"Stop yakking and keep tearing."

Finally the paper began to yield and she was introduced to a contraption with a long silvery pole attached to a large flat metal plate.

"Do you know what it is?" he asked, seeing her stunned face.

"Yes, of course I do . . . it's a metal detector. Wow, Jesus, I think I'm speechless!"

"I guess if you really want to be that archaeologist you talked about, you might need one of these and if nothing else it's a bit of fun. Thought you had enough shoes and bags and clothes to do you a lifetime." He laughed and she laughed too.

The mystery of her disappearing clothes had been solved, he had vacuum-packed them and put them in the attic while she was away, saying he couldn't bear to look at them every day, wondering if she was coming back or not.

"Thanks, Mark. It's the best present you've bought me in a very long time, because it says you believe in me, believe in my dreams," and she hugged him tight and jumped up and curled her legs around his waist and kissed him heartily.

"Jesus, not again, I'm not as young as I used to be, you know!"

"This isn't about sex, you idiot, this is about love. I love you, Mark Gleeson," she laughed as she saved his back and slipped back to the ground.

"All I want is for you to be happy and if you decide you don't want to do that open-university course and want to take your digging interest into horticulture or something else you can forget all about that metal detector and I'll buy you a few trowels or then again after your hospital stint if you want to become a nurse –"

"A nurse, oh I don't think so, that was just a once-off job, easy to chuck in. Although I miss them, you know – Johnny the Gent and his fighting fists, Alice and her chocolate bars, even Mrs Kinsella and her 'toilet, toilet, nurse' and poor, kind Mrs Redmond who used to be beautiful and who made me want to go and see my own mother – I'm glad I did too even though it was hard – it's better to face Rosemary the way she is than dream about the way she was and, even though she's not perfect, I love her, just as I love you, Mark. Mark, did you hear what I said? I love you."

"Sure why wouldn't you love me? Like attracts like, and now we've stopped fighting I can see it even more clearly – we're two of a kind, we belong."

Distractedly he looked out the window at Rebecca's twenty-five-year-old Porsche and shook his head half-admiringly, half in amusement. He was thinking of how he had pinched her car from outside Jen and Dan's house, using her spare set of keys, that day she had rung the Garda Station to report her loss. He had discovered her whereabouts by a fluke. Ollie had been asked to do a costing and a sketch for an extension to a house in Jennifer's neighbourhood. He had spotted Rebecca's car and let Mark know straight away where she was. After that, it was just a matter of turning up by cab early enough in the morning to do his *Gone in Sixty Seconds* act . . . she always had loved that film after all . . . He grinned now as he remembered the kick he had got out of dumping her flashy shopping bags full of clothes out on the pavement and gliding away in her fancy wheels.

"I know what you're grinning at!" she said, glowering at him. "You sneaky fecker! Taking my car was just not –"

"Nice? No, it's not nice but, you and me, we're not nice. Decent – I'd like to think I'm decent, but I'll do what I need to earn a buck. I'm a survivor, baby, that's why you married me, don't tell me any different. You're a survivor too – like I said we're two of a kind."

"Stop looking at my car! If you're a good boy one of these days I might let you drive it. Did I tell you I'm taking it to a track day next week on the racing circuit to burn some rubber, which is probably what I should have been doing all along."

"Yeah? Actually I'm not admiring it, I'm thinking of how it's really bad for my image."

"What image?" she teased, putting her finger in front of her mouth.

"My *green* image. That thing must drink petrol – we'll have to get you some kind of nice little hybrid so you'll look more the part."

"Your green image and what part? Hello, could you hand me back my husband, please?"

"Yeah, right, very funny. Look, myself and Ollie put in for planning to build a new green environmentally friendly village on the outskirts of town, near the woodlands west of the cross, and it's been accepted. It's seen as a showcase for the region – fifty high-quality units, all mod cons, all sophisticated finishings and extras."

"But you're not green – you couldn't care less about being green and environmentally friendly!"

"Ollie always had a leaning that way and I'll be anything I need to be if that's where the money is at."

"Jesus, Mark, you're a fecking rogue, do you know that?"

"Well, this rogue is meeting Ollie for dinner in the pub. I don't suppose you've called Lou since you got back in town?"

Rebecca shrugged her shoulders and picked up a cookery book from one of her kitchen shelves. She couldn't recall ever buying it, but the meals did look gorgeous. Her husband was staring at her, waiting for an answer. In agitation she shut the book and met his gaze.

"No, I haven't called her yet but obviously I will since she's married to your buddy and since they're having a baby and since we live in a small town where, for convenience sake, nobody can afford the luxury of falling out with anybody else."

"You're mad at her for working in the salon while you were away, aren't you? Don't be too hard on her, Rebecca. Things have been really slow for Ollie – bar the odd house extension he hasn't had much work coming in and she didn't go looking for the job at the salon, she was asked did she want a few hours and she thought it would help what with the baby coming."

"Well, all I remember is she wasn't exactly a rock of support when I went away. I could have done with a real friend then and she never even called. Anything for an easy life, Lou – she never goes where there's a hint of trouble."

"Maybe she's just focussed on the pregnancy and it hasn't been all plain sailing for her – carrying a baby has her looking wrecked and she hurt her back doing massage on a client. Ollie tells me *she* could do with some support right now."

"Look, I'll ring her, but to be honest – it may have taken me years to figure it out, but I don't think we're all that great friends, not really, not like the girls I played rugby with. They would have died for me, Mark, on or off the pitch, although Helen hasn't spoken to me since I stopped playing and they lost the semi-final – although I'm sure she'll come round – she's really just fuming 'cos they've lost the chance to move up a division."

"Whatever. Look, nobody says you and Lou have to be best mates but I'd like if you could be civil. After all,

Lou did save your precious fashion show at the tennis club. It mightn't be so important to you now, but it was important to you then."

"I'll ring her, okay – now get lost."

Flicking through some course guides on archaeology, Rebecca hardly heard the doorbell and when she opened her front door she found herself face to face with her cleaner, back cleaning the house with Rebecca's blessing as well as doing some commercial cleaning. Usually Rebecca wasn't around when Mariola cleaned, usually she would be working at the salon – not that they would be looking for her to come back any day soon or ever at Tranquillity.

"It is okay to clean now?" Mariola asked sweetly, a big happy smile on her face, her eyes sparkling.

Really, she was effortlessly beautiful. Without even thinking about it Rebecca's old jealousy button switched on and with difficulty she turned it off again. Nothing had happened between Mariola and Mark, nothing would ever happen. She was, as he said, just a nice girl doing her best to make a life for herself, and besides she was just newly married – she wasn't likely to be looking for anything on the side yet.

"Yes, it's okay to clean, come in," Rebecca answered, trying to keep the friendliness in her voice. The house was a state, much worse than if she had remembered Mariola was cleaning that day. "I will start with the windows and then the floors and then as many of the bathroom as I can. It is okay?"

"Sure . . . absolutely, whatever you do when . . . when I'm not here . . . I'll just be upstairs if you need me."

Restlessly, Rebecca headed for her bedroom, not sure

what she was meant to be doing as she heard Mariola banging around with the vacuum cleaner. Maybe she should have left the house and got out of her way but she felt obliged to stay now. Walking into her wardrobe she ran her hands down her beautiful clothes. Most of them held no appeal for her any more – she'd outgrown most, mentally at least and in some cases literally. Since she'd left she'd put on a few pounds and she liked it, especially since most of it had gone to her boobs – she'd gone up a cup size. Determinedly she pulled clothes off the hanger that had lost their appeal and laid them in organised piles on the bed, then collapsed down on her bed herself, lying on her back, just feeling happy. Smiling she looked at her pole fully assembled in a corner of a room. It wasn't a secret any more – she swung out of it whenever she wanted now, sometimes for Mark's benefit, sometimes just to get her own endorphins pumping for the day.

After two hours of sorting (she had far more clothes than she realised), and after a little bit of spinning off her shiny chrome god, she ventured downstairs and saw Mariola, up to her elbows in washing-up gloves, going over the floors one more time with a dry mop. There was no doubt about it – she was a brilliant worker, fast, efficient, uncomplaining.

"Tea, Mariola?"

"No, thank you, if it's okay, I'll keep going with the work."

"Just five minutes. I'm having tea anyway. Will you join me? If you don't like the ordinary stuff I have herbal. Chamomile, lemon, mint?"

"Oh . . . okay, mint, thank you, you are very kind."

Mariola put aside her mop, pulled off her gloves and waited a little nervously while Rebecca boiled the water.

Taking down her wedding china, which had been recently reinstated from its storage box in the garage, and flipping the top off her cookie jar, filled for once with gorgeous chocolate cookies, Rebecca arranged the cups and saucers at the breakfast bar, then made ordinary tea for herself and mint for her once-a-week employee.

"You got married – Mark told me. It must have been nice to go home for the wedding?"

"Yes . . . we spent time visiting family but then we had a week by the sea . . . it was very nice, thank you," Mariola said shyly, sipping her tea politely if a bit awkwardly.

"And you're staying here now you're married? Your husband, he is Polish too?"

"Yes, but I don't know for how long we will stay. We are back only a while and he has learned that his job is gone soon."

"Oh God, that's awful." Right, that meant there was no chance now she could inquire discreetly about her cream couch. It looked like she'd have to go shopping for another one and a few other nice items, once she had got Mark to dump his boy toys out of her lovely light-filled conservatory. Of course that might mean another row. Oh hell, she might just let him win this one on the furniture for the moment.

"Well, it hasn't happened yet . . . we might be lucky . . . he might get new job." Mariola was drinking her tea fast, not overly comfortable talking to her employer, clearly much happier doing what she did well – work.

Her body language told Rebecca that she wanted to get on with things but then Mariola's eyes were caught by the nearby fruit bowl filled to the brim with oranges – oranges that Rebecca, despite her best intentions, would probably end up binning in a day or two. Picking up one scented orange globe, Mariola placed it to her nose, closed her eyes and inhaled the scent deeply.

"I'm sorry, it just reminds me . . . when I was very little girl, there was nothing in the shops, no toys, nothing to buy, but at Christmas sometimes there would be oranges and people would queue to hope to buy. Not everyone would get the orange but if you got one it was so beautiful, almost too beautiful to eat. Every time I see oranges I remember this – oranges make me feel so happy I want to cry."

A lump was forming in the back of Rebecca's throat as she listened to Mariola's tale of Christmas happiness which seemed poignantly sad. Right there and then she wanted to give away all the oranges, all her useless clothes upstairs, another couch, her impossible-to-wash crystal glasses, all her useless chrome kitchen appliances, anything that hadn't given her real pleasure but which she thought she must have, but of course she did none of these things for fear of offending the quietly dignified woman in her kitchen.

"Excuse me, I go back to cleaning now. It's nice to talk to you. I'm sorry you did not come to my wedding but your husband met my mother, my cousins, my grandfather and everybody liked him very much. My grandmother said he was very handsome man. Family is very important in Poland, maybe the most important of all," Mariola quietly asserted as her eyes filled with a kind of sadness and then she whipped on her cleaning gloves again and resumed her dirt-busting mission around the house.

Back upstairs Rebecca lay on the bed and looked at her bedside phone. Her sister's number was ingrained in her brain, she had dialled it often enough since she had returned home and she never had to be afraid of that number again and that feeling filled her with joy, comfort and great relief.

From out of her handbag she took out a crumpled envelope, with the Spanish postmark, recently rescued from Jennifer's kitchen bin and read the letter within.

Hello, Jenny,

Your old dad Jimmy here. I know you're more used to getting the odd postcard from me over the years than a proper letter, but things are not so good at the moment. Lydia has been diagnosed with breast cancer – it doesn't look the best and she wants to come home to Ireland to be with her sisters. I will be in Dublin from the end of May. I know you're very busy but if you want to come and see me I'll be staying at her sister Mary's house – her children have grown up and she says it's no trouble. Would love to hear from you, love. Hope your sister Becky is well. I don't hear from your brother but I suppose he's still interested in his rock bands. Thinking of you always,

Love
Dad

Family is the most important, maybe the most important of all. Closing her eyes, Rebecca played the familiar scene over and over, her on the beach in the green swimsuit, clambering over rock-pools in the sun and her daddy up to his neck in sand, laughing, the crystals of grain in his beard and in his hair, that glorious red-brown hair he'd bestowed on her alone.

Forty-one

Jennifer turned the colourful postcard over in her hand and re-read the short happy message for the second time that morning.

"Hi, Sis, got hitched to a lovely American girl called Zoe Bright, well, she's Zoe Murphy now 'cos she's my missus. Vegas is cool, best place in the world to get married. Lee."

Vegas, a playground for adult children, and it seemed her brother Lee was not planning to grow up any day soon, preferring to be 'spontaneous' forever. Maybe there was something in that – doing things on a whim. At least he was always happy, had perhaps always been happier than his cautionary big sister. Well, as she'd told Dan, she was going to do something about that annoying cautionary streak now, bit by bit.

Madeline the Model Mammy was at the school grounds

early, swinging the keys of her tank, when Jennifer showed up with Abby ensconced in the pram and Adam trying to stand, gripping onto her trousers, determined to gnaw her knees. Surprisingly, Super Mammy actually initiated a conversation as they waited by the school gates for their children to escape. Maybe it was because Jennifer was beginning to dress better these days and accessorise, develop a visible waist and a tighter ass. Today, for example, she only had the slightest bit of baby sludge on her trendy top and because it was patterned it was hardly noticeable at all. At a push she could pass for a Yummy Mummy herself, with extra curves of course in all the right places – she'd never be without those curves.

"Won't be long before you're shot of the two girls, more time for yourself," Madeline began; her sunglasses as always glued to her head whatever the weather.

"Uhm . . ." Adam had just bitten her leg. Jesus, that's all she needed – another biter in the family with a taste for human flesh served rare.

"Miss Fitzpatrick is a marvellous teacher, isn't she? They come out learning so much under her instruction." Madeline was still swinging her keys so they jostled together and made an annoying clinky tune.

Jennifer grimaced as Adam dug in deeper with his teeth and then tore in with his sharp little fingernails. Actually she'd settle on Emma knowing less in school, knowing nothing at all if it meant she ran in the gates to school in the morning and came home with a smile on her face in the afternoon.

"Brilliant that they're getting her for a second year running, but not that everybody knows that yet,"

Madeline said, dropping her voice and indulging in her super-sleuth wink-wink 'informed sources' behaviour.

Oh Jesus, not another year of the young battleaxe teacher with opinions on everything and knowledge of nothing. As she pulled Adam into her arms and tried to keep an eye on Abby in case she tried some really dangerous stunts, Jennifer caught sight of her eldest daughter looking glum, standing outside the prefab, and her teacher grimacing in a display of enforced friendliness.

"*Bonjour*," Miss Fitzpatrick machine-gunned the words out then immediately reverted to English – there was no point going past the preliminaries with Jennifer and they both knew it. "I wonder if you could step inside for a moment, Madame O'Malley?"

"Well . . . actually . . ."

A look of impatience came over the teacher's face and Jennifer knew she couldn't avoid her forever. Perhaps it was just as well to succumb to whatever it was that the schoolmistress needed to get off her ample young chest.

Emma and Abby went off to the book corner while Jennifer perched her bum on a tiny desk at the front of the room and tried to control a wriggling Adam.

"The thing is, I was wondering how you would feel about changing Emma's name in school to Ém-il-ie?" The teacher drew out the Frenchified name slowly for the benefit of Jennifer's non-polyglot brain, making Jennifer feel like an idiot in the process. "Émilie for Emma – it's quite a close match really sound-wise."

For a moment Jennifer couldn't speak until she was sure she had heard what she'd heard and even then she was a bit stunned by the request.

"But that's not her name – *her* name is Emma," Jennifer stuttered, almost asphyxiating.

"Yes, well, most of the children have French or Norman names and if they don't, well, we like to help them along in the process. We think it might help in the grants process if we can be seen to do all we can to encourage the promotion of French as a language."

From afar Emma looked up a bit nervously and she was sshhing Abby into being quiet, not that Abby gave a damn. Jennifer could tell by her middle child's body movements that a cartwheel was threatening to break free at any moment.

"So perhaps if we tried it on a trial basis . . . the new name, that is . . . Émilie?"

"No," Jennifer could feel her cheeks burning.

"I'm sorry?"

"No, no, no way, absolutely not, it's an insult to me to even suggest it. I picked her name and it's good enough for me, in fact I *like* the name Emma, Emma likes the name Emma and we're not robbing Emma of her identity by calling her a name that she isn't."

"Really, I think you're being most –"

"No. I said no, it's not up for discussion, not now, not ever!"

"Well, I must remind you that the school board can review enrolment of any child –"

"I said no, and now I'm going. Emma, Abby, come on, we're going."

"Are we going to the burger place?" Emma asked, her eyes lighting up as she dragged her school bag by the handle and sat it at her mother's feet while her teacher smoothed down her skirt and openly fumed.

"Yes, yes, we are," Jennifer announced loudly, her body was almost shaking from rage as she said a brusque goodbye to Fitzpatrick in English and strode towards the door.

"Mammy, are we *really* going to get chips and fizzy drinks or just pretending like the last time?" Emma asked breathlessly as they walked towards the car parked on the street with Fitzpatrick's laser eyes boring hard and long into their disappearing backs.

"Absolutely, let's go there right now, let's not waste a single minute," Jennifer affirmed, feeling utterly and completely spontaneous and a teensy bit worried, knowing junk food would have Abby bouncing off the walls, ceilings and floors for the rest of the afternoon.

Having ordered the nutritiously deficient and exorbitantly priced meal, Jennifer made soft blowing noises as fast-food tea burnt the inside of her mouth. Soon her chicken burger had sunk to her stomach and promised to stay there for the rest of the day, making heavy work for her liver as it tried to break down the onslaught of animal fats. There was no need to get worked up about this name business, she calmed herself – it could all be solved in a completely rational manner. Watching Adam sucking his beaker in his pram and seeing that he was content, Jennifer turned her attention to Emma, laughing as she made rude slurping noises with her milkshake and in a rare display of spontaneity scribbled on her plastic hamburger carton with fries and ketchup.

"So, Ems, how are things at school, pet?"

Emma went quiet as her mother brought her school environment back into focus again. The little girl's eyes filled with tears and she shook her head, not able to answer her mother's questions. Even now with the school year almost finished, Emma had never really settled into the place and a few times Jennifer had tried to nab the principal and query him on the peculiar school policy, but he was wily when it came to dodging parents. Instinctively, she knew where he would stand on the current name issue: with the teacher.

"It's okay, Emma, it's okay . . ." Jennifer pulled the little girl towards her and stroked her hair. It was up to her to figure things out for the best and she would, starting this very moment.

A week later Jennifer swung round the supermarket roundabout and noticed with glee that there were several parent-and-child parking spots freely available. For about two seconds she felt guilty as she realised all her kids were home with Dan, so technically she would be stealing the place from another mother with real tots in seats. Still, if she didn't park there, it would be nicked from under her nose by one of the town's boy racers, so without any more guilt she parked.

By the time she had flicked through a few trashy novels, nearly had a multi-orgasm in the make-up section, brain-drunk from all the new-fangled products that promised to lift this and fill in that, and given the condoms the once-over (perhaps her and Dan should explore a few new naughty lines), she was feeling ridiculously impish. So much so that she found herself wandering in the luxury-biscuit section and there she came right up against Madeline, holding of all things an easy-bake bun mix in an attractively coloured box, the kind of easy-bake box that's big on chocolate buttons, jellies and gooey icing and stuffed with unpronounceable, scary ingredients. Madeline, who was famous for her bake-from-scratch cakes and buns, blushed as she caught Jennifer eyeing up her intended purchase.

The end of year charity-school bake sale (one of the many never-ending bake sales) was only one day away and Jennifer had decided to not even bother baking this time, despite having successfully nailed the Murphy scones recipe. This time shop-bought rubbish would do just fine and besides she'd already reconciled herself to the fact that, although her mother was a champion baker, it didn't mean that she had to continue the tradition.

"Hello there, Madeline."

Madeline was the colour of beetroot now, the easy-bake box the only item in her hands, its presence as embarrassing to her as running into the parish priest with a twelve-pack of condoms in one hand and a pregnancy test in the other.

"I've a lot on this week," Madeline blustered, looking at her easy-bake product and back again at Jen. "There's not always time," she continued as if she was pleading her case in some kind of court – the Mummy Court perhaps.

Peculiarly, Jennifer was filled with a kind of sisterly affection for her fellow-mother with the sunglasses implants. Always being perfect on the outside had to take its toll – nobody could be perfect all the time, not even, 'Look at me – I have it all under control' Madeline.

"And besides I don't want to turn out like Sophie Lloyd," Madeline stammered.

"Why, what's happened to Sophie Lloyd?" Jennifer asked, mystified.

"Poor, poor woman . . . I used to record all her cookery programmes to play back later . . . who would have known she found all that baking so stressful?" Madeline raved before sprinting for the checkout with her easy-bake box. "Got to go, I've three of them in the car."

Sophie Lloyd? What had happened to Sophie Lloyd? Maybe she'd split her French nails when breaking opening an egg for a freshly made meringue, or maybe she'd got her hair cut short and couldn't carry the new look? Then again, maybe it was her stomach. Yeah, that could be it. Maybe someone had let the cat out of the bag that Sophie really wore big knickers or that Spanx stuff 24-7 and her stomach was actually as saggy as an old maternity bra? Jennifer couldn't wait to sprint for the newspapers after she cleared the checkout.

It was hard to take it all in at first as her eyes were assaulted with headlines and photos for not just Sophie but for her hot meteorological fantasy, Pierre the Weatherman. Appalled, Jennifer read that Pierre the Weatherman, Euroman stuff of her fantasies, had been spotted frolicking on a gay beach in the US with a gorgeous young black buck. Caught in an embarrassing embrace, Pierre had come clean and admitted he was madly in love with Lucas Joshua Johnson the third, a twenty-two-year-old truck-driver from Tennessee whom he was planning to marry in a star-studded ceremony in Vegas.

To think of all the times she'd supposed Pierre was giving her and every woman in Europe the eye during his weather reports and here he was, not interested in female flesh one bit. Jennifer felt duped at all the wasted desire she'd tried to telepathically communicate through the TV screen over the last few months . . . and Sophie, was that picture of a wild-eyed woman with scruffy hair in the back of a car really the uber-elegant culinary extraordinaire, Sophie Lloyd?

The papers were full of the news that the lovely Sophie had been whisked off to a nice 'spa' suffering from nervous exhaustion, that her cookery programme was temporarily suspended and that the nuns at her local convent (Sophie was big with the official sisterhood ever since she ran the special on traditional soda bread) were offering up prayers for her speedy recovery. Well, if ever there was proof that too much baking and fancy cooking led to madness, this was it. Poor Sophie, Jennifer felt a twinge of real sympathy for her and for Madeline and for all muddle-through-it-day-by-day mums like herself who were lucky if they could find a clean shirt or a pair of trousers for the day. It seemed none of them had things worked out to perfection, even those who from the outside looked like they had. Perfection was too bloody hard, too tiring. Fun was the only way to go, fun was everything.

At home Dan was surfing the net looking up flight deals to Canada. He wanted the girls to know their Newfoundland heritage, to know where he was from and to know how they were part of somewhere other than Ireland. His initial holiday surfing over, he took off to their garage to sand down and glue his boat and he knew now that his yearning for boats had made him think of home and how much he needed to reconnect with his own family soon. Yet, he had a real talent for this hands-on lark. His seedlings in his greenhouse were thriving and his patchwork boat was beginning to look like something both saleable and sailable. It made Jennifer happy to see him work at something he loved, to see her man with passion in his eyes and strength in his arms, to see him being the man he was rather than the man family, friends and society told him he should be all his life.

"Okay, baby?" he asked, seeing her watching him from the garage door sharpen a chisel to peel back paint blistered by his heat gun.

"Just . . ."

She moved towards him.

"Yeah?"

"Just you look so bloody sexy and you make me want to do things to you," she whispered as she brushed her hand against his stubbly beard and winked at him seductively, hearing his deep laugh echo through the space behind her footsteps as she left.

Turning on the TV she searched for any news on Pierre the Weatherman, but he seemed to have been erased from the airspace completely and in his weathery place the TV channel was playing it safe by getting a balding, sexless man of about fifty-five with a hook nose, heavy-framed glasses and an accent as thick as stewed tea to do the weather forecast instead. Shaking her head at her gullibility, Jennifer berated herself for not being able to spot an on-air gay from the comfort of her own couch. Of course Pierre did dress particularly well for a man, but he was French and she'd always assumed his clothes choices were down to the TV station. Never in her life had she thought he actually relished getting dickied up every night. Still watching the TV screen from time to time, for any news about Pierre or the mad TV Cook, Jennifer scoured her mobile for the necessary contact details and waited for the phone at the other end of the line to connect.

"Birdie?"

"Jennifer, pet, how are you keeping?"

"Fine, fine, bit of news though. Just ringing to tell you your feckless nephew Lee sent me a postcard to say he got married in Vegas, so you can stop worrying about him being in prison or working in a rodeo."

"Well, isn't he the dark horse! Didn't know he had a special lady friend."

"Oh, believe me, he's had many a special lady friend, but it came as a bit of a surprise that he actually wanted to marry one of them – but there you go, all part of the rock 'n' roll lifestyle, no doubt – sure he'll probably be divorced by Christmas."

"And do you think he'll want a divorce? You don't think this marrying lark has something to do with citizenship, or that maybe he was going to be deported? Is she American, this one he's married?" Birdie was back in detective mode again.

"Birdie, will you stop worrying? Lee has spent his whole life being spontaneous, living for the day and it never did him any harm. In fact, I've started to believe myself it's the only way to live. Quite spontaneously I've decided to take Emma out of her flash hothouse school next year and send her to the country school on the edge of town. In fact, I dropped her into her new class already just so she could see what it's like. You'll be pleased to hear her new best friend, Nadia, is Russian."

"Oh, that's lovely. You can't beat the Russians – their long history of suffering has given them plenty of stamina. Nadia will probably be a loyal friend to Emma all her life."

"And there's a Chinese kid in the class as well, a Latvian, two Polish boys and a lovely little girl from India. I believe the First Communion in the school is like a day out for the United Nations – they all turn up in their national costumes."

"Oh, isn't that wonderful, and China, Poland and India are all the parts of the world that are set to boom – I saw it in a TV documentary only last week. Sure Emma will have all her contacts made if she ever becomes an international businesswoman. Why did you move her in the end?"

"Ah, I guess her going there was just extra pressure on me and her and the competition and stress would only get harder the further up Emma goes in the school. I think I kind of realised there's enough stress in life without adding more to it myself. It was like the baking, I've stopped baking completely since I found out how to make mum's scones, although the stress of trying to make them nearly killed me along the way!"

There was a long pause down the line, each one wondering who was going to bring up the topic, Birdie not wishing to push it, Jennifer not wanting to say anything to make the phantom real.

"I was just wondering . . . Rosemary . . ."

"Yes, pet?"

"Nothing." Her voice-box refused to make another

sound. It made her feel panicky like the time of the bronchitis and not being able to breathe all over again.

"Rosemary is still here, Jennifer. I'm still here, Jennifer."

"I know, Birdie, I know, but nothing is forever, Rosemary won't be forever," Jennifer whispered as her eyes filled up with tears.

Forty-two

Rebecca sat in her red sports car opposite the row of ex-local-authority houses and felt nauseated as she baked in the heat of the early summer sun. Across the road, the metal railings painted, white, black or silver hemmed in the small gardens, the front lawns neat with well-cared-for clipped green hedges or paved over to make room for the extra cars that were still a rarity when she was a child.

Nervously, she checked the number again and glanced over at the mid-terrace building, with the well-tended hanging baskets and white lace net-curtains which framed jugs of plastic flowers on the windowsills. The house was eerily reminiscent of her own modest childhood home, but that time seemed so long ago. For a moment she remembered skipping on a road like this from Easter till September and playing hand games till she was hoarse from singing and her hands tingled with the shockwaves of clapping.

The sounds of children laughing and playing filled her head with nostalgia as she remembered the days of her early and middle childhood. Those were the days when everything was right with the world, when her parents were still a united front, outside of the home at least, where her mother hadn't seemed so tired from working, sewing, cleaning, scrimping or saving. Maybe it was a mistake coming here. Maybe she should just leave now and no one would know the difference. She could start the car and just drive home to Mark – at least everything there seemed hopeful.

Yet the memory of past family life was so powerful it made her head spin. It was the second time that day that she felt light-headed and a strange kind of yearning for what might have been. The red-stained toilet bowl in her own home that morning was indication enough that she wasn't pregnant, despite being two days late. Since her time away she had become lax about taking the pill and taken a few chances with Mark. Since she'd come home she hadn't given it too much thought – after all, everyone knew coming off oral contraception and getting pregnant took time. Her heart had crashed through her chest from fear when she first realised she was late, but funnily enough she hadn't felt relief at getting her period this morning, much to her own surprise. She felt a weird sense of disappointment instead.

For the last few days she had moved from butterflies in her stomach into a kind of dream state where her belly swelled until her personal cinematic feature ended with a little baby in her arms, a pink-cheeked girl with red-brown hair, that mesmerising hair that belonged to her alone. For the last two days she'd said nothing to Mark about the phantom morning-sickness type afflictions that hit her stomach, hadn't alerted him to her suspicions that hormones had turned her off morning coffee or that the slightest trace of kitchen mess or stale food was enough to make her gag. Rebecca had even foreseen the moment when she'd ring Helen and tell her that her rugby career was definitely over either in Bannestown or Carrigmore while she was 'with child', but it seemed it was all just a shadow pregnancy, a figment of her imagination, and as she flushed the toilet and washed away the stain she felt peculiar, yes, definitely peculiar and definitely and perhaps illogically disappointed.

Now, sitting here watching the world go by it all seemed obvious. Stress had caused her period to arrive late, but there was really nothing to worry about.

Then she saw an old man in oversized cheap dark sunglasses amble past the terraced houses with a terrier at his heels. Paralysed with fear but wanting to run until her heart burst and her limbs ached, Rebecca felt herself shake and the shaking continued as she hauled herself out of the car and tried to lock the doors.

Up close, she noticed that the brasses of the front door were shining like a well-polished soldier's belt and that the stained glass was gleaming a rainbow in the bright sunlight – it was the kind of pride her mother took in the appearance of her own home, in a well-scrubbed step, cobwebs being brushed aside, front windows so clear it wasn't unusual for baby birds to collide with the glass . . .

Oh God she shouldn't have come, her feelings were too mixed up, too overwhelming. She was almost about to turn on her heel when he saw her from the window and he came to answer the door himself.

On the way up from Carrigmore she had practised what she would say to him. She would be polite, but she wouldn't be particularly affectionate, she would be somewhat reserved – after all this was the first man to break her heart – she would be . . .

"Rebecca?"

"Dad?"

He took her in his arms and hugged her tight and she forgot all about being reserved and polite, she cried like a little girl on the first day at school, she cried big sobs of relief that made her feel vulnerable, she cried until he kissed her cheek and took her inside the front room of a little house she didn't recognise but was so obviously familiar, this house of Mary with the grown-up children. She cried as she remembered the days before her father had fallen for the hated Lydia, the woman who had stolen her Dad away, the woman who now had breast cancer. She cried as she remembered the feel of sun on her skin, of being in the green swimsuit and digging for crabs in the rock pools, she cried as his faded red hair mingled with her own as without a word being said her body let them both know that in the end blood was thicker than all the bad and hurtful memories gone before, that in the end there is only one thing important: family and where you've come from.

It was the smell Jennifer noticed first, the smell of disinfectant and cleaning, the kind of cleaning smell that never comes from ordinary houses after a bottle of bleach and half a bottle of floor cleaner. Birdie, brightly painted and smiling as always, led her into the compact room, which had everything her mother needed and at the same time nothing much at all.

"Mum?" The word was said with so much hope but no recognition. The face she knew so well was still beautiful and kind but vacant as if the spirit inside was already flitting between two places.

Birdie looked at her niece in worry, but Jennifer was prepared. Rebecca had already told her that their mother knew more of the distant past than the time just recently gone by.

"I have something for you, Rosemary," Jennifer smiled as she sniffled away her tears.

From a purple paper bag with yellow ribbons parcelling the ends, Jennifer pulled out a baby-pink silk scarf threaded with gold, delicately embroidered with sequins and with a long, soft fringe ending. A light came on in Rosemary's eyes as she took the gift and ran the fringe across the back of a hand, crinkled with the years and mottled with liver spots.

"Beautiful, beautiful material. It would be lovely to finish off an outfit, a nice skirt, something simple like Audrey Hepburn would wear, maybe with black or navy heels and kid gloves . . ." Rosemary choked with tears and Jennifer just nodded and patted the papery hand.

"I'll wear it when I go dancing with my husband. Do you know my husband? Such a handsome man, everybody says so . . . oh, looking at this scarf really makes me want to dance!" Rosemary half-sighed, half-laughed and Jennifer couldn't help but smile herself.

It must be genetic, this looking at scarves and wanting to dance, and she smiled as she remembered her own night of the seven veils, the night of her wedding anniversary when her separation from Dan was more than just physical, it was a mindset, when it seemed that she would never again meet the Jennifer of the past or of the future, when dancing seemed a release from all the little constraints of life that told her what to do and how to act and how to be, when she was rigid but desperately wanted to be as fluid and as playfully happy as a scarf in dance.

"It's a beautiful scarf, Rosemary, it would make anyone want to dance," Jennifer said, pulling off her coat.

Bringing her mother an expensive silk scarf, seeing her eyes light up as her brain recognised beauty in her hands – was this the absolute ending of her childhood, the beginning of her being an adult to the one who had nurtured her through life, and could she stand that pain of role reversal now?

Seeing Rosemary again, there was the bond, the bond that isn't erased by time or lack of physical recognition, the bond that exists between mother and daughter for all time, the bond that just is, not like the bond with her father which had been damaged and broken, perhaps forever. Although when Rosemary talked about Jimmy, Jennifer didn't feel the anger she expected she would feel for a man who had walked out on his family for another woman. Perhaps feeling anger would be hypocritical, for hadn't she almost been tempted astray herself before realising that it would do her no good, that happiness came from the inside? But being tempted, wanting to sometimes walk away from marriage and start again, she could at least understand that now, even if she didn't want to, even if it made her feel something close to sympathy for a man who had made her life harder by not being around when it mattered. Maybe the anger for Jimmy was passing, although she felt a long way yet from forgiveness.

Helping her mother butter her toast, Jennifer knew that there are no perfect endings just as she knew that there are rarely perfect beginnings, and that life is no more than a series of jumps and starts where if joy and understanding are not a right, they are at least a possibility for all who make a sudden leap of faith.

The End

If you enjoyed *Two to Tango*
by Nuala Woulfe, why not try
Chasing Rainbows also published by Poolbeg?
Here's a sneak preview of Chapter One.

Chasing Rainbows

NUALA WOULFE

POOLBEG

One

It was not the first Monday morning that Ali Hughes had given some thought to deliberately falling down the metal stairs that led to her place of work. Not that she was thinking of throwing herself from the top – Jesus, that would be mad altogether – but perhaps she could manage a little skid as she approached the last few steps, a skilful wobble, and then it might be a sprained ankle, a bad back and some decent compensation from the dull little company that she worked for.

It could all be made to seem quite plausible really. After all, it was September in Dublin and the city-centre trees were shedding their foliage, leaving a greasy sludge of rot behind to tempt the accident-prone. Her brain went into an excited state of overdrive as she thought about the possibilities. Crikey, she might even meet a nice doctor in casualty and be married before she turned the dreaded thirty!

Of course she didn't need sympathy to get a date; she

wasn't that desperate. Ali was pretty enough, with shoulder-length dark-brown hair flecked with the odd strand of auburn, and with slate-blue eyes that many a gobshite had described as 'expressive'. No, it was just that bringing home a doctor would be the ultimate coup in making her mother tongue-tied for a week, particularly if he was some tall chap who'd significantly overshadow Ali's five-foot-five-inch frame.

The last step was approaching rapidly. It was now or never: to wobble or not to wobble? But even deliberately staging an accident on those steel steps could only be painful. Besides, she doubted whether the small firm she worked for actually had the money to pay her any decent compensation – they would say they didn't, that's for sure. The scabby bastards might even contest the case, she thought as she reached the basement of the Georgian building and the office.

Looming in front of her was the big heavy door that she desperately tried to forget about all weekend, every weekend, the door that once shut would have her in its grasp for another eight hours – eight valuable and wasted hours of her life. And she was late again, and even though the Irish transport system was conveniently unpredictable her excuses were beginning to shift from the somewhat ridiculous to the downright outrageous.

This time she reckoned she would have to own up to having overslept, not that that was the truth either: she had lain awake in bed for half an hour listening to the news programme *Morning Ireland*, letting her head take flight with one dream after another.

As she went to place her key in the lock, she noticed that the door was slightly ajar and that Maggie was inside the main office, rooting around in a pile of papers on her desk.

Maggie O'Shea looked up and smiled in her bemused manner at her old college acquaintance and Ali was struck for the thousandth time by the natural beauty of her friend who even without make-up could look stunning with her exotic "Black Irish" looks. Maggie's curly black hair framed her heart-shaped face and her eyes were big and dark with long dark lashes stroking her tanned cheeks. Even now at the end of summer Maggie was a dusky brown while Ali struggled to hold on to her freckly tan.

"Is he in?" Ali asked, hoping that Simon (or "Little Bastard" as she called him) had got caught in a traffic jam or that he had an early meeting with a client and hadn't yet graced the staff with his divine presence.

"He's been and gone, girl. Little Bastard noticed you were running late but he had to leave to meet some woman who runs a food business. Was so excited about it he didn't even have time for his Power Juice Special this morning!"

"Maybe I need to get power-juiced. My motivation is up me arse these days, Mags, and Little Bastard is chalking up every little thing he can against me so he can tell it all to the Big Boss the first chance he gets."

Maggie put down the book she was holding and lifted a paper cup to her lips, inhaling the exotic aroma of morning coffee. "I think you're exaggerating just a bit. Sure, what do you care? The *Real Boss* couldn't care less what you're doing, He's seldom here anyway."

It was true that the owner and chief executive of O'Grady Marketing was a man as elusive as Charlie from *Charlie's Angels*. Joe O'Grady, aka Charlie, was one of those invisible business magnates who was so busy making easy money that his marketing company was practically a hobby. Mostly Joe left the day-to-day running of the place to his second-in-command, his captain, his little general in the making, Simon Webb.

"I think I need a fix of coffee," said Ali. "Where's Luce?" she added, noticing that the receptionist's desk was unoccupied.

"Upstairs: photocopying something for a mail-shot."

"And Lucky Pam's still on holiday getting her arse roasted in the sun," quipped Ali as she exited the basement door before she was hardly five minutes inside it.

* * *

It was a lovely day, one of those September mornings that has some heat of sunshine in it and the throngs of people hurrying through the streets of Dublin still had their summer clothes on, with maybe just a light jacket or a cardigan slung over their shoulders. Watching them scurrying around like ants, Ali wondered what their lives were like and if they were happy with their lot.

In the shop around the corner Ali continued her musings as she waited for her coffee, inventing careers for the toned young guy in front of her, the self-assured young girls in tight skirts and heels and the thirty-five-plus brigade of women who looked tired around the eyes and jaw-lines despite the bit of slap on their faces.

The queue was moving slowly. It seemed to Ali that the entire city was gathered in the one coffee shop, all needing their Monday morning fix of caffeine to inspire some motivation into their hunched shoulders and shuffling feet. Motivation: it was getting harder and harder to drag herself out of bed these days and into the drippy shower of her one-bedroom apartment on Dublin's south-east coast. It didn't even matter what day of the working week it was. Ali found she was now leaving just enough time to shower, dress and brush her teeth before getting the train into the city. Breakfast had become a luxury that she was prepared to take on the hoof.

The woman at the counter took her order for a latte and Ali heard the machine swish into life as the milky froth was added to the large paper cup. The price was ferocious. Sometimes it was enough to make Ali think of unscrewing the cap of the coffee jar in the office kitchen but deep down she knew she'd just continue with the daily extortion. It was ludicrous, she knew it, but buying coffee she could barely afford sort of made her feel dangerous as if she was living on the edge and, considering the state of her bank balance, maybe she was.

Holding a paper napkin around her steaming coffee, Ali popped into the shop next door and bought a packet of luxury cookies for the office, trying to ignore the horrifically expensive price label and the grams of fat per bickie.

Back at the office, with the coffee already firing up her veins, she plonked the goodies a little too firmly on the communal desk that served as the general junk station and watched as they worked their usual magic.

"Oh, you're a pet!" squealed Lucy as her eyes landed on the unopened packet. "These are *so* yummy! Do you mind if I have two with a cuppa?"

Ali smiled. Lucy, the receptionist, was a tonic. She was

twenty-two with a wasp-like waist, huge boobs and slim but curvy hips and her crowning glory was undoubtedly her curly waist-length honey-blonde hair. Young and arrogant enough not to give a damn about anything, Lucy would flash a look of contempt at Simon which just dared him to fire her, every time he issued her with some petty administrative demand. When you're young jobs are just ten a penny as long as you can party and have fun. Ali sighed; she wasn't so old herself. These days your late twenties was practically babyhood, or so she'd been told. Plonking herself at her desk, she listened as her computer cranked into life. Poor fecker sounded like it too could do with a cup of coffee just to get it going.

The thump of feet was heard on the steps outside and they all saw him as his highly polished shoes then trouser legs appeared silhouetted in the giant basement Georgian window that let in the only natural light to the office. It was Simon. Suddenly everyone shut up and pretended they were busy. He was struggling with a large box which seemed to be sapping the strength out of his five-foot-six featherweight frame, but nobody was rushing to help him down the steps.

"Well, girls, start of the week again, what?" he said as he finally made it through the door, panting with the exertion.

He was greeted by a collective low mumbling, which could have been an acknowledgement or a form of mass indigestion.

"Well, Lucy, how's the head this Monday? On the pull again this weekend, were we? Like the top, is it new?"

Fluffing his white-blond hair with his hand in an

attempt to look sexy, Simon fixed his cold, dark eyes on the lovely Lucy. For some strange reason Simon thought he was God's gift to women. Well into his thirties, Little Bastard still lived at home with a maiden aunt. "We're like John Lennon and Aunt Mimi," he would joke. "But John Lennon was good-looking," Ali would say when they'd gossip and roll their eyes in the adjoining employee kitchen – or even better – the loos. "And talented," Lucy would add.

So as usual Lucy shot Simon one of her most contemptuous looks but Little Bastard either didn't notice or he really did have skin as thick as rhinoceros hide.

"Well, if anyone is under the weather from a bit of weekend overindulgence with the demon drink, I have the *perfect* cure right here. Rashers, sausages and pudding from the Perfect Pig company whose account I have just *personally* landed! Should save you girls a few pence during the week – you can all take some home with you when I work out how many we should each get."

He looked like he was waiting for a round of applause to acknowledge his double whammy, landing an account with a meat company and getting a few rashers thrown in by way of a bonus. He had probably asked for them and all, such was the way with Simon. The office remained resolutely silent. For a split second he looked annoyed and then he recovered himself.

"Put the kettle on and make us a cup of tea, will you, Maggie, and bring us in one or two of these as well." He gestured at Ali's biscuits which had cost her an arm and a leg.

He would never buy anything more expensive than

Marietta, thought Ali as she marvelled yet again at the arrogance of the little fecker, ordering his staff around like minions.

"Right, will I put everyone's name in the pot so?" asked Maggie to a chorus of assents and she disappeared into the nearby kitchen.

Simon was nearly out of the main office when he uttered a very deliberate aside. "Oh, by the way, Ali, I'd like to see you in my office for a chat and bring in that proposal you are working on for Sunshine Travel, the one you gave me a copy of on Friday. You can bring the tea with you."

How generous, maybe he would even let her bring in some of her own biscuits too. It took a few minutes to root out the file, a few minutes more than necessary, and then she followed him in reluctantly, trying desperately to disguise any signs of unease. *For God's sake, you're twenty-eight – you're not some school kid about to get a talking-to from the headmaster!*

Sitting down at the breakfast table which he'd recently installed in his spacious office for "friendly" brainstorming sessions with staff, she tried to hide as much of herself as possible behind her opened work file, knowing that no matter where she sat or how she tried to screen herself he would have a bull's-eye view of her famous bazookas. Annoyed, she crossed her arms in front of her chest as extra armour and waited for him to begin.

"As you know, Joe is mad to land this account and Sunshine Travel is desperate to capitalise on the youth market. Now, about this proposal, Ali, I've got some suggestions as to how you could *radically* improve it."

Simon leaned his forearms on the small table and pushed his upper body closer to Ali in an effort to show her the pieces of typed paper he had corrected.

"For example, see here where you say O'Grady would be assessing the average *income* of student youth – I would prefer if you would use the phrase '*spending power*' instead. Now down here where you recommend targeting the youth sector through beer-mat advertising in pubs, I've deleted *pubs* and put in *bars*."

Amazed, Ali watched as he continued to circle and delete and add words to her copy in luminous green marker until page after page was a mass of huge, untidy squiggles.

After an extensive monologue Simon smiled his fish-like smile and handed her back the sad piece of work, adding condescendingly that she could resubmit it for another once-over before the final deadline.

"Simon, while I appreciate your comments," – Ali didn't – "do you not think a lot of these suggested changes are superficial?"

Leaning back in his chair, Simon placed a hand to his chin as if he was thinking over what she was saying, while in reality she knew he was not. He clicked his ball-point-pen repeatedly in irritation and Ali felt her chest tighten as she closed her folder on the shameful mess of green circles and slashes.

"Don't forget the deadline is Friday." He smiled coldly, then turned his attention to his diary in a gesture which signalled that the meeting was now definitely over.

Fuming, Ali got up and left.

Something had to change. She knew that as she

headed out the door that evening and fought her way onto one of the commuter trains.

*   *   *

Back home, her answering machine was flashing red and, switching it on, she heard her best friend Karen cackle out their familiar greeting, "Seen any good willies lately?"

Ali sighed. Good willies had been in short supply ever since she had given that annoying policeman, Detective Garda Dave O'Connor, the bullet. He would have got her out of this black mood, he would have wrestled with her until she screamed, let her bang a few cushions and pretend it was Simon's head, kissed her and told her to cheer up. Struggling hard, she tried to remember why exactly they had broken up. For the life of her she couldn't remember.

If you enjoyed this chapter from
Chasing Rainbows by Nuala Woulfe
why not order the full book online
@ www.poolbeg.com